INTO THE TORN KINGDOMS

JUMPSTART DUCHY
BOOK 1

STEFON MEARS

Also by Stefon Mears

The Rise of Magic Series
Magician's Choice
Sleight of Mind
Lunar Alchemy
Three Fae Monte
The Sphinx Principle
Double Backed Magic
Mercury Fold (coming soon)

Cavan Oltblood Series
Half a Wizard
The Ice Dagger
Spells of Undeath

Power City Tales
Not Quite Bulletproof
No Money in Heroism

Standalones
Between the Cracks
Sects and the City
Prince of a Thousand Worlds
Devil's Night
Portal-Land, Oregon
Stealing from Pirates
Fade to Gold
With a Broken Sword
Twice Against the Dragon
The House on Cedar Street
Sudden Death
On the Edge of Faerie

Short Story Collections
Spell Slingers
Twisted Timelines
Longhairs and Short Tales: A Collection of Cat Stories
Confronting Legends (Spells & Swords Vol. 1)
The Patreon Collection, Vol. 1-8 (Vol. 9, coming soon)

Nonfiction
The 30-Day Novel and Beyond!

Spells for Hire Series
Devil's Shoestring
Zombie Powder
Spirit Trap
Dragon's Blood

The Telepath Trilogy
Surviving Telepathy
Immoral Telepathy
Targeting Telepathy

Edge of Humanity Series
Caught Between Monsters
Hunting Monsters

Jumpstart Duchy Series
Into the Torn Kingdoms
The Dragon's Gold
The Gift Castle
The Deadly Feast
The King's Test
Triumph in the Torn Kingdoms

Published by Thousand Faces Publishing, Portland, Oregon

http://1kfaces.com

Copyright © 2022 by Stefon Mears

Front cover image © Elena Kozyreva | Dreamstime.com (File ID: 101691792)

Hardback ISBN: 978-1-948490-43-6

Paperback ISBN: 978-1-948490-26-9

INTO THE TORN KINGDOMS

1

———

FLUSHED WITH VICTORY, KEIFER STRETCHED OUT ON THE TARMAC OF the basketball court and let the light rain kiss his sweaty, exhausted body.

What a game. Full court five-on-five. It was only supposed to go to eleven, but the rule at McKenzie Park — that little gem of pickup basketball tucked away in the hills of southwest Portland, Oregon — was that you had to win by two.

The final score: Keifer's team twenty-seven, the other guys twenty-five.

Man, when Tyrone's game-winning jumper hit from the top of the key, Keifer could've kissed him.

Instead he dropped down and stretched out right inside the three-point arc, panting and so hot he was steaming in the light drizzle.

The tarmac here always smelled like old rubber. Hot old rubber in the summer, but even on a cool spring day like this one, it still smelled like old rubber. As though the surface wasn't actually tarmac, but had been cobbled together out of old sneakers and cheap basketballs, then pressed into shape.

His four teammates gathered around him as though viewing a

corpse at a funeral. All of them sweaty and panting themselves, but still looking at him as though wondering if they needed to call a coroner.

Drew. Pale, freckled, and the shortest guy who played here, but he had such a good dribble and fake that he could get away with his five-foot frame. Most of the time.

Marcella. A skinny Latina with fast hands and a wicked hook shot. Oh, and she was a good six inches taller than Drew, and never let him forget it.

Tyrone. Their big man at close to six-eight — a full half-foot taller than Keifer — he could dominate around the rim, and when his jumper was falling, look out.

Finally, there was Dre-Dre. Dre-Dre's dad used to play for the Trailblazers, but Dre-Dre never would. He had the height, at around six-six, but even at twenty-five he still moved like a gawky teen. Sure, he had a wicked mid-range game and could kill from beyond the arc, but no ball control at all.

Drew handed Keifer his big, Costco-special water bottle, which they all knew was filled with that special electrolyte water that was all the rage.

Keifer wouldn't admit to this, but he actually bought the water because it was the only brand that could do black cherry flavoring just right.

Keifer chuckled and swirled some of that tasty water around in his mouth before swallowing.

"That was a sweet pass," Tyrone said, talking about Keifer's no-look, behind-the-back special that set up the game-winner. "But if you don't get your ass up off that court, we'll have to replace you for the next game."

Keifer sighed. Rules of the park. Winners played, losers went to the back of the line. If Keifer wanted to sit, he'd have to join another team and wait for his chance to rotate in.

Their impatience hardly seemed fair, though. He'd played two games in a row — both had gone overtime, with the first one ending seventeen-fifteen — while the others hadn't.

Of course, that was because the rest of his first team had split after only one game...

Still. A little rest would have been nice. His muscles were quivering from running the point for two games in a row — especially since that last game went more than *double* over-time — but he didn't want to sit and get cold in the rain, waiting for another chance to play...

Fine then. Once more into the breach.

"I'm good," he said, holding up his hand and getting a lift up. "Who's next?"

Just as the words left his mouth, the skies opened up. Apps and weatherpeople alike had predicted nothing more than a light drizzle that day, burning off by late morning, and leaving clear skies for the rest of the weekend.

Apparently somebody forgot to tell the weather. It went from a light drizzle to a torrential downpour in a matter of seconds.

No one had to say anything. Everyone ran for their cars.

Rain came down like it was December. So hard and fast that even Keifer's *socks* were squishy before he was halfway across the lawn toward the curb where his car was parked.

Blinding light flashed across the sky. Thunder roared loud enough to hurt Keifer's ears.

He made it to his car. Reached for his keys.

Damn. He'd forgotten his fanny pack.

He shielded his eyes against the downpour. There was his fanny pack. Still sitting out on the court, behind the basket.

Three nearby maple trees all flailed in the wind as though taking bets about whether Keifer would go for his keys or just seek shelter.

Not that he had great options for shelter. With the wind picking up, even hiding on a porch across the street wouldn't keep him dry.

Plus, it would be trespassing. Not exactly his sort of thing.

He turned back and looked toward the basketball courts again.

Well, at least he couldn't get any wetter.

Turned out that wasn't true.

Rains has been fairly light over the last few weeks. Pretty dry for

May in Portland, to be honest. And that had left the park's topsoil unprepared for this level of drenching.

Keifer slipped twice on his way back to the court. The first time just landing on his ass — and soaking his shorts and underwear beyond anything he wanted to think about.

The second time he went down face-first and slid three feet across the wet grass.

Lightning flashed and thunder laughed at him.

The rain hadn't been this bad for two minutes yet, and Keifer was so wet he felt as though he'd been dragged down to the bottom of a pool and kept there for half an hour.

Hell, his skin was probably pruning, he felt so wet.

But he made it to the court. Grabbed his fanny pack. Turned back toward his car.

That was when he heard the saddest sound he could think of. A plaintive little meow.

Oh, god. Some poor cat was stuck out in this?

The meow came again, and Keifer spotted a bit of orange near the roots of one of the maple trees. An orange cat was down there, trying unsuccessfully to find shelter from the rain.

Well, how much wetter could Keifer get anyway?

He strapped the fanny pack around his waist and started slowly toward the cat.

As he got closer, he could tell that it was a good-sized tom. Maybe twelve pounds, when the poor bedraggled thing wasn't sopping wet. Adult, but still on the young side. Maybe four or five years old.

Keifer started clucking his tongue as he got closer.

Lightning flashed and thunder rolled again. The cat's eyes went wild with fear.

"Hey there, big guy," Keifer said in as soothing a tone as he could manage, under the circumstances. "I don't know about you, but I hate sitting out here, getting wet. Want to come get warm and dry with me?"

The cat crouched low, ears back and eyes narrowed. But he wasn't making any territorial sounds. That was good. He didn't have a collar, and soaked as he was, it was difficult to tell if he looked like a stray.

Keifer used to have a cat, growing up. Amphitrite. Fee, for short. She was a sweet little tabby cat who saw Keifer through the roughest parts of adolescence.

Keifer held out a hand to the orange tom, while the rain continued to pound down on them. He'd started shivering, but did his best to keep his voice steady.

"Shh," he said, then clucked his tongue again. He started moving slowly closer. "Come on, big guy. Don't worry. I won't steal you. I'll just help you get warm and dry, and then I'll help you get back to your people. Unless you don't have any people. Then we'll figure something else out."

Oh, Keifer couldn't help selfishly feeling that that was a wonderful possibility. He'd been all alone since Andi died two years ago.

Probably only felt as though it took half a freaking day for the cat to trust Keifer enough to allow him to pet the big guy. But hard as it was raining, it took more than long enough.

Soon as Keifer felt he had enough trust for the attempt, he scooped up that orange cat and held him close.

The big orange lug snuggled right in against his chest and purred.

That was all the hint Keifer needed. He started back across the lawn for his car.

Wasn't easy to get himself, the cat, and his water bottle into Keifer's Subaru Crosstrek, but he managed. The cat was clinging to him by now, and Keifer hoped that the big guy's claws didn't do too much damage to his shirt.

It was the last shirt Keifer still had from his days of playing intramural ball at University of Oregon. He didn't really want holes in it.

Keifer started up the car and cranked the heater. The cat was shivering worse than he was, and clung as though Keifer's body heat was the only thing keeping the poor guy alive.

Maybe a few holes in the shirt wouldn't be such a big deal after all...

At least Keifer kept a towel on the front seat on basketball days. Just a hand towel, true, but it was better than nothing. And petting the cat with the hand towel would at least help get rid of the worst of the water soaking the poor thing's fur.

The heater helped. The towel helped. And soon the cat was sitting in the passenger seat like he belonged there, bathing his fur back to something closer to its normal glory.

"All right, big guy," Keifer said. "Don't have any cat food right now, but I'm pretty sure I have a few cans of tuna in the cabinets that should still be good. Sound like a plan?"

The cat, almost as though understanding, paused in bathing long enough to give Keifer a heavy-lidded look of approval.

KEIFER DIDN'T GO STRAIGHT HOME, THOUGH. HE KNEW IF HE GOT THAT cat into his home, he'd start getting attached. That would be bad, if the cat belonged to someone else.

So, instead, Keifer drove over to a nearby veterinary hospital, only about a dozen blocks from the park. Over on Barbur Boulevard, *the* major street running from near downtown and out into the suburbs.

Keifer parked near the entrance, under the dubious rain shield provided by the branches of an old Douglas fir.

The parking lot was half-empty, at least. He considered that a good sign, in terms of them having time to help with a stray cat.

The orange tom was curled up by now and gazing lazily up at Keifer. That was a good sign, in terms of how well they were getting along, but Keifer doubted it indicated a willingness to go back out in the pouring rain.

He sat there for a moment. Listening the rain on the roof. Watching the waves it made on his windshield. He was sitting in a car that smelled like, well, mostly wet *cat*, but he was pretty sure some of the wet smell was his own, too.

He took out his phone and called the front desk. Explained his situation and made the arrangements.

They had time, and so, fawning apologies, Keifer scooped up the cat and carried him into the waiting room.

The appointment didn't take long. The cat was healthy enough that it wasn't likely he was a stray. Not even a flea on the big guy, and he'd been snipped a long time ago.

He also didn't have a microchip, so there was no easy way to tell who might be responsible for the cat's good condition.

They offered to hold onto him, but Keifer wouldn't hear of it. If they could help him find the big guy's people, that was fine. But if not, Keifer didn't want anyone else adopting him.

They did set Keifer up with a temporary litter box, some proper cat food, and some cat toys as well.

On the drive home, Keifer got tired of calling the cat "big guy" and gave him a name. A temporary name, Keifer told himself, but a name nonetheless.

Zeus.

"Powerful name for a powerful cat, don't you think?" He asked Zeus while scritching him at a stoplight.

Zeus purred. Possibly in response. Possibly because he enjoyed the petting. Possibly both.

Keifer's place was a little two-bedroom, down near the border of Lake Osewgo. Wasn't much of a house, to be honest. Kitchen and living room downstairs, two bedrooms upstairs, and a postage stamp of a backyard out back. Though the latter was made nicer by a handful of Japanese maples, and the garden of colorful perennials that Andi'd planted.

Keifer parked in the garage, and carried Zeus inside.

The house still smelled like the scrambled eggs Keifer had microwaved for breakfast, before heading out to play basketball.

It was immediately clear that Zeus didn't trust the hardwood floors. Suggested that he was used to carpeting. Keifer tried not to think about that.

Keifer's living room doubled as his office. He kept a huge old teacher's desk butted up against the back of his old, brown college sofa. The one Andi'd tolerated, but never really liked. It was huge and comfortable, but it was also a couch you could literally sink into, in the wrong spots.

It went well with the big, dark, faux-wood coffee table, though.

His television was much fancier. Wall-mounted, and so were his speakers. Full surround sound.

Keifer desperately wanted a shower and fresh clothing, but he knew he had something more important to do first.

So he gave Zeus a chance to get used to the house while he did the responsible thing. Sat down at his computer and hit all the neighbor and pet websites. Posted a picture of Zeus (though not the name, obviously) and information about where he'd found him, how to contact Keifer and so forth.

Off to his right, as he sat at his desk, Zeus sniffed around in the little kitchen. And it was a little kitchen. Hardly any counter space or storage.

It was sunny and yellow, though. Which had been about the only things Andi'd liked about it.

This was supposed to be their starter home. Their chance to build equity so they could buy the kind of home they wanted to live the rest of their lives in.

Turned out to be the last home Andi ever had. And Keifer was pretty sure he was never leaving it.

Zeus was out of the kitchen, now. On past it and into the dining room, which was really a glorified kitchen nook. Big enough for their round kitchen table, as well as a row of cheap bookshelves full of paperbacks and gaming books.

Zeus jumped up onto the table and sniffed around. Keifer couldn't remember the last time he'd used that table.

After he'd done his due diligence toward finding out whether anyone was looking for Zeus, Keifer took a much-needed hot shower, and put on his red-and-white striped terrycloth bathrobe.

He flopped on the couch next to where Zeus had curled up, and checked his email and social media.

Hey.

Del Baker was running a Jumpstart!

Del Baker was Keifer's favorite game developer. The man responsible for all of Keifer's favorite modules — and so much more — going back his teenage years when he was just discovering *Dungeons and Dragons* and its ilk.

Del Baker had developed a living, breathing campaign world called Qorunn for a setting called *Torn Kingdoms*. Over the years it had spawned hundreds of novels, a line of videogames and more, but Keifer's favorites had always been the sourcebooks themselves.

The maps, the descriptions, the world. Keifer just loved to read about the place as though it were real. He'd grown up with Qorunn, and knew its people, places and history at least as well as he knew his own world. Maybe better.

Especially since Andi died. When Keifer was reading about Qorunn, he didn't feel the crushing loneliness of life without her.

He just ... felt the childhood joy of fantasy all over again.

And if Del Baker was crowdfunding his next big project through Jumpstart, Keifer was damn sure going to get in on it.

He was just about to open the link and check out what Del Baker was up to when Zeus strolled onto his lap.

"Hey," Keifer said, laughing. "Feeling ignored? All right, big guy, I can take a hint."

Keifer petted the cat for a while. And then they played together with a feather dangling from a stick. When dinner time came around, Zeus got the can of tuna he'd been promised, and Keifer made himself a pair of grilled cheddar sandwiches, with extra sharp cheddar and more butter than was probably a good idea.

He and Zeus passed the evening on the couch watching reruns of a show about people competing in classic knightly skills like jousting, riding, melee combat, and more.

When bedtime came, Zeus forewent his spot on the couch and curled up on Andi's pillow like he belonged there.

Keifer seriously thought about moving him. If he tried, sometimes, he thought he could still smell a hint of Andi on that pillow. He didn't wash its pillowcase when he did his laundry. Figured he didn't use it, so it wasn't getting any dirtier, and he didn't want to lose that smell. That last little touch of her.

But Zeus looked so comfortable, Keifer couldn't bring himself to move the big guy.

"All right," he said softly. "Just tonight, though. I'll get you your own pillow tomorrow."

Zeus didn't reply to that. He was too busy sleeping.

KEIFER DREAMED HE WAS CLAD IN ARMOR. NOT THE FULL PLATE ARMOR of historical knights, or even the fantasy equivalent. No, he was clad in the light, half-plate armor worn by would-be knights on that contest show he'd been watching.

From the waist down, he was wearing good, thick blue jeans, with sneakers. But above the waist, gleaming armor. With a full helm, visor down. He even wore a shield on his left arm, shaped like an arrowhead, point down.

Something was written on the outside of the shield, but Keifer wasn't sure what. He tried to look a couple of times, as he mounted the roan stallion he'd been provided for the joust, but the letters never made any sense.

Someone handed him a lance. Keifer raised it in salute.

At the other end of the jousting run was the show's top competitor. Edna Johnson, a retired WNBA star. She'd beaten every opponent she'd faced so far and was the early favorite to win the tournament. She sat astride the black charger who'd served her so well on the show, and returned Keifer's salute.

They set up at their ends of the field, waiting for the signal.

Someone started hammering. Weren't the stands ready yet?

No. That couldn't have been it. The stands were full of fans. Jumping and shouting and cheering. Some of them looked vaguely familiar.

What was that hammering sound?

A woodpecker.

A giant red-crested woodpecker had landed on the side of the stands, and begun hammering away.

That was too much. Keifer woke up, puzzled. His dry mouth tasted lingeringly of iced tea. Had he forgotten to brush his teeth last night?

He shook his head. Tried to ease back to sleep. Wondering why a giant woodpecker had invaded his dream. Wondering if that had been Andi, dressed as a queen and presiding over the joust.

When the knock came again, Keifer jumped hard enough that Zeus meowed a complaint.

What? Awake? What time was it?

He glanced at his phone in its wireless charging cradle, proudly informing him that it was nearly eight o'clock on a Sunday morning.

Who the hell was knocking on his door at this hour?

Grumbling, he stumbled out of bed and into his striped robe. He started across the landing for the stairs. Stopped himself. Tied his robe closed. Ran his fingers through his short blonde hair to make it something like presentable.

He kept one hand on the wooden rail as he made his way down the stairs.

The knock came again.

"I'm coming, damn it," he grumbled. Or said. It sounded like a shout in his head, but he wasn't sure how loud it actually came out once those words got past his lips.

He failed on his first attempt to tear the door open, because he'd forgotten to undo the deadbolt.

Teeth gritted and shoulders tensed, he twisted the deadbolt to the unlocked position, and opened the door more slowly.

Three people. On his doorstep. All of them looking way too damned excited for eight o'clock on a Sunday morning.

They were obviously a family. A young couple only a couple of years older than Keifer was — putting them in their late twenties — and their ... maybe five-year-old daughter.

The man was in a sharp blue suit. The woman and little girl were both in matching dresses of spring green.

They were all so blonde and bright they could have been advertising shampoo and toothpaste at the same time. They even smelled clean.

"If you're selling religion," Keifer said, "I don't want any."

"I'm sorry if we woke you up," the man said with more patience than he'd shown in his knocking.

"You saved our Tommy!" the little girl said. "Where is he? Puss puss!"

Keifer's heart and stomach both tried to drop out of his body at the same time. He sagged.

These bright shiny people had come to take Zeus away from him.

Keifer wanted to slam the door in their bright, shiny faces. But that would be wrong. Zeus belonged with his family. Assuming Zeus *was* their cat...

"I'm happy to return him to the right family" — which was only half a lie — "but how can I be sure he's yours?"

The woman, still smiling, said, "Oh, we wouldn't come without proof. Show him, honey."

The man held up his phone, showing a series of pictures of an orange cat as a kitten and as an adult. Alone and with each of the three of them.

And the markings on the cat were a perfect match for Zeus.

Whose name was never Zeus in the first place. Apparently, the orange cat's name was Tommy.

Tommy the Tom Cat. Little girl probably named him.

Speaking of, that little girl was showing remarkable restraint while Keifer double-checked the pictures. She was twisting and craning to look around Keifer and into the house, but she didn't actually try to push past him and go hunting for her cat.

Keifer wondered if he would have been so patient, when he was her age.

He sighed and forced a smile onto his face. "I'll go get him."

Keifer didn't invite them in, but he didn't close the door in their faces either.

He found Ze— He found Tommy still curled up on Andi's pillow, but looking up with interest, past Keifer and toward the stairs.

Sure. Of course. He heard their voices. He knew they'd come for him.

"Come on, big guy," Keifer said, scooping the cat up and carrying him back down the stairs.

"Tommy!" The little girl ran forward the second she set eyes on the cat.

"Marcy!" her mother called after her, but Keifer wedged another smile and waved that it was all right, that they should come in too.

"Here he is," Keifer said, handing the cat to the little girl, to Marcy, who barely looked big enough to hold him. "Safe and sound."

The cat immediately buffed Marcy's face and started purring. Marcy's parents approached, smiling, and looking around at the mess Keifer had left last night. From there at the bottom of the stairs, he imagined they could see the open tuna can on his kitchen counter. His empty glass and ice cream bowl on the coffee table.

Hell, they were probably counting the dust motes in the air, since he hadn't swept lately.

Then the father spotted the cat toys and the temporary litter pan.

"Hope you didn't go to all that expense for Tommy," he said, and he actually sounded concerned.

The sound of concern made it more real. When was the last time anyone had shown Keifer concern? The funeral? Maybe just after the settlement?

"It's nothing," he mumbled, barely shaking his head. "Didn't want the little guy getting bored."

"Well, let us give you something for your trouble," the father said, reaching for his wallet.

Keifer shook his head sharply. "No. Really."

"You're sure?" the woman asked. Marcy was lost in a world of Tommy, who looked thrilled to be back with his people.

"'m sure," Keifer managed, with a nod.

"We'll get out of your hair then," the man said, while his wife began herding Marcy and Tommy back toward the front door.

He shook Keifer's hand. He had a firm, confident grip. Like a salesman. "Thank you so much for finding Tommy and keeping him safe. You're a good person."

Keifer managed to keep something like a smile on his face as he shepherded the happy family out of his house.

Then they were gone, and he went back to bed.

Andi's pillow smelled like Andi and Tommy now.

KEIFER WOKE UP CLOSE TO NOON, FEELING DEPRESSED.

He stared at the polar bear white ceiling. That was the compromise color he and Andi had chosen. She'd wanted something bright and pretty. He'd wanted something that didn't make him feel like he was waking up in a tampon commercial.

He tried to keep his mind on the paint, but he kept thinking about Tommy nee Zeus.

What had he been thinking? Naming the cat. Rookie mistake. Everyone knew that naming an animal was part of the bonding process. He should've just called him "cat" and not given it any more thought.

But done was done. The cat was back with his family, and Keifer was left with nothing but some orange hairs on Andi's pillow, some cat litter he needed to throw out, and some cat toys he didn't need.

Maybe he should get his own cat?

Maybe.

That thought was enough to drag him out of bed and into the shower.

Ten minutes of hot water and loudly sung Iron Maiden songs helped. Convinced Keifer to put on actual clothes. Some cargo shorts and a Timbers tee shirt.

Soon he was downstairs, eating peanut butter toast over the sink and drinking more iced tea.

When he realized he'd started remembering playing stick with

Zeus — Tommy might have been Marcy's cat, but Keifer's, he decided, was Zeus — he started cleaning.

He swept the whole house. Washed the kitchen counter. Threw out some old moldy Havarti cheese, and washed the inside of the fridge.

Keifer dusted and scrubbed and washed everything he could think of until he collapsed on his sofa. Heat came off him in waves. He had a light sweat on his forehead. His heart thumped harder as it slowed from its cleaning pace.

The couch tried to suck Keifer inside, just the way Andi used to complain about. He knew, though, that it just meant he was lying at the wrong angle. He wrestled around and adjusted until he felt comfortable.

By that point, he'd even stopped sweating.

Maybe what he needed was to adopt a cat of his own.

Wasn't the first time he'd had that thought. He and Andi used to talk about getting a pet — either a dog or a cat, they hadn't decided — but she insisted that they wait until they lived someplace bigger.

Was that why he hadn't done it yet?

Or was it just that he didn't want something else to die and leave him, the way Andi had?

Drunk driver. Andi'd been coming out of her favorite downtown coffee shop at three o'clock on a Wednesday freaking afternoon.

The place was right in the middle of the block. Not even on a corner. Not even a busy street, for downtown.

In fact, that was the problem. If there'd been cars parked along the curb that day, the driver would have hit them and Andi'd be alive.

There were no cars parked at the curb. Even Andi's little Miata was three blocks away, over by Powell's City of Books.

The drunk bastard jumped the curb and...

The settlement had made Keifer a rich man.

He'd trade it all to have Andi back. But that wasn't an option.

He felt so untethered, since Andi died. He'd quit working. He didn't need to, after all. And editing reseller contracts for a shoe company didn't matter anymore. Plus, it wasn't like he made lots of work friends.

Five years with that company and he'd never stopped feeling like the contractor he'd been before they took him on full-time.

In fact, all Keifer's real friends were people he'd met gaming, and they only played together a few times a month. They were good people, and good friends, but ... they'd been distant since Andi died.

Or maybe Keifer was the one who'd grown distant. Either way, it amounted to the same.

Lots of time to himself, and little motivation to seek more social activities.

Maybe it was time to get a cat. Maybe a little fuzzy friend could help wrestle Keifer out of his bouts of depression and loneliness.

He pulled out his phone to start looking at nearby animal shelters.

When he unlocked his phone, the first screen he saw was that Jumpstart page for Del Baker's new project.

Torn Kingdoms Sixth Edition!

Keifer was smiling before he knew it. He'd heard that a sixth edition was in the works, but he'd written that off to idle internet gossip.

He watched the video, where Del Baker teased about changes to the world of Qorunn since the Godswalk Wars, and how those changes would be reflected in the new edition of the game.

Ah, the Godswalk Wars. When the magic fell asunder, and the gods themselves had to come down from their heavens and hells and wage war across Qorunn. Each faction bent on determining how magic would return, what it would mean, and who would control it.

That had been the plan. Except that the Silver Arrows, the eight mightiest heroes of Qorunn, had stolen the secrets of magic while the gods were busy warring.

It was one of the Silver Arrows, the great sorceress Kalinda, who became the new goddess of magic. She ended the war and forced peace on the gods, returning them to their home planes of existence.

Keifer started looking through the pledge levels and their rewards.

He was able to skip past the low-level stuff. That was for the pikers and newbies. Old sourcebooks and adventures in electronic format. Old novels, the same way. Then came the paper levels.

Then the more interesting stuff. The new material in print and ebook. Plus maps. Plus one level that had a huge, six-foot-by-eight-foot wall map...

That would look great over his desk. But maybe he shouldn't—

Fuck it. Who was going to object?

Keifer marked that one a maybe and kept going.

Fancy, signed, limited edition copies of the new books. Good, good. A virtual one-on-one with Del Baker. Better still.

And then came the best stuff. The levels that had all the other goodies — even that wall map — but included the one-of-a-kind extras.

Five people could pledge seven hundred fifty dollars each and play in a virtual game run by Del Baker, with their characters guaranteed minor NPC roles in later sourcebooks.

That was tempting. It would've been more tempting if it were an in-person game. But that would probably have been a logistical nightmare.

What was this?

The top pledge level possible, coming in at five thousand dollars, was called Duke/Duchess of Deepwater. And the description...

This is the ultimate Tuckerization opportunity. Not only will you get all the goodies talked about above, including every stretch goal in the highest quality form we offer, but you, personally, get to become part of the Torn Kingdoms — as the Duke or Duchess of Deepwater, in the kingdom of Armyr!

Not only will your name and likeness live on in sourcebooks and fiction, you'll also receive your own patent of nobility, as well as an authentic representation of the ducal seal, done in at least fourteen karat gold, and a signet ring.

There was a little legalese following the description. The kind of thing to make sure that the new duke didn't end up with an obscene name or something.

But Keifer smiled as he thought about the possibilities here. He'd been reading about and playing in the *Torn Kingdoms* since he'd first discovered roleplaying games.

And now, now he had the chance to make himself a part of that world. To know that future sourcebooks would include Keifer McShane, Duke of Deepwater. Peer of the kingdom of Armyr.

Gods, Armyr. With its knightly orders and noble families...

That was right. The Godswalk Wars had claimed the life of Arinda Soulfist, Duchess of Deepwater. She had been a mighty wizard, and died defending her borders from reavers in service to Xazik the Flayer, god of chaos.

She'd died without an heir. Last thing Keifer could remember, there was some question about whether the king of Armyr, Colm Stronghand, had the right to appoint his choice for a new duke or duchess, or whether the old laws held and the duke of Silverlake and the Duchess of Merrek would have some say in who became their new peer.

Keifer wondered how Del Baker would play it. If Colm would simply appoint Keifer, meaning that his character would start his tenure at odds with his peers, or whether the duke and duchess would push for his ascension, putting the new duke at odds with his monarch and liege lord.

And what would the counts and countesses and barons think, either way? Would they feel that they, too, had a right to a say?

Only one person could claim this pledge level, of course. There could be only one duke of Deepwater.

Five thousand dollars was a lot of money...

No, he realized. Five thousand dollars *was* a lot of money. When Andi was alive, and they were saving to get a bigger house.

Nowadays, since the settlement, five thousand dollars was nothing. Especially since he wasn't exactly burning through money. He lived cheap. He ate cheap. Hell, he probably spent less every month now than he had back in college.

He could afford this. It wasn't a good, practical use of his money, but he could more than afford it.

And right now, he needed something that would make him smile.

He entered his pledge, claiming the duchy of Deepwater before anyone else could.

He lay back, then, and imagined how it would all come together. How he'd have a video chat with Del Baker about what kind of character would best suit Keifer. What kind of background to give the character in the fiction.

Keifer imagined that maybe his character could have come from a lowborn family. Been knighted during the Godswalk Wars. Maybe had a torrid love affair in the field with the gorgeous duchess of Merrek, Ashling Fyrenn.

Yes. That was just the kind of character he'd want associated with his name. Dashing. Adventurous. Maybe he didn't even have to be a swordsman. Maybe a wizard, instead. Apprenticed to some wandering wonder-worker, maybe, or a student at one of the great schools of magic down the coast at the Towers of Lund.

The world of Qorunn certainly had room for one more wizard...

Keifer hopped up off the couch and put his dining room table to use for the first time in months. He spread *Torn Kingdoms* game books across it, and maps, and started reviewing all he could about the kingdom of Armyr and the duchy of Deepwater.

And even though he knew Del Baker would make the ultimate choices about what kind of character "Keifer McShane" would be when he became Duke Keifer of Deepwater, Keifer couldn't help building his ideal character for the role all the same.

Made for a pleasant way to spend the day. Going through class and build options, and imagining different possibilities for the fictional Keifer to come.

He even got a smile when Marcy and her parents came back that afternoon. They'd baked him a batch of homemade chocolate chip cookies, and topped them with a thank-you card, hand drawn by Marcy. It featured a crayon depiction of Keifer with a cape holding an orange cat.

Yes, the day turned out to be pretty good after all.

The evening, however, got a little weird.

<hr>

THAT NIGHT KEIFER SAT AT HIS DESK. EATING A DELIVERY PIZZA WITH pepperoni, black olives, and extra cheese. Drinking Diet Eruption Cola. And making up a background for Keifer McShane, Duke of Deepwater.

The fictional Keifer had been just another peasant farmer in Armyr when the Godswalk Wars started. He'd been drafted into service by Baron Karmody. Given the basic training to handle leather armor and a spear, and sent off to war.

The fictional Keifer had acquitted himself well on the battlefield, and saved the life of his commander. This commander, a knight, had been wounded badly and was at the mercy of three taroc warriors when Keifer took up a fallen sword and shield and managed to fight off all three, killing one and wounding another in the process.

The fictional Keifer was knighted on the spot. And it was discovered that he was a natural *dweomerblade*, one of those rare individuals who found magic through swordplay.

The actual Keifer was sipping some soda and trying to decide if his character should, instead, have saved the beautiful Duchess Ashling Fyrenn — thus starting their torrid affair — or whether that should happen later, when his phone pinged with a text message.

The message was from Zan, his regular Friday night game master. It read, "What's this about you being the next Duke of Deepwater?"

Keifer smiled. Let the question hang through a cheesy, spicy bite of pizza. He'd sent out an email earlier, telling everyone in the group about the Del Baker Jumpstart — he knew they'd want in on it too — and casually mentioning that he'd already claimed the Duke of Deepwater reward.

"No shit," Keifer texted back. "No one had claimed it, so I jumped on it. Can't wait to see what Del Baker comes up with for me."

Keifer smiled at his phone, waiting for the reply. Jealousy, maybe, or even just congratulations. Zan wasn't as into *Torn Kingdoms* as Keifer was — Zan was more of a space opera gamer by nature — but still, Keifer had no doubt Zan would appreciate the cool factor involved.

"...Looking at the JS right now. Don't see any Duke of Deepwater reward."

Keifer frowned. Opened up his browser to the Jumpstart page...

Huh.

Keifer was listed up at the top as a five-thousand-dollar backer, for the Duke/Duchess of Deepwater reward. But when he scrolled down the sidebar, looking at the reward levels, that reward wasn't listed. Not even at the bottom, where the expired rewards were, for the early-bird backers.

The expired rewards were there, down at the bottom, where they were supposed to be. Scrolling back up, though, the top level listed was the "Game with Del Baker" reward at seven hundred fifty dollars.

That was weird.

Keifer then checked the site on another browser. One where Keifer wasn't logged in. Sure enough, there was no sign at all that the Duke/Duchess of Deepwater reward level had ever been available.

That was even weirder. Wasn't part of the point of these reward levels social proof? Demonstrating to potential backers how many others had backed this reward level or that one? Showing off how much money some fanatical individuals were willing to throw at the project?

Oh, well. No matter. If Del Baker didn't want the general public to know that they no longer had a shot at being the next duke or duchess of Deepwater, that was his call to make.

Keifer could still prove what he'd done.

Keifer brought up the Jumpstart page on his phone, took a screenshot, and sent it to Zan.

"It's visible on my page," Keifer included as text with the screenshot. "I can show you the email confirmation, you don't believe me."

Zan didn't respond immediately. When he did, he just said, "That's all right. I believe you."

That was all he said. Nothing about how cool it was. Nothing about how jealous he felt, that Keifer was going to be immortalized in gaming, while Zan wasn't.

Hell. Even his "I believe you" seemed almost condescending. As though he didn't believe Keifer at all, and was just humoring him.

Keifer was still considering a reply when a different text message came in. This one was from Nikki, who was, if possible, even more into the *Torn Kingdoms* than Keifer was. She had not just some, but *all* the novels. And she'd read them all. And she'd played the video games to death. She could give Keifer a run for his money, whenever they had their little trivia matches.

"There's no Duke of Deepwater reward," she wrote. "What are you talking about?"

Keifer didn't bother arguing. Just sent her a copy of the screenshot.

"Nice fake," she wrote back. "But I call bullshit."

Keifer, flustered, just stared slack-jawed at his phone through several long blinks. He was just formulating a properly outraged response when Nikki wrote a follow-up.

She attached a picture of her own reward confirmation. It was the Early-Bird Qorunni Noble level, which cost a couple of hundred and would get her fancy copies of everything.

With the picture came her message. "Check out my backer number."

Fine. Her backer number was eight. So she'd been on the page when it went live. Big deal.

Another message followed immediately. "I checked out every level at the time. There was no Duke of Deepwater option."

"So you missed it," Keifer sent back. "Too much of a hurry to get a low backer number, I guess."

"Or ... you're full of shit. Guess which I believe."

"Fine," Keifer wrote. "Can't wait to bring you proof when I get it."

"You do and I'll buy your dinner that night."

"You're on. And if I can't, I'll buy yours."

Technically, Deon didn't weigh in on whether it was real or not. His text message read simply, "Sweet!"

But by that point, even that one-word comment felt like condemnation.

As though Keifer would make something like this up.

Well, to hell with all three of them, then. They didn't believe him? Fine. They didn't have to. Keifer would bring the ducal seal, signet ring and the patent of nobility to a game night.

That would show them.

And that night, Keifer would order an extra special victory dinner, on Nikki's dime.

In the meantime, Keifer went back to working on the background for his fictional namesake.

Maybe Del Baker would let Keifer do some of the writing, even, when it came to his character...

KEIFER BEGGED OFF THE FRIDAY NIGHT GAME THAT WEEK. HE DIDN'T want to face Zan and the others until he had some tangible proof to point to about his new status as the Duke of Deepwater, a peer of the Kingdom of Armyr.

Fortunately, he knew he wouldn't have to wait long. The Jumpstart campaign was due to end on Monday night. And according to the reward level, even though none of the new *Torn Kingdoms* books would be available until the fall, *Keifer's* reward would be available as soon as the Jumpstart funded.

And it funded all right. More than ten times over, with three days still to go.

So Keifer waited with bated breath for news of his oncoming ascension to the ranks of nobility. And as he did, he played with the mental image of himself as a mighty, but fair, duke. Dispensing justice. Playing politics. Advising King Colm on matters of trade and war.

He even fooled around with a desktop publishing program,

designing ducal stationary, using a version of the Deepwater seal he found online.

He considered changing his email sign-off from "Catch you later, Keifer" to "from the desk of his grace, Keifer McShane, Duke of Deepwater."

Naw. That would be taking things too far. They'd all make fun of him if he did that. And, honestly, they'd be right to do it.

Still. These things were fun to think about. Say, when, he was stir-frying up some chicken with veggies, or cleaning out the coffee maker. Or going for a run through the hills of southwest Portland.

One thing he did do was buy some sealing wax. Could be fun to send out some letters sealed with the signet of Deepwater. That wouldn't be going too far. Anyone had a problem with him doing that, it was on *them*, not him. Some people had no sense of humor.

Best part about all of this duke of Deepwater stuff? Andi would have loved it.

Oh, she would never have approved of him blowing five grand on a title that had no meaning or use in this world. Not when they were saving to upgrade their house.

But setting the cost aside, she'd've loved it. She knew how much the *Torn Kingdoms* meant to Keifer, and she would have smiled that special little smile of hers at the thought of his getting to become a permanent part of the setting.

Oh, the incoming six-foot-by-eight-foot map would have been too much for her. No way she would have let him wall-mount that anywhere but the garage. Or maybe the man cave they'd talked about setting up for him, once they'd gotten a bigger house.

But the idea of Keifer having that golden seal, and the signet ring, and the patent of nobility. She'd have loved all that.

Andi even would have laughed with joy at the way he was carrying on. The stationary. The email signature. The sealing wax. And Andi would have *savored* introducing herself at conventions as "Duchess Andrea McShane, of Deepwater."

Ooh. That was a thought. Would Del Baker let Keifer's character be married to an Andrea? Then Andi could be a permanent part of the setting as well. If Duke Keifer was a former adventurer, maybe Duchess Andrea grew up Princess Andrea, and they fell so madly in love the king allowed them to marry.

A little extra tribute to Andi, embedded in something Keifer loved.

Yeah. That sounded perfect. And Keifer was sure he could sell Del Baker on the idea. He always seemed like a cool guy online, and surely he wouldn't deny a widower a little request like this. Especially not when that widower was blowing five grand for the privilege.

When at long last the clock on the Jumpstart started ticking away its final minutes, Keifer sat at his desk, watching the countdown. He had an open glass of Diet Cherry Eruption Cola on the desk, fizzing away, and a small, one-person bottle of sparkling wine, ready to go.

He even had a little assortment of chocolates for the occasion, each with a fruit cream filling like raspberry or lemon or lime.

The lime one he'd snuck earlier was delicious, and even played well with the cherry cola taste on his tongue. He had the album *Light Me Up* by The Pretty Reckless playing, but he had "O Fortuna" from *Carmina Burana* queued up and ready to go when the moment came.

His nerves were jangling in the best way. He had this stupid smile on his face, and kept laughing at himself as the minutes ticked closer to the zero hour. His heart was racing, and he could feel a good kind of tension singing down to his fingers and toes.

Five minutes left.

Laughing louder, he had to get up and pace around to keep his legs from bouncing.

Three minutes left. He killed the music. It was a distraction now. He imagined himself sitting in a waiting room, while in some great ducal hall crowds of nobles gathered and waited for his...

Coronation? No. That was for kings. There was probably a proper term for it, but the only one he could think of was "installment."

Could that be right?

He could look it up.

No. We were in the final minute of the countdown. No time to worry about the details.

Forty seconds and counting.

Thirty.

Twenty.

Keifer was so excited he tried to drum his fingers against each other, just to give them movement, but he kept missing.

Ten seconds.

Five.

Zero.

There was a little celebration animation, and the icons changed from "Live" to "Funded!"

Keifer reached for the sparkling wine bottle...

No. He'd wait for the confirmation.

It came a couple of torturous minutes later. First notifying him that his card had been charged. And then confirming that he'd supported at the five thousand dollar level, designated Duke/Duchess of Deepwater.

He started up "O Fortuna" and popped the sparkling wine.

"Here's to me!" he said. "Duke Keifer of Deepwater!"

But when he looked around, he had no one to share his joy with. Andi was dead. Zan, Nikki and Deon didn't believe him for some reason. And he'd never even gotten that cat.

Well, to hell with it. He'd celebrate on his own.

And maybe in the morning, he'd finally go see about getting a cat.

2

———————

Tuesday morning kind of snuck up on Keifer. He'd been lingering in bed, not even willing to glance at his phone and find out if he'd woken up early or overslept.

He had a slight pounding in his head. He'd never liked champagne. It always seemed to hit him faster and harder than even a good stout beer, and it always left him with an imprecise ache the next morning.

He'd hoped that sparkling wine — not being true champagne — would be kinder. But no. As he lay there, mostly warm and comfortable in his tangle of sheets, staring out the window at the wind in the elm trees, he had that familiar champagne headache.

It wasn't sharp or heavy, but it was just enough to be annoying. It didn't settle at the front of his head, nor at the back, nor even at his temples. It just seemed to move more or less among all three, as though sloshing about every time he tried shifting to a more comfortable position.

Currently it was behind his eyes, as he closed them and tried to persuade himself to go back to sleep. After all, the headache could last only so long. If he could get back to sleep, maybe it would be gone the next time he woke up.

He rolled over. Looked at Andi's pillow. He could just make out several little orange hairs, left behind by Zeus in his one night here.

If Keifer got out of bed, he could go check out animal shelters. It was springtime. Kitten season had probably begun.

Plus, if he got up, maybe he could even sweat out the headache in a good, hot shower.

Oh, and there could be coffee. Coffee would make everything better.

Of course, first, he'd have to get out of bed. Which would mean shaking the lethargy out of his recalcitrant limbs...

Someone knocked on the front door. Three sharp, loud raps.

"You've got to be kidding me," Keifer grumbled. Yes, the cookies had been lovely. And yes, he'd put that little thank-you drawing on his fridge. But he wasn't in any hurry to see Marcy and her parents again.

Unless, maybe, they decided they couldn't keep Tommy?

No. That family believed in proper forever homes for their pets. Tommy had a good home.

The rapid triple-knock came again.

Well, it wasn't the knock of Marcy's father anyway. It was probably nothing. Maybe somebody had a pest service out, and the pest service decided to knock on every door in the neighborhood and try to peddle their service. That always happened in the spring around here, when the spiders all started giving birth to thousands of baby spiders at a time.

Well, if that was all it was, the knocker would likely quit now and leave a card or something.

And the position Keifer had found — on his side, with one leg forward, the other back, and both hands under his pillow — was the most comfortable he'd managed in a while now. Even the throbbing of his head seemed to ease back a bit. Perhaps going back to sleep was an option after all...

The triple-knock came again. Louder.

"Fine," Keifer grumbled. He jerked himself out of bed, thrust his arms into his terrycloth bathrobe and tied the belt tight around his waist. "Need to pee anyway."

He didn't really, but saying so made him feel better about getting up.

Barefoot, he scuffled his way across the hardwood of the landing and down the stairs. His house still smelled like last-night's pizza. Speaking of, there were still a couple of slices in the fridge. Perfect for breakfast, once he got rid of the joker at his door.

That thought put a spring in Keifer's step. Cold pizza. The breakfast of champions.

"What?" He asked as he opened the door.

Standing on his doorstep was a portly old man in an orange robe with red trim. The trim had symbols sewn into it with golden thread. His boots were leather, old and worn but still intact. His belt looked the same, and from that belt hung dozens of pouches of various sizes.

The man was bald, but he made up for his lack of hair with a long, snow-white beard that hung nearly to his belt. His eyes were periwinkle blue, and seemed to sparkle when he smiled at Keifer, as he did now.

He leaned on a gnarly oaken staff that had to have been seven feet tall, a good foot-and-a-half taller than the man carrying it. At his feet was a leather backpack covered in pouches and pockets.

"Not a morning person I see," the old man said in a jovial voice as he looked Keifer over. And his eyes continued to sparkle.

"Can I help you?" That came out much politer sounding, Keifer thought. Well, it wasn't quite a *growl*, anyway.

"Now that's an interesting question," the old man said. "And I suspect the answer will prove even more interesting, when we come back to it. For right now, though, I did not come here to seek your help."

"Then why *are* you here?" Why, that sounded downright patient of Keifer, if he did say so himself.

The old man chuckled. As he did, Keifer examined the man a little closer. Couldn't quite guess his age. Somewhere between ... maybe sixty and eighty?

He seemed full of life, though, almost bursting with energy. He had more than his share of wrinkles, but mostly around the eyes and neck.

And his smile lines were getting a workout this morning.

"I think you'll likely be able to guess my purpose here, as soon as you realize who I am."

"Have we met?"

"Never had the pleasure of your acquaintance," the old man said, and from the sound of his voice he was enjoying himself thoroughly. "But I should think that you know well who I am. It's just that I suspect you were not expecting to meet me on your doorstep this morning."

Keifer shook his head, puzzled.

The old man raised one eyebrow above an eye that was somehow still sparkling. Shifted his stance so that his left shoulder was forward. He held the staff close to his right side, and shaded his eyes with his left hand as though looking off into the horizon.

There *was* something familiar about the old man. And that outfit. And that pose.

It was from the cover of *To Tour the Torn Kingdoms*, one of the most important Qorunn sourcebooks to come out of the first edition. It set the standard for all the books to follow.

Which meant that this man was — or was made up to be—

"Kainemorton," Keifer said, though really the word came out in a breath of awe.

Kainemorton. The Mage of Marrisford. The most ancient and powerful wizard in all Qorunn.

"The very same," the old man said with a bow, "and at your service."

"It's a fantastic costume," Keifer said, jaw slack as he looked the old man up and down with a more critical eye. "How do you get that effect with the eyes? The way they never stop twinkling. Special contacts?"

"I'm afraid the story behind my eyes is rather a private one," the actor said. And he had to be an actor. He had that kind of presence and stage voice. "Speaking of private matters, I suspect that the reason I'm here is not for public consumption."

"Oh, of course," Keifer said, standing back and gesturing for the actor to come inside. "You must be here about the Del Baker Jumpstart. My duke of Deepwater credentials. Have to say, I didn't expect a personal visit, but this is totally cool."

"Aye," the actor said, looking around at Keifer's house as he crossed the threshold and came inside. "Your status as the next duke of Deepwater is the very reason I've come."

Keifer smelled an aroma of lingering pipe smoke about the actor as he passed. But the actor had left his backpack on the porch.

Just as Keifer started forward to pick it up, the actor seemed to realize his mistake. But instead of turning around, or even saying a word, he just whistled. As though calling a dog.

The backpack floated up into the air and bobbed after him.

KEIFER SHUT HIS FRONT DOOR QUICKLY, NOT TAKING HIS EYES OFF THE backpack. If some trick had been set up on his porch, it should have cut off with the closing of his door.

But the backpack continued to bob in the air as it followed the actor down Keifer's short hallway, toward his living room and kitchen.

Couldn't be wires. There certainly weren't any wires between Keifer's ceiling and the backpack.

A drone maybe?

Keifer stood still. Tried to listen past his shallow breaths. He heard the surprisingly heavy tread of the actor, down the hall. He could hear the distant humming whirr of his refrigerator.

Could he hear any other humming?

No.

Wait. Couldn't be a drone *inside* the backpack. Displacing air from the inside wouldn't give the backpack any lift.

So how was the actor pulling this off?

One thing for sure. Del Baker was definitely trying to give Keifer his five thousand dollars' worth.

By the time he stopped gawking and followed the actor — and the floating backpack — down the hall, the actor was already sitting comfortably on Keifer's couch.

The backpack floated in the air beside him. Next to his staff, which seemed to be standing on its own.

And that wasn't all.

Keifer could smell coffee brewing in the kitchen. He could hear and smell bacon sizzling on his stove, in a pan alongside frying eggs.

Eggs that flipped themselves. Bacon that turned itself.

The toaster popped up, and slices of whole wheat toast floated through the air where a knife buttered them, before they landed on plates.

"Breakfast'll be along when it's ready," the ... actor? ... said. "You're free to enjoy the show, if you like, but really we ought not to wait too long to get down to business. And there's another matter that must be settled before we can do that."

Keifer took a seat at the other end of the couch from what he was no longer at all sure was an actor. He stared at the old man suspiciously, but the old man only smiled back, with those ever twinkling, periwinkle blue eyes of his.

"Go ahead and ask, lad," the old man said kindly. "Ask before the question bursts out of you on its own."

"You're not ... I mean you can't be..." Keifer swallowed. "How are you doing all this?"

"That's not the question you need to ask," the old man said, smiling. "In fact, it's a question that you know the answer to, if you'll allow yourself to admit it."

So the old man was saying that he really was doing all this by magic?

But then, what was the alternative explanation? That the old man had somehow snuck inside while Keifer was sleeping and rigged his kitchen to make breakfast?

"Are you..." Keifer swallowed again. The sparkling wine ache was back, hovering behind his eyeballs and making all of this seem more and more like a dream.

Was that it?

"Am I dreaming?" Keifer asked, and immediately tried to find something to read.

There. A fifth edition copy of *Gods of the Torn Kingdoms*. While the old man chuckled, Keifer opened to a random page and started reading. It was a depiction of Astryma, the old goddess of magic, before the Godswalk Wars.

Keifer read a paragraph about her mischievous personality. He looked away, and started again. The words were exactly the same, down to the font.

He read the passage a third time, focusing on each individual word and its letters.

Nothing jumped. Nothing shifted. Everything was as consistent as consistent could be.

"I'm not dreaming then," Keifer said softly.

"Nay, lad," the old man said. "Now ask the question before it burns you."

"Are you really Kainemorton?"

Two breakfast plates floated over the old man's head, each loaded with eggs and bacon and toast, complete with utensils and napkins. The plates were followed by two glasses of water, two glasses of orange juice, and two cups of coffee.

Keifer was pretty sure he hadn't bought any orange juice lately...

"I've already told you I am," Kainemorton said, sounding more amused than cross. "Is my word not good enough for you?"

"It's not that I'm doubting your word," Keifer said so quickly that the old man chuckled. "It's just that, well, I thought you were an actor, portraying a fictional character."

"I see," Kainemorton said — for Keifer could no longer deny the man's identity — "And tell me, lad. Do you believe there's only one universe out there?"

"I..." Keifer sighed and admitted the truth. "I never *wanted* to believe there was only one universe. Deep down, I think I wanted to believe that Middle Earth, and Westeros, and Qorunn were all real. Somewhere."

"Now," Kainemorton said, raising an index finger as though Keifer had made a point worth emphasizing. "If that's true, why should you be so surprised to see me here?" He made a show of glancing around at some of Keifer's *Torn Kingdoms* books. "Surely you know that the magics of planar travel are known to us on Qorunn."

"Knowing it could theoretically be possible," Keifer said, "isn't the same thing as seeing the Mage of Marrisford show up on my doorstep."

"Nay," Kainemorton said with a smile, "I'll wager it's not. But" — he raised that index finger again, just exactly the way Del Baker had described the way Kainemorton loved to make a point — "now that you know — and I mean you've properly accepted — who I am, then you must know why I've come."

"Am I..." Keifer's eyes widened in shock. "You mean I'm going to *really* become the duke of Deepwater?"

"I should say so," Kainemorton said. "If you're not, I've wasted a good deal of time and effort."

Roughly two thousand eight hundred and seventy-six questions all tried to come out of Keifer's mouth at the same time. But before he could organize his tongue enough to give voice to any of them, Kainemorton held up a forestalling hand.

"Speaking of not wasting time and effort. What say you and I delay the rest of this particular conversation until after we've given proper due to this hearty repast? With all we've got to do today, we're going to want some proper fortification in our bellies."

Kainemorton cocked an eyebrow at Keifer.

"Aye," he added, looking over Keifer's bathrobe, "and I think you'll want a change of clothes before we leave."

SITTING ON HIS OWN LIVING ROOM COUCH, EATING BREAKFAST WITH THE actual freaking *Kainemorton*, was easily the most surreal experience of Keifer's life to that point.

The breakfast itself was simple, but good. The eggs were runny and peppery, and their yolks tasted perfect when sopped up with buttered wheat toast. The bacon was even better. Crispy and just the way Keifer liked it.

The coffee was stronger than Keifer made, but it was still his own blend of two-parts medium roast to one-part hazelnut. The orange juice, though, was beyond compare. Keifer would have believed that it was fresh squeezed from plump, juicy, just-picked oranges. Possibly from trees in his own backyard.

Except, of course, that Keifer didn't have any orange trees. Or any orange juice in his fridge, for that matter.

Kainemorton seemed to enjoy the shifting expressions of wonder and disbelief on Keifer's face while they ate. And the greatest mage Qorunn had ever known ate patiently, giving Keifer time to adjust to unexpected realities.

It was all real. Qorunn. Kainemorton. All of it.

Wait...

"So," Keifer said around a mouthful of bacon, "everything in those books is true? The places, the people, the events?"

Kainemorton twirled one finger in his beard while he considered that question.

"I'd say at least as accurate as any history text," he said, "and more accurate than some by a fair piece. But no text every truly captures all the nuances of an event."

"How so?" Keifer asked, then took a sip of juice that might have ruined him for all other orange juice. It was just that good.

"Take a war," Kainemorton said. "Any war. The texts will only cover the larger, more obvious causes that led to it. But the smaller issues, the personal matters among the leaders, they tend to get missed."

"Can you give me an example? Maybe the War of Red Gold?"

That one always seemed straightforward to Keifer. It involved two neighboring counties within the duchy of Deepwater — Goldenfall and Motte. As a result of adventure *J13, King of the Deepmines*, gold had been discovered among the Threepeaks Mountains, the range that formed the northern edge of both counties.

Naturally, the discovery was close to the border between the two counties. The counts had disagreed over who had claim to the gold, and gone to war to press their claims.

Keifer didn't see any nuance there.

"Ah, already worried about your vassals?" Kainemorton asked with a grin. "Wise of you. And a good question. Because the gold was clearly on the Goldenfall side. But the Count of Motte…"

"Ferrin," Keifer prompted.

"The very same," Kainemorton said with an approving nod. "Ferrin was a young count, and hated the reputation his father had as a drinker and a coward. He was far more interested in an excuse to fight than in gold he had no claim to."

That made Keifer frown. None of that had been mentioned in the afterward of the adventure, nor the sourcebooks that followed.

"But he had those papers," Keifer said, talking about the reason that *did* show up in his books. "The ones showing his family's ancient claim to the land west to—"

"Papers he wrote himself," Kainemorton said. "Well, had a scribe write, with Ferrin himself dictating."

"No," Keifer said, more from astonishment than actual denial.

"Ink was barely dry when he started waving them in everyone's face," Kainemorton said with a chuckle. "Brazen one, that boy. You'll want to keep an eye on him."

Keifer was still absorbing that when Kainemorton chuckled again.

"'Boy,' I call him, but you better not. He's right about your own age."

"So, wait," Keifer said. "Why did none of the texts mention the forged claim? That'd be easy enough to prove."

"Because her grace the duchess chose not to make an issue of those papers when she forced peace on her vassals. You see, Goldenfall is well-named. It's the richest county in all of Armyr, and money brings power."

"So," Keifer said slowly, "by not refuting the claim..." He sat up straight. "She wanted to keep the option of backing Motte, if Goldenfall became a problem?"

"Now you're thinking like a duke," Kainemorton said.

"But that mountain range forms a natural border entirely within her duchy. Couldn't she have declared the range ducal land?"

"She could have, aye," Kainemorton said, "but she had other problems pressing for her attention. D'you know which?"

Keifer closed his eyes, trying to remember past his throbbing, sparkling wine headache. Food had helped, and coffee had helped even more, but thinking like this seemed to exacerbate it.

"Was this..." Keifer thought back to adventure *K12*. It was called *Red Tides Rolling*, and the villain was one of the big bads of Qorunn... "The pirate queen Nelazzi?"

"Very good," Kainemorton said with a smile and another approving nod. "You do know your history. Yes. Duchess Arinda needed to focus most of her military might on fighting the pirates, which meant she couldn't have enforced a claim on the mountain range, if both those counts united against her."

"Which they would have done," Keifer said, "because Ferrin was spoiling for a fight, and didn't care who he fought?"

"Well, yes," Kainemorton admitted. "There's that. But they would have opposed her ruling anyway, because it was clear at the time that they could. That she couldn't afford to enforce it."

"And so she didn't press, because she didn't want to fail and look weak."

Tough choice. Even another sip of orange juice couldn't make Keifer feel better about picturing himself in her position.

Which was just where he was about to be?

"So what did she do instead?" Kainemorton asked, bringing Keifer's attention back to the conversation.

"I don't know," he said, stress already tightening his shoulders and gut. "This part wasn't covered in the modules or sourcebooks."

"All right," Kainemorton said soothingly. "That's fine. So. If you were duke when it happened, what would *you* have done to assert yourself, while still not contesting the rights to that gold?"

Keifer took a long, slow breath. Then needed another.

That wasn't enough.

Keifer thought about the question through a slowly eaten slice of wheat toast, liberally washed down with coffee from a cup that seemed to be refilling itself.

For that matter, so were his breakfast plate and orange juice.

Kainemorton winked at Keifer. "Focus on the question, lad."

All right. If this had happened while Keifer was playing *Torn Kingdoms: Dynasties*, what would he have done?

"I'd ... I'd've levied a one-time war tax on both the counties — both money and soldiers — to defray the cost of fighting off pirates and preserving trade that benefited the counties. Obviously both counts could afford it, since they had the resources to fight each other while the duchy was under such an extant threat. Plus, they were flush with the new gold from the peace agreement."

"Which is what her grace did," Kainemorton said, and his eyes twinkled even brighter when he smiled. "Though she gave them the option of paying with gold or troops, rather than taking both."

"So my way was too harsh?"

"That's for you to decide. Should you ever face a similar problem."

At his gesture, slices of bacon began to stand tall on his plate. Then slices began to bend slightly, and seemed to jump atop each other until they stood as one, eight strips tall. They wobbled slightly, but stayed erect.

"Politics is a balancing act," Kainemorton said, while a slice of toast jumped up to lay flat across the top edge of the bacon, and spin. "You have to know when to be assertive and strong, and when to yield and compromise."

He snapped his fingers, and his tower fell down to his plate. He picked up and munched on a slice of bacon, while Keifer considered the message.

"You'll make mistakes," Kainemorton said. "Everyone does, myself included. Though I'll wager I make fewer than most. But then, I've also lived longer than most. The key is to *learn* from your mistakes. Most folks miss that part."

"But..."

"Go on," Kainemorton said, encouragingly.

"But how can I judge beforehand what's a mistake and what isn't? I mean, when it's something I haven't done before." Keifer shook his head. "Which all of this will be. I mean, I've *pretended* to handle situations like these, but I've never *actually*—"

"You won't be able to tell beforehand," Kainemorton said with an infuriatingly unconcerned shrug. Then he looked Keifer over and nodded. "I'd say, though, that in your case, you'll do fine. Seem a good sort, and you have a decent head on your shoulders. Even if you *have* allowed yourself to wallow entirely too much lately."

"What—"

"Most important for you to remember, is that any action is better than none. Especially in a crisis. Trust your gut, your heart, and your head. You'll do fine, lad."

Keifer wanted to get back this "wallowing" thing, but Kainemorton was looking him over critically.

"Right," Kainemorton said. "I'd say you've had enough breakfast. Unless, of course, you want to grow a proper belly like mine." He patted his belly for emphasis, and let out a loud belch.

Keifer couldn't help laughing at that. "No, I'm not ready for a belly like yours."

"Probably a good call," Kainemorton said. "Not every man can carry it off as well as I do." He winked at Keifer, then said, "Now. Go clean yourself up and put on something decent. When you come back down, I think we'll be ready to finally discuss this duchy of yours."

Keifer showered on autopilot, his mind a chaotic swirl of excitement and fear.

How could he possibly become a duke? He wasn't raised to run a duchy. He had no training or experience at any kind of politics, let alone feudal politics.

Well, except what he'd done in roleplaying games, and those didn't count.

Did they?

No.

The sourcebooks weren't perfect pictures of the nations and peoples of Qorunn. In much the same way, playing at being a noble and working through political problems couldn't possibly be as complex and dangerous as the real thing.

Dangerous.

God. People murdered nobles they didn't like. Poison. Assassins. These would be real threats where Keifer was going, wouldn't they? He'd have to learn the hard way who he could trust and who he couldn't.

And he'd be the outsider. What if they didn't accept him? What if everyone from his vassals to his staff and advisers turned against him?

Keifer shook himself, realizing he'd crouched down in the shower and was rocking back and forth with his arms around his legs. His heart pounding, and his skin clammy from fear sweat, despite the hot water beating down on him. Steam was everywhere.

He didn't have to do this. He could always refuse the reward. Continue living here ... in safety...

Did what Keifer did here count as *living*?

He forced himself to stand up. Start showering again, while he considered his life.

And he didn't like it.

Truth was, Keifer hadn't been *living* since Andi died. Not really. He'd been existing. A ghost, haunting a house that was little more than a shrine to his dead wife.

Keifer didn't leave the house anymore, except to run, buy

groceries and go to games. And hell, sometimes he even had the groceries delivered.

He never had guests over. Marcy's family had been the first other human beings to set foot inside Keifer's house since the funeral reception.

Even his own family back in Minnesota didn't come visit.

Not that Keifer wanted them to. Lots of people knew about the Michigan Militia, but not many people seemed to know that there was a Minnesota equivalent. If much smaller and more insular.

Part of the reason Keifer had moved to Oregon for college had been to get away from all that. Andi'd made staying out here easy.

Now Andi was dead. And Keifer spent all his time online, or reading, or gaming.

Life here was just waiting to die anyway.

But if Keifer accepted the duchy...

Nobody here would miss him. Not his family, certainly. And even his gaming friends — how much could they miss him if they thought he'd lie about something as presumably inconsequential as a Jumpstart reward?

No. Keifer wouldn't be leaving much behind. And to look forward to, *real adventure.*

He'd get to travel to *Qorunn.* Breathe its air. Walk on its dirt. Eat its food. Meet its people. And all *for real.*

He wouldn't be some nobody who could just hide in his home and read. He'd be a duke. He'd have real responsibilities. He'd *have* to meet people. Attend social events, as well as political ones.

And hell, even if the locals all turned on him and killed Keifer on his very first day there — which he doubted would happen, if *Kainemorton* was his escort — he'd still die having proven beyond the shadow of a doubt that the world he loved so well wasn't just a work of fiction.

And hey. If they killed him, he'd get to be with Andi on the other side. Kind of a no-lose situation.

Buoyed by that admittedly macabre thought, Keifer found his fears calming and his excitement growing as he dried off and dressed.

He even put some thought into what he would wear, for the first time since the funeral.

Back when Andi was alive, she loved for them to go to places like the Renaissance Faire and the Highland Games dressed in appropriate garb. Both her and Keifer.

All those clothes had gathered more than a little dust since her death, but he could shake them out easily enough.

"Should I pack a bag?" Keifer called down the stairs.

"No need for that," Kainemorton called back in a carrying voice. "Though feel free to bring any special mementos you'd like at hand."

Keifer put on a white poet shirt, with the blue-and-green tartan half-kilt Andi'd said made his legs look amazing. He had socks that matched it, and black shoes that really needed a proper polish. But they still more or less matched his belt. Adding a sporran, he felt dressed in a decently appropriate fashion.

True, kilts weren't the fashion in Armyr, but he was an outsider anyway. Might as well steer into the curve.

As for keepsakes, he kept the small crystal pendant Andi'd gotten him for their first anniversary, and the gold chain it hung from.

He thought about bringing more, but all he really needed was a memento of Andi. Except...

Keifer walked out onto the landing and looked over the rail down at where Kainemorton was standing in the dining room, reading something from Keifer's bookshelf.

"Can I bring my *Torn Kingdoms* books?"

"Certainly not," Kainemorton said. "Can't risk other people getting their hands on them. Could bring all sorts of questions."

Kainemorton looked up at Keifer. "Lose the kilt. The tartan doesn't fit any clan on Qorunn." He frowned. "Not that it would be better if it did."

"Fine," Keifer said, then went back into his bedroom and traded the kilt for dark brown leggings, and the tartan socks for white ones. But now the shirt looked plain, so he traded it out for a pale blue shirt that had laces toward the collar and gave Keifer a classier look.

He redid the belt over the shirt, and kept the sporran.

The shoes he traded out for soft leather boots that laced all the way up to the knee. Much more comfortable, for walking, which Keifer imagined he'd be doing quite a bit.

Finally dressed, he came back downstairs, eager to talk about his new duchy.

By the time Keifer was dressed and downstairs once more, Kainemorton was back on the couch, halfway through a superhero game sourcebook that was really just a collection of powers, demonstrating how to build them using that system.

"You play that game?" Keifer asked.

"Not in the least," Kainemorton said, still reading. "But it does provide interesting ideas for future spells." He closed the book. "Though the designers ought to be ashamed of some of them. Certain of those powers could be abused worse than any spells I've ever heard of."

Kainemorton looked Keifer up and down with those twinkling eyes of his. He nodded.

"That'll do," he said. "We can find you something more appropriate to your new rank once you've settled in."

"Find?" Keifer asked, settling back in place at the other end of the couch from the great mage. "Don't you mean 'have made?'"

Kainemorton smiled. "Do I?"

Keifer shook his head, deciding he wouldn't get a better answer anytime soon.

"So," he said instead. "About the duchy. Where do we start?"

"Well," Kainemorton said, tossing the book into the air, where it zoomed back to its proper place on Keifer's bookshelf. "We do have a little detail to attend to first."

Kainemorton clapped his hands. The light in the room — which was all coming from outside, through the windows — dimmed. He made a quick gesture and spoke a word, and they were surrounded by floating, burning white candles.

Those candles had to be illusory, but they smelled like beeswax, and Keifer even felt a little bit of heat coming from them.

"Keifer Alan McShane," Kainemorton said, "if you accept the position of duke of Deepwater, you must first leave behind your life in this world. The day may come when you find a way of returning under your own power, but you should leave with the expectation that you will never again see the lands and people of your birth. Do you understand?"

"I do," Keifer said. He'd been thinking about nothing else since that shower. "I have a question about that, though."

"Ask." Kainemorton seemed to expect this.

"What happens to all of this? My house. My money. The rest of it."

Kainemorton leaned forward, and this time his smile gave Keifer a shiver.

"You won't be coming back. Why do you care?"

"I don't," Keifer said, frowning. "Not really. It's just... All I have to remember Andi is this necklace." He pulled it out of his shirt. "I'm not sure I'm ready to lose our wedding photos and video. Or—"

Kainemorton laughed, but it wasn't a mocking laugh. If anything, he sounded pleased.

"Good, good," he said, smiling. "Wanted to make sure you weren't worried about foolish things like money you won't be spending or land you won't be using. *Personal* items are a different breed altogether."

"But you said—"

"I said I didn't want you packing a bunch of clothes you won't be using or books you shouldn't have. And I don't. However. I can offer you a chest to fill with those personal items you might find you want someday. *That* you can bring with you."

Keifer started to get up, but Kainemorton stayed him with a raised hand.

"*After* we've finished our discussion, of course."

"Sorry," Keifer said, chagrined. "Where were we?"

· "Well, I'd say we've made it clear enough that you won't be expecting to run home if life gets difficult. And that's important."

"Burn the boats behind so we can't sail away, eh?" Keifer said with a grin.

Kainemorton cocked an eyebrow. "Interesting thought. Something from your history here?"

Keifer nodded and started to explain, but Kainemorton raised a forestalling hand again.

"Let's not get sidetracked." His face grew serious again. Or at least, as serious as it could get with those twinkling periwinkle eyes. "If you accept the position of duke of Deepwater, you will be accountable to your liege lord, the monarch of Armyr, to your vassals, and to all the people of Deepwater. Do you understand?"

"I ... think so," Keifer said. "I will owe feudal allegiance, as well as taxes, to the king. My vassals will owe feudal allegiance to me, as well as taxes. And I will owe them my protection and my just rule. Which I will also owe to the people of Deepwater."

"Very good," Kainemorton said. "But not everything. Do you understand the other responsibility you will take on?"

Keifer drew a blank. Shook his head.

"Put it this way, lad. The duchy is, traditionally, an inherited position. By rights it should have gone to the son or daughter of her grace, Duchess Arinda Soulfist, and would have, save that she died without acknowledged issue."

"She wouldn't marry any man who couldn't outdo her with spells," Keifer said, recalling the reason given in her description in one of the sourcebooks.

"True, as far as it goes," Kainemorton said. "But she was very picky about those she let try." He shook his head. "Truth was, she just didn't want to be a mother. She took too much pleasure in using the possibility of a marriage-alliance as a bargaining tool."

Kainemorton shook his head again. "Mages, lad, tend to think of themselves as immortal, because we can live a very, very long time. And I'm guilty of it myself, I don't deny it. But even the best of us can die. And because old age is rarely the culprit, death often comes for us unexpectedly. Such was the case with poor Arinda."

"Part of the agreement is that I can't make that mistake. Is that it?"

"His Majesty King Colm of Armyr will be installing you as duke. This will not sit well with the duke of Silverlake nor the duchess of Merrek, both of whom feel they should get some say in the matter. What does that tell you?"

"It tells me I'll be starting my political career with two major enemies."

"Well," Kainemorton said, chuckling. "*Enemies* might be putting it a bit too strongly. You'll have to prove yourself to them, though, that's true enough. But it's also not the point I was going for."

"The king is going to expect me to marry and produce offspring, so he doesn't have to make a decision like this again, should something happen to me."

"Just so," Kainemorton said, his face serious once more. "No one will expect you to rush into anything, you understand. Just don't make a game of it, the way Arinda did."

"But I'm—"

"A widower, I know," Kainemorton said. "And it's obvious to anyone who looks at you how much you loved your lost wife. But tell me something, lad. Would that Andi of yours want you to go the rest of your life without love? Without companionship? Without children?"

Keifer hated the answer to that question, but he couldn't lie. Not about Andi.

"No. She'd ... she'd hate to see me living the way I am."

"And a good woman she was then," Kainemorton said, gently. "Life is for the living, lad. Remember that. You're young, strong, and pleasant to look upon. Even without the title you'd not lack for options, when it comes to a bride."

The stress of this subject seemed to be tightening every muscle in Keifer's body. A couple of deep breaths helped, but not enough.

Damn it, though, it was true. Andi wouldn't want him to go the rest of his life without love.

"All right," Keifer said, forcing the words out of a reluctant mouth. "I guess I can agree to that. Marriage and children are part of the deal. As long as I don't have to rush into anything."

"Good," Kainemorton said. "Wasn't sure you'd agree to that part." He clapped his hands. The candles vanished the sunlight resumed its normal, bright level. "Now, lad. Tell me. What do all of the nobles of Armyr have in common?"

"They're all humans," Keifer said quickly.

"Well, that's true, I'll grant you," Kainemorton said with a chuckle. "Not what I was going for, though. What else do they all have in common?"

"Well," Keifer said, "I'm not sure. Most of them were born into noble families. But not all of them—"

"Aye," Kainemorton said, "what about the others?"

"They were all former adventurers, given their titles and lands as thanks for some great accomplishment."

"*That's* what I was looking for," Kainemorton said. "The nobles in Armyr were all either born to their position, or had it granted through achievement."

"But I'm not—"

"Born from a noble Armyrian family?" Kainemorton said with a smile. "Nay, I should say not. They'd certainly remember you."

"But my only accomplishment is supporting a Jumpstart campaign."

"Aye," Kainemorton said, his eyes twinkling even brighter for a moment. "You played a critical role in the success of an important campaign that will affect all of Qorunn."

"Wait," Keifer said, feeling as though he'd just had a glass of cold water thrown in his face. "They're going to think I'm an *adventurer*? But I'm not! And they'll expect me to have the skills and—"

"Ah, lad," Kainemorton said with a wink, "you've spent more time adventuring than most, I'd wager."

"Yeah," Keifer said, "but with *dice*. Not with actual enemies trying to kill me."

"And did you take the lives of your characters any less serious than you take your own?"

"Well ... no, but—"

"Just so." Kainemorton smiled. "Lad, not everyone was offered the opportunity to become duke of Deepwater. Only those who both knew the world well enough to fit in, and had the kind of adventurous souls we need."

"Let me guess," Keifer said with a grimace, "and wouldn't be missed here in this world?"

"I'd not have said that myself," Kainemorton said, "but I won't deny that it helps."

"So, what?" Keifer said. "We tell people I'm a former adventurer and just hope I never have to prove it?"

"Now, what fun would that be?" Kainemorton rubbed his hands together. "Let's talk about what sort of adventuring career would suit you best."

KEIFER EXPECTED TO GRAB PENCIL, PAPER AND DICE AND START BUILDING a character. Well, building *himself*, but *as* a character.

Though, when he stopped later and thought back on this moment, he realized that he wouldn't have needed dice for that. He would have been expected to assign himself scores and have the game master — most likely Kainemorton in this case — correct them, if necessary.

But none of that was what Kainemorton had in mind.

He didn't even start asking Keifer a series of questions, like some social media quiz. Which, honestly, Keifer half-expected him to do, once Kainemorton stopped Keifer from getting up to go get those things he usually used when creating characters.

Kind of a funny thought, really. The great Kainemorton asking questions like, "A borog warrior bursts through the door. Do you a) reach for your sword, b) reach for your spells, or c) reach for your holy symbol?

Honestly, Keifer's mind was just flailing out for reference points to make some sense out of what he was going through.

After all, he was sitting on his own old, half-broken brown couch. That relic of his college days. In his own house. The one he'd shared with Andi.

And he wasn't only talking to the Mage of Marrisford himself. The one. The only. *Kainemorton.* No. He'd had breakfast with Kainemorton — a breakfast prepared magically, no less, including the fantastic orange juice that Keifer could still taste, if he thought about it — and now was preparing to magically become some kind of adventurer?

Had Keifer been struck by lighting in that sudden storm the other day? That would make as much sense as anything else. That Keifer were having some kind of coma dream.

That smell of bacon lingering in the air. Could that be one of the signs of a stroke?

Kainemorton snapped his fingers, drawing Keifer's attention.

"Wake up, lad," the old mage said. "This is all real enough. And we've important decisions to make before we leave for Qorunn."

Keifer shook himself. Gave Kainemorton a shaky smile.

"Good. Now. What was that spell..." Kainemorton twiddled one finger in his beard while he thought, mumbling to himself.

Keifer was about to offer to gather his *Torn Kingdoms* books of spells when Kainemorton snapped his fingers again.

"Of course." He twirled his hands as though sorting through files in a filing cabinet while he mumbled some words to himself

His hands began to glow a vivid greenish purple. As they did, the character sheets of all of the characters Keifer had ever made flew out of their binders and folders and boxes and swirled in the air over the Mage of Marrisford.

As they circled in the air, it was though Keifer could see great moments of his gaming history played out in flashes above each sheet.

Here the warrior Grakin, the last member of his party still standing when he dealt the deathblow to the Lich of Liveston.

There his eldrani skald Nulesin spellbinding the great dragon Vermithraxis for four whole combat rounds, buying time for the cleric to heal the party to full strength. They'd have lost the fight without that skald's song...

Kainemorton continued to mumble to himself as he looked up at the swirling sheets of paper and the scenes that played out above them.

Some of those papers were formal character sheets, printed and copied out of books (with explicit permission of the publisher). Others were handwritten. Still others were printouts from character-building programs.

The wizard Randolf Eibswitch, the first character Keifer had ever made back in high school, who'd never made it beyond seventh rank, no matter what Keifer later told his friends. Every single character Keifer had ever played, all the way to Lunn, the barbarian he'd been playing in Zan's current campaign.

Keifer found himself thinking about his gaming career. All the characters and campaigns he'd played and run. Which ones had been the most fun, and which ... hadn't really seemed to suit him. Which ones had pushed him to try new things and think along new lines, and which had felt like coming home. Natural and easy.

The papers began to swirl faster and faster. It sounded as though a hundred angry crows were all flapping around Keifer's living room. The scenes that played out above them began to run together, speeding faster through their great moments and blurring into incomprehensibility.

The greenish-purple glow from Kainemorton's hands grew brighter. Began to spread from his hands up to among the papers.

Individual sheets of paper began flying away. Back to their boxes and binders and folders, each of which whipped open to swallow whole the papers as they arrived, closing with a loud *clap*.

Sounded as though the audience was giving the angry crows a standing ovation.

Finally, the last piece of paper flew away. But as soon as it did, another appeared in the middle to the greenish-purple glow up above Kainemorton's head.

The old mage stopped his incanting and gesturing. The glow died from his hands, and vanished slowly upward, until it faded from around that final, spinning sheet of paper.

The paper floated gently down to Kainemorton's waiting hands.

He read it over, nodding, and making small *mmm-hmmm* sounds.

He held the paper up, blank side facing Keifer.

"This contains an analysis of all the characters you've ever played, including the types, races, accomplishments and total time spent playing each type of character."

He lowered it, leaning a little closer. His periwinkle eyes twinkling.

"From the information on this sheet, I can make a reasonable guess about what kind of adventurer you'd best make." He smiled. "But I'd like you to tell me what you think the data here concludes."

That ... wasn't what Keifer was expecting at all.

He'd played so many characters over the years.

A friend of his was fond of saying that people always played themselves, and that they always tended toward the same one or two basic characters over and over.

Keifer had fought hard against that stereotype through the years. Varied his races — which properly should have been called "species" but convention in roleplaying games kept them as "races" — and classes, even his gender a time or two. Found what fun he could find in every option available.

He knew he did play wizards more often than other classes, but that was just because other players often avoided the spellcasters as too difficult.

Or was that just an excuse? Maybe covering some deep-seated desire to practice actual magic himself?

Keifer snuck a glance at Kainemorton, but the old mage gave him nothing to work with. Not so much as a hint about what that paper might say about him.

Wait.

Maybe that was the answer. Maybe that had all been a sound and lights show to throw Keifer off-balance, when the whole point was to make him choose the adventuring career that would suit him best.

Especially since, like claiming the duchy itself, Keifer suspected there'd be no chance to change his mind...

"This isn't a trick," Kainemorton said softly, as though reading Keifer's mind. "I do have an answer here. But I want to know what you think all the same."

When Keifer frowned, trying to figure out how to begin to answer that question, Kainemorton spoke again, still in that soft voice.

"Think of it this way, lad. You've played every character whose depiction floated over my head not a few minutes past. Which ones most captured you? Which ones did you sink into easiest? And why was that? What did they have in common?"

Keifer thought about that, but he wasn't sure it helped. How well he sank into characters, sometimes that came down to the group, or the game master, or even an individual scene.

No.

That wasn't entirely true.

His favorite characters were the lost ones. The children of fallen noble houses. The orphans who didn't know their past, or whose past was dead and gone.

That was just the kind of situation he was going into. Wasn't it? When Keifer arrived in Armyr, he'd be a man lost to his past and his homelands, where he'd been a wealthy landowner.

And every time he played a character like that, they fell into three categories: skalds, wizards, and dweomerblades.

Skald was out. No way Keifer wanted to deal with the realities of having to weave spells with his words and songs. Especially the songs and epic poems that would be expected of him.

No, sir. Next.

Wizards and dweomerblades. The former were the masters of magic. The learned men and women who studied the Art in depth and mastered its intricacies.

That would be ... that would be beyond cool. To go from a world where magic was no more than a children's story to a life where actual spells were at his fingertips?

Yeah, that was a maybe.

The other, though. The dweomerblades. Natural sorcerers, who found their magic through battle and physical movement.

If he chose wizard, he'd trade a life of books for a life of books, though, wouldn't he? Only study and experimentation could increase his mastery of the Art.

On the other hand, if he went with the dweomerblade, all his magic would be involved in battle. And how often would he ever...

Qorunn was a world of adventure. If he went there as a dweomerblade, no doubt there'd be chances to use his skills. And plenty of risk, as well.

"I'm torn," Keifer admitted, "between wizard and dweomerblade."

"You know yourself well then," Kainemorton said. "I'd been curious."

He turned the paper around, showing that wizard led the way, in a virtual tie with the dweomerblade, with skald lagging behind, a reasonably close third.

"So what does that mean?" Keifer asked. "Do I cross-class between wizard and dweomerblade?"

Kainemorton chuckled. "Cross-classing. An interesting way to describe those who find their talents lie along more lines than one. Those who fight as well as they pick locks. Or those whose magic comes from both their arcane studies and their faith in the gods."

"So..." Keifer began, but trailed off when Kainemorton shook his head.

"Nay, lad," he said. "You'll have enough to focus on in your new world without having to split your training."

"Wizard," Keifer said, suddenly.

"Shall I trust," Kainemorton asked, "that you mean something more than merely addressing me impudently?"

"I'm traveling to a world filled with magic," Keifer said. "A world where I won't be sure who I can trust and who I can't."

Kainemorton looked as though he wanted to say something then, but Keifer continued.

"Magic plays a key role across all of the Torn Kingdoms. If I'm going to rule a duchy in Qorunn, I'll need some understanding of how it works. More than I'd get as a dweomerblade. I choose wizard."

No sooner had he made the decision, than Keifer felt his heart sink a little bit. Dweomerblades were the truest swashbucklers of Qorunn. The most daring. The most wild.

It was a career for those who loved to live life to the fullest. And given how badly Keifer needed a change—

Kainemorton chuckled.

"I'm afraid you misunderstood me a bit," he said. "I wanted your opinion, true enough. I'd not want to consign a man to a career he'd hate. But never was I asking you to choose here and now."

"But—"

"This is a choice you made long ago," Kainemorton said, gently, with humor rising in his voice as he continued. "I mostly wanted to know if you recognized it. You did, and this pleases me, because it makes my job that much easier."

"So," Keifer said, "wizard came in first in that list, though not by a big margin over dweomerblade. Does that mean I'll be a wizard?"

"Close," Kainemorton said. "You'll be something new, my lad, though not entirely unique. You'll be the first of the dweomerblood in Qorunn."

KEIFER WAS STILL A BIT STUNNED AS HE GATHERED CERTAIN PRECIOUS possessions to go into the only crate he'd keep from the world of his birth.

A dweomerblood. The *first* dweomerblood.

As Kainemorton described it, the dweomerblood were born to magic. It infused their very natures and beings. Some abilities would come to them naturally because of this.

But they could study magic as wizards did, and gain and refine their powers in this way. Though they might never be as ... varied in their powers as a dedicated wizard.

Further, the dweomerblood could find aspects of their magic through combat as well, as the dweomerblades did. Though again, without their dedicated focus.

In fact, Keifer suspected that when the sixth edition of *Torn Kingdoms* came out — no doubt including the brand new dweomerblood adventuring career — dweomerblade would be considered a subcategory of dweomerblood.

A nervous chuckle escaped Keifer's dry lips. He truly was making a new character for the next edition of *Torn Kingdoms*. It would just be the last character he ever made.

He tried to keep his attention on where he was and what he was doing right now.

That was the sixth and final photo album from his life with Andi, that he'd just placed into the chest. She'd so loved her printed pictures. Hardly took a picture that she didn't print out and put into her photo albums.

Nevertheless, Keifer downloaded all his old documents, office files, and pictures and videos from his life and stored them on a series of thumb drives and duplicated on microSD cards. His music, as well.

Just in case.

After that, it was just a question of a handful of favorite books (nothing involving the *Torn Kingdoms*), certain meaningful articles of clothing, and favored jewelry of Andi's.

The last thing to go into the chest were the wedding rings. Andi's, and his own.

That last one was harder than he expected. He stood there over the chest on the edge of his dining room, considering the simple platinum band, engraved on the inside with his name and Andi's.

He hadn't taken that ring off since they were married. Not when he was sleeping. Not even when he showered.

And trying to take it off now, to put it in the chest with the rest of the meaningful things from his life — how few and small they seemed — he felt like Frodo, trying to destroy the ring at Mount Doom.

Well, Keifer's ring wasn't evil. But now that it came time for him to remove it once and for all, he found himself reluctant.

"Twere best done quickly, lad," Kainemorton said, gently, from just behind Keifer and to his left. "The lass is dead, and it's time for you to let her go."

"It's only been two years," Keifer said. "I'm not ready."

"You cannot go to Deepwater bearing a ring of marriage," Kainemorton said. "You must remove it, or you'll have to decline the duchy."

Keifer's face felt hot. He had the sudden urge to turn and strike the old mage, who seemed so ready to just erase Andi from ever having existed.

"Every year," Keifer said, softly, trying to ignore the wetness flowing down his cheeks. "Every year I will light a candle in memory of my beloved Andi. Even if I marry another, I will do this in memory of my first true love, who was stolen from me."

"The dead live on only so long as they are remembered," Kainemorton said softly. "There's nothing wrong with you lighting a candle in memory of your lost love."

They stood there in silence a moment. Though whether Kainemorton intended it as a moment of silence of just a moment for Keifer to gather himself, Keifer didn't know. He chose to assume the former.

Finally, he removed the ring, kissed it, and laid it in the chest beside Andi's ring.

Silently, he said goodbye to Andi one last time.

He closed the chest, and fastened the clasps.

He turned to Kainemorton. Nodded.

"All right. I'm ready."

<h1 style="text-align:center">3</h1>

———————

WHEN IT CAME TIME AT LAST FOR KEIFER TO TRAVEL TO QORUNN, HE expected a major sound and light show.

I mean, this was *planar travel.* He'd be going from one world to another. This had to involve intricate incantations, maybe incense and candles. Maybe even a pentagram or something drawn on the hardwood floor of Keifer's living room.

Keifer even smiled to imagine that, to be honest. That he'd disappear, and all that would remain to show what happened to him would be the smell of bacon in the air and a pentagram drawn on the floor.

But that wasn't what happened at all.

As soon as Keifer closed the chest that would contain his last belongings from Earth, and turned to announce his readiness to Kainemorton, the old mage merely smiled.

"Good, good," he said. He cracked his fingers, then his wrists. He frowned. Snapped his fingers. The floating backpack bobbed its way around in front of him. Its straps undid themselves and the main flap opened wide.

Kainemorton pointed into the backpack, and the chest lifted up off the floor, shrank down as it went, and flew straight into the backpack.

Keifer craned his neck to see what else might be in there, but he couldn't see anything. Despite all the late morning light filtering in through his windows, the interior of that backpack appeared dark as midnight on a moonless night.

The flap snapped shut, and the straps fastened themselves. Keifer had the fleeting notion that the backpack didn't like him looking. Which sounded ridiculous...

...but was it? Some magical swords were famous for having personalities. Could a magical backpack have one as well?

Well why not?

"Should I give you some room?" Keifer asked.

Kainemorton smiled, his periwinkle eyes twinkling with mischief.

"No, my boy," he said. "You should *sleep*."

And with that last word, Kainemorton slapped Keifer's forehead with his palm.

Everything went black. But didn't stay that way.

A life passed before Keifer's eyes. It wasn't a life he'd known before, but it flew past as though he'd lived it all himself.

Childhood as an orphan on the streets of Sartis. That city might be known as the "shining beacon on the southern sea," but for an orphan, life there was hard.

Still. Even as a boy, his magic began manifesting itself in times of need. Enough to keep him in food and water, for himself and those he was willing to call friends. As well as to protect himself and his own from those who'd prey on children.

For the streets of Sartis weren't entirely free from such predators.

The boy came to the attention of a wandering wizard named Karbin, whose skin was the blue-black of lands the boy had never heard of. Karbin took the boy on as an apprentice, to travel with him and his band of adventurers, but the ways of wizardry ill-suited the boy.

Or perhaps it was merely the training techniques known to Karbin that ill-suited the boy.

Either way, Karbin had to place the boy — now on the verge of adolescence — with the Iron Wands, an order of wizard-knights who had among their number a branch of dweomerblades.

The hope was that one of their number would succeed with the boy where Karbin had failed.

But the boy never lamented a moment of his time with Karbin. Karbin had been the first adult who'd been kind to the boy. Treated him well. Taught him to laugh, as well as teaching him about the world.

It was also Karbin who named that little street rat of a boy: Aefric.

The apprenticeship might not have taken, but Aefric missed Karbin, and wrote to him as often as he could, during his time with the Iron Wands.

The Iron Wands, alas, had little more success with Aefric than Karbin, himself, had had. The boy seemed to have some of the talents of a dweomerblade but a range of abilities closer to that of a young wizard.

It was the Iron Wands who reached out to Kainemorton, and Kainemorton himself who had come to see about training the boy. To help young Aefric learn to understand and wield his magic.

Somewhere about the summer of his sixteenth year — difficult to say how old Aefric truly was — he set out on his own, joining an adventuring crew.

The crews came and went over the years. Sometimes into retirement, after looting some amazing treasure or other. Sometimes falling to injury or death. But Aefric continued to wander, to ply his magics and work wonders where he was needed.

He even traveled again with Karbin for a time, when Aefric was finally of age and Karbin looked not a single day older than the thirtyish he'd looked when Aefric first met him.

Aefric really wasn't powerful enough to fight alongside the likes of Karbin and his fellows — not against such mighty foes as they faced — but the youth found ways to make himself useful all the same.

And so he traveled with Karbin and his friends for a number of years, learning and growing as he went.

Aefric and Karbin were separated when the Godswalk Wars came. Aefric had ridden back to the fortress of the Iron Wands, to report on what he'd learned of the world and of magic, but found that the whole of their order had been called to war.

Aefric wanted to ride out and join them ... but he'd never been officially made a part of the order. And so the servants refused to give him information about where the Iron Wands had gone and what they were doing.

Gnolda, the very same old matron who'd tucked young Aefric into bed at night, sang him songs and told him stories — and even slipped him the occasional extra cookie when he'd been good — was the same woman who now slammed the iron door in his face and sent him away without even a bed for the night or a meal for his belly.

Aefric found his ways into the wars on his own. Fighting here among the noble warriors and wizards of the eldrani. Shorter than humans by a half-head on average, but so beautiful they seemed almost to glow in the dark.

Fighting there among the na'shek, so tall and broad, with skin gray as slate and braids down to their waists. Almost entirely bereft of magic, they made their wonders through their magnificent smithing.

Aefric had been separated from the na'shek company he'd been aiding when a spearhead thrust of borog warriors — their skin and heads and horns like the rhinos of Earth, but humanoid and between humans and na'shek in size — split the battle lines in half.

The battle was chaos. The next thing Aefric knew, he was fighting — glowing staff in hand and clad in armor of leather — alongside humans against the mighty borogs.

But the wars had taught Aefric much of battle and of magic. Even surrounded and on his own, he fought through the lines of borogs to find a front where humans were pressed hard.

The tattered remains of a human army, so spent they could barely hold up a standard so torn and dirty that Aefric could make no sense of its device.

That army was caught between the borogs and what Aefric at the time took to be the sea.

The humans fought well and fought hard, but the borogs were too numerous. It was only a matter of time before the human army was crushed.

The borogs carried the standard of Xazik the Flayer, a bloody, skinless man on a green background.

Aefric could not give the Flayer victory here.

Aefric stomped hard on the matted grass of a hilltop, and thrust his staff toward the sky, crying out words of magic he'd never dared utter before.

From the cloudless sky answered the ringing booms of thunder, as a series of lightning bolts crashed down among the borog ranks.

Five strikes.

Ten strikes.

A dozen in all. And when the last one fell, all was quiet on the battlefield for a moment, as both sides of the battle before Aefric turned to stare at him, standing alone on the hill. Surrounded by the play of lightning and the stench of ozone.

In a ringing voice, Aefric called out to the same nearby regiment of na'shek he'd fought beside only hours ago.

The na'shek. The most ancient enemies of the borogs.

"Meara nash, rogo nek hai!" Aefric called in Na'shese, which meant, "Come with me and kill your enemies."

Alone, Aefric went running down the hill at the borog forces.

A moment later, roaring cries of challenge, a thousand battle hardened na'shek followed in his wake.

The ground shook with the na'shek charge.

The borog lines broke.

The tide of the battle turned.

And King Colm Stronghand of Armyr survived the battle, determining right there and then that he'd found his new duke of Deepwater.

———

KEIFER'S EYES FLUTTERED OPEN. HE FOUND HIMSELF LAYING BACK ON A red divan — a surprisingly comfortable red divan — in a round room no more than twenty feet across, at its widest.

The walls of the room were a pale gray stone, with a series of small, arched windows bringing in a stiff breeze of the freshest, cleanest air Keifer had ever smelled.

Cleaner even than the air atop Mount Hood, which was hard to believe. Oregon had good air to begin with, and at that height...

And yet *this* air was so clean that pollution might have been nothing but a nasty rumor.

Keifer could hear songbirds singing outside, but they weren't songs he knew from either Minnesota or Oregon. Chirps and trills in patterns he couldn't place.

The sound of trees moving with the wind, that was familiar. Comforting. The branches rustled like evergreens. Those trees could have been Douglas firs.

The floor of the room was stone, but covered in wide rectangles of rich red rugs. On a small brown table beside the divan was a chased silver bowl full of water, and a pair of hand towels that looked like linen.

Standing at the foot of the divan was a little old man in a simple gray robe knotted with faded black cord, and leather slippers. He was almost bald, but not quite. Tonsured. That was the term. He was bald, for the most part, but he had a ring of pure white hair around his scalp.

His skin was a nutty brown color, and his eyes were a bright hazel. His arms were folded into his sleeves, in front of him, but he smiled kindly at Keifer.

"I am glad to see you are awake, my lord," he said with a small nod. His voice was surprisingly firm, for as old as he looked. "Shall I tell my lord Kainemorton that you've roused? Or do you require anything first?"

Keifer thought about it. No. He still felt full from breakfast. He could even taste bacon, peppered eggs and especially that orange juice in his mouth, now that he was trying.

"I think I'm ready to see him," Keifer said, then shook himself. "I'm sorry. What's your name?"

"Vel, my lord," Vel said with a small nod, then moved off toward a door Keifer hadn't noticed. Which was strange. It was a plain wooden door, but until Vel started toward it, Keifer would have sworn that the wall in that place was unbroken stone.

Keifer shook his head.

Vel. Of course the old man was Vel. How could Keifer have forgotten the name of Kainemorton's old retainer?

Keifer stood sharply.

Vel.

And these surroundings.

They were here! Qorunn.

And Keifer would have to get sharper. He knew this setting at least as well as he knew his native United States, and he'd better start acting like it.

That door. Why had he missed...

Magic.

Now that he thought about it, Keifer realized he could *feel* the magic of this place. Like a faint hum of electricity, and a change in air pressure, not far from where he stood...

Wait. Magic? Was he actually *sensing magic*?

Well, obviously. Of course Aefric could sense magic. Just as he had most of his life. He'd first learned that as an orphan on the ... streets of Sartis...

Aefric. He'd just thought of himself as Aefric. Like the boy from his dream.

That boy was an orphan. And for a moment, Keifer had believed that he, too, was an orphan.

But that wasn't true. Keifer's parents were very much alive, back in Minnesota. And he'd grown up not on the streets, but in a middle-class house on the edges of Elk River.

And yet that dream had been vivid as any memory...

Keifer looked at his hands. They were tanned, as though he'd spent a lot more time outside than he ever did back in Oregon. And his fingers, callused.

He ran those fingers through his hair. Still that sandy blonde color he was used to. Longer though. His hair hung past his shoulders now.

His shoulders. He looked down.

He was wearing the same clothes he'd worn when he dressed ... that morning? ... in his — Keifer's — house in Portland. The high, soft leather boots that laced up nearly to his knee. The brown leggings, under the pale blue, medieval-style shirt.

Did Aefric own clothes like these? And Aefric certainly had other possessions...

Possessions! Keifer's hand darted to his chest.

Yes. The crystal Andi'd given him was still dangling on the gold chain about his neck.

Keifer blew out a deep breath that almost doubled him over, releasing some deep-seated tension.

For a moment, the whirling in his head stopped and his mind cleared...

Then Keifer — Aefric — noticed a warmer buzz than the general background sense of magic, here in what had to be Kainemorton's tower in Marrisford.

He turned and saw it. A staff. *His* staff. Carved from a single, six-foot branch of white thunderwood. A brown leather wrap, where he most liked to hold it, while walking.

Or casting spells. This staff was enchanted. Heavily enchanted. It not only carried magics of its own, but also augmented his own spells.

Keifer. Knew. Spells!

Or ... rather ... *Aefric* knew spells. But Keifer ... was also Aefric?

The staff leaned against the wall beside a sword belt — Aefric's sword belt, with longsword — and a leather backpack.

Keifer raised his hand and the staff flew to his grip. Embedded in its top was a yellow diamond, big as the last joint of his thumb.

"I'll ask you not to go casting spells in my tower," Kainemorton said from behind Keifer. "Not unless there's a need more pressing than proving to yourself that you can."

Keifer turned, holding the staff in both hands, and feeling its smoothness. He saw that Kainemorton had entered soundlessly through the same door Vel had left through.

The old mage was dressed in the same clothes he'd worn in Keifer's living room. The orange robe with gold-embroidered red trim. The old leather boots. The belt of many pouches. No staff in his hand, though, and no floating backpack.

Keifer turned his attention back to the staff in his own hands.

"I remember finding this staff," Keifer said, looking it over and not entirely sure it was real. Or that he was. Or that any of this was.

"Tell me the tale," Kainemorton said, as though doing so were more important than one of Keifer's old "no shit, there I was" gaming stories.

How important, though, he didn't yet understand.

KEIFER'S ATTENTION SHIFTED. HE WAS STILL HALF-AWARE THAT HE stood in that high room in Kainemorton's tower in Marrisford. Smelling that so-fresh air and listening to birdsongs he'd never heard before.

But half his awareness was in a past he was only just remembering. Of dank underground hallways hewn from rough stone. Halls that linked ancient, lost crypts, where the only creatures that moved had never known love or joy. And those that had known life, had left it behind ages past.

"I was traveling with the Last Sons," Aefric said. "Karbin's group. But we'd been separated during a battle with a lich..."

That battle. The crypt of the great lich itself. Cavernous. Large enough to house a dragon, with its sides littered with a maze of tunnels that had taken the Lost Sons more than an aett — the eight-day week that they kept in Qorunn — to understand and navigate. Even with all their faculties available.

And that battle. Karbin, throwing the mightiest spells that Aefric had ever seen. Until the lich outdid him, wielding death itself as spells, with crackling power.

The twin warriors, Ulik and Krolik, straining just to approach through the undead wizard's repelling aura. The eldrani warpriest Lishnasal chanting prayers nonstop just to counter even some of that dread lich's powers.

Aefric shivered at even the thought of saying the name—

"Nez'karak," Kainemorton prompted. "I'd heard that it was your group that took that foul thing down."

"Karbin's group," Keifer said. "I wasn't much more than an occasionally useful mascot." He shook his head. "At least, up until that fight."

"Tell me," Kainemorton said.

"Lishnasal had found a way to unweave the lich's repelling aura. Ulik and Krolik came in close, swinging their great, glowing claymores. I was throwing spells of red lightning that never even approached the lich, but it was the biggest spell I could cast.

"Karbin's eyes gleamed with triumph. He wasn't casting anything more complex than a kind of paralysis, but he must've been certain it would take..."

"Did it?" Kainemorton asked.

"We never got to find out. Not then. The lich cried out a spell of exploding darkness."

"Exploding darkness?" Kainemorton asked.

"Had to have been something it researched itself," Aefric said with a shrug. "Never heard of it before or since. But it was like being caught in an avalanche that not only battered the body, but plunged the world into darkness."

Aefric huddled against the memory of the way his whole body had been pummeled at once and flung through the air. The way the hard-packed dirt jarred him as well as stealing his breath. He could barely stand, even with his staff. He bled from at least a dozen places...

"What did you do, lad?" Kainemorton said softly.

"I didn't know what to do. I couldn't see. I couldn't hear anyone or anything. It was all I could do not to give in to panic." Aefric shook his head. "I wandered in darkness that denied all my spells. Certain the lich was right behind me. Sweat stung my eyes. Fear tasted like steel on my tongue. My heart beat so fast I couldn't tell one beat from the next, wetting my clothes with fresh blood in a dozen or more places.

"I remember finding a rock wall with my right hand, and clinging to it for dear life."

Aefric tilted his head. "I'd been thrown so far I ended up in one of the tunnels. No idea which. No idea which way I was going. But all I could do was continue on. One step at a time. My right hand on the wall. My left testing the floor with my staff, to make sure I didn't fall down some unseen pit."

"Did you make it back to the battle?"

"Yes. And no." Aefric shook his head. "Seemed like the purest chance. My hand on the wall found just the right stone. A grinding sound. An opening. I risked taking it."

Aefric — Keifer? — tilted his head as he pondered what he was saying. This felt so much like a true memory. Every bit as true as his high school prom, or his marriage to Andi.

And yet, it couldn't be...

"Go on, lad," Kainemorton said gently.

"Two torches sprang to life as I left that cursed hallway. Their light didn't leave the room, but I could see. And what I saw looked like the lich, except not quite."

"How?"

"The lich we'd been fighting. Nez'karak. When not moving, it seemed little more than a skeleton wearing a tattered purple robe, and a crown whose multicolored gems shone with power." Keifer frowned, remembering. "But the one I saw in that room. It, too, was a skeleton. And it, too, wore a tattered robe. But the color was more of an indigo than a purple. And it wore no crown."

Keifer held up his staff. "It did carry this staff, though."

"What happened next?"

"I raised my old, oaken staff. Called up my own power from within. Ready to do battle. But this lich, it issued no threats. Made no move to attack." Aefric gave a breathless laugh. "Instead, it asked my name and purpose. When I told it I'd come with a group to defeat Nez'karak, it called me a liar. Called me a coward, who fled at the first sign of trouble."

Aefric clutched the staff tighter.

"I defied the lich before me. Said, 'I'll be happy to go fight Nez'karak if you'll get rid of the darkness.'"

"What did this second lich do?"

"It tapped its staff — this staff — on the ground, and white fire blazed all around it."

Aefric tapped the staff's butt on the floor and summoned the white fire himself. Kainemorton nodded.

"The lich challenged me. 'This staff will light your way. Take it, if you dare.'"

"I dropped my oaken staff and seized this one, my hands right beside those old bony hands." Keifer shivered. "Oh, how the cold burned. But I held on, staring the old lich in its green-glowing eye sockets and willing it to let go first."

"And it did," Kainemorton said.

"Oh, it did. But not until the white flames engulfed us both." Keifer looked up at Kainemorton's twinkling eyes. "The fire, its cold wasn't burning our flesh. It was ... whatever it was doing, it was doing to our essences."

"Aye, lad," Kainemorton said. "It was testing you both. Go on."

"On an impulse, I jerked with both hands. The lich let go with, as weird as this sounds, a sigh."

"It's not weird, lad. I'll explain when you've finished. Go on."

"When the staff blazes white," Aefric said. "No magical darkness can stand against it. And the power of the staff made the difference in that fight. The white fire and lightning I called from it were the key to our defeat of Nez'karak."

"The creature sighed when you defeated its will," Kainemorton said, "because it was not a lich, but a guardian. Nez'karak sought that staff for himself, and if he'd found it first, even I might not have been able to stand against him, with all the Silver Arrows fighting alongside me. But *you* found the staff — in truth, I think it called to you — and you overcame the will of its guardian."

Kainemorton smiled. "A fine accomplishment, lad. And one to be proud of."

"But I didn't really *do* it, did I?" Keifer asked. "Any more than I grew up on the streets of Sartis, or trained with Karbin, and the Iron Wands, and you. I remember these things, but—"

"Oh, you did them, true enough," Kainemorton said, eyes twinkling with mischief. "I carried you away from the world of your birth as an adult, that I do confess. But I brought you here to this world as a child once more."

Keifer extinguished the staff and leaned on it as the implications of what Kainemorton just said reverberated through him. He'd lived two lives? Each just as real as the other?

In one, college and Andi and gaming and friends.

In another, adventure and magic and—

"Wait," Keifer said. "You brought me to this world as a child?"

"I did," Kainemorton said, nodding. "Go on and ask."

"And you just abandoned me in the streets of Sartis as an infant?"

"And if I'd raised you as my own, you'd've had all the enemies that come with being my child, and not just one of many who've apprenticed to me for a few years."

"You *abandoned* me. On the *streets*. As an *infant*."

"Where you learned to be strong and smart, to rely on yourself, and to watch out for others." Kainemorton winked. "And maybe, just maybe, you did this under the unseen but watchful eyes of the Bowstrings."

The Bowstrings.

The Silver Arrows might've been known as the greatest heroes of the Torn Kingdoms, but they owed at least part of that reputation to the work of the Bowstrings. That network of allies, spies and informants. Some adventurers, and others shopkeepers and barmaids, sailors and swineherds and more.

The Silver Arrows were said to have eyes, ears, and hands in every town and city across Qorunn. And those eyes, ears, and hands were those of the Bowstrings.

It was entirely possible that Keifer's — or rather Aefric's — childhood had indeed been under the watchful eyes of the Bowstrings, without his ever having known it.

"So..." Keifer frowned. "I really am both? Keifer and—"

"Not quite," Kainemorton said. "On the world you know as Earth, you are Keifer Alan McShane. But here in Qorunn, you are Aefric, called the Brightstaff after that very staff in your hands."

Even through the echoes of that idea, ringing through his head, a question still emerged.

"Wait," Keifer — or rather Aefric — said. "Why the streets of Sartis? Why not the Towers of Lund, where they could have taught me—"

"Politics? In Lund they practice that even more than they practice their spells." Kainemorton snorted, then nodded his head back and forth. "Maybe that would have served a purpose or two. And certainly the Towers of Lund are a cutthroat enough place to learn. But truth is, lad, not a wizard in this world would truly know what to do with you. For you aren't a wizard. You're the first of the dweomerblood."

Aefric paled. "They'd've killed me, wouldn't they?"

"Likely," Kainemorton said. "If the wrong one figured out the truth of you. Wouldn't have stopped there either. You'd've been vivisected on multiple levels."

Aefric swallowed.

Kainemorton clapped a hand on Aefric's shoulder.

"Now, lad, will you trust that I made good, if not perfect decisions in how to handle your upbringing, and let us get on with why you've come?"

"You mean..."

"I mean Colm Stronghand awaits your arrival in Armyr even now."

"Oh," Aefric said, hurrying to buckle on his sword belt and grab his leather backpack. "I guess we're teleporting then?"

Kainemorton chuckled.

"You're thinking like Keifer," Kainemorton said. "Expecting travel and information to flow as swiftly here as they do back on Earth. So tell me, *Aefric*, do you expect me to teleport you to Armyr?"

Aefric stopped, backpack over only one shoulder, as he realized he knew the answer. He'd been taught about situations like this by none other than the great mage currently asking him the question.

"No," he said. "Teleportation is for when matters are urgent. A wizard who teleports everywhere forgets that between any two places are the lands, the people, and the problems of the world."

"And you should..." Kainemorton prompted.

"See the lands. Meet the people. Solve the problems."

"Just so," Kainemorton said, pulling a pointed, wide-brimmed hat out of nowhere. "So shall we?"

As Aefric, he knew that that, by horse, the outskirts of Armyr were about five days ride from Marrisford. Assuming the roads were in good repair, and the horses healthy.

As Keifer, he knew that the distance from Marrisford to Armyr was about two hundred fifty miles. Though he couldn't, for the life of him, remember how far into Marrisford Kainemorton's tower was, nor how far into Armyr the royal palace was.

For the sake of argument, he concluded that he was in for a horseback ride of about an aett with stops every night at friendly inns or keeps. Unless Kainemorton was in more of a mood to sleep out of doors, in which case, it'd be bedrolls and camp dinner every night.

Keifer hadn't been camping in years, but Aefric was well-used to that lifestyle.

It was a contrast that still played strangely in his head. That double sense of a life. As Keifer he knew he was about six weeks away from his twenty-sixth birthday, but as Aefric ... well ... it had to be about the same, didn't it?

He'd been brought to Qorunn as a young child... Yes. Based on the earliest of Aefric's memories — a soft voice telling him that every-thing would be all right — he'd've been about three or four when that happened. Which meant he must have about twenty-two or twenty-three years of experience living in this world.

Call it twenty-three, to be safe. That meant twenty-three years of double-memories.

And yet, so far at least, they didn't seem to conflict with each other in his head. Somehow they managed to maneuver around each other.

If Keifer thought of this past Christmas, he remembered the bottle of eggnog he drank in front of the yule log on television, toasting Andi who loved the idea of having a silly burning log on a television screen.

If Aefric thought of the last Winter Festival, he remembered sitting around a campfire with a mixed group of humans and eldrani, toasting the god Liskavan, who brought to both races the secret of fire. Albeit at very different times, for the eldrani were the much younger race.

The war was over, but word hadn't reached that campfire yet.

Both these memories were clear in his head. Neither one clashed with the other. And yet, they were both memories of the same man, living different, simultaneous lives.

These were the things that Aefric thought about as he and Kainemorton descended the stairs of Kainemorton's tower.

The stairs of Kainemorton's tower weren't like the stairs of most towers Aefric had seen. Nor did Keifer remember their description from any sourcebook he'd seen. (Perhaps they'd been detailed in a novel he'd missed?)

The walls of the tower were about six feet thick. The windows were either cut straight out of the walls, leaving a six-foot channel for each, or, in a few places, the outer wall tapered to the window.

Those were the kind of windows that had been in the room where Aefric awoke. The tapering kind.

The stairs themselves were within the outer wall. So even if a whole floor was dedicated to a single room, as Aefric had seen, the door to the stairs was on the outer wall.

The stairs themselves were narrow and entirely enclosed, with handrails on both sides — not that Kainemorton needed them — and modestly lit by magic. They smelled faintly of old fires and camaraderie.

When the two of them — Kainemorton and Aefric — reached the kitchen and dining area — the bottom floor of the tower — Vel already had a pack ready to hand Kainemorton.

This was a cloth backpack, not the leather one that had floated after him on Earth. Not the backpack that held Keifer's chest of important possessions.

Aefric was about to ask about that when Kainemorton turned and smiled.

"Don't dawdle, lad. It's best not to keep kings waiting any longer than you have to. Important lesson for a new duke to learn."

With that, Kainemorton turned and walked out through the double-door that led to outside.

Aefric found himself caught between Keifer's desire to ask questions, to understand every little detail that might become important later, and Aefric's own eagerness to be on his way to the next great adventure.

"Hush, my lord," Vel said, laying a gentle, wrinkled hand on Aefric's arm. "Your thoughts are so loud I can almost hear them."

Aefric/Keifer turned to Vel, and a dozen or so questions collided on their way out of his mouth.

"Peace, my lord," Vel said, smiling as though he had found his own perfect, internal peace that he carried with him wherever he went. "Much has changed for you this day. But whether you walk in this world or another, whether you call yourself Aefric or by some other name, you are still yourself. Every experience, every decision.

It's always been you. You know more answers than you think, and you are capable of more than you know."

Vel removed his hand and nodded toward the open double-doors. "You will do great things, my lord. But first, you must walk through those doors."

Aefric chuckled. How many times over the years had Vel offered him just the piece of advice he needed? More than he wanted to count.

"Thank you, Vel," Aefric said, smiling, and walked out through the double-doors.

The grass outside Kainemorton's tower was thick, soft, and a rich, dark green. The grass extended about a hundred yards in each direction from the tower itself, before the trees began.

The trees were evergreens, but not the Douglas firs of Oregon. They were much more like the redwoods of California. In color, in the bunching of the leaves, and certainly in size. Though their smell was different. Just a touch sweeter, on the gentle, easterly breeze.

The sky above was a welcoming blue, where small, fluffy white clouds chased each other toward the west.

West. West of Marrisford was the great forest Dellwood, where hills rolled beneath the trees for at least a hundred miles before giving way to ... the Free Baronies of Olwich.

Kainemorton's tower. It was just north of Marrisford itself, surrounded by a grove of trees that weren't really a part of the Dellwood, but had been planted by Kainemorton close to a thousand years ago.

There was a small road that ran the thousand yards or so between Marrisford proper and the tower.

All this information, a blend of Aefric's knowledge and Keifer's. And yet it all came together smoothly.

Perhaps Vel was right once more.

Aefric smiled as he turned to Kainemorton, who was watching him with a small smile on his face.

The old mage cocked an eyebrow.

"Everything settling in well together, lad?"

Aefric knew without asking that Kainemorton meant the twin sets of memories in his own head.

Aefric nodded with a smile, then showed off how well things were coming together. He turned and with no more than a few words and a sweep of his hand, summoned his *magaunt*, an ephemeral steed, bright red in color with glowing orange eyes and hooves that faded into pale red smoke.

Those who weren't spellcasters called them "ghost steeds," which Aefric always took as a mark of jealousy.

Before Aefric could mount the ready steed, Kainemorton cleared his throat.

Aefric turned, the question so visible on his face that Kainemorton smiled broadly.

"Much as I would enjoy riding with your once more, alas, I cannot spare an aett or more getting you to the royal palace at Armityr."

"You said we weren't teleporting."

"And we're not," Kainemorton said with a chuckle. "But there's a middle ground I find much more reasonable."

He turned, raised his staff, and called forth something Aefric had seen only a handful of times in his four years or so of apprenticeship to the old mage.

The *magari*. A flying, fiery chariot, pulled by a pair of *magaunts* (a vivid sea green, in Kainemorton's case).

"You really must teach me that spell," Aefric said, not trying to hide the wonder in his voice.

"Now now," Kainemorton said. "Even if you were still my student, this is hardly the time for a lesson."

4

The *magari* did not simply speed across the ground. No. As soon as Aefric and Kainemorton took their places in the fiery chariot — which fires did not burn, Aefric was glad to note — the bright, sea green horses leapt straight into the air, leaving a brief, fiery trail in the *magari's* wake.

Up they flew, above those trees that weren't quite redwoods — they were called gnalla trees, Aefric remembered, and were noted for the quality and orange hue of their hardwoods — and into the bright sky above.

Aefric couldn't help laughing at the startled, undignified squawk of a raptor, adjusting its dive to avoid the fires that wouldn't have burned it.

The view was spectacular. The mighty forest. The broad, swift river Jann. Aefric smiled to see these things, feeling the joy Keifer felt at seeing these things for the first time, even though Aefric, of course, had seen these sights many times.

Though, admittedly, only rarely from this angle.

The *magari* carried them to the northwest past flocks of migrating rika birds, with their bright red crests only now coming in with the spring.

For it was spring in this part of Qorunn. Aefric knew that. Early spring, when the rains would still come down so often it seemed as though the sky gods all argued among themselves about whether the springtime should have clear skies or driving rain, and kept changing their consensus.

Kainemorton drove the *magari*, but it required little of his attention, it seemed, for he seemed to be watching Aefric as much as his reins.

Within an hour they were past the outer edges of the Dellwood, and over the rolling plains of Kesh. Kesh was a kingdom, at least nominally, but the views of the free baronies to the south had seeped in, with the barons and their people demanding more and more freedoms, and the monarch — Jotohn, a king barely old enough to be crowned — ceding more and more of his traditional rights and powers to the barons and their city mayors.

"That will come to a head, soon," Kainemorton said, pointing down at a dispute beside a bridge over the Jann. Aefric could pick out two different banners, and perhaps a hundred armed men supporting each.

"The barons of Kesh have no true interest in the politics of free baronies," Kainemorton explained. "They don't want to cede any of their power to the mayors and the people. They just want to take more power from the king who, like a fool, is letting them."

"What's going on at the river crossing?" Aefric asked.

"Each of two barons is claiming the bridge and the right to charge a toll." Kainemorton shook his head. "It's the king's bridge, but none of those soldiers are flying the king's colors."

"Should we intervene?"

"Certainly not," Kainemorton said firmly. "This is politics, and it doesn't need a foreign wizard — or a foreign dweomerblood — interfering."

"But if they go to war—"

"The king will have to find his courage and stop it."

The river was behind them now, as they flew over rolling farmland and ranchland. Including sections that had been burned, or ruined by war.

"They're still recovering from the Godswalk Wars," Aefric said, "and they're looking for more?"

"Some will look at an aftermath and see a chance to seize power," Kainemorton said. "Remember that, lad, for the place we're going has seen worse than a little scorching and scarring."

Aefric swallowed. He hadn't considered that. He was going to be taking charge of a duchy not long after a major war that had involved all of Qorunn. He had no idea what to expect. How bad things would be.

Cold shock wove through him at the thought of taking charge of a duchy populated only by the dead.

"Easy, lad," Kainemorton said. "You're not arriving under the best and happiest of circumstances, tis true, but I'm not throwing you into a volcano and expecting you to swim."

Aefric chuckled, despite himself, at that mental image.

He realized then that they were talking without raising their voices. And that, despite their altitude and speed, they weren't being buffeted by the wind.

This was definitely a heck of a spell.

"So," Aefric said, "will you be staying on a bit to help me settle in?"

"Certainly not," Kainemorton said. "My bringing you here was a favor. But I don't have time to play court wizard for you." He smiled. "Besides, you'll already have a court wizard."

"You mean me?" Aefric asked. True, *he* knew he wasn't a wizard, properly speaking, but most wouldn't know the difference.

"Not in the least," Kainemorton said. "But I'd hate to spoil the surprise."

Aefric tried thinking back to all the sourcebooks he'd accumulated at Keifer, but for the life of him he couldn't remember who was the court wizard under Duchess Arinda Soulfist. Or even if she had one, considering that she was, herself, a wizard.

Probably a moot point, given the tumult of the Godswalk Wars...

They passed over another forest, and then along a series of grasslands that edged a swamp. These were wilder areas. Aefric couldn't remember who claimed them, but they were just south and east of Armyr. With the border of Armyr starting at the Indecisive River, called such because it curved more than it had any right to.

It widened and narrowed seemingly at random, and some of it was not much wider than a large stream. And yet, it maintained its flow and integrity, despite all attempts of weather to widen it, or of people or animals to dam or direct it.

There were at least three places that Aefric could see efforts at damming had been made, each near towns just inside the Armyrian border.

In each case, the river moved around the dam.

"Three," Kainemorton said, laughing, apparently at the count of dams. "Those will each have been placed since winter, lad, and the river defies them all."

"Why?"

"None know for certain," Kainemorton said. "Though I hold to the belief that the river is sacred to some lost god of persistence or independence."

"Then why do they keep trying?"

"Because there are always those who won't believe something doesn't work until they try it themselves."

Aefric smiled at that, but lost his smile as he looked out over the countryside of Armyr.

He could see some signs of what Kainemorton meant about the effects of the war here. The two of them were barely across the border and yet he could see scars in the land from battles. Whole farmlands trampled under the feet of passing armies — or perhaps looted of their bounty in none too kind a fashion.

Aefric drew a deep breath and steadied himself

Whatever he was getting into, he could handle it.

What was it Kainemorton had taught him about action in a crisis? Even the wrong action was better than none.

And with no duke or duchess to make those decisions, no doubt the people of Deepwater were suffering.

Aefric wouldn't stand for that.

THE PALACE AT ARMITYR WAS THE LARGEST, OLDEST CONSTRUCTION built entirely by human hands in all of Qorunn. Long before Armyr — the kingdom — had existed.

Thousands of years ago, this was the first land that humans called their own, and this palace was their way of saying to the other races, "We're here. We're not going anywhere. We are a force you must reckon with."

And at its peak, no doubt it was one of the most splendid sights in all of the Torn Kingdoms. Mighty gray and white stones, fitted close together without need for mortar. Thick walls, crenellated where soldiers would stand guard. Arrow slits down low and broad windows up high.

At its peak, it must have been inspiring.

Aefric had never seen it at its peak.

And what he saw as he and Kainemorton descended from the skies in Kainemorton's *magari* was a half-collapsed castle badly in need of even more repairs than it was undergoing.

He estimated that there had once been five or six towers, soaring hundreds of feet into the sky. Only two of those towers still stood, and one, well, listed.

The main part of the keep must have stood a hundred fifty feet tall, and perhaps five hundred feet across. Where the outer walls had not been collapsed, and taken some of the structure with them.

Half ... *perhaps* as much as two-thirds of the palace remained intact.

In fact, all of the city of Armityr had been ill-used by the Godswalk Wars. The great wall surrounding the city — seventy feet high and twenty feet wide — had been collapsed in no fewer than four places that Aefric could see.

Whole sections of the vast city had been burned, trampled, or sunk into the ground. Tents and camps filled much of those places now, as people worked feverishly to restore what had been lost.

They had even brought in hosts of na'shek to help raise the sunken areas, restoring and fortifying the lands beneath.

For in all of Qorunn, none knew more of the ways of dirt and rock and mountain than the na'shek.

Well, there were those who said that the borogs knew as much of those ways as the na'shek. Some might even have said that the borogs knew more.

But only a fool said such things in the presence of the na'shek.

Workers were everywhere, moving about the city and the walls. But none could be seen working on the castle itself.

"King Colm," Aefric said as the *magari* rode lower still, then rose up above the walls of the palace itself, revealing that a courtyard lay within its center. "Instead of repairing his castle, he has all available workers repairing the city first, doesn't he?"

"And what think you of that?"

"That's how I'd do it."

Kainemorton only nodded. And Aefric wasn't sure if that nod meant agreement, or only acknowledgment of what Aefric had said.

Not that it mattered. If Kainemorton would have done otherwise, Aefric decided, then Kainemorton would have been wrong.

No huge crowd waited for them in the courtyard below. It looked as though a small dais had been erected at one end of a row of fruit trees, with no more than a dozen finely dressed onlookers and about as many attending servants hustling about.

Kainemorton set the *magari* down on the grass at the other end of the courtyard from the dais. The nobles were apparently all sufficiently used to magic that, though they looked with some interest at the newcomers, none seemed overwhelmed. None even appeared as impressed by the *magari* itself as Aefric had been.

It was odd to think that, for some, magic was so commonplace that they'd lost the wonder of it...

...or perhaps they, as nobles, made a habit of looking unimpressed by much of anything.

Interesting. Aefric would have to figure out which was the case. The distinction could prove important.

He could smell roasting meats and fresh-baked breads and pies, though he didn't see the source of these marvelous aromas.

No musicians, either, which Aefric found odd. Didn't events like this one always have musicians?

Then again, given the state of the capital city, perhaps minimizing the celebration was in order.

Certainly there were not to be very many witnesses.

Aefric didn't recognize everyone in the courtyard, but he was confident that he could spot the major players. The gaming source-books Keifer had read so assiduously might never have had color interior illustrations, but the portraits they showed for the major non-player characters had all been pretty spot-on.

First, up the dais, was King Colm Stronghand. Still quite ruggedly handsome, though making his way into middle age. A few gray hairs now in evidence among the rich black of his hair and mustache. The man had led his armies into battle no fewer than a half-dozen times *before* the Godswalk Wars, and now was likely as seasoned a warrior himself as one would find anywhere among the nobility of Qorunn.

He didn't dress in his armor, today. He wore a finely embroidered yellow shirt along with light brown leggings, under a cloth-of-gold belt with what looked to be a slender, ceremonial sword at his side.

He wore a crown of fairly simple design, though it was anchored in the front by three upward rays: one above a diamond, the other two above rubies. They matched the jewels in his rings. The diamond of his wedding ring — on the middle finger of his right hand — and the rubies in a twisting snake ring, also gold, on his left hand.

Over his shoulders he wore a cloak made from some kind of soft-looking white fur, trimmed with cloth-of-gold.

Standing beside him was his new queen, Eppida Fyrenn, younger sister to the duchess of Merrek — though both were close to Aefric's age — and at least her equal in beauty. Both women had the pale skin so favored by Armyrian nobles — despite the wartime tan of their king — and both were tall and willowy.

Queen Eppida's long curls were blonde. Duchess Ashling's were raven black. Queen Eppida wore a gown of yellow to match her husband's shirt — though far more elaborate in design, with folds and ruffles and brocade — along with a similar cloak to his, and a crown that could have been a smaller version of his own.

Her wedding ring had a diamond that matched the king's. She wore no other ring though, only a golden torc, inscribed with something Aefric could not read, but could sense was magical.

In fact, none of the nobles present were without magic, though probing to find out the details of such items as they carried would have been the height of rudeness.

Aefric noted that neither of the twins, Prince Killian and Princess Maev, were present. They were the children of Colm's first wife, the late Queen Zinerva Haltallan, who'd been born a princess of neighboring Rethneryl.

The twins would have come of age sometime during the Godswalk Wars (the sourcebooks had been unclear about their exact age). Certainly they should have been present for an event of this magnitude...

Standing below the dais were the other nobles present.

Duchess Ashling stood with two ... well, they were well-dressed for retainers. They might have been lesser nobles. Aefric decided to think of them as "companions" for want of a more precise word. Either way, they were a man and a woman. The duchess herself was clad in a simple gown that matched her hair, which made the sapphire dangling from her golden pendant shine out all the brighter, as well as catching and showing off all the blues in her eyes.

Her companions also favored simple garb. In fact, Aefric quickly realized that the companions present were all dressed simpler than the nobles they accompanied, and none seemed to wear any jewelry or carry any magic at this event.

Aefric wondered if that were a matter of fashion, or a statement of some kind. Not that he felt he could ask.

Chatting with the duchess of Merrek was the duke of Silverlake, Wylyn Stormsent.

Aefric would have picked this man out as a former adventurer, even without the surname (or the advantage of having read of him in sourcebooks). His chestnut brown beard was split on both cheeks by scars. He kept his hair cut battlefield short, and his smoke gray eyes never stopped moving.

Aefric knew that those scars came from a trap Wylyn had failed to disarm in a crypt down in the badlands south of Nereth-Te. Couldn't remember what he'd done to get himself appointed a duke, but it had been long ago, during the time of King Colm's father, King Ceolwulf. He was the oldest person present, with the obvious exception of Kainemorton.

Despite the still-chestnut color of Wylyn's hair and beard, it was clear that his face had earned its many lines and wrinkles.

Still, the man looked lean and fierce beneath his embroidered, pale red shirt, and he wore daggers at his belt that looked more wicked than ceremonial.

Aefric noticed that Duke Wylyn's two companions both stood in positions that, among the three of them, they could watch every direction at once. Both men looked more like soldiers than advisers. And like their duke, their eyes never stopped moving.

Duke Wylyn was the shortest of the nobles present. Which made Aefric wonder about the rumors that he had kindaren heritage, somewhere in his background.

Of course, given that kindaren adults rarely grew much taller than waist-height to most humans, that didn't seem very ... feasible.

The only other noble present was one that Aefric didn't recognize.

She was tall, likely taller than Duchess Ashling, with soft brown hair woven into a series of braids that came together as one down her back.

She stood with the posture of a warrior, not a courtier, in her surprisingly simple royal blue gown, but she had the open, accepting brown eyes of a cleric. She lacked the glamor of the Fyrenn sisters, but she possessed a quiet, confident beauty all the same.

Her two companions, both women, seemed to be keeping up a hushed, nonstop commentary, to which she listened while still paying attention to the rest of what went on about her.

In all, not a large crowd to see Aefric named the duke of Deepwater. But maybe that was for the best. Fewer witnesses, if Aefric committed some kind of major mistake.

"Ah," King Colm said, and just like that the rest of the conversation in the courtyard died away. "I see the great mage Kainemorton has arrived with the man we've been waiting for. The man who saved not only my own life, but the lives of countless of my soldiers and citizens with his quick thinking and mighty spells."

He raised his hand. Four trumpet notes rang out, three of the same note, and the fourth a higher pitch.

Ah. There were the trumpeters. Up on a balcony overlooking the courtyard.

"Come, Aefric Brightstaff," King Colm said. "Come to me and be made Duke of Deepwater."

THIS WAS IT. THE MOMENT COME AT LAST. AEFRIC'S NERVES RACED about like servants preparing for an unexpected royal visit. His heart pounded like war drums.

Wait. Were those drums? Could there have been drummers hiding up there on the balcony, with the trumpeters?

No. That was just his heartbeat.

His mouth was suddenly dry. Why was his mouth so dry? Given the luscious smells of the roasting meats and fresh-baked pastries, Aefric would have expected his mouth to be watering.

And yet, his mouth felt dry as a sepulcher.

Didn't help that the air here in the courtyard was so still. Almost as though the skies were holding their breath. Even the clouds up high had stopped streaking across the sky, as though they wanted to stop and gawk at the unworthy man about to be made a duke.

Because Aefric felt unworthy.

Who was he, to be made a noble?

He was Keifer. An American citizen, but the equivalent of a commoner. Landed, yes, and rich, but common nonetheless. Keifer had never held public office. Never had to make decisions that affected anyone other than himself, and maybe Andi.

He was Aefric. That orphan boy from the streets of Sartis, with magic in his blood. He'd faced death many times, but he'd never been a ruler. Never even worked with a group larger than five.

He was no duke. And he had the distinct feeling that everyone looking at him knew it.

King Colm smiled, yes, but what did that really mean? Was he appointing Aefric out of a belief that he'd make a good duke? Was he appointing a presumed ally against Merrek and Silverlake? Or worse, did he plan to rule the duchy himself, through advisers already in place?

Queen Eppida smiled as well, but Aefric couldn't tell for sure if that smile reached her eyes. What plans might she have, that involved Aefric? Was he *her* choice to take the duchy? And if so, why had she chosen him?

And if not, if she favored another, did that mean she would work against Aefric? Perhaps in favor of her sister, the duchess of Merrek?

Speaking of the duchess of Merrek, she regarded Aefric with her sapphire eyes remote and her expression nothing more than polite interest and perhaps curiosity.

Which was more than he got from the duke of Silverlake, whose lip curled in a slight sneer as he took Aefric's measure.

The unknown noblewoman, though. Her smile seemed sincere. Her brown eyes, encouraging.

Though that might have meant she was the most dangerous of them all.

"It's all right, lad," Kainemorton whispered softly beside him. "You've nothing to fear."

Looking out over the faces of those assembled — including the companions, whose expressions ranged from skeptical to politely interested — Aefric doubted that a great deal.

But he had never backed down from a challenge, and he wouldn't start now.

Aefric straightened himself. Smiled at those assembled. He stepped out of the fiery chariot of the *magari* and began to walk down the center of the grass of the courtyard.

He kept his steps measured. Slow. Certainly much slower than his speeding heart. He tried to force his breaths to come in deeper. They'd gotten rapid and shallow in there somewhere, and that was no good.

Couldn't hyperventilate. That would be bad. Mustn't pass out in front of the king.

The fruit trees were nava fruit. A type of citrus popular with sailors and campaigners, because they stayed fresh a long time, and their sweet taste had a bite to their undercurrent.

By the time Aefric reached the stairs of the dais, he felt more confident in his breathing. His heart had even slowed to something close to a normal beat, though he felt too warm from the torso on up.

Still. At least he no longer worried about passing out.

Aefric stopped on the grass at the foot of the stairs. He bowed low to their majesties and held that bow until King Colm said, "Rise."

Aefric stood. Unsure what to do next. Should he ascend the dais? Wait for the king to come to him? Should he—

He heard a soft, throat-clearing beside him, just behind his right shoulder. A quick glance told him that a page in the green-and-gold livery of Armyr — featuring a golden oak tree on a field of forest green — had approached.

"Ascend to the third step, my lord," the page said softly, "but do not step onto the dais itself."

As Aefric did this, he heard a soft rustling off to his left, from the direction of the duke and duchess, and their companions. Amusement, perhaps, at Aefric's ignorance of courtly ways.

He stopped on the third step, as instructed. His heart had started racing again.

The trumpeters played their flourish again.

The king and queen both smiled.

"Aefric Brightstaff," King Colm said, and his voice rang out in the courtyard. "You have done this kingdom a greater service than it can repay. You may not realize this, but after our victory at Deepwater — the victory you brought us — the tide of the war turned in this part of the world. The advance of the Flayer's forces was stayed. Not just stayed. They were driven back."

"Your actions," Queen Eppida said, and she certainly *sounded* as though she were grateful, "saved the kingdom from playing host to the depredations of the Flayer's forces. Our people, our lands, and ourselves are all in your debt."

"Your actions were noble," King Colm continued. "And today we recognize that by granting you the title and lands to go with the nobility of heart and spirit you have already displayed."

"Kneel," Queen Eppida said.

Aefric knelt.

King Colm drew forth his ceremonial sword. Softly, to Aefric, he said, "First the knighting, because you deserve that too. Don't stand when I'm done."

He reached out and tapped Aefric on both shoulders.

"In acknowledgment of your bravery in battle, I, Colm Strong-hand, King of Armyr, do hereby grant you the right to keep and bear arms as a knight of Armyr. I further charge you to answer the call to battle, to protect the weak, to defend the innocent, and to take up arms in defense of the realm. Hereafter you shall be known as Ser Aefric Brightstaff."

Scattered applause from the witnesses, though it sounded more sincere on the side of the unknown noble and more perfunctory on the side of Aefric's new peers.

"Now," King Colm said softly, while sheathing his sword, "we get to the main bout of the tourney."

Unless it was Aefric's imagination, King Colm was enjoying this a great deal.

Much louder, the king continued.

"And now, in acknowledgment of the great service you have done my kingdom, I, Colm Stronghand, King of Armyr, would name you Duke of Deepwater."

"This is a responsibility, as well as a gift," Queen Eppida said. "For while you will hold lands and titles, with all rights, incomes, and entitlements thereto, you will also have all attendant responsibilities."

"As duke, you will be my vassal," King Colm continued, "and I your liege lord. A reciprocal relationship of rights, duties and responsibilities. You will be under the aegis of my protection, but you must also enforce my laws and stand ready to answer the call to war, should it come."

"You will have the right of high justice within your lands," Queen Eppida continued, "as well as the terrible responsibility of high justice."

"You will be liege lord to vassals of your own," King Colm continued, "and you must hold those relationships in the same sacred trust that I hold yours."

"The responsibility owed to your people will be no less than that owed to your vassals. If you are fair and just, they will prosper. And as they prosper, so shall you."

The king and queen spoke the next words together.

"Are you, Aefric Brightstaff, willing to accept these rights and responsibilities?"

Half a lifetime of Keifer's jokes made during roleplaying games gave Aefric a momentary urge to say no, and laugh. But he knew this was no joking matter. Lives would change based on whether he said yes or no, and not just his own.

The truth was, he could back out here and now. He knew that. He had the right to say no, if he didn't feel he was up to this.

Mind you, he couldn't go back to Keifer's house in Portland. That much was clear to him. But if he backed out now, he could resume Aefric's life of adventure. That was certainly an option, if he wanted it.

Still, he had known since he clicked the pledge button on Del Baker's Jumpstart campaign that he was looking for something more than the treading water that Keifer's life had become.

He might become a great duke. He might be an abject failure. But he had to try.

"I am," he said.

"And you are ready to swear the oaths?" Queen Eppida asked.

"I am."

The oaths were long, and formal, but Aefric was amazed to realize that when they were done, they only really covered what the king and queen had already gone over with him moments before.

And Aefric wasn't the only one swearing oaths. The oaths were reciprocal, and the king and queen really did swear to uphold their end of the feudal arrangement.

"Excellent," King Colm said, once the oaths were complete. "Then I have the distinct pleasure of naming you, Ser Aefric Brightstaff, Duke of Deepwater. I grant to you in perpetuity all lands and titles associated with this position, to be passed down to your children and children's children until the end of time."

The same page from before approached now, and handed items to the queen that she named before handing them to Aefric.

"Here, the golden seal of your office," she said, and handed Aefric the ducal seal. It was done as a round medal, made of gold, hanging from a chain of gold. The seal itself was the image of a lake, with a sword sticking out of it, hilt first.

"And here," King Colm said, "your signet ring. You may note it bears a new device, in your honor."

The symbol on the ring was image of a staff, with two bolts of lighting coming from it, upward and to the left and right.

"Use the lake and sword for ducal matters and the lightning staff for personal matters," the king advised softly, with a wink.

"And now," the king said loudly. "Arise, Ser Aefric Brightstaff, Duke of Deepwater."

The applause was louder this time, but Aefric wasn't sure it was any more sincere.

KAINEMORTON DIDN'T STAY FOR THE CELEBRATION. NO SOONER WAS THE ceremony over than he and his *magari* launched back into the air. No doubt about some matter of such import that it would shake the foundations of Qorunn.

He just always seemed like that kind of character.

But then, Aefric realized, as servants rapidly set up a pair of tables in the courtyard, Kainemorton wasn't just a character.

As Keifer, he'd always thought of Kainemorton — just like all the other non-player characters of Qorunn — as plot devices for the game master to use. They showed up when the game master needed them to do something in the campaign, and then they were off again. Ostensibly doing things "of great import."

Truth was, though, that in games, once Kainemorton did whatever the game master needed him to do, he was just gone. Forgotten about. Put back in the box of NPCs, to be pulled out again only when needed to further the story of the campaign.

But Aefric had met the *real* Kainemorton. Hells, Aefric had *apprenticed* to the old mage. Traveled with him for years. Knew well that he wasn't just a plot device, but a person with hopes, fears, aspirations, regrets.

Once Kainemorton left the royal castle at Armityr, he wasn't just disappearing into a holding pattern until the game master needed a plot device. He really was off someplace, taking care of something important.

The man had a seemingly never-ending to-do list.

Even so, Kainemorton was a person. Just like all these others around Aefric now were actual people, not just stat blocks with lists of motivations and a few paragraphs of history.

King Colm, Queen Eppida, Duchess Ashling, Duke Wylyn — all of them people he'd read about in sourcebooks, but all of them so much more than that now.

Just like Kainemorton.

And then there were the others, the ones Aefric didn't know yet. The unknown noblewoman with the brown braids. All the companions attached to the obvious nobles. Plus the servants and pages.

Not an NPC in the bunch. Not anymore. Every one of them a person. Every one of them real. They had families, and dreams, failures and aspirations and—

"Are you all right?" King Colm asked with a smile. He clapped Aefric on the shoulder. "I know, it's not much of an investiture. Certainly I'd've preferred to honor you with every noble of the realm present, as well as thousands of onlookers. A tournament, as well. With a proper feast to follow, with drinking and dancing, rather than this small banquet."

"That's quite all right, your majesty," Aefric said, deciding not to mention that he'd been thinking about something else entirely. "A nation recovering from war the way ours is, a large celebration might be ill-received."

"It's good that you recognize that," Queen Eppida said, then smiled. "But we will have more gifts for you before you leave."

"If I might ask," Aefric said, "where are the prince and princess?"

King Colm chuckled, but Queen Eppida's sapphire eyes tightened just a little. A point of contention between them?

"Getting some much-needed experience," King Colm said with a smile. "Killian is holding your duchy for you, while Maev sits regent in Fyretti for its new countess."

The county of Fyretti sounded familiar, but the details there paled beside the import of what the king had just said.

The prince and princess? Temporarily holding a duchy and a county? That was a job that certainly could have gone to a lesser noble. Perhaps even a majordomo or seneschal or constable.

Why send the prince and princess?

A page got the king's and queen's attention then, and they stepped back to speak to servants about something. So Aefric tried to stop worrying about the politics of regency and turned to look at the arrangements in the courtyard.

The tables were set up now. Both rectangular, covered in white cloth, and each with a vase of red roses in the center. The settings had forest green placemats beneath golden plates. Forest green napkins beneath golden utensils. Crystal goblets for both wine and water.

Both tables had six places set, but arranged differently. The table nearest the dais had a seat at each end, and two chairs to a side. The other table had three chairs to a side.

One table for the nobles, and one for the companions. Interesting. If the companions were nobles, then clearly they were lesser nobles, so far as Armyr was concerned.

Aefric was just wondering which seat would be his when the duke and duchess approached.

"Greetings, Aefric Brightstaff," Duchess Ashling said, in a high, clear voice. "Excuse me. I should rather say, greetings, your grace. I am Duchess Ashling Fyrenn, of Merrek."

"It is a great pleasure to make your acquaintance, Duchess Ashling," Aefric said, shaking her hand as an equal, in the Armyrian fashion, rather than offering to kiss it because she was a woman, as would be done across most of Qorunn.

A decision, he noticed, that had not been lost on her. One of her eyebrows rose just the barest fraction, and the look in her sapphire eyes grew considering.

In fact, unless Aefric was mistaken, she looked him over anew as Duke Wylyn spoke in a voice that was rougher than his words.

"And I am Duke Wylyn, of Silverlake," he said offering his own hand to shake. His grip was strong, but more gauging than challenging. "It is a pleasure to finally meet the Hero of Deepwater."

"Hardly a hero," Aefric said. "Even the best I could do with my lightning would have amounted to nothing if a host of na'shek had not answered my call to arms."

"And why did they answer?" asked the unknown noble, whose voice had the lilt of a singer. "Because you'd already earned their respect in battle." She smiled. "I am Faenella Darkwalker, newly made countess of Fyretti."

"Fyretti," Aefric said, and as he kissed her hand — he was pretty sure that was the right Armyrian greeting for a lesser noble — he now recognized the county from the reading he'd done as Keifer after supporting the Jumpstart. "That's a county in my duchy, if I'm not mistaken."

"Yes, your grace," she said. "Though I don't know if I'm to swear the oaths of vassalage here, or whether that will be handled when we reach Deepwater."

"Oh, let it wait," Duchess Ashling said. "Those oaths take forever and our luncheon will be ruined."

No sooner were those words out of her mouth than another short fanfare was played by the trumpeters, and all were called to eat.

The nobles took the table nearer the dais, with the king at the head of the table, the queen at the foot. Aefric sat at the king's right hand, Ashling at his left. Duke Wylyn sat beside Ashling, and Countess Faenella beside Aefric.

They were served first a salad of beets and greens, seasoned with something spicy that Aefric didn't recognize, and dressed with a light, tangy dressing.

The main course of the meal was roast venison that practically melted in Aefric's mouth, with a rich, full taste that went perfectly with the strong red wine. Served with the venison was a medley of roasted vegetables, root vegetables from the eldrani lands, seasoned with that same sharp spice as the salad.

For dessert, a pie made with strawberries and cream.

And with the lunch, a conversation that never got very serious. It only ever covered the basics of how repairs were going in the capital, as well as in the duchies of Merrek and Silverlake. Apparently Merrek had been largely spared by the war, but Silverlake had been harmed greatly by incursions from below.

It seemed that the evil dybbungstad — a race long believed to have been destroyed by constant warfare and internal conflicts — yet lived somewhere beneath the surface of Qorunn. And one of their gods had brought them to the surface once more within the confines of Silverlake.

And the dybbungstad hadn't come alone. They'd summoned their demon twins, and made such war on the surface that Silverlake hadn't been able to answer the king's call to arms.

They'd been too busy trying to survive.

Countess Faenella turned out to be another adventurer like

Aefric. She had demurred from discussing the feat that had made King Colm grant her a county. Aefric had been able to determine, at least, that she was either a warpriest, or from the Order of the Blessed Knights, warriors bound by oaths of service to their gods.

Though if she were the latter, could she accept a position as countess? Which oaths would take precedence?

Badly as Aefric wanted to ask those questions, he knew he could not. Conversation at the luncheon was kept light. Even what he had learned about the return of the dybbungstad, he'd had to piece together from Duke Wylyn's discussions of how repairs went.

Badly. They went badly. It was pretty clear from the way Duke Wylyn spoke that his duchy had come out the worst of all of Armyr. That he would dearly love aid, but either he a) was too proud to ask, b) didn't want to ask the king only to be refused because of repairs needed by Armyr itself, or c) had already asked and gotten all the aid he would get, for the time being.

Aefric noted that Duchess Ashling, though admitting that her own lands had suffered little from the Godswalk Wars, had not been quick to offer aid to either her peer or her liege.

Of course, perhaps she already had. Aefric couldn't know for certain...

Once they had all finished with their dessert and presented their compliments on the meal, the king stood.

He raised his glass.

"To new beginnings," he said. "Both for our new duke and countess, but for us all. For the Godswalk Wars are over. And from the wreckage they have wrought, let us build a new era of peace and prosperity. Let us rebuild Armyr such that all the nations and peoples of Qorunn will look upon us with admiration. To Armyr!"

Aefric stood, along with the others. All raised their glasses and toasted.

"To Armyr!"

THE DUCHESS OF MERREK AND THE DUKE OF SILVERLAKE LEFT SHORTLY after the toast, both speaking of affairs back home that needed their attention.

Similarly, the queen left to tend to some matter involving the repairs. Though before she did, she congratulated the new duke and countess once more, and gave each of them golden rings woven from some sixteen different shades of gold. The ring she gave the countess was anchored by a small diamond, and the ring she gave Aefric was anchored by a large emerald.

The workmanship of those rings was inspiring.

Aefric and Countess Faenella were still admiring their new rings when the queen gave her king a kiss on the cheek, and left him with a smile that Aefric would have sworn meant *have fun.*

The king then, along with a small squad of royal guards and a handful of pages, escorted Aefric and Countess Faenella through long, wide halls and down even longer — though narrower — stairs.

It was a long, twisting journey, that involved several detours around portions of the castle that were either too damaged to use, or currently under at least a token level of repair work.

The king even apologized for that, at one point, expressing that, really, he didn't feel right about using *any* workers to effect repairs on the castle until, at the very least, every citizen of Armityr had more than a tent between themselves and the night air.

However, time and efficiency were pressing. Parts of the keep itself were on the verge of collapse. Twenty journeymen stonemasons, with apprentices, working for two aetts right now could stave off the need for hundreds of stonemasons working for seasons. Perhaps years.

In the king's opinion, there would be more than enough work for stonemasons in the coming seasons without needlessly creating more.

Also along the way, interspersed with comments about the state of rebuilding within Armityr and its environs, the king offered advice, quietly, to Aefric.

"The counts of Motte and Goldenfall should have been here for your installment." He shook his head. "Oh, they claimed to be busy with their own repairs and the needs of their people, but mark my words. Their not coming was a message."

"That's why you sent the crown prince to sit regent for me. To keep them in check."

"That's one reason," King Colm admitted. "I needed regents in Deepwater and Fyretti that your other nobles would have to respect." He shook his head. "You're a new noble, and rest assured. They're going to test you. Your counts, and possibly your barons. You'll want their oaths of fealty as soon as you can get them."

"Will they respect those oaths?" Aefric asked.

"Oh, they will," King Colm said with a grimace. "Though Motte and Goldenfall will certainly push the definitions of duty and responsibility, if you let them. But until you have their oaths, they'll be worse. And I'm not sure they'll ever be truly trustworthy."

"Marvelous," Aefric said through a sigh. "All right. I'll summon them as soon as I reach my new castle."

"And if they don't come?" King Colm asked.

"I'm not sure yet," Aefric admitted. "Though I may just declare the Threepeaks mountain range entirely ducal territory."

"Ah," King Colm said with a smile. "You know about the War of Red Gold, and how it was resolved?"

"Not everything, I'm sure, but the basics."

"Do you know about the ... *history* of the claims presented by Count Ferrin of Motte?"

"Kainemorton said something about them being of, shall we say, questionable veracity."

"'Questionable' is being kind about it. I still think Arinda played that one wrong." King Colm cleared his throat. "In any event, be careful. Claiming the Threepeaks might unite them, and united they could pose a real problem for you."

"Assuming he stands alone," Countess Faenella said, joining the conversation. "But he will not. Fyretti will stand with the new duke."

"Thank you," Aefric said.

"Nothing less than my duty and nothing more than my pleasure,"

Countess Faenella said with a smile. "I've heard tales of you, your grace, and all of them speak of a good man. In fact, I will be happy to swear my oaths of fealty before we leave."

"And I'll be happy to witness them," the king said.

"Thank you, your excellency, your majesty," Aefric said, giving them bows in turn. "This might not be so desperate a situation as I feared."

"Even with her aid," King Colm said, "Goldenfall and Motte united won't be easy for you to deal with. Not with the scarring Deepwater has taken from the war. Your barons could be an aid, but they'll likely wait and watch as long as they can, before weighing in on either side."

"I'll think of something," Aefric said. "Oh, and Kainemorton also said something about finding me a court wizard. Do you know anything about this?"

"He has not taken me into his confidence on the matter," King Colm said. "I hadn't even known the two of you were acquainted until he showed up two aetts ago and told me he knew where to find you."

Interesting. Could that have coincided with the Jumpstart?

And just where did Del Baker fit into all this?

And why, oh *why*, hadn't Aefric asked Kainemorton that last question when he had the chance?

At last they reached the foot of one more staircase, and instead of going down yet another hall, they turned and passed through a door into an area outside the keep itself.

The stables. They'd reached the royal stables. Still well inside a rare, intact section of castle wall — as opposed to the city walls, which were a good distance away yet — the royal stables were large enough to host at least two hundred horses. Dozens of grooms bustled about, under the command of the avener.

The smell of horses and hay was almost overpowering. Fortunately, the walls of the castle — such as they were — and the castle wall outside them created a bit of a wind tunnel, and fresh air came whistling through.

A page ran ahead into the stables, calling instructions to the avener, a well-muscled woman of middle years, who passed them on to the grooms.

"Before we do anything further," the king said. "If our new countess would be so good as to kneel, we can see about those oaths."

DUCHESS ASHLING HAD BEEN RIGHT ABOUT ONE THING, AT LEAST. THE oaths of fealty really did seem to take forever.

Or maybe it was just too surreal for Aefric, who had — not two hours past — given the vassalage half of the oath for the first time.

And now here he was, on the receiving end of those same oaths. Listening to Countess Faenella going through all the words he'd recently said to the king, and waiting for his turn to say the words that the king had said to him. The liege lord half of the oaths of fealty, with promises just as important and just as binding.

And all this was taking place not on a dais in front of even a dozen noble witnesses. It was taking place just outside an intact portion of the royal keep in the palace at Armityr. The huge royal stables (and attendant odors) not a dozen paces away. The springtime sun directly overhead making the day seem hotter than it probably was.

Only one witness, but a witness whose quality was beyond dispute — King Colm Stronghand himself, who had a small smile on his face through the whole procedure.

Odd, that something so important could be happening while life went on as normal in the background. In the distance, Aefric could hear stonemasons and other workers calling to each other, and a great deal of hammering.

Faenella was only halfway through her oaths when that page — the one who'd broken off and hurried ahead into the stables — came speeding out of those stables on a gelding.

Still, through it all, Aefric had to admit. Giving and receiving these oaths all felt quite serious and, well, good.

Back in Portland, as Keifer, he'd only felt half-connected to his life. But here in Armyr, as Aefric, he'd already sworn greater commitments than anything Keifer had undertaken since his marriage vows.

As Aefric finished his portion, he felt a kind of solemn peace wash through him. It lasted only a moment, though, because the king spoke.

"Now," King Colm said, turning to Aefric and Countess Faenella. "Faenella, I've given you your gifts, have I not?"

"You have, your majesty, and you've been most gracious. I am particularly grateful for the sword."

Aefric saw no sign of this sword, which he felt was a pity, for she described a longsword of surpassing beauty and quality, that had been enchanted to an edge beyond anything that a smith could sharpen.

"May it serve you well," King Colm said. He turned to Aefric. "Now. Though you do, as I understand it, use a blade from time to time..."

"That's true, your majesty." Aefric, after all, wore his longsword at his hip even now, every bit as comfortable in its place as the leather backpack on his back.

"I thought so. But obviously your preferred weapon is in your hand right now."

"It is difficult to sheathe a staff, your majesty."

"Too true," the king said with a chuckle. "However, a wand might sheathe more easily."

The king held out his hand, and page placed a wand in it. A wand that was, true enough, sheathed in leather, with a loop that was clearly intended to fit on a belt.

"This is Garram," the king said, holding up the wand, "the wand that was wielded by my great great grandfather, King Iounn Strong-hand. He had not his father's gift for swordplay, but he made a fine battle wizard."

He handed the wand to Aefric, adding, "He specialized in the magics of ice and fire. May this wand serve you as well as it did him."

"Your majesty ... is too kind," Aefric said as a true sense of being honored arose within him, well beyond anything he'd felt when he'd been granted the duchy.

The title and lands. Those were kingly gifts, true — though in a sense, Aefric as Keifer had bought them in the Jumpstart — but this wand was a piece of Stronghand family history.

A truly personal gift, as well as a wand whose power might be invaluable, once Aefric had time to learn its ways.

"It is nothing less than you deserve." The king held out his hand again, and a page placed a small, velvet pouch in it. He handed the pouch to Aefric.

Inside was a small, toy replica of an enclosed carriage, of the sort used by nobles and wealthy merchants throughout Qorunn. Though no figures of horses accompanied it.

"Look on the bottom," the king said.

Aefric did. On the bottom was engraved the word *Arcoa*. Aefric smiled, feeling the buzz of magic the moment he thought the word.

"This is no mere toy," Aefric said.

"Not in the least," King Colm said, smiling. "Speak the word and it becomes a coach that will tirelessly and unerringly whisk you to any destination you name."

"Thank you, your majesty."

"You're quite welcome, my friend. I keep one myself, for emergencies." The king smiled. "I'd use it more, but I like horses, and I like keeping drivers employed."

Aefric chuckled, and so did Countess Faenella.

The king held out his hand one more time. A much larger, heavier velvet pouch was placed on his palm.

"Oh, no, your majesty," Aefric said. "This is really too much."

"It is bad luck to refuse a royal gift," the king said with an arched eyebrow. "I don't know the state of your finances, and I won't have my new duke destitute when he takes on his post. You'll likely need your duchy treasury to rebuild. But you must keep personal funds on hand to see to your own welfare."

He handed Aefric the pouch. Aefric didn't look at the contents. Just tied it to his belt and said, "Thank you, your majesty."

The pouch was heavy enough to make his belt sag.

"You are quite welcome. Both of you," the king added, before Faenella could thank him again. "And, your grace, you will find one more gift waiting for you between here and the road. But now, alas, I must be about less pleasant, though no less important duties of state. Best of luck to you both."

The king turned and left then, taking his entourage of guards and pages with him. Save for one page, who handed Aefric and Countess Faenella each a pair of scroll cases before he too turned and left.

Two of the scrolls were their official patents of nobility, signed and sealed by the king himself. The other two scrolls were maps, with the paths to their ducal and county keeps, respectively, marked clearly.

As they looked over those patents and maps, a thought occurred to Aefric.

"Your excellency, where are your two companions?"

"Fetching my horses, your grace. More gifts from his majesty."

"Well," Aefric said, transferring that new money pouch to a safer location in his backpack, along with the smaller velvet pouch and its contents. "I guess we won't be taking my new coach, then."

"Oh ... your grace..." she said, visibly flustered, as a groom brought forward a brilliant, speckled white stallion.

"Let us ride together," Aefric said with a smile. "I'll try out my new toy another time."

"Thank you, your grace," Countess Faenella said, and Aefric pretended not to notice the way her cheeks had reddened.

He'd have to be careful. He hadn't meant anything by the comment about the coach, but he wasn't talking to a friend. He was talking to a vassal.

Without even thinking, he'd put her in an awkward position. He'd have to take care not to do that again.

There might be a time to put his vassals in awkward positions, but it was never something to do by accident.

He smiled reassuringly as he looked over her new horse. He had to admit, the stallion was magnificent. And its saddlebags already bulged, likely with her adventuring gear.

Two more horses trotted up out of the stables, ridden by the two women who'd been with the countess at the ceremony. Both were young. Likely somewhere about the age of majority. One had skin of a deep brown, and long black hair. The other had fair skin dusted with freckles, and long, shimmering red hair that hung nearly to her waist.

Neither wore the gowns they'd worn for the installation. Rather they were dressed for riding, with leather breeches, and fine silk shirts of soft gray, as well as riding half-cloaks.

"Your grace," Countess Faenella said, "may I present two of my ladies in waiting, the eldest daughters of my two barons. This is Sighild Ol'Masarkor," — she indicated the redhead — "and this is Oswen Ol'Ulinnis" — she indicated the brunette.

"It is a pleasure to meet you both," Aefric said, kissing their hands in turn.

"The pleasure is ours, your grace," Oswen said, while Sighild only managed a shy smile.

"Mind if I take a moment to change into something better suited for riding?" Faenella asked, and Aefric smiled to hear her sound more like a confident adventurer than an overwhelmed noble.

"By all means," he said, and before she could dig into a saddlebag, both her ladies in waiting were off their horses — reins handed to grooms who showed up almost as though by magic — and they quickly pulled out proper outfitting and whisked her into what appeared to be a changing room in the stables themselves.

While he waited, Aefric attached his new wand to his belt, beside his sword and belt pouch.

When the ladies returned, the countess looked far more comfortable. She wore chainmail with a white tabard emblazoned with the Watchful Eye of Vera. She wore a kite shield on her back, and a sword at her side.

So. Definitely of the Order of Blessed Knights, then. Vera's warpriests were known to favor the mace and morningstar.

Her ladies in waiting appeared to have different opinions of their countess' choice of riding apparel. Oswen smiled and nodded, as though pleased that she would be serving a warrior countess. Aefric noted that Oswen herself had added a short sword to her riding outfit.

Sighild, on the other hand, had paled, and looked as though something from lunch was not sitting right in her belly. And she had not added a weapon to her belt.

"Your horse, your grace?" Countess Faenella asked.

Aefric smiled was about to summon his *magaunt*, when the avener called out to him.

"Here, your grace," she said, leading a glorious young stallion of midnight black. "His name is Windsong, and he is your gift from her majesty, the queen."

Aefric shook his head in smiling disbelief. Another gift?

"Please," he said to the avener. "Convey my thanks to her majesty for this magnificent horse."

"I'll be only too glad to, your grace," the avener said with a smile.

Aefric slid his backpack into a saddlebag and mounted. He was ready to turn and ride away then, but the page stopped him with a subtle movement of his hand and bow of his head.

Puzzled, Aefric turned to see the rest of the countess' party arriving.

Apparently the two ladies in waiting, when they had come to the capital, had come with a retinue for their new countess. Maidservants for the ladies and their countess. A dozen mounted soldiers, both men and women, with one carrying her banner. A cook with great drooping mustaches, two assistants, and his own wagon. And last but not least, a cleric of Ulna, goddess of travel.

The cleric was a portly man named Nyorngyth, with light brown skin and dark brown hair, who seemed to take delight in everything around him.

Such a crowd. Aefric, it seemed, would have to get used to traveling as a noble, instead of an adventurer.

At least, to judge by her expression, Countess Faenella was as uncomfortable with the crowd as he was.

5

———————

IT SEEMED THAT NOT ALL OF THE DAMAGE TO ARMITYR WAS SIMPLY being repaired. Changes were being made to the city, reshaping it into something new.

The route that Aefric rode, along with Countess Faenella and her entourage, was only one example of the changes taking place.

Aefric knew from Keifer's old maps that, before the Godswalk Wars, the Kingsroad started at the royal palace and led through the city of Armityr to the western gate and out into the country of Armyr.

The Kingsroad had been the only direct road leading into Armityr. Even roads coming in from the neighboring countries of Rethneryl, to the east, and ... Malimfar! That was the kingdom that claimed those swamps and grasslands he'd flown over with Kainemorton!

What else could he remember about Malimfar?

Not much. As Aefric, he'd had little reason to think about it. But as Keifer, he'd known it from the *Torn Kingdoms* sourcebooks, of course...

They were a decent sea power, or had been before the Godswalk Wars. They reminded Keifer of Vikings...

That was it. At least, at the moment.

The road from Malimfar to the south, had to meet up with the

Kingsroad west of Amityr, just as the road from Rethneryl, from the east, had to.

In this way, all roads to Armityr had to join and cross the Maiden's Blood River, watched over by a fairly impressive keep in its own right.

However, the page who led Aefric and his company out of the capital city did not take them around the castle and immediately to the Kingsroad.

Rather he took them directly south, through recently cleared rubble that had once been buildings. And would be again soon, from the way hundreds and hundreds of men and women bustled about, rebuilding what was lost.

Despite all the activity, Aefric noted that there was a smooth, straight road leading from the royal palace to the southern wall, and that a gate and gatehouse were being built where once stood only wall.

It seemed that the road from Malimfar now came directly to the capital. Or at the very least, the road from those woods near the border.

"The king will need a new keep," Countess Faenella observed, "if he intends to keep this road."

"Do you think?" Aefric asked. His mind was less on the strategic matters of roads than on the clear skies above him. The gentle breeze coming from the southwest, carrying fresh scents from the river and fields.

"For centuries the only way to reach the capital by road was to cross the Maiden's Blood or the Indecisive, and the king controlled both crossings well." She shook her head. "Adding a southern road and an extra gate might add convenience now, but he may pay for it if he ever goes to war with Malimfar, or a force that crosses Malimfar."

"Overland is certainly an option," Aefric said.

"True," the countess said, "but slower than the roads. Especially with siege equipment." She shook her head. "Hope King Colm knows what he's doing."

The page led them out past the construction and onto that new road, which also branched around the outer walls of the city to the west, to join up with the Kingsroad shy of the Maiden's Blood River.

Construction truly was everywhere, around Armityr. Despite the direction of the breeze, the smells of human sweat and sawdust, horse sweat and pitch and more all swelled until the ladies in waiting, as well as their maids, held scented handkerchiefs to their noses.

Countess Faenella frowned at that, as though wondering if she, too, should hold a handkerchief to her nose.

"They aren't used to the harder life of an adventurer," Aefric said to her, but not loudly enough for the others to hear. "You and I, we've smelled much worse than this."

She shared a smile with him.

Finally, though, they rode past the construction and began to approach the Maiden's Blood and Riverkeep.

Riverkeep was a broad, squat, gray stone keep that controlled access to both the Kingsroad and the wide Maiden's Blood River. Its hexagonal outer walls featured ballistae at every corner, and chain nets across the river. Inside those walls, drawbridge access for the Kingsroad. The keep itself had at least four huge catapults that Aefric could see.

From his old reading, he knew that Riverkeep housed over a hundred soldiers, as well as support staff, and entire flocks of sheep and pigs, as well as two small farms. It was almost self-supporting. And anyone wanting to cross the river not only had to deal with guards and portcullises at both ends, they had to pass a gauntlet of murder holes that could take down an invading army. And had, at least once that Aefric knew of.

The page rode ahead of them, calling to the guards at the near side of the bridge.

"All these precautions," Aefric said, thinking not only of the impressive keep before him, but also the conversation he and Faenella had had earlier about roads. "And yet, the borog army of the Flayer never once used the road. They tunneled under the rivers, and struck where they would."

"No defense is perfect," Countess Faenella said. "Especially when the attackers are spurred on by a god."

The page rode back in the company of a about a score of soldiers, one of whom carried the flag of Armyr.

"Ah," Oswen said. "This must be our formal escort from the king. I was wondering where they were."

"Here is where I leave you," the page said. "But his majesty wishes me to convey to your grace his last gift." His chin jerked down sharply in self-rebuke. "Excuse me. His last gift *for now*."

Gift?

The page swept his hand out to indicate the soldiers around him, then handed a scroll to Aefric.

Aefric, puzzled, unrolled the scroll and began to read.

My Dear Duke of Deepwater,

As none of your own troops were present for your installation, tradition would generally see me providing my new duke with an escort to see him safely to his own lands for the first time.

However, in your case, I decided to make an exception.

It occurred to me that there might be others who were grateful to you for saving their lives at the Battle of Deepwater.

Thus, I had my constable seek out a dozen volunteers to leave my service for yours.

In truth, he could have found fourfold what I asked of him. Such is the gratitude of the people of Armyr, as well as its soldiery.

The twenty-four you see before you were chosen for their dedication to the Hero of Deepwater. You may assign them as you will, but I suggest you make of them your personal guard. They are all battle-tested, and you will not find any more loyal soldiers anywhere on Qorunn.

May they serve you well.

By the hand of His Majesty,

Colm Stronghand

King of Armyr

"Do you accept his gift?" the page asked.

"I do," Aefric said, touched by the fire he saw in the eyes of the soldiers around him. "And please convey to his majesty my utmost gratitude."

The page bowed and rode off, while Aefric looked around at his new soldiers. They all wore chainmail armor and coifs, with simple tabards in muted colors. Sixteen of them looked to be men, and eight women. All human, and mostly young. Perhaps a handful were as old as Aefric, or older.

All of them wore crossbows on their backs. Half of them carried spears, and the others swords or maces or axes.

One of the soldiers rode closer. He was an older man than the rest, with the rough features and old scars of one who had served as a soldier for most of his close to forty years. He favored a sword, and had a shield strapped to his horse. He wore full plate armor instead of chainmail, and his graying black hair battlefield short.

"Your grace," he said, and his voice was surprisingly strong and clear. "I am Ser Beornric Ol'Sandallas. On behalf of my company, may I say that we are deeply honored to serve you. Every one of us survived the Battle of Deepwater only because you turned the tide."

Before Aefric could reply, the knight called out a sound.

As one, Aefric's new solders all saluted with a right fist held high.

Aefric returned their salute.

The soldiers then pulled down the patches from their right shoulders. The patches that bore the sigil of the kingdom of Armyr.

Sewn into place underneath those patches waited the sigil of the duchy of Deepwater.

The flag bearer took down the king's standard, and raised the duke's instead.

"Thank you all," Aefric said, meeting the eyes of each of his new soldiers in turn as he spoke. "They call me the Hero of Deepwater. But in truth, I would not have survived that battle without you. Without all of you. No battles are won or lost by an individual. They are won only by the whole, *fighting* as an individual."

Aefric drew a deep breath.

"I pray that I find as much success as a duke as I found on the battlefield. It is an entirely different arena, but no less a war."

At that he was met with soft laughter.

"And as such, I can promise you only that I will keep that same principle in mind. If the duchy pulls together as an individual, we will be greater than any of us could be on our own."

The cheer that Aefric got in response was inspiring.

Now he hoped he could live up to such ideals.

ARMYR WAS A LOT WIDER THAN IT LOOKED ON THE GAMING MAPS, BACK on Earth.

Oh, when he'd poured over them as Keifer, he'd known intellectually that Armyr was over three hundred miles across at its widest east-west point and something like two hundred eighty miles across at its widest north-south point.

But those were maps being read by a man used to casually covering seventy miles in an hour, in his car. Three hundred miles, that wasn't even five hours of driving.

It was a lot longer, by horse.

And as Aefric, who had traveled everywhere first by horse and later by *magaunt*, which rode somewhat faster than a horse, he *knew* that these distances were long.

He'd just never cared before how long those distances were because he'd never been in that much of a hurry to get anywhere.

No. Scratch that. There had been times for hurry. But at those times, he'd teleported. Not on his own, of course. He didn't have command of that magic. Not for great distances. But he'd teleported via the magic of Kainemorton, or Karbin.

For the most part, though, for Aefric, travel had been its own reward. Seeing the sights. Finding adventure.

This trip was different. Now he was riding *to* something. His own duchy. He'd sworn the oaths, and he carried the piece of paper, but that duchy wouldn't really be *his* until he formally took possession of it.

And he couldn't do that until he covered the almost two hundred fifty miles of road between the capital and his ducal seat at Water's End.

Alone, on his *magaunt*, he could probably cover that distance in five or six days. Cold camp at night. Trail rations. Short sleep. He'd done it more times than he could count. And he could cover it even faster by flying.

But he was riding this splendid new stallion, Windsong, not his *magaunt*.

And he wasn't riding alone.

Not only did he have twenty-four new soldiers of his own, but he was traveling with his vassal, Faenella, Countess of Fyretti, and her entire retinue.

No. Scratch that. This was a pretty small retinue, for any traveling noble. Two ladies in waiting, a handful of maids, a cook and assistants, a dozen soldiers, and a cleric of Ulna.

Pretty bare bones, as noble retinues went. Of course, his own was even more spartan. One knight and a company of soldiers.

With a crowd like this to think of, this trip would likely take an aett. But it couldn't be helped.

Fortunately, the oaths involved in taking a landless knight into his service were much shorter and more direct than the formal oaths of vassalage. They'd amounted to Ser Beornric swearing to serve Aefric loyally and honorably to the best of his ability unto death or dismissal, while Aefric in return swore to protect and provide for Ser Beornric, and to give him opportunity to gain honor in Aefric's service.

Honestly, the portions of the oaths about honor took the longest, but the whole process was still short enough to take care of there on the road, during a pause to rest the horses.

At least the slower travel gave Aefric the chance to look over the countryside as a duke, not an adventurer. At least, what he could see of the countryside from the Kingsroad.

It was clear that an immense army had marched straight across the farmlands and towns nearest the capital. Repair efforts were underway, but the areas where crops and homes had been put to the torch were still plainly visible.

There would be a lot to do, recovering from the Godswalk Wars. Aefric found himself worrying about those who would take advantage of this time. Overcharge for food or supplies. Or worse, raid those supplies, then sell them back to the victims.

There might even be entire countries left relatively untouched. And those countries might be eyeing their weaker neighbors with thoughts of expanding their borders...

No. This was not the direction he could afford to think. Not now. Now he had to turn his attention to his own duchy. Most of Armyr's seacoast was within Deepwater. Aefric's problems with raiders would far more likely be from pirates than from bandits.

But even that concern would have to wait for now.

By the end of the first day's travel, they had reached the fork, where branches of the Kingsroad split off toward Silverlake and Merrek, while the main branch continued on toward Deepwater.

Their party took over the Red Hand Inn, taking all available rooms. Unfortunately, even so, half the soldiers had to sleep out under the stars or in the stables.

Aefric was surprised to see that the parties of Duchess Ashling and Duke Wylyn were not boarding at that inn for the night. They'd had no more than an hour's head start. Clearly they had either pushed on farther or made other arrangements, because the innkeeper pled ignorance when asked about them.

Aefric's second night on the road, his party was hosted by the grace of Baroness Slishan, a matronly woman who seemed to feel she'd never aged past the prime of her youth. And its attendant attitudes.

She spent most of dinner that night — a sparse affair of thin beef stew and hard bread, with watered wine — complaining like a spoiled child about the sorry state of her finances and the aid she would need to repair her own lands, let alone those of her tenants.

And when she was not complaining, she was trying to flirt with

Aefric and Beornric in ways that made Countess Faenella finally hush the giggling of her ladies and maids.

Aefric sealed his door with magic that night, unwilling to risk an unwelcome midnight visit from his hostess.

Riding through the baroness' lands the next day, Aefric did have to admit that they were in a sorry state. However, they didn't look so much war-torn as they did ill-kept. The fields hadn't been burned, they'd been overgrown with weeds, or perhaps abused with entirely the wrong kind of crop for their soil.

They passed two small towns along the Kingsroad that had been partially burnt and razed during the war. But repairs hardly seemed to be underway. Aefric couldn't tell, as they passed, if it were a question of priority — such as helping the nearby farms first to keep the food flowing — or just that the damaged parts of those towns had been abandoned.

There were, at least, goatherds that seemed to fare well enough, along the hills toward the western side. So perhaps all was not yet lost for Baroness Slishan.

Midway through the day's riding, they passed a set of territory stones, marking that they were crossing from the baroness' lands into the king's lands once more. And the moment they passed those territory stones, the land changed. Or, at least, the feel of the land did. Gone was that sense of desperation, and in its place a sense of order.

The hills here that were not grazed by goats or sheep were quarried for stone. Granite, from the look of it.

"You'd think the baroness would take the hint and see about the contents of a few of her own hills," Countess Faenella said, still visibly bristling about the behavior of the baroness.

"I wouldn't be surprised if she had," Aefric said, "but took no action when it was clear that their contents weren't easily mined veins of gold."

She snorted, but Ser Beornric said, "Think not too harshly on her, your grace. She was never meant to rule. Her sister was to be baroness, and her sister's son after her, but both died in the wars.

Slishan mourns them, but more than that she mourns the years she wasted on frippery when she could have been learning to rule."

"Perhaps," Countess Faenella said, "instead of mourning her lost years, she should see about finding worthwhile advisers and learning to rule now."

"She has them," Ser Beornric said, then shook his head. "But she worries so about every decision that she does nothing. You've seen the result all about you in her lands."

"You seem to know a good deal about this," Aefric said.

"A cousin, your grace. Though I daresay she's forgotten me."

Aefric tried not to think too much about that as they rode on.

They stayed that night at Towerkeep, named for its central tower which stood some three hundred feet tall. The tower was crowned by a watchfire that, it was said, burned so bright it could be seen by day all the way from the capital to the east, and beyond the forest Kerrik, to the west, the start of which was only a few hours away.

The keep itself was not nearly so impressive as even Riverkeep had been, but it had more than enough room to host their entire party in moderate, if simple, comfort. And the fare they were provided was much better than they'd tasted while staying with the baroness.

And the next day, they would finally cross the border into Aefric's ducal lands.

***

That night, Aefric stayed late in Towerkeep's dining hall.

The fire had gone out in the large hearth, but its heat lingered on in the chilly spring evening. This room was in the heart of the keep, at the foot of the tower itself, and held its heat well.

The room was round. And unlike many feasting halls, it wasn't built around a handful of long tables. Instead, there were two dozen round tables that each sat eight on armless, backless bench seats, two to a seat.

The hall was lit by five chandeliers, which hung from the high ceiling. The central was the largest, easily a dozen paces across. The others were perhaps two-thirds its size.

Few decorations on the walls of the hall. Two banners flanked the hearth. One featured the royal sigil, the other the sigil of the keep — a black tower on a red background. Across from the hearth, a tapestry commemorated an old battle that featured the tower prominently with its signal fire blazing up above.

The smallest decoration was the one that Aefric himself found most meaningful. On the hearth was mounted a sheet of parchment, listing the names of every castellan who had held Towerkeep in the king's name, along with their years of service.

Five hundred years this keep had served Armyr. And in that time, there had been twenty castellans.

Looking over that parchment had been a moment of double-memory for Aefric. As Keifer, he marveled at standing within a keep that had served for twice as long as his own country had been in existence.

As Aefric, he marveled at the battles this keep must have seen and survived. Even the Godswalk Wars, which had taken down sections of the great royal palace at Armityr, had failed to knock down this ancient tower.

It was thoughts of history that keep Aefric late in the dining hall that night. He was a duke now. He would be featured in histories someday. Not just the sourcebooks on Earth that Keifer had loved so well, but actual books here in Qorunn, written not by Del Baker, but by historians of this world.

They'd get some things right. Others they'd miss completely. But their overall tenor — what would that be?

What kind of duke would he make?

He pondered that for a time, staring into the banked coals of the fire.

Then he pulled out the map given him by the king, and began looking over the lands that would soon be his. Were his now, technically.

He tried to grasp the scope of what it all really meant. To be a noble. To rule, in his own right and in the name of the king.

Once they crossed the border tomorrow, Aefric himself would be the authority. Everyone would be looking to him for leadership. To set the tune that others would have to dance to.

How many lives would be depending on him? How much trade? How many decisions?

How much trust could he count on? How much trust could he afford to give?

When he had backed the Jumpstart, it had seemed a small thing. A new twist on a game he'd played most of his life.

But here now, it was no game. If he made the wrong call, he couldn't argue with the game master. He would have to live with the consequences.

"We cross into your lands tomorrow, your grace," a voice said from across the room, over near the door to the tower stairs.

Aefric shook himself out of his reverie. Looked up at the speaker.

Nyorngyth.

The cleric of Ulna wore what looked to be the same brown traveling robes he'd worn for the whole of their trip. They were likely comfortable, at least. They even split front and back, and would likely have revealed far too much of the cleric, were he not wearing matching leggings.

Probably easier to ride that way, in a robe.

"Forgive me, your grace," Nyorngyth said, offering a bow. "I didn't mean to disturb you."

"That's quite all right, Nyorngyth," Aefric said. "Please. Join me."

"Thank you, your grace." The cleric, despite his portly stature, moved with a swift and graceful stride.

He looked over the map Aefric had laid out on the table.

"As soon as we reach the Kerrik Forest," Nyorngyth said, "we'll be in your lands, your grace."

"I've just been considering what that means," Aefric admitted.

"Ulna has blessed you most of your life, your grace," Nyorngyth said with a smile as he took a seat near Aefric, but not so near as to presume familiarity. "She smiles on adventurers."

"Ah, but I've given that up, haven't I?" Aefric said with a grimace. "I'm sure a duke can't afford to exploring haunted mines and delving into forgotten ruins."

"And is your new undertaking any less an adventure?"

"Ulna is a goddess of travel," Aefric said. "I won't be doing nearly as much, once I reach Water's End. Not compared to what I'm used to."

"But others will be traveling in your name, your grace. Soldiers, messengers, agents, and more, I'm certain."

Aefric chuckled. "Trying to make sure the new duke keeps up his offerings?"

"Of course," Nyorngyth said with an open smile. "But offering reassurances as well. Both are part and parcel to my calling."

"I don't suppose that speeding horses is part and parcel to your calling."

"I'm afraid not, your grace," Nyorngyth said, still smiling. "Shortening travel? Ulna forfend. Travel is a gift unto itself."

"I've had a lot of gifts, lately," Aefric said, shaking his head.

"With good reason," Ser Beornric said from the door to the kitchens. He entered carrying two copper mugs full of ale. "May I join you, your grace?"

"Certainly, Ser Beornric," Aefric said, "so long as you finish that thought."

Beornric called over his shoulder for more ale, and took a seat on the other side of Aefric from Nyorngyth, handing one of his mugs to Aefric, who took it gratefully and drank a long pull.

The ale was rich, and nutty, and had been stored in such a way to keep it just the least bit chilly to the taste.

A tower servant came in with another mug and a copper pitcher, both of which were full of ale.

Once the servant was gone, Ser Beornric glanced at the cleric, suspiciously.

"I assure you, good knight," Nyorngyth said. "While we clerics of

Ulna will happily share news on our travels, not a one of us will reveal any secrets we hear in our travels. To do so would be a crime against the goddess."

"In that case," Ser Beornric said, "please consider this conversation such a secret."

Nyorngyth sketched the symbol of Ulna — a crossroads — in the air, and said, "In Ulna's name I swear to hold as secret anything I hear tonight from either of you, from the time I first entered this room to the time I leave it."

Ser Beornric looked at Aefric. Aefric nodded.

"The king has taken a risk in naming you duke," Ser Beornric said, leaning closer and lowering his voice. "The choice is popular with his subjects and his knights, of course. The Hero of Deepwater. But Merrek and Silverlake both likely take it as a slap in the face, for they were not consulted."

"How do you know they weren't consulted?"

"Well," Ser Beornric said. "I do not know it of a certainty. But I have gathered as much from things said by the constable when he was seeking volunteers to enter your service."

"It does make sense, your grace," Nyorngyth said, leaning in and speaking more quietly. "You would not have been their choice, and they gain nothing by your installation."

"They were known to be lobbying to expand their duchies," Ser Beornric said. "Duchess Ashling wanted to annex the county of Fyretti."

"Her family has been pushing for that for ages," Nyorngyth said. "After all, her family once ruled the principality of Fyr, which included Fyretti, as well as your grace's baronies of Norra, Felspark and Riverbreak. Not to mention land that is now part of Malimfar, to the south."

Aefric considered that through a long breath. That would have given Duchess Ashling all the land north to the Haven River and the Kingsroad. A full third of his duchy.

"And Duke Wylyn," Aefric said. "What did he want?"

Ser Beornric pointed to a long, wide canyon on the map.

"Right now, your land is divided from his by the Dragonscar, which is technically yours. He would want at least to extend his realm south to the Threepeaks, including their mines."

"Taking land and gold at once," Aefric said, shaking his head.

"Not to mention silver," Ser Beornric said. "There are silver mines in those mountains as well. And possibly others not yet discovered."

Aefric couldn't remember anything from the sourcebooks about silver mines. Interesting.

"In giving you the whole of the largest duchy in Armyr—" Ser Beornric began, but Nyorngyth interrupted.

"Though not the richest. That honor goes to Merrek and its extensive trade network."

"Still," Ser Beornric said, arching an eyebrow at the cleric. "The largest duchy in Armyr. And in giving it to you, the king needs to assure himself of your allegiance. The peers will not forget his decision in this matter. And they have long, long memories."

"That's why he gave Fyretti to Faenella," Aefric said. "She's a warrior, and she already respects me."

"Giving you an ally along Merrek's border," Ser Beornric confirmed with a nod. "A wise move."

"Two of my barons still border Merrek," Aefric said. "Norra and Felspark."

"They border your counties as well," Ser Beornric said. "And likely the counts have been in their ears since the death of Duchess Arinda."

Aefric sighed and shook his head. But then he smiled at Nyorngyth.

"As you said. An adventure."

* * *

AEFRIC AND HIS PARTY HADN'T BEEN ON THE ROAD MORE THAN AN HOUR the next day before they reached the Kerrik Forest, and the border between the king's lands and those held by vassals for the duke of Deepwater.

Which made it something of a surprise to see construction underway for a small fort, just at the edge of the tree line, complete with a metal gate, closing the road.

Two men in chainmail stood guard over the gate, each armed with a halberd.

Above the gate flew the banner of Motte — alternating bars of black and purple, descending to the sinister.

Not the sigil of Motte, but the battle flag.

This sight caused no little stir among the countess' retinue.

"Oswen," Aefric said, without looking away from the sight before him, "was this gate here when you left Fyretti?"

"No, your grace," she said. "Neither was any construction at all."

"I thought as much," Aefric said softly.

"Shall I enquire?" Ser Beornric asked.

"No," Aefric said, "I'll do it myself."

He spurred Windsong forward, with Countess Faenella and Ser Beornric following just behind, along with a soldier bearing the Deepwater banner.

Aefric stopped his horse no more than fifty feet from the gate.

"What is the meaning of this?" Aefric called out.

"Safe passage through the Kerrik and the county of Motte will require a toll of one silver apiece," responded one of the guards, while the other called a signal back behind him.

Construction on the fort stopped.

More soldiers came out of the woods. Six, armed with crossbows.

"The count of Motte does not have jurisdiction over the Kingsroad," Aefric said, having confirmed this very issue only last night with the cleric of Ulna. "That is the province of the duke of Deepwater."

"I have my orders," the soldier said, though he didn't sound happy about it. "No one crosses without paying. No exceptions were made for nobility."

"Do you know who I am?" Aefric asked.

"I know that banner," the soldier said. "So I assume you must be the new duke. But I don't serve you, your grace. I serve Count Ferrin. And I have my orders."

"You also don't have enough support to enforce those orders," Ser Beornric said, nodding at the thirty five soldiers riding with Aefric and Faenella. "Think, man."

Aefric reached down and pulled out his staff from where it was lashed to his saddle. He stood tall in his stirrups, holding the staff high.

"I am Ser Aefric Brightstaff," he called in a ringing voice. "Hero of the Battle of Deepwater, and newly made Duke of Deepwater. And I have no intention of paying a toll to enter my own duchy."

The yellow diamond at the top of the Brightstaff began to glow.

"Furthermore," he said, while the count's soldiers looked back and forth, as though each wanted another to be the first to either fire a shot or defy the count. "I will not have *my* vassals charging tolls on *my* road."

He took the staff in both hands.

"Stand away from the gate," he ordered.

"What's going on here?" Another soldier came out of the woods. This one older, and bearing the star of a sergeant on the left shoulder of his tabard.

Aefric chose not to explain himself further.

"Your last warning, stand away from the gate."

"I'll have you know this is the count's—"

The count's sergeant never got to finish that sentence.

A tease of lightning played about the Brightstaff, then lanced out and demolished the gate in a single, booming stroke.

The two guards with halberds were too near. They were burned and thrown by the blast.

There was a moment of silence, in which all that could be heard was the smoldering of the gate's remains.

Some of the count's soldiers raised their crossbows.

"Any one of you shoots," Ser Beornric called in a loud voice, "you'll be declaring war on your count's behalf."

"He already—" The count's sergeant began, but Ser Beornric cut him off.

"The road is his by law," he said. "Your count had no right to bar it, and his grace was good enough to warn your men to move away."

Countess Faenella whistled, and her soldiers rode up behind her. Not to be outdone, Aefric's soldiers rode up as well. Every one of these soldiers already had crossbows loaded and aimed.

"Stand. Down," Aefric said to the count's soldiers.

The count's sergeant grimaced. Appeared to run a quick calculation of his chances. Shook his head.

"You heard his grace," the sergeant said. "Lower your weapons, men. And I think we'll be waiving the toll."

The soldiers did as ordered, and stepped off of the road.

"Carry news of this back to your count," Aefric said. "I'll not have him charging a toll to those who would use my road."

"His excellency's men keep the forest safe to ride through," the sergeant said, showing an admirable amount of loyalty, in Aefric's opinion. "Is he to receive no compensation for that?"

"A fair question," Aefric said, raising one hand to forestall Ser Beornric's response. "And you may tell his excellency that the new duke will ensure that he does not bear that cost alone."

The sergeant nodded. "Thank you, your grace."

Aefric spurred his horse forward, and led his company past the remains of the gate and into the forest.

The forest on either side of the road was really quite lovely. Mostly composed of oaks and ashes, along with the occasional copse of yew and beech, and the rare ironwood here and there. There were even places where the canopy stretched across the road, though those were few.

The birdsongs here were striking in two ways. They were both somewhat like birdsongs Keifer knew on Earth — a few reminded him of the robin and the western meadowlark — but not entirely like any he knew back in Oregon or Minnesota.

And yet, he recognized them all, as Aefric. He could only name one of the birds involved — the pekethrush — because Aefric had never bothered worrying too much about the birds behind the songs.

Aefric only recognized the pekethrush because in his travels with the Last Sons, the forest maven Krolik had emphasized that the pekethrush's cry got sharper and higher when unnatural creatures were around.

The pekethrushes didn't sound worried today.

"At least there shouldn't be any bandits," Countess Faenella observed. "Not if the count is trying to claim a toll."

"A toll he no doubt divided with Norra," Ser Beornric growled. "The forest south of the road is hers. Only the northern side is Motte's to claim, which means they're both involved in this venture."

The knight shook his head.

"I confess, your grace," he said, "I don't like the idea of you paying the count to do what he should be doing anyway. And the baroness of Norra will likely be irritated that you're compensating the count, but not her."

"Not at all, good Ser Beornric," Aefric said with a smile. "The road is mine to guard and maintain, after all. And if Motte wishes to invite me to send soldiers to patrol his border, then who am I to object?"

Ser Beornric laughed.

"Speaking of which," Aefric said. "My soldiers will need a base to work from, and I think that fort will do nicely. So. Once we reach Deepwater proper, I'll want you to send workers to finish construction and soldiers to make clear that it is *my* banner that will fly over *my* fort, not Motte's."

"Happily, your grace," Ser Beornric said. "I think I'm going to like serving you."

"That fort *is* on the count's land," Countess Faenella said, and though her words were neutral, Aefric had no doubt she had a strong opinion about what Aefric was doing.

"The count tried to seize control of the primary land route into my duchy," Aefric said. "He chose to move against me before even meeting me. He needs to pay a price for that. Both for himself, and as a lesson to others."

"A price that could last a very long time."

"That depends on him," Aefric said. "If we develop a good working relationship, I'll turn the fort over to him at some point. But not until I know he can be trusted."

The countess did not look any more convinced.

Aefric sighed.

"The fort, in and of itself, doesn't bother me," he said. "The signal fires of Towerkeep keep it from being strictly necessary, but having a fort there isn't a bad idea. Still, for the time being at least, I need to control that fort. If I don't have soldiers there keeping Motte in line, he'll start up with that 'toll' nonsense again."

Countess Faenella gave a considering nod that Aefric hoped was agreement.

Ser Beornric, however, laughed and said, "Forgive me, your grace, but if that fort is yours until you can trust Motte, I suspect the Deepwater banner will still fly over that fort when your grace's grandchildren hold the duchy."

And that might be true, but Aefric hoped it wouldn't come to that.

***

Riding the Kingsroad through Kerrik Forest proved to be a pleasant enough experience. Most of the trees growing near the road were oaks and ashes, and the familiarity of those scents — both as Keifer and as Aefric — gave him a pleasant feeling.

The spring weather was still mild, and the morning breezes gentle. Adding in the songs of the local birds and the first hours of riding through his own lands felt pleasantly bucolic.

And Aefric had to admit. The count, and likely the baroness, were doing a decent job of keeping the forest safe to ride through. Even as they approached their noontime break, he hadn't seen hide nor hair of any bandits, brigands, nor thieves.

Then again, there might never have been any in these woods to begin with.

"We're being followed," Ser Beornric said, after taking a report. "Lone rider, lightly armored, and staying a good distance back."

"Scout?" Countess Faenella asked. "Keeping an eye on us?"

These seemed reasonable enough questions that Aefric merely added a cocked eyebrow and a look at Beornric.

"Possible," he said, "though I think a messenger is more likely."

"Why wouldn't a messenger just ride past us?" Aefric asked.

"Because then we'd know for sure he was a messenger, carrying word to the count. Or at least to someone senior to the sergeant back there."

"So what if he does?" Aefric asked. "The count will know sooner or later anyway."

"We have only twenty-four soldiers," Ser Beornric said. "And they know that. If they meet us with—"

"Thirty six," Countess Faenella corrected him. "Not to mention myself and his grace."

"I didn't wish to presume, your excellency."

"I won't lie," Countess Faenella said. "I have mixed feelings about your claiming the fort." She raised a forestalling hand. "I understand your logic, your grace, and concede that you may have a point, though I personally believe that there may have been a less intrusive way to assert yourself there."

Aefric considered answering that, but Faenella wasn't done.

"However, setting aside that issue, I have no intention of standing by in the event that some baron or count along this road attempts to threaten our new duke with force."

"Very good, your excellency," Ser Beornric said with a nod before turning back to Aefric. "Nevertheless, Motte could certainly muster more than thirty-six, especially if Norra stands with him."

"We will let the messenger pass," Aefric said. "I have no intention of seizing control of the radio stations in my first act as duke."

"Excuse me, your grace?" Ser Beornric asked, and Countess Faenella looked just as puzzled.

"Never mind," Aefric said, silently chastising himself for using one of Keifer's expressions. It wasn't as though anyone else in this world knew what a radio was, much less a radio station. "It is a reference to becoming a tyrant. I have no intention of it."

Word was passed back along the line, though if it was passed to the trailing rider, Aefric couldn't tell. The rider stayed well back as they rode.

But when they did stop at highsun to rest the horses and eat some of the cook's roast lamb, the rider went speeding past, riding low in his saddle.

"About that fort, your grace," Countess Faenella said, as they sat down to eat on blankets spread out by the countess' maids. "Would it not serve just as well to share the fort? You would be able to keep as strong an eye on Motte's activities, while provoking less ill will. It is his first move against you, after all. Likely just a test."

"His second move," Aefric corrected her. "His first was not attending my installation. And construction on that fort was well-underway. Likely he'd been rushing, hoping to finish it before I came to claim my duchy. He'd hoped to be able to force me to pay to enter my own lands."

"True," she said, frowning. "Still. He must be going to considerable effort and expense, but that only stands to my point."

"There's another factor," Aefric said. "That's all new construction. During a time when the priority *should* be on repairing and rebuilding. It's not as though a fort there is strictly necessary for defense. The signal fire from Towerkeep could be seen well on the other side of this forest."

Countess Faenella frowned, but nodded.

"You heard his majesty," Aefric said, softly. "Goldenfall and Motte are likely to move against me. If I gave an inch here, I would only encourage them."

"That's true..."

"And there's Norra to consider. Norra controls more of this forest than Motte. Which means that either Norra is a silent partner in that fort, or risks losing control of part of the forest to Motte."

"If the former, then you've given Norra an informal lesson,"

Countess Faenella said, "and if the latter, you've done her a service. Is that it?"

"That's my thinking," Aefric said with a sigh. "No telling if I'm right though."

They lapsed into thoughtful silence through most of their lunch, though they did hold a little light discourse. Discussions of the trees of the Kerrik, the condition of the road. Little things like those.

Until they all had eaten, the horses were rested, and the company was ready to set out again. *Then*, the countess spoke as they mounted their horses.

"You may well be right about Motte, your grace," she said. "Though I hope the count will not be so set against you as the king implied."

"I would like to think not, but what I've seen so far doesn't give me much hope."

"With that in mind," she said, "may I have your leave to discuss the fort with Motte?"

Aefric frowned, and reined Windsong in, rather than taking his place near the front of the procession once more.

"I'm not ready to negotiate anything about that fort."

"Of course not," she said. "I just want to make sure that he understands the lesson you're trying to impart, and that your seizure of his fort need not be forever."

Aefric thought about that. On the one hand, he really wanted to handle Motte and Goldenfall himself. On the other, Countess Faenella was, right now, his only ally among his vassals. And he could not afford to alienate her...

"Forgive me, your excellency," Ser Beornric said, "but Motte will understand why his grace is seizing the fort—"

"A moment, Ser Beornric," Aefric said, not continuing until Ser Beornric nodded. "Your excellency, you have my trust, and my leave to discuss whatever you desire, so long as you don't make promises on my behalf."

"Thank you, your grace," she said with a smile that lit up her face. Could she really have imagined herself in Motte's position?

"I do make one request, though," Aefric said, and drew a deep breath. "You and I are both new to being nobles. I don't know about you, but I need some time to settle in, learn what it means to be a duke, and decide for myself if I've done the right thing. So, please, Faenella. Give me a year and a day before you broach the topic of the fort with Motte."

"Certainly, Aefric," she said, looking far more reassured than Aefric expected. Or perhaps more comfortable with him as duke?

"Then let us ride. We've a long way to go before we leave this forest."

Kerrik Forest was too broad to cross in a single day. Not riding with the company that Aefric rode with on that first trip to Water's End.

It also didn't seem to attract much traffic right now. But then, there hadn't been much traffic on the road since they passed through Baroness Slishan's lands. The occasional farmer or two, carting goods. A handful of peddlers and wandering craftsmen, traveling without the benefit of a caravan, and only a few guards for protection.

Aefric suspected that trade was suffering in the wake of the Godswalk Wars. Just another problem he'd have to resolve as duke.

And thoughts like those kept him from enjoying the warm afternoon's ride among the beeches and yews, oaks and ashes, as they continued along the Kingsroad through the forest.

Countess Faenella, it seemed, didn't have this problem. She appeared to find the forest inspiring. She led her ladies in a series of songs about travel, about forests and forest nymphs who longed for the love of human men.

During a break in the singing, Aefric did ask a question of Ser Beornric.

"Odd," he said. "We've seen so much damage from the wars, but the forest looks pristine. Untouched. Why do you think that is?"

"Simple," Ser Beornric said. "Just north of the Kerrik are miles and miles of swampland."

Countess Faenella laughed. "Of course. Given a choice between trees and swamps, the borogs will choose swamps every time."

That led her into a song about an eldrani tailor who got lost in the swamps, only to be saved by a borog woman. It was a song, so of course they fell in star-crossed love that led to a poignantly beautiful ending.

As the afternoon grew late, still well within the forest, they found an inn on the Norra side of the road. The Ironwood Inn.

The smells of the Ironwood Inn were detectable well before the inn itself could be seen. It seemed as though the smell of fresh-baked rye bread carried like birdsong through the forest.

But when they reached it, the Ironwood Inn was a sight worth seeing. Old and beautiful. It looked as though every ounce of the wood that had been cleared to build it had gone into its making.

Fully three stories tall — more likely made of oak than ironwood, despite its name — with two small, single-story wings out behind the main building. Arched roofing with wooden shingles painted a bright blue, the same shade as the shutters for the many windows.

It looked so homey that, despite his depressing line of thought that afternoon, Aefric found his heart lightening and his face smiling as he regarded the inn.

"May we see about accommodations?" Sighild asked.

She must have found some courage in her singing with the countess, for this was the first time that Aefric could remember hearing her speak. She had a good, clear voice, much like the countess'. A voice made for singing.

Countess Faenella looked the question to Aefric, who nodded, and said, "Ser Beornric, accompany them if you would."

"If I may," Countess Faenella said.

Aefric nodded for her to go ahead.

"Rather than Ser Beornric, may I send my own knight, Ser Arcy?"

Aefric blinked. Of course at least one knight led her company of soldiers. They were escorting nobles, after all. There might be as many as two or three knights among her number, even if they were not clad in full plate, as Ser Beornric was.

Though why they wouldn't be, he couldn't imagine. Knights were generally expected to wear the best armor available.

"By all means," Aefric said. "I did not meant to presume."

"No presumption was involved, your grace," Faenella said, smoothly. "You are the senior noble present and he is your senior knight. You do my ladies honor by offering Ser Beornric as their escort."

"But it is certainly proper for your ladies to be escorted by your own knight," Aefric said, as much to remind himself to watch out for stumbling blocks like this one in the future as to accede the point.

Ser Arcy dismounted then. She was tall. Even taller than Aefric, and even broader through the shoulders. In fact, she was so large that she might have had na'shek blood, though her skin looked tanned rather than na'shek gray.

She carried a two-handed greatsword strapped to her back, and Aefric wondered if she could handle it just as easy with one hand.

Perhaps she eschewed plate armor because human armorers couldn't make it in her size...

The knight and the ladies returned shortly, having secured rooms for all, as well as meals, and the news that out back were stables more than large enough to accommodate their horses with room to spare.

They were not the only travelers staying at the Ironwood Inn that night. A caravan was staying there as well, taking up a greater portion of the common room, with intentions to push on east out of the forest the next day.

Aefric took that opportunity — and only a trifle of the money the king had given him — to buy several bolts of silk, in a variety of colors. Some for himself, but mostly for the countess and her ladies in waiting.

"A small gift of congratulations on your own installment," Aefric said, presenting most of the fabric to the countess. "And a thank you for your lovely singing," he added, giving smaller amounts to Oswen and Sighild.

In making his purchase, he learned that the caravan made the trip from Deepwater to Armityr and back once a season, selling materials they'd brought in by ship from Sartis, to the south.

And if the merchants ended up discussing the generosity of the new duke of Deepwater, so much the better.

The innkeep, a grizzled old man named Andrel, apologized for the lack of musicians while they ate a decent, if not inspiring, rabbit stew with a surprisingly good array of vegetables. Custom had been down since the war, and he hadn't been able to afford to keep musicians.

But the beds were comfortable, and the rooms quiet. And the next morning, bright and early, Aefric and his company were on the road once more.

AEFRIC FELT CHEERED BY THE COOL MORNING AIR AS THEY SET OUT from the Ironwood Inn early the next day. From what the caravan had said, the town of Drywood waited for them just outside the forest.

They should reach it before highsun. An opportunity to stop. Get news of the events in the county, and perhaps the duchy.

The caravan had been surprisingly light on news. Likely because they were stopping as little as they could before crossing into the king's lands. They hadn't given any overt reason for this, but Aefric gathered that the merchants feared being charged a duty if they sold Deepwater goods in Motte.

Such was the tension between Motte and Deepwater. Which made Aefric wonder if the caravan had done any selling in the baronies, or in Goldenfall.

Alas, he'd already told them who he was. If he'd asked then, they might have told him what they thought he wanted to hear, rather than the truth.

He would just have to wait until he reached those lands to find out.

And as for Motte, if Aefric rode into Drywood flying his banner, smiling and spending money on food and perhaps some goods to bring back to Water's End, he might be able to take the first steps in dispelling some of that tension.

This made him eager to get clear of the forest, despite its natural beauty. His spirits were high enough that he even added his own bass to a chorus or two of the ladies' singing.

It was just shy of highsun when they came out of the Kerrik Forest...

...and found a hundred soldiers waiting for them.

Aefric's high spirits sank so that he felt his belly must have fallen down into his horse.

The soldiers flew the banner of Motte, of course. Most of them were clad in chainmail, but the three dozen archers split between the two sides of the road favored leather armor instead, including leather caps instead of mail coifs.

In the center, three knights. Armored in full plate, on chargers clad in plates of barding. All three had lances at the ready. And they had to be knights. They had their own devices on their armor, though Aefric didn't take time to study them in the moment.

Leather-clad squires, on smaller horses, sat behind the knights on the road, just shy of the rest of the troops. Near enough to be ready, if their masters called, but not near enough to get in the way.

Well, not the knights' way, at least, Aefric decided. If the soldiers behind them lowered their spears and charged, the squires would either have to draw swords and join the charge or get trampled.

The knight in the center of the trio raised her visor. She had hard, but handsome, features. Light brown skin and strong brown eyes.

"Aefric Brightstaff," she began, in a voice used to giving commands.

"You address the Duke of Deepwater," Ser Beornric snapped. "You will give him his courtesies or meet me on the field of honor."

"Very well," she said. "*Duke* Aefric Brightstaff, you have committed an act of war against the county of Motte. You have—"

"Who accuses?" Aefric said.

"I am Ser Pemith," she said. "Knight in service to his excellency Ferrin Ol'Nylla, the Count of Motte."

"Well, Ser Pemith," Aefric said, "you have been misinformed."

"Did you or did you not attack soldiers of the count without provocation?"

"I did no such thing," Aefric said.

Ser Pemith pulled a small scroll from her belt and held it up.

"I have here the sworn testimony of the sergeant on duty, as well as a dozen of his men. With one voice they say that you attacked them without provocation."

"You say you are a sworn knight. Is that correct, Ser Pemith?"

She nodded only once in answer to what was, frankly, an insulting question. But then, she'd started the insults.

"Then on your honor I charge you to answer truly. Who is responsible for the Kingsroad in the duchy of Deepwater?"

"The duke of Deepwater," she said, then quickly added, "but until today there has been no duke nor duchess of Deepwater since the death of her grace, Arinda Soulfist. In that absence, the count did only what was necessary to maintain the road. As such, he should be compensated for his efforts. A modest toll addresses that concern without drawing funds away from rebuilding efforts."

"I question that a silver per traveler can be construed as a 'modest toll,' but that's another issue," Aefric said. "Water's End has not sat empty. Prince Killian has held it in regency. If the prince approved that toll gate, show me his letter of permission. If you cannot, you must agree that Motte had no right to build that gate, nor charge tolls on a road he cannot claim."

Ser Pemith drew breath to speak. Aefric cut in ahead of her.

"Mind you, even if you have such proof, as duke it is within my power to countermand the regent in this matter. And, as duke, I and mine should certainly not be expected to pay a toll on my own road."

Ser Pemith frowned.

"You cannot deny the truth," Aefric said. "I was well within my rights to destroy that gate at my own leisure, and therefore took no action that could constitute an act of war."

"I grant that your grace is within his rights to deny the count payment of the toll. I will even grant that your grace had the right to destroy the toll gate. But your standing as duke of Deepwater does not grant your grace leave to attack the count's soldiers with impunity."

"I say again, I did no such thing." Aefric raised his hand to forestall the knight's rejoinder. "The count's soldiers intended to insist, at the point of a crossbow, that I and my party pay them a toll to ride the Kingsroad. Even after having positively identified who it was they intended to charge."

"Nevertheless—"

"Let me finish," Aefric said, snapping the words so that they rang out on the air.

Ser Pemith nodded, reluctantly.

"Despite confirmation of my identity, the count's soldiers refused to yield the road to me. Furthermore, they continued to point crossbows at us, menacing myself, the countess of Fyretti, the two eldest daughters of Fyretti's barons, and the rest of our party."

As Ser Pemith drew breath to speak, Aefric spoke louder.

"*And yet*," he said. "I *still* did not attack them. Rather, I warned them to move away from the gate. They refused. I repeated my warning. They refused again."

Aefric let those words hang a moment, while Ser Pemith regarded him through narrowed eyes.

"I then destroyed the gate with lightning." Aefric shook his head. "Because they refused to heed my warning, two of the count's men were injured, though Ser Beornric informed me that their injuries did not look fatal."

"Some burning and scarring," Ser Beornric said. "Likely a few bruised or broken ribs from the concussion. But they'll recover."

"Directly or indirectly," Ser Pemith said, "you did attack the count's men. And—"

"By your own admission," Aefric said, "the count's men met me on *my* territory. They stood barring *my* way on *my* road. They refused to move. They menaced me with crossbows. What I did unquestionably counts as defending myself."

"I am Faenella Darkwalker," the countess said, from Aefric's left hand, "newly made countess of Fyretti. And I confirm everything the duke has said. Furthermore, if Motte thinks to use this as an excuse to begin a war, he will be fighting it with Fyretti as well."

"With the full support of Fyretti's barons," Oswen called out. Sighild, next to her, looked pale as midnight mist, but gave a shaky nod of confirmation.

"Keep in mind," Ser Beornric lied. "We already sent a rider back to Towerkeep. So the king will already know the truth of what happened at the other edge of Kerrik Forest."

Of everything said so far, only that truly seemed to give Ser Pemith pause. She turned and consulted with her two colleague knights who, notably, did not raise their visors.

At last, she turned back to Aefric's party and nodded.

"Very well," she called out. "We will advise the count to give this matter further consideration. However, I suggest that your grace consider how best to compensate his excellency for the injuries suffered by two of his soldiers."

"His excellency," Ser Beornric said, "should be grateful that only two of his soldiers suffered from their bout of idiocy. Or is it your contention, Ser Pemith, that the soldiers were acting properly and *on the count's orders* when they barred the road to his grace, and leveled crossbows at him without cause?"

Ser Pemith grimaced, but gave no response. Instead, she gave a hand sign and the road cleared of soldiers and opposition.

Ser Beornric gave a humorless chuckle.

"I thought as much," he muttered.

As the soldiers cleared the road, a rider near their back took off down the road to the west.

"The county seat is north of us, yes?" Aefric asked.

"That's correct, your grace," Ser Beornric said. "More likely one of Norra's scouts, carrying a report of how things went."

Wonderful. Perhaps Norra wished to get in on the game of roadblocks.

It wasn't the scout, though, that gave Aefric an urge to speed the horses. It was the need to pass all these armed soldiers.

Still, he fought that urge, and led the way into the middle of all those armed people before calling a halt, near to Ser Pemith.

"So long as I have you here," Aefric said to Ser Pemith, "please tell Count Ferrin that he was missed at my installation. Furthermore, that I shall expect him to appear at my court within the next aett to offer me his formal oath of vassalage."

"I..." Ser Pemith swallowed whatever she started to say. "Yes, your grace. I shall convey your words to my liege."

"Thank you, Ser Pemith," he said.

Having pushed his luck as far as he intended, Aefric led his party away at what he hoped was a dignified trot. At least it wasn't a gallop.

Nevertheless, he gave up thoughts of stopping at Drywood. He wanted to be well clear of this place before calling the halt again.

A shame. Drywood looked to be a decent-sized town with a bustling community. What was more, it didn't look to have been hit hard by the war. It would have been a nice place to stop.

Why had this town been spared? Chance? Proximity to the Kerrik? Because it was true that the town was built almost entirely of wood from that forest, and the town sat not an arrows flight from the nearest trees.

Just something else for Aefric to wonder about.

Soon enough they were riding past farms that looked to have been recently restored, though those on the Motte side of the road looked to be further into recovery than those on the Norra side of the road.

While they rode, Aefric took the opportunity to thank Ser Beornric for his quick thinking back at the confrontation, coming up with that lie about the rider.

"It shouldn't have been a lie," Ser Beornric said with a grimace. "I should have sent that rider. I was just too shocked at Motte's audacity.

In fact, your grace, please accept my apology for not having sent that rider in truth."

"There's no need for an apology," Aefric said. "And I intend to take that lie from you at our next stop."

"How?" Countess Faenella said, "If I may inquire, your grace."

"Oh," Aefric said with a smile he'd smiled many times over the course of his years of adventuring. "I'll think of something."

<hr>

As they took to the road again, Aefric instructed Ser Beornric to treat this as a ride through hostile territory. He hated doing so. It was all his own duchy, after all. But he didn't want to be caught unawares again.

And so, Ser Beornric tasked two riders to ride ahead as advance scouts, and two to trail and keep an eye on the rear.

The best practice, of course, would be to have more outriders off the road to their sides, but as they were riding through farmland, Aefric decided that was a bad idea. He didn't want to anger the farmers and risk their crops just because one count was acting foolish.

Aefric and his party stopped for luncheon late that day, as all agreed that putting an extra hour or two of farmland between themselves and Motte's forces at Drywood sounded like a good idea.

They mostly grew grains along here. Grains that gave the air a sweet smell. Some variety of berry wheat, perhaps. Though again, the farms on Motte's side seemed to be doing better than their counterparts across the road in Norra.

Water might also have been a factor, there. When the breeze shifted to come down from the north, it carried more humidity than the southern breeze. Possibly because they were nearing more of Motte's swamps. Though if the king's map was accurate, the swamps shouldn't come that close to the road...

Aefric and his party were trailed by a scout along the road. Aefric received regular reports about this, though that scout stayed well back.

He held off asking questions about the scout until the group stopped, finally, for luncheon, near a small farmers market on the Norra side of the road. A dozen wagons full of assorted fruits and vegetables, as well as a selection of chickens and pigs, both those still living and those freshly butchered.

The countess' cook and assistants went over to refresh their stores. Aefric offered to pay for what they bought, but the countess wouldn't hear of it.

So while she dealt with that, he turned to the subject of the scout.

"Another of Norra's?" Aefric asked, as he rubbed down Windsong.

"Possible," Ser Beornric replied, "though my money would be on Motte. Likely Ser Pemith wanting to keep an eye on our movements while she waits for her next orders from the count. Pemith herself might be as close as a half-day behind us."

That was enough to make Aefric sigh. He would be away from Motte tomorrow, but he was days still from Water's End.

Just how many more problems would he face before formally taking possession of his ducal seat?

"Your grace," Countess Faenella said formally, after they'd dealt with their horses, the cook's stores had been replenished, and the company was ready to sit down to a lunch of freshly roasted chicken, with rosemary and thyme, served with a salad of fresh apples, spiced pears, and plums.

"Yes, your excellency?" Aefric asked, frowning at her formal tone as he sat — noticing in the process that she stayed standing, and that it was too late for him to reverse course.

"I wish to offer you a formal apology," she said with a small bow. "Based on the conduct of Ser Pemith, as well as the forces at her command, at Drywood, I can only conclude that Count Ferrin of Motte was attempting to goad you into war. What was more, like a coward, he sought to do so before you even took formal possession of your duchy, and command of its armies."

"I don't see how Count Ferrin's foolishness should require an apology from you, Countess Faenella."

"I challenged the way you intend to handle the fort Motte is building on the eastern edge of Kerrik Forest. I was wrong to do so. It is clear to me now that Count Ferrin will need an expensive lesson in manners." She grimaced. "If anything, your grace might have to go further than taking his fort."

"I could claim his share of Kerrik Forest," Aefric said with a laugh, "but I suspect that would be more trouble than it's worth."

He gestured to the blanket, inviting her to sit.

"Countess Faenella," he said, still smiling, "You owe me no apology. I had more information about the count than you did, because I'd discussed both Motte and Goldenfall with Kainemorton previously. I saw a troublemaker in need of a lesson. You saw a peer losing claim to land. You had reason to question that."

"Thank you, your grace," she said with a half-smile, and sat on the blanket. Which then allowed her ladies in waiting to join them, as they'd done at each break over the last two days. The portly cleric of Ulna, Nyorngyth, joined them as well.

Which was something of a pity. As Aefric shared a smile with Faenella, what he really wanted to do was tell her to forgo formalities and call him by his name. They were traveling companions and allies. It seemed only right.

But with her ladies in waiting looking on, not to mention a cleric who would treat such gossip as news, such a request might have been misinterpreted as an overture of affection.

The last thing he wanted to do was risk miscommunication with Faenella.

Aefric did his best to be cordial and hospitable through the meal, but his thoughts were elsewhere. He'd started thinking about those scouts again. One ahead of them, and one behind.

Further, they'd already met one small army along this road. And even if they made it past the border of Motte without facing another, there would still be Goldenfall. A less impulsive count, but likely more cunning.

He might meet Aefric's party not with his own soldiers, but a band of mercenaries masquerading as bandits. Perhaps to claim hostages. Perhaps simply to get rid of the new duke. Possibly in favor of a known factor. One more amenable.

Perhaps Count Cyneric of Goldenfall was already making overtures that direction to the king's advisers. After all, Goldenfall was aptly named, even without the additional mines in the Threepeaks. The hills in Goldenfall were full of gold and tin. Cyneric likely had money to spread around and buy influence...

No. Aefric couldn't wait until tonight to solve the problem of long-distance messages. He needed to send two of them, and the sooner he could send them, the better.

The problem, though, was not simply resolved.

Across most of the Torn Kingdoms, long-distance communication was primarily handled three ways. The first was the least reliable — letters and packages given to travelers, caravans and the like. Prone to all manner of mischief.

The second was the most common, and more reliable, but far from perfect. Rika birds, strong fliers who naturally migrated thousands of miles on their own, could be domesticated and trained to carry messages.

This was common among nobles, leaders of larger towns and cities, and some of the wealthier merchant families. Rika birds, though, for all their good flying, still suffered the depredations of hawks, eagles and the like, as well as interception by the arrows of ... ill-meaning parties.

The third was the most reliable, but also the slowest and most expensive. Personal messengers.

There was, of course, a fourth way: magic. Wizards had long ago worked out ways to send missives of perhaps fifty or a hundred words to a listener anywhere on Qorunn.

But there were two problems with this.

The first was that the spellcaster had to have some level of personal acquaintance with the receiver. A personal item could serve for this purpose, but that wasn't much help, when it came to casting the spell on behalf of a non-wizard. Few people were in the habit of traveling with the personal items of everyone they might wish to contact.

(Kainemorton had suggested to Aefric long ago that wizards could resolve this issue easily enough — if they were willing to be turned into professional messengers. Which they weren't.)

The second was that this spell left no evidence behind. The spoken words would be heard by the receiver, once, and then they were gone.

This was fine for the purposes of most wizards. They tended to have excellent memories as a professional requirement, and only rarely needed to offer proof to anyone about where and how they'd obtained information.

The lack of evidence, however, made this spell useless to nobles and merchants, who felt that any message worth the expense of paying a wizard to send was important enough that it ought to leave a written record.

Preferably with appropriate signatures and seals.

Rumor had it that certain nobles who also happened to be wizards, such as Lord Orlance of the Ruby, down in Sartis, had resolved this issue.

But if they had, they were keeping the secret to themselves.

Aefric, of course, knew the spell to send a spoken message. He even knew a variant, that allowed for a response from the receiver. And even his brief acquaintance with King Colm was probably sufficient connection that Aefric could use that spell to contact his majesty.

However. He would, as other nobles had complained, not be able to send a written message that way. And this was the sort of message that really ought to leave a record.

Further, he had no acquaintance with Prince Killian at all. And Aefric dearly wished to contact his ducal regent as well.

With these thoughts in mind, he returned to a problem he'd been puzzling over off and on since they'd left Ser Pemith's forces at Drywood.

How to send a written message.

If Aefric had known the secret of long-distance teleportation, he could likely solve this problem in the snap of his fingers.

But that kind of teleportation was a closely guarded secret among the greater wizards of Qorunn. As Kainemorton put it, *The last thing any of us needs is to have fools popping around the world any time they get a notion.*

Aefric did, however, understand the basics of the concept well enough to transport himself — and as much as a horse, or another person or two — a few hundred yards.

But that wasn't what he needed.

But maybe he wasn't as far from his solution as he thought...

There was a time around the beginning of the Godswalk Wars, when Aefric had found himself trapped inside a collapsed ruin.

His own fault, really. Following rumors of lost spellbooks and a ring of power, when he knew full well that both borogs and na'shek had mined the area for irons and harder metals both heavily and recently.

Somewhere beneath him, one of those mines had collapsed. And when it did, it had brought down a wall of solid stone — and the dust of a thousand years — at such an angle that Aefric, by all rights, should have been crushed.

But he'd been lucky that day. He'd been in a position where two stones happened to come together — both at least twice as large as he was — and they'd created a gap that protected him. Kept him from getting crushed.

Of course, they'd also trapped him in a place where he had enough air to last perhaps three hours. Likely less, considering how much air he wasted coughing and sneezing away the dust of a thousand years.

Aefric had, with his life on the line, puzzled through a kind of reverse summoning. A means of opening a gateway from where he was to somewhere he knew well.

He'd done it. Gotten himself safely to not just the surface, but the first place he'd thought of — the fortress of the Iron Wands.

A good two hundred miles or more from where he'd been trapped under the ground.

The gateway — a doorway of shimmering green energy — vanished behind him, of course.

This was not true teleportation. Not the simple matter of conveying someone or something uncounted distances in the blink of an eye. This was...

Aefric knew that he'd traveled *through* something. The trip had been timeless for him, and he had no frame of reference to know how long it had taken, as time passed on Qorunn.

And yet, it was certainly immensely faster than a rider...

Aefric had not attempted that form of travel since. It felt too risky.

But this, this would not truly carry the same level of risk. He didn't wish to transport himself, after all, but a scroll of parchment.

Could he do it?

There was only one way to find out.

* * *

As Aefric had been taught by Karbin, the Iron Wands, and Kainemorton himself, wizards developed their spells through a combination of applied logic, understanding of the interrelationships of forces, and a touch of artistic talent.

Though they despaired of imparting the first to Aefric, they all conceded that he had the last in large enough quantity that — to their eternal frustration — he seemed to be able to compensate for his logical gaps with artistic flourishes.

Only Kainemorton seemed to understand that this was part of his nature as a dweomerblood.

What this meant was that, for so long as any of them could handle attempting to teach Aefric magic, they focused heavily on the second, attempted to beat him over the head with the first, and accepted with gnashed teeth that his command of the third would be forever beyond their reach.

Aefric devoutly hoped they were right about the overcompensation of his magical artistic streak. Because he had no idea how to approach this spell from the perspective of logical development. He had only ever learned a handful of summoning spells, because they were not the kind of magic he personally enjoyed.

Which, in his case, made a difference in the effectiveness of his spells.

So he let the factors involved play about in the back of his mind while he took parchment in hand — along with a personally enchanted quill that needed neither ink nor sand to leave a good, steady, unblotted line — and wrote two letters. One to King Colm, and the other to Prince Killian.

In the letter to King Colm, Aefric detailed first his encounter at the toll gate and fort, and second his encounter just outside Drywood. He made clear that he was not asking for aid, but only making clear the actions of his count to date, in case matters escalated.

He signed and sealed the letter, then invited Countess Faenella to read it. As she agreed with the facts as Aefric laid them out, she signed and sealed at the bottom that she, too, bore witness to the actions described above.

Aefric couldn't help but consider how much easier matters would have been if he could have chosen the adventurer's solution to Motte and simply killed the count himself.

But no. He was a duke now. He had to look for the duke's solution.

More was the pity.

After that letter was complete, Aefric penned a second letter, this time to Prince Killian. Without going into extensive detail, he explained that the count of Motte had taken military action against him. He requested that Killian send a detachment of troops to ensure that the new duke arrived safely at his ducal seat. He also gave instructions about the fort on the east edge of Kerrik Forest.

He signed and sealed this one as well.

Then, the easy part was finished. Now he had to figure out *how* to send these scrolls to their destinations.

He began with his letter to the king.

A reverse summoning...

Well, that would give him his target, at least. The king himself. Colm Stronghand.

Of course, summoning spells, properly speaking, did not target human beings. And certainly not human beings here in Qorunn. Summoning spells were supposed to bring creatures from *other* worlds.

But that was logic talking. And logic could be the enemy, when it came to Aefric's spellwork.

The interrelationships of forces. That was the place to start.

With that in mind, Aefric sketched out a circle in dirt beside the Kingsroad, while the countess and the others looked on.

The circle wasn't necessary for all summonings. But it helped balance and contain the forces involved. So, in this instance, Aefric used it.

He set within the circle his letter to the king.

He chanted then, drawing first on the power of certain ancient words he knew. Words that channeled and contained a power of their own no matter who said them, so long as they were pronounced with the proper rhythm and inflection.

However, Aefric had determined early in his studies that when *he* used those ancient chants, he got more power in response than most wizards. It wasn't until he studied with Kainemorton that he came to understand that those chants resonated with his nature as a dweomerblood, calling power from within himself to increase the power of the words alone.

That extra power might be important in this spell. For those chants would form a foundation for his working.

Their power spread outward beneath his message scroll in a sheen that crackled bright and red against the borders of his dirt circle.

Good.

Next, he sang parts of two songs of power he'd learned in his travels. The first was a na'shek song of the grounds and the lands beneath them all. The second was a kindaren song in praise of the skies and the stars, and the powers they, too, contained.

Aefric wove the two powers like a net, and linked them to the crackling red power in his circle.

Twin hums, like the aftermath of two ringing bells. One high and clear and beautiful. The other, deep and resonant in a way that made Aefric's teeth ache.

The power of the circle shifted to a deep orange, with sparks of blue.

Aefric could only hope that was right.

Next, he considered the king, and the power held and wielded by monarchs everywhere. The power of authority.

Yes. Authority. Aefric was a duke now. He had authority. And his authority came from the king. Was connected to the king. His power as duke, part of the power of the king, even unto high justice in the king's name.

This power was a new thing to Aefric, but the artist in him understood it. Understood that it weighed heavily, as lead did.

Aefric cast about him for that weight. That power. Felt it settle in a ring about his head. Like a crown. Heavy enough to bow his neck. To ache within his skull.

Aefric reached up with his fingertips and removed that power like a crown. Voices around him oohed softly. In his fingertips was a coruscating ring of white fire.

Aefric reached out and set the crown of white fire on his circle, while focusing with every ounce of will he possessed on the image of the king. On opening the way to the king. On reaching the king with the scroll in his circle.

When the crown of white fire reached the flaring orange power of the circle, with its sparks of blue, it all came together in a blinding flare of bright green.

In the instant that the power flared up, Aefric cried out words of command. An improvisation. A derivation of the words that would banish a summoned creature.

A cracking sound rent the air, like the sudden snapping of a tree trunk ten feet wide.

All around Aefric came startled cries, but even as Sers Beornric and Arcy called for calm, Aefric quickly regained his composure and his eyesight.

The dirt circle remained. The scroll, however, was gone.

He smiled, and pumped his fist in a manner far more familiar to Keifer, after sinking a three-pointer on the basketball court, than to Aefric when working magic.

But in the moment it felt right on every level.

"Did it work?" Countess Faenella asked.

"I have to hope so," he said, panting just a little, and feeling sweat trickling down his forehead. "And I imagine that if it did, we'll be hearing something about it from the king at some point."

Aefric worried at his lip, then, considering the prince he hadn't met. Surely there was some way of reaching him. The authority concept wouldn't work here, but...

Or would it?

Not the same way, surely. But right now Prince Killian sat regent for him. He sat in the ducal seat, held the ducal seal. And Aefric, of course, was the rightful duke. Also holding the ducal seal...

Ser Beornric cleared his throat. Apparently Aefric had simply been standing there for a time, considering how he might modify his efforts to work with Prince Killian.

"So what do we do now, your grace?" Ser Beornric prompted.

"Do?" Aefric asked with a smile. "Why I have to do it again, of course. I wrote two letters, after all."

6

———

After that second message-transportation spell — the more demanding spell, in terms of pure magical effort — Aefric was only too glad to be back astride Windsong and riding the Kingsroad once more.

He and his party were past the halfway point in his trek from Armityr to Water's End. That was the good news.

The bad news was that they would not pass Motte's border until early tomorrow. And Aefric was certain that somewhere before that border, Count Ferrin would move against him one more time.

The worse news was that once they passed that border, it would be Goldenfall's turn to make whatever moves *its* count felt appropriate.

Aefric was already developing a strong dislike for two of his counts. And he hadn't even met the men yet, let alone accepted their vows of vassalage.

Assuming they were willing to give those vows, and not rise up in open rebellion.

An extreme possibility, to be sure. But after the last two days, it was one Aefric found himself unwilling to discount. Especially since he doubted he could count on either of his peers for assistance. And the king's forces were days away, even if he both could and would muster them on Aefric's behalf.

The weather was with them still, at least. The skies above were mostly clear, and the day was warming as the afternoon wore on.

The Kingsroad in this region mostly ran through farmland. No towns between Drywood and ... Norrtarr? Was he remembering that right? If so, Norrtarr would be a town they would reach somewhere about dusk that night. A town on the Norra side of the road, and near to the baronial seat itself.

In the meantime, the monotony of farms was broken up by small, side roads every so often, and occasional cleared circles beside the road, likely for farmers and traders markets. Though none of the circles they passed were in use that day. Not since the one near their stop for lunch.

Earlier in the day, Aefric had been worried a bit about the barony of Norra. The farms he'd seen on the Norra side of the road had been in sad shape, back closer to Kerrik Forest.

Through the ride that afternoon, though, those farms on the Norra side of the road began to look in better and better shape. As though the funds for repairs simply hadn't reached as far as the Kerrik yet.

But that was speculation on his part. And the truth was, Aefric had no idea if it was reasonable speculation. For all he knew, the difference between the farms currently doing badly and the ones currently doing well had less to do with the war than it had to do with the farmers and their choice of crops, the effects of the local weather patterns, or any of a hundred other things that a farmer would know immediately, and an adventurer would never think of in a million years.

And yet, somehow, as duke, he might be expected to know?

No. That would be why he had advisers. Had to be. Advisers he would have to find a way to vet. After all, Motte might not be subtle enough to seek influence in Deepwater through the new duke's advisers, but that didn't mean Goldenfall wasn't.

For that matter, even without outside influence, there was still the question of whether the locals in Deepwater would mean Aefric well or ill. The only people he knew that he could trust right now were riding with him.

In fact, Aefric could probably ask one of the other riders about those farms...

Probably not Countess Faenella. She was another adventurer, like he was. Unless she'd been raised farming, she wouldn't likely know either. Much the same reason he didn't feel he could ask one of the knights.

The ladies in waiting, perhaps? Fyretti's baronies couldn't be very large. Perhaps their nobles had to know such things.

Aefric was just considering whether asking another noble's ladies in waiting about the health of farms in a completely different barony would be a good or bad decision when Ser Beornric called for his attention.

One of the advance scouts had returned.

"Soldiers in the road ahead, your grace," Ser Beornric said. "Riding this way and flying the banner of Norra."

"How many?"

"A score. Led by three knights and someone in a cloak. No armor. Might be a spellcaster."

"Might also be an emissary from the baroness," Countess Faenella said. "If that was her scout back at Drywood, she'll know you're coming."

"Given the way this ride has gone so far," Aefric said with one eyebrow raised, "which do you expect it to be? A spellcaster or an emissary?"

She chuckled. "Spellcaster it is, then."

"Right," Aefric said through a sigh. "That's the only thing they haven't thrown at us so far. Magic." He shook his head. "All right. Be wary, everyone, but I'm not stopping now."

Ser Beornric made small adjustments to their formation as they rode. The forward scouts returned, riding now no more than a hundred yards ahead of the group.

Aefric and Countess Faenella rode side by side at the head of the party, with Ser Beornric on Aefric's right hand, and Ser Arcy on Faenella's left hand.

A dozen soldiers rode behind the pack, and the remainder rode spread out along the sides of the group, protecting the nobles and their entourage from all sides.

The waiting was difficult. Aefric found his heart beating faster. His mouth growing dry. His fingers itched for a sword or a spell.

In all of his years of adventuring, Aefric had hated most those times when something was *about* to happen. Would happen *soon*.

But. Not. Yet.

If he'd hoped to leave that distasteful experience behind him when he became a duke, it seemed he was to be disappointed.

He could only hope the waiting wouldn't get worse.

There was a hell he didn't wish to face.

Finally, though, he saw the clouds of dust in the road ahead. The afternoon sun was hanging lower in the sky, and as he was riding almost due west, he had to squint to try to gauge those riders in the distance.

No good. More waiting.

At last, they came into view, and Aefric called the halt. Not so much to make the oncoming soldiers come to him — although, he decided on reflection, that was probably a good move — but because they had reached a spot on the Kingsroad between two circles where traders or farmers markets were held.

If there was to be a battle, it might as well take place where they had room to maneuver without trampling anyone's crops.

THE SUN WAS IN AEFRIC'S EYES AS HE WAITED FOR THE APPROACHING troops of the baroness of Norra. He couldn't stop thinking about that detail.

The sun was in his eyes.

Yes, it was a warm day. Yes, he was dusty and dry-mouthed from the day's ride. Yes, he was looking forward to reaching Norrtarr and calling the halt for the day.

But there were troops approaching.

And the sun was in his eyes.

It was just that morning that Motte had met Aefric's party at Drywood with a hundred soldiers and an accusation that Aefric had committed an act of war.

Much as Aefric would have loved to have settled that problem the adventurer's way — with swift and blinding violence — he'd been good. He'd used his words. Made his points, and finally gotten through that little problem without the need for bloodshed.

Thanks, in no small part, to the quick thinking of Ser Beornric.

However.

A scout had ridden away from that scene in a hurry. A scout riding not for Motte, but down the Kingsroad.

A scout riding for Norrtarr? For the baroness of Norra?

It seemed likely.

One rider with a good, well-rested horse. One rider, not stopping for breaks along the way. Such a rider could have pushed his horse. Reached Norrtarr ... perhaps around the time that Aefric and his party had stopped for lunch.

The report would take time. Perhaps a debate among the baroness and her advisers. They would want to act quickly, but they would know they had time to consider their move.

Suppose they meant to support Motte...

If so, they might present a token force up front. Say, a score of soldiers, plus a few knights and one "ambassador," who was actually a battle wizard.

And they might have troops along the side roads. Perhaps hidden among the farms. Perhaps waiting for a signal, given by the battle wizard.

Troops from Norra. Troops from Motte. Working together against a common foe...

"Ser Beornric," Aefric said, "tell me this isn't a trap."

"Would that I could, your grace. The corn and tara they're

growing along here stand more than tall enough to hide a crouching archer."

"No," Countess Faenella said, though more out of disbelief than denial. "You think they'd give up trying to get the law on their side and just assault us?"

"I don't believe it," Sighild said, her denial so surprisingly firm that Aefric practically wrenched his neck, whipping around to look back at where she and Oswen rode behind him and Faenella.

"Baroness Herewyn is a cousin, on mother's side," she said, stringing more spoken words together than Aefric had heard from her the whole ride. "I spent a summer with her not three years past. I saw her in court. I saw her in council. I saw her at a dance. And on my honor I say my cousin is not a woman who will assault a man she's never met, on the word of another."

"What about the promise of another?" Aefric said. "If Goldenfall or Motte made her promises—"

"She'd still meet your grace first," Sighild said, and Aefric was so surprised that she cut him off that he chuckled without thinking.

Apparently that made Sighild realize what she'd done, and she flushed a red so bright her hair looked brown by comparison.

She tried to mumble an apology then, but Aefric wouldn't have it.

"My dear Sighild," he said with a small bow, hoping she didn't misinterpret his smile as insulting, "please believe me when I say that your counsel is well taken. Solid information is worth more than gold out here, and you've just given me a *treasure*. Thank you."

Ser Beornric cleared his throat. Aefric turned back around, and as he did he heard Oswen say something to Sighild in hushed, excited tones.

The delegation from Norra was arriving. The banner of Norra — a white horse rampant against a sky blue background — flew tall and proud above them.

True to the scout's report, the — delegation or assault team, Aefric wasn't sure which yet — consisted of a score of soldiers, all mounted, and all carrying spears.

Spears. And they weren't carrying extra spears strapped to their saddles. Just the one spear per soldier.

Spears. Not bows or crossbows?

Looking about with more purpose now, Aefric didn't spot a crossbow or bow among the lot of them. He hoped that was as good a sign as it appeared to be.

What was more, the three knights rode without weapons in hand. Even better news. Oh, they had weapons at their sides — two of them swords and one a war axe — as well as shields strapped to their horses.

But no weapons *in hand*. And they weren't wearing their helms, either...

Two of them were men, and one a woman. And though none of them had open, welcoming expressions, neither did they look ready to issue a challenge.

Of course, if any of the group were likely to issue a challenge, it would be the remaining member of their party.

She rode without armor, and without device on her simple clothing, all shades of brown. Made it difficult to tell, in places, where the cloth ended and her skin began. For her skin, too, was different shades of brown.

Even her cloak continued the theme, though her cloak was a darker brown than even her high, thick boots.

She was a woman who wore her decades proudly. The lines on her face, the silver streaking her dark brown hair. She had a quality of solidity to her that made her seem as though she should have been stout of body and thick of limb. But she was surprisingly lean.

"That is Burrew," Sighild said, in what Keifer would have called a stage whisper. "She's the court wizard."

"A *vholcairn*. A wizard of clay and stone," Aefric specified, nodding. "Yes."

That would have been obvious to him, even if he could not feel her considerable power. From her mode of dress to her sense of solidity, everything about the woman screamed *vohlcairn* to him.

Well, that explained why they didn't bother with ranged weapons.

If Burrew was as powerful as she appeared, her side of a fight might consist of her opening the ground beneath them and swallowing Aefric's party whole.

On the other hand, he couldn't help but wonder why a wizard of her power was working for a small barony...

The advancing party from Norra came to a halt. Close enough now for moderately comfortable speech, Burrew began the conversation.

"I am Burrew," she said. "Court wizard and adviser to her lordship, Herewyn Ol'Norette, Baroness of Norra. Do I have the pleasure of addressing his grace, Ser Aefric Brightstaff, newly installed Duke of Deepwater?"

"You do," Aefric said. "As well as her excellency, Faenella Darkwalker, the new Countess of Fyretti."

As they exchanged a couple of more pleasantries, Aefric kept glancing about for the hammer. Clearly they were on the anvil now. Where was the hammer?

"Your grace, your excellency," Burrew said, finally getting to the point, "on behalf of her lordship, I welcome you to Norra and offer you hospitality at Norrtarr. For tonight, at the least, but for so long as you are willing to stay."

"I thank you kindly," Aefric said, "though I'm afraid it will have to be for the one night. I am anxious to reach Water's End and take formal possession of Deepwater."

"Of course, your grace," she said with a nod, then gestured to the soldiers and knights riding with her. "I hope you will forgive the size of my company. I have been given to understand that the roads ... have not been safe for you. And her lordship is eager to see you safely through her lands."

"There is nothing to forgive, *Vohlcairna* Burrew."

Burrew's eyebrows raised slightly at being addressed with the proper declension of the ancient na'shek term for a wizard of her nature. She nodded in acknowledgment.

"With that in mind," she said, "with whom shall I coordinate our combined forces for the ride to Norrtarr?"

"With the commander of my personal guard, Ser Beornric."

Ser Beornric's eyes widened.

"The threats may not end when we reach Deepwater," Aefric said quietly to his astonished new commander. "I'll need people I can trust around me. So the company you brought me are now my personal guard, and you, Ser Beornric, are their commander."

Aefric smiled. "A position you've more than earned already, I assure you."

Ser Beornric smiled broadly and spurred his horse ahead.

"All right," he called in a strong voice. "Let's see about getting everyone safely to Norrtarr."

———

THE RIDE THE REST OF THE WAY TO NORRTARR WAS SURPRISINGLY QUIET. Perhaps because, with the active participation of Norra, Aefric felt more confident that Motte wouldn't try any further shenanigans. Not that day, at any rate.

Of course, it probably helped that Aefric now rode with more than fifty soldiers and five knights. Plus the countess, who was of the Order of Blessed Knights. Plus Burrew, a *vohlcairn* of not inconsiderable power.

And, of course, Aefric himself.

Yes, they made a fairly formidable force at that point, riding through the late afternoon sun.

In fact, Aefric got the distinct impression that Ser Beornric was disappointed not to get to test his new title in battle that day.

Just as well. Aefric felt confident that his new personal guard and their commander would find themselves tested all too soon.

The sun was just beginning to burn the western sky orange as they approached the town of Norrtarr. A town with no walls of its own, and yet it looked to have been missed by the wars.

Must've been fortunate positioning.

The town was built around a large, open center square, built from old stonework. In fact, the older parts of the town were easily distinguished by their cobblestone streets and dark, granite buildings. The newer parts of the town were largely wooden construction, or wood over granite, for those rarer buildings that reached a second or third story.

The town had the smell of people. Dirt and sweat, fire and smoke, cooking and baking. The coke and heat of smithing, and more besides. A number of smells that all warred in Aefric's nose, but still made him smile.

When was the last time he'd ridden through a town? Had to have been aetts ago. Perhaps the better part of a season.

Something itched at the part of him that was Keifer, though. Something in the smells was wrong. Or at least, not what he was expecting.

And yet, the smells were exactly what he should've been expecting. The part of him that was Aefric knew that with an absolute certainty.

Even the huge city of Sartis itself hadn't smelled much different than—

Waste. That was the smell that Keifer kept expecting. The smell of human waste. Urine and excrement and the like.

Oh, now that he was thinking about it, he could detect *slight* smells of such. But they weren't *strong* smells, the way he would have expected from a medieval...

No.

That was the disconnection.

The part of him that was Keifer was still thinking of this as a vaguely medieval world. But despite a similar — though not identical — form of feudalism, this world had nothing to do with medieval Western Europe. And the towns here, they had versions of what Keifer would have considered Roman aqueducts.

Not as good as modern American plumbing, but a hell of a lot better than what Keifer would have found in, say, twelfth century London.

As Aefric, of course, he knew all this. But the man who was both those men was still getting small moments of cognitive dissonance, trying to reconcile the thoughts and experiences of two separate lives, lived — for all intents and purposes — simultaneously.

That disconnection was worrying. If it hit him at the wrong time — distracted him during a battle, say — it could mean the difference between life and death.

Aefric picked at the disconnection as he rode. Tried to analyze and approach it, mentally, from as many angles as he could.

The more he could resolve of this conflict now, the smaller the chances that it would hurt him later.

Or at least, that was his reasoning.

Either way, the task required enough of his attention that they had passed through the town before he knew it and were ascending the hill toward the keep of Norrtarr proper.

The hill was thick with fragrant spring grass, but also had a handful of small groves of spreading, leafy trees. Groves no more than a hundred yards or so from the keep's outer wall. That struck Aefric as odd.

Why would they leave cover available to potential invaders as close a hundred yards away?

The wall was stone. More granite, but otherwise not very impressive. No more than perhaps fifteen feet high, and though it circled the hill around the keep, it lacked strong points for defense. No proper crenellations, either.

As they passed through the gate — wood, and not more than a foot thick — Aefric noted that there were internal ramps that could at least allow the defenders to stand crossbowmen at a height that they could shoot over the wall, while still keeping to decent cover.

Still. Not the most defensible structure around.

He was two-thirds the way up the hill when the answer hit him.

The *vohlcairn*.

With a powerful wizard of clay and stone on their side, the entire hill beneath the keep became an active part of their defenses.

Of course, if anything happened to their *vohlcairn*, they were in trouble...

Norrtarr proper, on the other hand, was a small but solid keep.

Three stories tall. Good stonework, with crenellated parapets for defense, and four squat towers at the corners.

Getting to the keep might be too easy, but taking the keep would be another matter. And from the look of it, it hadn't been taken often, if ever. The stonework looked quite old — centuries old, most likely — and all original granite.

If Aefric had seen the keep first, he might not have expected Norra to meet him with force of arms. This didn't look like the keep of someone who sought out fights.

As they approached the portcullis at the entrance to the keep, it was clear that a reception had been arranged. Red carpeting had been laid out over the dirt and grass outside. A ring of torches worked to banish the shadows of growing twilight. Musicians with string instruments played a gentle, haunting melody.

Perhaps two dozen well-dressed courtiers — mostly petty nobles, Aefric suspected, but likely a handful of well-to-do merchants as well — stood about, waiting.

Standing alone in the center of it all, directly in front of the portcullis — which Aefric couldn't help but notice was down — had to have been the baroness.

He could immediately see the family resemblance to Sighild. The baroness had the same pale skin and the same shimmering red hair. Hers was not so long as Sighild's — only halfway down her back — and crowned with a simple golden diadem.

The baroness was not yet a full decade older than Sighild, and she had the confidence and bearing of her title, to go with the grace and form that womanhood had given her.

She wore a gown of dark, forest green that set off the emeralds at her throat and the green in her eyes.

This was a woman who knew how to present herself to fullest effect. She stood just at the edge of the light from her torches, giving her almost a glow in the growing dusk. Separated just enough from her fellow nobles that, combined with the lighting, she gained an almost otherworldly look.

Aefric was impressed despite himself. And he felt dirty and road worn by comparison.

Burrew took on the herald's duties then, riding out ahead and stopping between the two groups. From there, she called out the names and titles of the visitors — although she restricted herself to the countess and the duke — and then that of the baroness.

"Your grace," the baroness said, her voice a smoky contralto. "Your excellency. My humble barony is made greater by your presence. Thank you for accepting my offer of hospitality."

"Your offer was most gracious," Aefric said, dismounting, approaching and kissing her hand. "And most welcome. The road from Armityr is long. And has seemed even longer of late."

That brought a smile from the baroness and soft, appreciative laughter from her court.

Countess Faenella looked uncertain about whether or not she should speak, so Aefric gave her a small nod.

"I wish to thank you especially for the escort," Countess Faenella said, coming up to stand beside Aefric. "Though I have never been one to refuse a fight, I would prefer not risk my companions to the aspirations of my peers."

Another soft laugh from the court, though Aefric wasn't sure that Motte was a laughing matter.

"Your grace," the baroness said. "Normally at this point I would say that Norrtarr is yours. But properly speaking that is something I could only say to my liege lord. Which you are not yet."

She smiled, and knelt where she stood on the carpet.

"Shall we rectify that situation?"

By the time Aefric had finished accepting the oaths of vassalage from Baroness Herewyn, and offering his oaths as his liege lord in return, the sky had reached full dark.

But there, on the red carpet outside the portcullis of Norrtarr, there was still light. Some of it firelight coming from torches on the other side of the portcullis, but more of it coming from the ring of torches set up for the event.

The witnesses assembled by the baroness — the local petty lords and wealthier merchants — managed to make it through the whole of the exchange of oaths without any sounds of impatience that attracted Aefric's attention.

Would that he could say his own party was so patient. But after that confrontation near Drywood, and a long, dusty day's ride spent largely expecting more trouble, they were more than ready to go inside and eat.

Oh, the nobles acquitted themselves well enough, including the knights. But the rustling of soldiers' chainmail had provided a constant background sound through the whole of the oaths.

At last, though, they were done, and Aefric was helping the baroness to her feet.

She kept his hand then, as she turned toward the portcullis and said, with a gesture of offering, "Your grace, Norrtarr is yours."

The portcullis rose smoothly, and with impressive silence. Aefric could hardly hear the gears turning or the creaking of the ropes.

Still holding his hand, Baroness Herewyn led Aefric through the portcullis, past about a dozen strides worth of murder holes and through a second portcullis into a small courtyard.

Acfric had to smile then, as he realized the optical illusion he'd fallen for.

The keep wasn't as squat as it looked, though it was a good deal narrower.

The outer wall was separate, and a good thirty feet thick, although Aefric suspected that a section of the middle was hollow, for archers to move about and shoot from. Likely through narrow arrow slots he hadn't spotted in the dimming light of the late afternoon.

The squat towers at the corners were all part of the outer wall, and not part of the keep itself.

Yes, this little keep was more defensible than he'd thought. And Aefric approved.

He could hear similar thoughts expressed softly, behind him, from Countess Faenella. Likely to Ser Arcy, but possibly also to Ser Beornric.

The rest of the baroness' court followed the core members of Aefric's party, and the soldiers followed along behind.

The wide main doors of the keep stood perhaps fifteen feet tall, arching together to form a point. They were also strapped and supported by iron bands in three places, he noted.

"Your grace," Baroness Herewyn said with a smile, "the doors await your command."

This woman was going awfully far to show that she was a loyal vassal. Aefric couldn't help but wonder if that was a mask, or if it was simply a way of distancing herself from Motte's behavior.

After all, she certainly had to know about Motte's little fort at the edge of Kerrik Forest. Which meant either she was a partner in his toll scheme, or that his move had been against her as well. Laying claim to more of the forest than was properly his.

No way to tell here and now, alas...

He returned her smile and turned to the keep.

"Let the doors be opened," he called.

From within, two servants swiftly opened those doors, which had plainly been oiled in preparation for this.

Wait. She'd had a crowd gathered to witness her oaths of vassalage. The portcullises and the main doors of the keep had plainly been freshly oiled...

The doors opened to reveal the main hall of the keep. Wide and tall and long it was. It must have run the length of the keep, and at least half its width.

Large chandeliers hung from the ceiling, giving the darkening evening a welcoming warm glow.

The stone of the hall looked fresh and clean. Both on the flooring, and where it could be seen between tapestries on the walls.

The tapestries on the walls were not of battle scenes. Two of them involved hunting, a third appeared to be a scene from a classic tale of love, and the others portrayed moments out of myth or folklore.

Odd, that so soon after the Godswalk Wars someone would

display mythic scenes. Lent credence in Aefric's mind to the idea that the wars had largely not harmed Norra directly.

Aefric could sense the low background hum of some kind of magic. Likely magic of clay and stone. The hum lacked the edge of a threat, though, and investigating it might cause offense, so he opted to trust his hostess for the time being.

A series of long tables were set up across the middle of the hall, with another table on a raised platform at the far end. Likely the platform where she normally sat her baronial throne and held court. Some sort of green carpeting was laid out on the dais.

With the hall in this arrangement, there was clearly more than enough seating for the number of guests who'd been gathered here.

Including the soldiers.

She'd gathered quite a crowd. Likely more than her normal courtiers. She'd had the portcullises and doors oiled. A feast arranged. Musicians.

Either Baroness Herewyn had been planning this feast since well before that little incident outside Drywood, or she excelled at last-minute planning.

No. Even an impressive planner could not gather a crowd of nobles and merchants this size on a few hours notice.

In the back, right-hand corner of the hall, a set of four trumpeters played a flourish of welcome.

"My keep is nothing to Water's End, of course," Baroness Herewyn said as she escorted Aefric to his place at her right hand at the feast table on the dais. "But I'm quite fond of my little barony. My family has held it for generations. My people are good workers, and quite loyal."

"I've been most pleased so far, I must say," Aefric said, which made her smile. He continued, "But before I leave, I do hope to discuss Kerrik Forest with you."

"I was hoping you would, your grace," she said. "But let us save that topic for the morning, before you leave. If you're certain you must be leaving us so soon."

"I must," Aefric said, wondering if this woman was that good an actress or if she really was sincere about wanting to host his party for some time. "Prince Killian has been keeping my seat warm long enough. The poor man deserves a break."

The baroness had a good laugh. Aefric had to give her that.

She was a good hostess, as well. She paid plenty of attention to Countess Faenella, seated to her left, and even managed to engage Sighild and Oswen — the next two farthest out at the table — as often as she could.

Aefric noted that Oswen was seated to his other side, not Sighild. Was that a reflection of their relative ranks, or something else? Because Aefric had no doubt that every seat at this table was chosen with great deliberation.

Including the four other persons important enough to be seated at the baroness' high table. Aefric never got to meet those four. And by the time the feast was done and he was being escorted to his rooms, he would wonder about them.

Why those four? If they were important enough to be seated on the dais, why was he not introduced to them? Informally, at least, if not formally. Or was it merely happenstance that he never had the opportunity to engage any of those four in conversation?

Perhaps. Though Aefric doubted much about that feast was left to chance. Certainly, the news discussed at the table wasn't happenstance.

First and foremost, of course, the condition of her own barony. This included her losses during the war. Although no battles had taken place in Norra, she'd lost her share of soldiers in the wars. Including both professional men-at-arms, and those mustered from the peasantry.

Baroness Herewyn gave only token mention to her concerns about "bandits" in Kerrik Forest. And she said the word "bandits" while giving Aefric a knowing look, as though to imply that she knew Motte was behind her supposed problems in Kerrik.

She shifted topics quickly, though, ensuring that Aefric felt no need to address that issue during the meal.

Through the course of dinner, Aefric noted that all her news came from Norra and Motte. The falloff of most trade, and its slow recovery. Her efforts to restore her farms, forestry and quarries, following her losses to the war. Talk of a traveling carnival that had come through in the past aett, which had done much to raise spirits.

She gave no news from even from the nearby barony of Felspark, let alone Goldenfall, which was certainly close enough that news should have traveled from there.

Aefric didn't know how to interpret this. If there simply was little news from the western part of his duchy, or if she wanted to focus on her own first, and leave the issues of others for another time.

Either way, the feast itself confirmed for Aefric that she could not have thrown this together at the last minute. Not unless she'd been lucky enough to have enough deer slaughtered at just the right time for them to be roasted to perfection. The deer were served with boiled ears of corn and sweet tara, along with a salad of greens and root vegetables dressed with a spicy mix of oils.

For dessert, a mixed berry compote that managed a hint of tang beneath its refreshing sweetness.

To drink, she'd broken out sharabi, a magnificent green wine that she said came from her own vineyards. This sharabi was light and crisp, and went very well with the meat, the side dishes, and the dessert. Which Aefric considered an accomplishment.

Of course, he'd never actually tasted sharabi before. He'd had the red and white varieties of wine, but in all his travels he'd never realized it came in green. Made him wonder what other colors and flavors he might have missed.

Which also helped him realize that the sharabi was stronger than he expected. Which made him slow down his consumption.

For entertainment during the feast, the same string musicians from outside had taken up residence in the back corner and played soft, sweet songs. And at the change between courses, a kindaren singer stepped forward.

The kindaren were of a height — and often a slenderness — that made humans and eldrani occasionally mistake them for children, even when fully grown.

The tallest kindaren Aefric had ever met still could have stared Aerfic straight in the sternum.

With their smaller size, their voices tended to be higher. And when they could sing with a clear, strong voice — as this male kindaren did — they seemed to sing with the voices of river and sky spirits themselves.

Lending to that image, the singer was clad in gauzy, silvery robes, and his long, silvery hair hung past his elbows. His song was danced as much as it was sung, with every line accompanied by movements of the hips and wrists, fingers and neck.

At times he seemed almost to be one of those spirits himself.

At last, though, the meal was finished, the songs were sung, and Aefric and his party were escorted to their rooms for the night. Those rooms were on the third floor of the keep, which meant a lot of stairs at the end of the day. But the prospect of a good night's sleep made those steps practically fly by for Aefric.

At Ser Beornric's insistence, four of Aefric's personal guard accompanied him, inspected his rooms, and stood guard outside his bedroom door.

Technically, this meant they were still in his rooms. He had two. An outer room for changing and informal talks, and an inner room that was just for sleeping.

The outer room featured more of those fresh green carpets, which appeared to have been skillfully woven from leaves of some sort, despite having a strength akin to linen.

This room also included a wash basin, with shaving mirror and towels. A copper tub, near a fireplace with a hearth large enough to heat pots of water.

On the other side of the room, near to the two shuttered windows, an armoire and a pair of wooden couches with dark red pillows.

Aefric almost wondered about the couches being so far from the hearth, but then he realized what that background hum of magic was.

A warming enchantment. Heat from the ground beneath the keep, being brought up into the stones themselves. Burrew's work, no doubt.

The bedroom was smaller. Large enough for a canopied bed, with four wooden posts. Red, woven fabric carpets in here, all freshly laid down, with some sort of sweet herbs underneath them to give the room a subtle, but pleasant fragrance.

And the bed itself was most inviting. The mattress was thick with soft feathers. The sheets weren't actual silk, but they were so soft and smooth that the difference was slight. And there were enough blankets and comforters for the dead of winter, let alone a pleasant spring evening in a keep kept warm through magic.

Aefric was just preparing to turn in when there was a knock at his door.

Already half-naked, he only opened his bedroom door enough to see that it was one of his soldiers knocking. What was the woman's name?

Arda. That was it.

"Yes, Arda?" he asked.

"There's a servant here for you, your grace. She says it's not a matter that can wait until morning."

Aefric sighed. "Send her in, then."

The servant was young, and looked nervous. Playing a bit with the sleeves of her pale blue frock.

"Yes?" Aefric asked.

"Sorry to disturb your grace," she said with a small bow, "but I've come to offer you *leaba*."

Leaba. That word sounded vaguely familiar. Aefric had never encountered the term, but Keifer had read of it. Years ago. Though he couldn't remember what it was...

"*Leaba*?" he said. "I'm sorry. I'm not familiar with the word."

"It's a very old custom, your grace," she said, her cheeks coloring prettily. "It is the pleasure of a bed mate."

Aefric was suddenly uncomfortably aware of three things. First, that this woman was *very* pretty, with big blue eyes, a tumble of chestnut curls, a sweet smile and a lovely form. Second, that Aefric had not had sex in at least three or four aetts. Third, that it had been much, much longer for Keifer...

"What is your name?"

"Octave, your grace," she said with a deeper bow that he was pretty sure she was using to give him a good look at her décolletage.

"Forgive me, Octave," Aefric said, "but I will not have anyone ordered to my bed."

"Oh, no, your grace," she said quickly, both hands coming up with all fingers crossed, a local gesture used to ward away evil. "*Leaba* can only be offered freely." She smiled as she looked at Aefric's bare chest in frank appreciation. "Anyone who offers it is a volunteer."

"And is this *leaba* being offered to the countess Faenella as well?"

"Of course, your grace," she said. "Both you and she had a number of eager volunteers."

"Was it offered to the knights?"

"No, your grace. Only ranking members of the nobility of Armyr. *Leaba* is never offered to knights, nor to foreign nobles, nor to Armyrian nobles who hold no ranking titles of their own."

"Dare I ask how you were chosen?"

"I was not told the reason for my selection among the volunteers, your grace," she said. "And I confess I did not question it."

Aefric couldn't resist chuckling at that.

"Who made the selection, if I might ask?"

"The baroness herself, your grace."

Interesting. Which made Aefric wonder if the selection of Octave was about Octave, or about Aefric.

Not that he had any way of knowing.

"Will your grace ... accept my offer of *leaba*?" she asked, hope as evident in her tone as in her eyes.

"Tell me this, first," he said. "As the tradition goes, is there honor or dishonor in either accepting or refusing *leaba*? I want to make sure I understand fully what I'll be saying before I answer."

Hope looked to be dying in her big blue eyes, but she held her chin high as she answered.

"It is not a matter of honor, your grace," she said, "but of pleasure. *Leaba* must be offered freely, and it must be accepted or refused freely. You cannot shame me either by sharing your bed with me or by sending me away."

She held herself steady, awaiting his answer. Her posture true, but the set of her jaw and the disappointment in her eyes suggested certainty that he'd send her away.

And the truth was, the part of him that was Keifer wanted to refuse her. This woman wasn't Andi. He shouldn't sleep with her. It was that simple.

The part of him that was Aefric was more than happy to say yes. This woman was very good looking, and he'd been without sex for far too long.

But there was a simple fact that brought both sides together on this matter.

As Keifer he'd promised that he would fulfill *all* of the duties he'd undertake as a duke.

That meant he'd have to marry and produce offspring.

That meant that, at some point, he'd have to accept the touch of a woman who wasn't Andi.

Octave was pretty, young, willing, but otherwise nothing at all like Andi. Which made her the perfect place to start.

Aefric smiled at Octave.

"Thank you for your patience," he said. "And for helping me to understand exactly what *leaba* is and how it works. Now that I understand, let me give you my answer."

Aefric allowed his eyes to track up and down Octave's body the way she'd already been looking him over, and let his appreciation of her beauty settle in his smile and his tone as he next spoke.

"Octave, my dear, I'm *delighted* to accept your offer of *leaba*. It would be my great pleasure to share my bed with you tonight."

"Thank you, your grace," she said, sounding both relieved and excited. "And I promise you. It will be."

She started to reach for the ties of her frock, but he stopped her with a gesture.

"The road is ... much with me," Aefric said, referring to his day's dirt and sweat. He considered using magic to address this, but had a better idea. "Would your offer of *leaba* extend to helping me wash the dirt and grime from my skin before we go to bed?"

"Oh, your grace," she said with a broad smile. "Of course it does."

***

Only one of Aefric's guards had heard of *leaba*. But he quickly — and quietly — explained it to the others. They were then most accommodating to the thought of their duke having his *leaba*. They found a pair of folding screens behind the armoire, and set them up around the copper bathtub to give Aefric and Octave their privacy for the first part, as well.

As they did this, Octave called for buckets of water, and got them heating. And all the while, she kept giving Aefric smiles that were themselves hot enough to boil water. Even though he was still only half-naked.

Aefric watched her work. Studied her, as she moved about her task with swift, crisp efficiency.

She was most definitely *not* Andi.

Andi was taller. About five-foot-six. Octave, she was a good three inches shorter. Andi's eyes were hazel. Octave's, blue. And much wider.

Andi did have curly hair, like Octave, but not *quite* like Octave. Andi's was darker. More ... mahogany than chestnut.

Andi's hair curled in tighter, too. She'd sometimes smile and pull a curl straight, showing that her hair really should have hung down past her shoulders, instead of just framing her face. But it seemed the more Andi tried to grow her hair, the tighter it curled in. As though her hair insisted on fighting the pull of gravity.

Octave's curls were looser, bouncing freely as she moved.

He wondered for a moment what it would feel like to run his

fingers through her hair. How different would it feel? The strands looked finer than Andi's. Perhaps softer...

Guilt pushed him back to cataloging differences.

Andi was slender and small-breasted. Octave's curves ... were a little more generous...

Guilt came rushing back from the Keifer part of him, and brought shame with it this time.

How could he stand here, ogling this woman who was years younger than him? Old enough to vote, maybe, but not likely old enough to drink. Not in ... not in Oregon...

He wasn't in Oregon. Not anymore. He was in the barony of Norra. In the duchy of Deepwater. In the kingdom of Armyr. In the world of Qorunn.

Here he was not Keifer. Here he was Aefric.

Aefric had never found his Andi. Never married.

Aefric had known love as only fleeting. Not lasting. The Aefric part of him felt no guilt or shame at admiring the beauty of this young woman who seemed so very eager to share his bed.

It was right. It was natural.

And anyway, no one in Armyr voted, except maybe for councils or mayors in some towns. Maybe. And likely alcohol had been available to Octave for years.

She was old enough to volunteer to give him *leaba*. Which meant she must have reached the age of majority. Certainly the baroness wouldn't risk offending Aefric by sending him someone too young.

But there was no harm in finding out.

"How old are you, Octave?" Aefric asked, as she poured the third bucket into the copper tub.

"Just celebrated my majority not three aetts past, your grace," she said, that heated smile of hers still in place. "Might be her lordship selected me for this pleasure as a present for reaching majority."

Pleasure. Not duty. And she was undoubtedly old enough.

Reassuring on one front, but the conflict within him was not so simply resolved.

The part of him that was Aefric was more than eager to get this young woman out of her blue frock and enjoy a night of mutual exploration and satisfaction.

The part of him that was Keifer, in contrast, was shaking and on the verge of throwing up. This wasn't Andi. He'd committed himself to Andi. He loved his wife. And her being dead didn't mean he loved her any less. How could he betray her with this girl?

Some of the conflict must've shown on his face, because as Octave prepared his bath, her smile grew puzzled from time to time.

Aefric shook himself when he saw that puzzled look. He couldn't explain Andi to her. Aefric had never known Andi. That was Keifer's life. Keifer's love. And he couldn't let the fact that he was both these men become known to anyone here in Qorunn.

That might be dangerous in ways he couldn't begin to imagine.

But then Aefric realized that the bath was ready, and Octave was frowning at him.

"You have many cares, your grace," she said softly.

Aefric started to speak, but she closed the gap between them and put her fingers to his lips.

Just that little touch alone made him shiver. When was the last time a woman had stood kissably close to Keifer? Touched his face? His lips?

He knew the answer. Andi. Andi, who smelled like raspberries from that body wash she so loved.

Octave smelled like lavender. Likely she'd had her own bath, before coming up here.

The different smell helped. He drew it in through a shaky breath as she spoke softly to him.

"No need to list those cares for me now, your grace. Come. Let me wash them from you."

Aefric nodded.

Octave couldn't possibly understand his conflict. Couldn't know the truths about his dual lives and conflicting emotions. But she seemed to understand something of them anyway. Or at least, enough to understand that right there, right then, what he needed most was her gentle touch.

And so she stripped him with quick, efficient hands. And even though his body stood more than ready for what his emotions were so conflicted about, she didn't tease. Not then.

Instead, she guided him into the tub, singing something under her breath.

The bath helped. The constant touching. Her hands going places no woman's hands had been since Andi. She scrubbed, but she did more than that. She stroked his skin. Massaged knots in his shoulders and neck. Ran her fingers along Aefric's old scars and through his hair.

And as the bath continued, he found himself relaxing. First, the part of him that was Aefric, who had been treated to such a bath only once before, and was enjoying this immensely.

Then, slowly, the part of him that was Keifer. That part of him had never been bathed by a woman this way. She was doing something Andi had never done, and that helped.

Somewhere during the bath, the second time Octave rubbed at angry muscles in his shoulders, he found himself making a low moan of pleasure.

It was the first sound he'd made since she'd hushed him. And it encouraged her. Octave began cooing little appreciations about his body as she washed him. His muscles. His scars. His jaw. His eyes. His hair.

Never while meeting his eyes. And all the time, her hands on him. The bath slowly turning from a simple matter of hygiene to a more overt form of foreplay.

The part of him that was Aefric began to burn with lust in earnest. That part of him was growing tired of the bath. Wanted his hands starting to explore Octave. And more than his hands.

The part of him that was Keifer was spinning. Unsure. Savoring the almost forgotten feel of a woman's hands on his body. Guilt warred with reason. He knew that Andi would want him to move on. Knew that she was probably cheering Octave on from the afterlife. But still unable to reconcile the idea of making love with a woman who wasn't Andi.

Oddly, that phrase turned out to be the key.

Maybe he wasn't ready to make love. But that wasn't what was being offered to him tonight. This young woman, Octave, she wasn't in love with him and wasn't pretending to be.

She wanted him. Lust, pure and clean and simple.

This was not a night for love. This was a night for lust.

Aefric knew lust well. Keifer ... much as he tried to deny it out of loyalty to Andi, he knew lust too. There had been women before Andi, after all. And his time with them hadn't always been about love.

No. He wouldn't make love to this woman, Octave. But perhaps he could have sex with her. Could he fuck her? Maybe. But only if she was fucking him right back.

The part of him that was Aefric leapt on this concession. Touched Octave's cheek and turned her face to his. Enjoyed the heat of desire in her eyes. The smell of lavender — not raspberries — from her skin.

He kissed her.

Octave's lips parted for him almost immediately. Invited him into her mouth. Her tongue twined with his, while she made humming sounds of pleasure.

She still tasted of the slightly bitter nysta tea that would ensure this night produced no offspring.

Her kiss was different from Andi's. Wilder. Octave kissed with abandon, as though trying to make clear to Aefric that she was more than eager to give herself to him that night.

When he pulled back from the kiss, Aefric almost didn't recognize the low, lustful growl as his own voice as he said, "I think I'm clean enough."

"Yes, your grace," she breathed back into his mouth.

Octave groped him with the towel as she quickly dried his body. Then her fingers flew over the laces of her frock as the two of them hurried into the bedroom.

Once she was naked and the door was closed behind them, Aefric refused to hurry.

He looked her over, slowly. Trying to show her as much heat with his eyes as she'd been showing him.

The way she smiled told him he'd come close enough.

Then, it was his turn to explore her, with hands and mouth while she encouraged him with gasps and moans.

No, despite some guilty urgings from deep inside, he would not just "get this over with."

If he was going to have sex with Octave, he would go slowly. Really enjoy this beautiful woman who was so eager to share his bed. And he would do his best to make sure he gave her every bit as much pleasure as she gave him.

He still felt that conflict within. The twists of love and loyalty. But he was committed to his course now. To finally taking the first step toward moving on in a world without Andi.

When the time came for more than exploration, Octave proved once more that she was nothing like Andi. Everything she did. Every movement. All of them different from what he'd known so many times.

And that helped too.

Late that night, when they'd both had their fill of pleasure, they were lying entwined in his bed when Octave surprised Aefric.

"Who was she, your grace?" she asked softly. She reached out and touched the crystal pendant still hanging from its gold chain around his neck. "The woman who gave you this."

"How did—"

She smiled, and this smile was different. Friendly.

"Something was holding you back. Before the bath. Something almost made you send me away, and I knew it wasn't cares of the office." She traced her fingers over his chest. Played with the scar left by an old spear wound along his ribs. "The look in your eyes. The anguish. Had to be a woman. A woman lost to you."

Aefric's throat felt tight. He was pretty sure he wanted to speak, but no way any words were getting out.

"When I bathed you," Octave continued, "your namesake staff — and all your trinkets and magic too — they were all in here. Not close at hand. But this" — she touched the crystal pendant gently — "this you kept on. A token of love, I'm thinking. And if your grace would like to talk about her, I'm of a mind to listen…"

Aefric chuckled softly and shook his head.

"You're a smart woman."

"I'm a woman, your grace," she said with a shrug. "We have a sense about these things."

"She was very special to me." Aefric shook his head. "Beyond that, I'm not really ready to say."

"You loved her very much."

"I did. I do."

Aefric could see one more question burning in her blue eyes, but Octave nodded and let the subject drop. Aefric half wondered if she would leave then. He wondered also if he wanted her to. He was tired enough that he could no longer tell.

Octave settled the issue by snuggling in with her head on his chest and sighing contentedly.

Aefric could feel the conflict inside him emerging again. Sex was one thing, but this kind of cuddling, was that going too far? Was it disloyal to Andi's memory?

Aefric shifted his attention away from the thoughts and emotions trying to swell within his exhausted mind and heart. He focused instead on the pleasurable sensations of Octave's company. The smooth warmth of her body against his, the contact of their flesh, the soft sound of her breathing as she drifted off to sleep.

Eventually sleep managed to come for him, too.

7

———————

The next morning, Aefric was gently wakened by Octave. She was clothed again, but smiling.

"I hate to wake you, your grace," she said warmly, "but her lordship insisted you be awake and dressed in time for breakfast."

Aefric wasn't sure about wakefulness. The comfortable featherbed called him to close his eyes and sleep some more. And the part of him that was Keifer figured he still had some processing to do about last night.

The part of him that was Aefric was enjoying the view down the front of Octave's pale blue frock.

Octave caught his glance and laughed with pleasure.

"Alas, your grace," she said. "I'd be more than happy to extend your *leaba* through the whole of today, but her lordship was quite clear about how she hoped to have your grace's presence at her breakfast table. And further that I was not to ... delay your grace's arrival. Plus, I do have my duties to see to."

She tilted her head and put one wrist on her hip.

"Course, if your grace were willing to extend his stay a second night..."

"No," he said through a sigh. "Much as I would enjoy a second night with you, sweet Octave, I have to get to Water's End." He stretched his arms as he continued, "Can't leave poor Prince Killian minding my seat while I'm here having fun."

The conflict inside him about Octave was still present, but its edge felt dulled this morning. In fact, Aefric found that he felt good about the night before.

The part of him that was Keifer might not have fully agreed, but it was too busy trying to understand it all and what it meant going forward to be able to drive home spikes of guilt for enjoying a little flirtation with a pretty woman.

And when he stood naked from his bed, he even got to enjoy the hungry way her eyes roved over him. In fact, he found himself responding.

"We'll have to put that beast away, your grace," Octave said with a laugh, "or they'll be calling you Aefric Readystaff."

Aefric chuckled, and expected that to mean he'd dress himself. But as he reached for his undergarments, Octave cleared her throat.

"'Tis *my* duty to dress you, your grace, as provider of your *leaba*," she said with a bow and a wink. "As well as my pleasure."

She washed him first, at the copper basin, then dressed him in his leather pants and his darkest red shirt, taking extra care to make sure that the fabric lay *just right* against his skin.

"Am I allowed to give you a gift?" He asked. "According to the rules of *leaba?*"

"You certainly are, your grace," Octave said, sounding pleased. "So long as it isn't coin or something similar."

While Aefric certainly didn't want her to feel *paid* for their night together, the truth was that he was traveling without much in the way of jewelry worthy of gifts.

He did have some gemstones within the special bag inside his backpack — part of his private money — but without knowing the state of his new duchy's finances, he wasn't sure he could risk giving any of them away.

He found himself grateful that he'd thought to buy fabric from those traveling merchants.

He gave her a small bolt of silk that matched the blue of her eyes.

"Oh," she said, sounding astonished. "Oh, it's lovely, your grace. Too fine for—"

He pressed the bolt of cloth into her hands.

She smiled widely. Then suddenly threw her arms around Aefric's neck and kissed him hard and deep, pressing the line of her body against his.

"Oh," she murmured when she pulled back from the kiss. "If I didn't have duties to get to, your grace, I'd show you how much I appreciate my gift."

"Then I guess," he said with a sigh, "I'll just have to imagine."

She gave him another kiss and a saucy smile before sighing and leaving to start her own day's work.

Aefric, with nothing more to delay him, stepped out of his room and allowed a page to lead him and his guards to breakfast.

BREAKFAST FOR AEFRIC THAT MORNING WOULDN'T TAKE PLACE IN THE main feasting hall. Instead, a page escorted him and his four guards to a courtyard up on the third floor. A small section of the keep — no more than fifteen feet long or across — that was open to the sky, which showed signs of oncoming rain clouds.

His guards took up positions in the hallway as Aefric entered the courtyard.

It was decorated along its edges with bright, colorful flowers in pots. In all, a cheerful place of privacy, at the top of the keep.

Or maybe Aefric was just feeling good that morning.

In the center of the courtyard stood a round, wooden table, set for three places. The other two seats were already filled. Apparently he was the last to arrive.

His breakfast companions were the baroness, of course, and Countess Faenella.

The baroness was wearing a modest gown of sky blue, with her shimmering red hair restrained behind her in a fragile-looking net of gold, studded with small gems. At her throat, a silver choker with a single emerald.

The countess was dressed for the road, though, in her chainmail over good, solid clothes in shades of brown. She looked, Aefric was amused to note, even more relaxed and cheerful this morning than he felt.

Apparently he hadn't been alone in enjoying the offer of *leaba* the night before.

"Good morning to you both," he said, then kissed their hands in turn before standing the Brightstaff beside the table, just behind his chair, and taking his seat.

They returned his greetings, and Baroness Herewyn smiled and cocked an eyebrow at them both.

"Few nobles these days are thoughtful enough to offer *leaba* to their guests," she said. "And I wasn't sure that lifelong adventurers such as yourselves would even be familiar with the concept." She made a show of looking at both Aefric and Faenella. "But I assume by those smiles that you approve of the tradition? That I could expect the offer returned in kind, should I find myself hosted in your lands?"

"Most certainly," Countess Faenella said.

"I should say so," Aefric said. "And you would be welcome to accompany me to Water's End when we leave this morning, if you wish."

"Alas," she said. "I have too much to attend to here. But we can speak of that after we eat."

Their breakfast was simple, but good. Fresh wheat bread sweetened with honey. Fried ham. A selection of sliced fruits and cheeses. And to drink, fine, clear water.

As they finished, Aefric began the discussion.

"I presume we should begin by addressing Kerrik Forest?"

"I had nothing to do with that fort of Ferrin's," Baroness Herewyn said, irritated enough to deny the count his title. "Nor that toll gate of his. I want to make those points clear at the outset."

She shook her head. "I won't deny, though, that I could use some help with bandits in the forest."

"We encountered no bandits on the road," Aefric said.

"Of course not, your grace," the baroness continued. "His soldiers drive them well south across the Kingsroad. So instead of harrying travelers, they harry my three timber towns along the forest edge. Some even range far enough to bother my quarries."

"You don't think they're all bandits, do you." Aefric didn't make it a question.

"They're certainly all bandits," she answered with a frown. "But I would not take surprise to learn that some of them spend their days wearing the livery of Motte."

"What of Merrek?" Aefric asked, while Countess Faenella watched the exchange, keeping her own counsel so far.

"I don't know for sure, your grace," Baroness Herewyn said with a small sigh. "I have no proof, and don't wish to speak against a duchess without some."

"I am not asking you to make a formal accusation," he said. "I'm asking informally. As informally as possible. In your opinion—"

"*Yes,*" she said harshly. "The Fyrenn family has troubled us for generations. Whenever they've felt they could get away with it. And now that one of them is queen, Duchess Ashling's emboldened. I've no doubt some of those 'bandits' are her people."

"All right," Aefric said, as reassuringly as possible. "I can't do much until I get to Water's End and take formal possession of the duchy."

"Of course, your grace," Baroness Herewyn said, and she seemed to be folding back into herself. As though expecting to be told she was on her own.

"*However,*" Aefric said, sharply enough to draw her suspicious gaze back to him. "Motte has already complained, though a sergeant and a knight, about the expense of holding the Kingsroad through Kerrik."

Baroness Hewewyn scoffed.

"So I've already decided to bear some of that cost." He smiled at her. "As soon as I'm at Water's End, I'll be sending workers to finish that fort, and soldiers to make clear that it is now *my* fort, not his."

Baroness Herewyn allowed herself a small smile. But Aefric wasn't finished.

"My soldiers there can coordinate with yours to see about those bandits in the forest."

"*Thank* you, your grace," the baroness said, sounding astonished. But before she could continue, Aefric kept talking.

"Now," he said, frowning. "About Merrek. I'm not sure yet, what my options are."

"If your grace can assist me with Kerrik," she said, "I'll have more soldiers available to see about my southern border."

"That's good," Aefric said, thinking about how he'd love to come investigate this himself. It sounded like the kind of adventure he'd done many times. But perhaps he could do it by proxy. "Though I might want to send an investigator, as well."

"Your investigator will be most welcome, your grace," the baroness said, holding out her hands to him, as though to take his hand.

She couldn't be going to *kiss* his hand. He outranked her.

Curious, Aefric gave her his hand.

She took his hand in both of hers and pressed her forehead against his knuckles.

It came together for Aefric then. That movement was part of the oaths of fealty. Apparently it also served as a gesture of gratitude to someone of superior rank, here in Armyr.

"Your grace," Countess Faenella said. "May I have the task of investigating this matter?"

"You have a county to see to," Aefric said. "I shouldn't think you'd have time."

"A full third of my county borders Merrek," she said. "So I'll need to see about my own border as well. And I suspect that Felspark might be seeing a rise in banditry worth investigating. And if they aren't, that might be information of its own."

Aefric hesitated, worrying at his lip.

"Your grace," she added softly. "While I would certainly not bring charges to this, I cannot help but think that if Motte is harrying that far into Norra at the same time that Merrek is, there may be coordination."

"I confess," Baroness Herewyn said, just as softly, "I've had that thought myself."

Aefric sighed, wondering where Goldenfall fit into all this.

"That makes sense," he said. "Might also explain why Motte has been so bold with me. And in case it's true, I'll need to cut Motte off from Merrek if I'm going to bring him to heel."

"I have a couple of friends who could assist me with the investigation," Countess Faenella said with a smile. "In fact, I suspect they'd love to ride with me once more."

"While teasing you about your new rank?" Aefric asked. "I know the type."

"If I may, your grace," the baroness said, arching her eyebrow again, "you *are* the type."

"True," he said with a chuckle, then sobered through a quick breath. "All right. Get me parchment and I'll draw up the order before we leave."

"With pleasure, your grace," the baroness said. And from the look in her eye, Aefric felt confident that he'd made a new ally.

Baroness Herewyn made sure that Aefric and his party were freshly provisioned when they left, perhaps an hour after breakfast. With smiles and well-wishes from the baroness and several of her courtiers, it was the best send-off Aefric had had on this journey so far.

And it was feeling like a journey to him. Not merely a matter of riding the road for an aett to get someplace, but something closer to the kind of travel he knew from his adventuring days. Where nothing was certain, and danger seemed to lurk around every corner.

In that sense, it felt like home.

And, acquainted with this sensation as he was, he did not let his good mood dull his awareness of his surroundings.

This, he suspected, was why he noticed the rider pacing his party — now escorted by a dozen of the baroness' knights, and *Vohlcairna Burrew* — as they entered the township of Norrtarr.

The rider sat a fast-looking horse, and he wore no armor to slow him down, nor any obvious livery. He did wear a short sword at his side.

The town was busy that morning. A farmers market was taking place in the town center, and Aefric used that as an excuse to turn and take his party around the western edge of town, rather than press on through its center.

Toward the edge of town, the roads were dirt, but well-packed and kept free of ruts. The smell of dirt was strong in the warm morning air. Beyond the town limits, there were only a few farms between Norrtarr and the cliffs of Felspark.

Sure enough, the rider was more than just some curious idler. He kept his distance, but he paced them as they rode.

Aefric was just about to call Countess Faenella's attention to the rider when she said, without looking away from the street ahead of them, "I see him, your grace."

"Just the one rider," Ser Beornric said. "Likely a scout from Motte, watching our progress. Assuming he's not an outrider for another group of Motte's waiting soldiers."

"Could be from Goldenfall," Countess Faenella said, "keeping an eye as we approach."

"I don't think so," Aefric said. "Motte had a scout following us yesterday. Likely the same rider."

"Worth worrying about?" Ser Beornric asked. "We could capture him, easily enough."

"No," Aefric said. "He'd learn more riding with us than watching. Just keep an eye on him."

"What if he's a scout for the bandits?" Countess Faenella asked.

"I don't think it's likely," Aefric said. "The baroness made no mention of bandits daring so close as Norrtarr. No. Let Motte think he's keeping up with current information. He can't know I've already set things in motion."

Countess Faenella frowned at that, then asked, "How, your grace? Your letter to Prince Killian?"

Aefric nodded. "Assuming the spell worked — and I think it did — he's likely riding our direction right now." He frowned. "At least, I hope so. Depends on what kind of man he is."

"If you asked him to meet you with troops," Ser Beornric said, "then his highness set out as soon as possible. He's a thirst for action, that one."

"I like him already," Aefric said, with a chuckle.

The sky overhead and to the west was fairly clear, but those rain clouds he'd seen at breakfast looked to be coming from the east. He could only hope they wouldn't catch up.

Once Norrtarr was behind them, the Kingsroad was clear that morning. The scout who tailed them had no way to hide his movements unless he wanted to risk the wrath of farmers and their corn and tara fields.

Apparently the scout opted to simply ride well behind them, instead.

Ahead of them, the cliff faces that formed the border between Norra and Felspark, and between Motte and Goldenfall. The Kingsroad cut a narrow canyon between the cliff faces, and ascended a slow grade up the five hundred feet or so to the elevation of Felspark and Goldenfall.

Wonderful, in terms of defense for Felspark and Goldenfall. Each of them kept a fort near the cliff's edge, and between them they could rain down death on any invading army trying to march up the Kingsroad.

Hadn't helped during the Godswalk Wars. The borogs had made their own way from Motte into Goldenfall, by digging tunnels through the cliffs.

Had Goldenfall and Motte collapsed those tunnels? Or were they looking at using those tunnels as new roads to connect their counties?

Something Aefric might ask about. If he ever felt on good enough terms with either of the counts. For now, just something to wonder about as they approached the cliffs.

"Your grace," Burrew said, riding in close to him and the countess. "My instructions are to escort you safely to the border. Beyond that, I have leave to follow my own judgment."

She made a show of looking up at the two forts, both of which were obviously occupied. "Further, if we have reason to expect an attack from above, I have leave to assist you."

"Thank you, *Vohlcairna* Burrew," Aefric said. "I don't think that will be necessary. Felspark isn't strong enough to risk attacking. And I think Goldenfall's challenge won't be as *overt* as Motte's."

"As you say, your grace," she said, bowing slightly while still astride her horse. "Will you object to our remaining nearby, just in case?"

"Not in the least," Aefric said. "In fact, I appreciate the show of support." He gave her a lopsided smile. "Who knows? Might even make them nicer."

"One can only hope, your grace."

No soldiers met them at the border.

As Aefric's party proceeded up the incline, they were not hailed by either of the two forts, where soldiers watched from above.

Aefric felt his neck and shoulders itch the entire way up that incline. How many times had he been riding through just such a pass when he'd been set upon by enemies of one sort or another?

And even on those occasions when the attacks didn't come, there was still the awful waiting. The tense expectation. That certainty that at any moment the world would explode into violence.

He felt all those sensations again that day. Even though he rode now as a duke, and not a wandering adventurer. Even though he rode through lands that were supposedly his. And safe.

He *should* have had reason to feel safe, even riding up that incline. Instead, he felt himself on the anvil once more. Waiting for the hammer to fall.

But it didn't. Not on the incline that day.

Aefric and his party came up out of the shadows of the twin cliffs to the higher elevation of the prairies of Felspark and Goldenfall.

Like below, the land looked a little drier south of the Kingsroad. And yet, Goldenfall didn't have swampland, the way Motte did. So Aefric wasn't sure why that was.

He was just puzzling over the difference when Ser Beornric got his attention.

"Riders, your grace. Approaching from the Felspark fort."

Sure enough, a party of a half-dozen approached, all on horseback. Five of them clearly soldiers — though wearing leather armor sewn with rings and steel studs, instead of the chainmail that had been so prevalent so far. The soldiers carried spears, and wore short swords at their sides. They had bucklers strapped to their saddles.

One of the soldiers carried the banner of Felspark. Three white stars descending to the sinister, on a background of goldenrod.

The other rider was clearly a noble of some sort. His clothing was of a far better grade, from his white shirt with its frills and lace, to his tight-fitting gray pants and cloth-of-gold sash belt. His leather boots looked soft enough to melt in the sun.

His blonde hair sat on his head in tight curls that moved little as he rode. No way those curls were natural. His goatee, too, was slicked, and curled inward to point at the bottom of his neck.

He wore a rapier at his side, as well as a dueling dagger.

"Your grace," the standard bearer called out. "May I present Ler Ordnoth Ol'Felruun, brother to her lordship, Baroness Blaewyn Ol'Felruun."

Ler. Ler...

As Aefric he had never come across "Ler" as either a name or a title. But as Keifer, his memory stretched back to his sourcebooks...

Yes. "Ler" was an Armyrian term for a minor, landholding noble. Ranked beneath a baron, and about equal with a knight. Possibly comparable to the Scottish *laird*, although he was less certain of that.

So. Not someone who'd get offered *leaba*...

"Your grace," Ler Ordnoth said with a bow that involved more hand-waving than Aefric was used to. Seemed to be the man's style though. He repeated every wave of his hands, as he bowed in greeting to Countess Faenella.

Aefric and Faenella returned their courtesies, while inside Aefric wanted to simply grab the man by the collar and say, *what do you want?*

Patience. He was going to have to learn patience. It would be good for his blood pressure.

Not that anyone in Qorunn measured blood pressure.

Still. It would be good for keeping his heartbeat at a reasonable rhythm.

Ler Ordnoth placed one hand over his heart and hung his head just the least bit as he next spoke.

"Her lordship regrets that offering your grace hospitality at Ruunkeep, her baronial seat, would add several days to your journey to Water's End."

"I understand entirely, of course," Aefric said. "And though I would enjoy meeting her lordship at Ruunkeep, that pleasure will have to wait for another time."

"Indeed," Ler Ordnoth said, then smiled. "So instead her lordship wishes to offer you hospitality at her castle at Tafarac. It's not nearly so large and fine as Ruunkeep, but it's much closer to the road."

Aefric held back an urge to grimace, and an even stronger urge to throttle the man. Perhaps Ordnoth had intended to give Aefric a pleasant surprise. Instead, he found the presentation a cheap ploy.

"Well," Aefric said. "In that case I would be glad to accept her lordship's offer of hospitality." He let Ler Ordnoth open his mouth to reply before turning to Faenella and saying, "Countess Faenella? Will you and yours be joining us?"

He turned back to Ler Ordnoth, one eyebrow high. "I do presume her lordship's invitation includes the countess' party as well."

Petty, on Aefric's part? Perhaps. But he refused to let this minor nobleman steal the conversational advantage during their first meeting. Not when he could avoid it.

"Of course, of course," Ler Ordnoth said quickly. "Forgive me, your excellency, for not being clear about that in the beginning. Her lordship would be delighted to host you as well."

Aefric almost — *almost* —asked if that meant her lordship wasn't *delighted* to host *him*. But he decided that there were limits to his pettiness.

Countess Faenella agreed of course.

Ler Ordnoth's soldiers took point, with their standard bearer. Ser Beornric immediately sent Aefric's and Faenella's standard bearers to ride up front with them. Aefric wasn't best pleased about that — he preferred the standards riding back with the main part of the group — but he was even less pleased about his next discovery.

Ler Ordnoth intended to ride the whole way beside himself and Countess Faenella.

Aefric began to wonder if he'd been ambushed after all...

BY THE TIME AEFRIC AND HIS PARTY STOPPED FOR LUNCH THAT DAY, HE was ready to kill Ler Ordnoth.

The man. Would not. Shut up.

It might not have been so bad, had he been talking about anything of consequence. The recovery process following the Godswalk Wars. Hints about whether or not the barony was beset by bandits. Indications, perhaps, about what Goldenfall or Merrek might have been up to.

But those were topics Aefric could only daydream of getting answers to, as he rode beside the nonstop blathering of Ler Ordnoth Ol'Felruun.

Instead, by the time they finally did stop for lunch on a pleasant patch of grass warmed by the strong midday sun, perhaps a hundred feet to the Felspark side of the Kingsroad, Aefric found he was hard pressed to recall anything specific the man had said as they rode.

Something about this or that ancient ancestor. Not about battles won, or great achievements, of course. No, that might have risked becoming interesting.

Instead Ler Ordnoth had spoken of rumored affairs with famous people, intermarriages with other noble families, and the supposed "even keel" that had been the hallmark of Felspark rulers going back a thousand years or more.

At least, that was what Aefric *thought* the man had been saying. But as he rubbed down Windsong for their break, he realized that reconstructing the conversations wasn't easy. The man's topics rolled into one another as he spoke, and seemed to range far and wide.

At least Aefric had managed to draw some conclusions about the countryside as he'd ridden along that morning.

It was in bad shape. On both sides of the Kingsroad. So far they'd passed the burned out remains of two towns — one on each side of the road — and at least a dozen farms.

That tracked with what Aefric remembered about the Godswalk Wars. After their defeat at Deepwater, the borog armies of the Flayer were said to have turned south and taken out their fury on the countryside even as they fled.

Perhaps Norra, down below the cliffs, had been spared. But it seemed that Goldenfall and Felspark hadn't been so lucky. And Aefric found himself already worried about Riverbreak and Fyretti.

The most frustrating thing about seeing such devastation during his ride was that Ler Ordnoth seemed entirely disinclined to discuss it.

Three times during the ride, Aefric had asked about the towns and farms, and what was being done to restore what had been lost. Especially once it was clear that more was being done to rebuild some of the farms on the Goldenfall side of the road.

And yet, all three times, Ler Ordnoth put his hand over his heart, sagged his head slightly with a sigh, and said only, "A tragedy, to be sure, your grace."

He then immediately changed the subject and pushed on.

A lifetime of adventuring had given Aefric little patience for that kind of blather. Especially when there was useful information to be had, if the man were willing to just shut up about the past and talk about the present. Or even just the recent past.

But Aefric took this ride as a learning experience.

He couldn't just beat answers out of this man, no matter how minor a noble he was. And even pressuring him might not be a smart move. Aefric was too new to his duchy. Too uncertain in his standing among his nobles.

Pushing too hard too soon might serve only to aid his enemies.

So Aefric practiced the patience he knew he needed.

And he hated every minute of it.

Jaw clenched and teeth gritted. Knuckles white, where they held Windsong's reins. His shoulders had given up all the relaxation that Octave had given them, and knotted themselves up tight once more.

But then they sat down to lunch, on blankets spread out by the countess' people. A meal of roasted lamb was laid out before them, along with a good, sharp cheese and fresh wheat bread sweetened with honey.

And a blessing came with the meal. Nyorngyth sat down to lunch with them.

Ler Ordnoth might have been skilled at blather, but a traveling priest of Ulna had conversational skills of his own. And Nyorngyth brought them to bear on the tiresome nobleman.

He asked about trade along the Fyrsa River, which flowed through a valley in central Felspark, coming down from Norra.

He asked about the drummers of Felspark, who were apparently renowned for their complicated patterns.

In short, he asked about things that didn't involve Ol'Feruun family pride or ancient history. And he asked questions in such a way that Ler Ordnoth actually answered.

The most interesting of those answers was about trade along the river. Baroness Herewyn had noted that trade was down in her barony, and Aefric had no reason to doubt her.

But Ler Ordnoth had answered Nyorngyth's question with a shrug and a simple comment. "Trade is trade. So long as the river flows, the trade flows with it. Like the river, sometimes it flows higher, sometimes lower, but always it flows."

Ler Ordnoth turned his line of conversation then to rainfall and the river. To times that drought had dimmed its flow to a bare trickle of its normal might. And to other times when the rains had come so swift and strong that the river overflowed and threatened to flood the whole of the river valley.

But Aefric focused on *how* Ler Ordnoth had spoken about trade along the river. He had sounded entirely unconcerned about the state of trade. No mention of this being an "ebb" time. No defensiveness, or over-compensation.

He truly seemed unconcerned about the state of trade in Felspark.

Now, that *could* have been cover. Ler Ordnoth had clearly been given instructions not to tell Aefric anything of the current status of Felspark. So it could well have been that trade had fallen off entirely, and Ler Ordnoth was trying hard to persuade Aefric and the others that this was not the case.

But what if it *wasn't* cover?

That would mean that Felspark's trade had to be stronger than Norra's.

If so, how?

Perhaps river trade was coming in from Riverbreak and Fyretti at normal rates. That was *possible*. But if so, why was that level of trade not continuing on into Norra?

Perhaps because the trade was coming in from Merrek? Trade that Merrek didn't *want* to have continue on into Norra right now?

There were possibilities in this that Aefric didn't like. And the officious, blathering style of Ler Ordnoth did nothing to reassure him.

After lunch, Nyorngyth smiled broadly at Aefric's invitation to ride up with the countess and himself. And he had volunteered to position his horse between Aefric and Ler Ordnoth, forming a buffer that made the afternoon ride almost peaceful.

Almost. The damage done by the Godswalk Wars was too visible as they rode along. Two more burned out towns. More destroyed farms. The spring air smelled too much of ashes and devastation.

Felspark looked to have suffered greatly during the wars. Recovery here would not likely be a quick process.

Was the same true in Goldenfall? Once away from the Kingsroad?

If so, perhaps Count Cyneric had not skipped Aefric's installation as a slight. Perhaps he had truly been working in his county and unable to leave. Was Aefric judging Goldenfall too harshly, too soon?

Something to consider.

Not to say that there were no signs of recovery, as they rode through the warm afternoon sunshine.

The brightest of these was off to the right, in Goldenfall. The early phases of construction had begun on a new town. It was not being built on the ashes and husks of its predecessors, but in a spot between two towns that had once graced the Goldenfall side of Kingsroad.

Alas, though Aefric would have been happy to stop and spend a little money there, the town was not yet built up enough for visitors. In fact, it was not yet really built up at all.

The land had been cleared, and leveled out to a respectable distance. They had workers bringing in stone and wood, but they hadn't begun any actual building. Not so much as digging out or laying out a single foundation.

Aefric wondered why not, and made the mistake of wondering aloud.

Ler Ordnoth took that question as a cue to talk, at length, about the historical problems of Goldenfall nobility in making decisions. To hear him tell it, none of the Goldenfall nobles would even be able to dress in the morning, if servants could not choose their clothing for them.

And, heavens forbid, if two of them disagreed about so much as the most fashionable color of the season, it would lead to arguments that would shake the Threepeaks with their volume, if not their coherence.

This, of course, was entirely unlike the nobles of Felspark...

He was off again, delving into the history of Felspark. Not saying anything of consequence, as usual, but praising how quick and how often right Felspark nobles were in their decision-making. Not to mention how forward-thinking in their fashions.

The other sign of encouragement were the goats.

Herds of goats on both sides of the road. Grazing the ruined land that had once held so many farms. It was a sight that got Aefric his first piece of actual, interesting information all day.

It came, of course, from Nyorngyth. Not Ler Ordnoth.

"Ah, good," Nyorngyth said with an open smile. "They've brought in the goats."

Ler Ordnoth tried to run away with that into a story of a goat and a nobleman and a lost document proving land ownership, but he'd covered that story already that day, so Aefric felt justified waving him to silence and asking Nyorngyth, "What do you mean?"

"Well," Nyorngyth said, drawing out the word with a smile. "One of the great crimes the borogs committed as they fled Deepwater was salting the land where they could. Especially farmland. But they didn't have time to actually *sow* the salt, of course. They scattered it, and called down rain to do the rest."

"Horrible," Countess Faenella said.

"But goats," Nyorngyth said, raising a finger as he made his point, "wonderful creatures that they are, they love the taste of salt. So, they graze the land that's been salted. They get their meals, and the land gets less salty. Another year of this, perhaps, along with certain other treatments such as the blessing of Halstaffur the Green Lord, and the land will take crops again."

Alas, Ler Ordnoth was ready with another story about goats and crops, and the rest of the conversation became less productive.

Aefric was, at least, reassured that steps were being taken to address the damage done by the war. From there, he allowed himself to tune out most of Ler Ordnoth's ramblings. Contenting himself with the taste of lamb and honey bread still on his tongue from lunch, and sweet memories of Octave from the night before.

The part of him that was Keifer tried to reassert some guilt at that point. But in the short term, at least, his guilt had lost some of its teeth.

By late afternoon, they at last were approaching a large town that had to be Tafarac.

Ler Ordnoth even confirmed it, saying his first useful thing of the day. "Ah, there she is. I knew we hadn't lost her. Tafarac. That town's been standing since my grandfather five generations back decided to expand our overland trade with more towns close to the Kingsroad. Tafarac was the first of these, and the jewel of the lot."

Tafarac sat no more than three miles or so off the Kingsroad. And unlike Norrtarr, it was a town built with defense in mind.

In the center of the town, at the highest elevation, stood the castle. From a distance, it looked to have been built following a hexagonal, motte and bailey design, with its own walls standing tall, and short towers at each point on the hexagon.

Then came a lower level, and what Nyorngyth described as the older part of the town. The castle had come first, as he explained it, and the first ring of town followed. Practically a motte and bailey town, it was, built on ground that had been raised up for that purpose.

How long must that have taken?

Definitely the action of someone thinking of defense before trade, no matter what Ler Ordnoth said. Which meant that the castle, and likely the town, were here as much to keep an eye on Riverbreak and Goldenfall as for any expansion of trade.

The older section of town was surrounded by its own stone wall. Tall and strong, it looked, even in the distance.

The newer section of town was spread across the ground below the old town. And its wall was wooden, though reasonably tall and strong-looking.

The gates of the town were closed as Aefric's party approached, and guarded by guards clad in leather armor and armed with longbows.

Closed gates. Even though the sun would not set for at least another hour. Another interesting point, for a town "built for trade."

Nevertheless, as soon as Felspark's standard bearer announced them, the gates were opened for them. They must have been waiting for Ler Ordnoth to return with the duke in tow, because as the gates opened, riders went ahead and began to clear the main street through town.

That main street was narrow enough that only three could ride abreast. And it wound through the town instead of cutting straight across.

Aefric also noted guard posts stationed along the way. Clearly any invaders trying to take the main road through town would be slowed, and face reinforcements for the defenders.

A military design, perhaps. But the townsfolk didn't seem worried. Those who stood watching waved and smiled and called out "Your grace!" as he rode past. Some even threw flowers.

Had they done that in Norrtarr as well? He'd been so preoccupied at the time that he hadn't noticed. He suspected, though, that if they had it would have drawn his attention. So likely they had not.

The route Aefric and his party followed did not lead through any kind of open marketplace. It stayed narrow, passing between low buildings that likely had the least valuable real estate in all of Tafarac. Because invaders coming through would probably hit those buildings first.

Invaders.

Aefric wasn't seeing damage from the Godswalk Wars. No burned out buildings. Not even any new construction.

Even the smells were just normal town smells. Fires and cooking. Coke and smithing. Sweat and dirt and the like.

This had to be where Felspark made its stand and turned the armies of the borogs aside. Aided, perhaps by the armies who pursued them from Deepwater.

Aefric's party passed on up a steep incline, through another set of gates, and on into the older section of Tafarac. Here the only wood used in construction was in roofs, doors, and windows. Otherwise, it was all stone. Even the streets here weren't packed dirt, like down below. They were cobblestones.

The street they rode was wider, but still diverted around the larger gathering places and important buildings. Not that any of the two and three story structures around them were likely deemed "unimportant." This was where the old money of Tafarac lived. The lers, and the better artisans and craftsmen. The councilmembers, the mayor, and the like. The finer restaurants, taverns, and inns, as well.

Here, fewer people watched and waved as Aefric and his party rode past. Few smiled, and none of them threw flowers.

Finally, they reached the impressively large stone wall of the castle itself. Its gate was wood and iron, and sat closed as they approached. Guards on the walls watched with arrows nocked, but not pointed.

"Open the gates," the standard bearer called, "for Ler Ordnoth and his guests, the Duke of Deepwater and the Countess of Fyretti."

The delay lasted long enough that Aefric thought they'd refuse. What they did instead was almost worse.

***

GATES OF WOOD AND IRON. LARGE AND THICK, SHOWING SCARS FROM ancient battles. They looked impressive. And the longer they stayed closed, the more Aefric wondered how well they'd do, struck by, say, a dozen bolts of lightning…

Ler Ordnoth's standard bearer had already called for the gates to be opened. And yet, Aefric remained on his horse in the warm late afternoon sun. Waiting for those gates to open.

He was tired and dirty from the day's ride. His stomach growled. Memories of lunch seemed as distant as Oregon. He itched in a dozen places that he was pretty sure a duke should not scratch. Not in public. And certainly not in this small square outside the gates, where he could feel eyes watching from nearby windows.

Even Windsong pawed at the cobblestones, irritated at having to wait out here, for the gate captain to do his damned job.

All around him, Aefric could hear the sounds of impatience. More horses, wanting either movement or a rubdown. Voices grumbling, too soft for their words to carry, but their meanings all close to identical.

Open the damn gates already.

"Is there a problem?" Aefric asked Ler Ordnoth with one eyebrow raised.

"Of course not, your grace," he responded with a smile that sat much easier on his lips than it did in his eyes. "Probably wishing to confirm that everything is in order on their side, before allowing your grace his first proper look at the castle. First impressions and all that."

"And you think keeping me waiting makes a better first impression?"

Ler Ordnoth drew breath for what, no doubt, would have been a long-winded and entirely uninformative answer.

For better or worse, he never got the chance to give that answer.

"Nobles alone may enter, with their retainers," the gate captain called down. "The only soldiers allowed inside the castle walls are those of her lordship."

"Of course," Ler Ordnoth started to say, and all of Aefric's irritation and impatience with the man came boiling out of him at once.

"*Then her lordship's offer is a lie,*" he called out in a ringing voice.

He heard several sharp intakes of breath around him. The loudest came from Ler Ordnoth, who'd gone several shades paler, which, by all rights, should have rendered him transparent.

Aefric continued, looking from Ordnoth to the gate captain and back again as he spoke.

"I have ridden all day with Baroness Blaewyn's brother. Ler Ordnoth Ol'Felruun. He is the one who conveyed to me her offer of hospitality. Ler Ordnoth, do you deny this?"

"Of course not, your grace, but—"

"I come here riding not with an army at my back, but supported only by my personal guard. Soldiers sworn to me who have stood between me and harm *here in the lands of my own duchy.* Do you understand this, Ler Ordnoth?"

"I ... certainly do, your grace, and assure you that—"

"Did you at any time warn me that this offer of supposed hospitality would be so insulting as to imply that I come as an invader presenting a threat to her lordship?"

Ler Ordnoth, who had proven himself an able improvisational speaker on any number of topics that day, sputtered.

"Your grace," he finally managed, "I assure you—"

"Am I offered true hospitality or not?"

"Yes, your grace."

"Then I expect that my soldiers will pass through those gates" — Aefric pointed for emphasis — "where they will be given their proper care for the night."

"But, your grace—"

"That is the proper way for a vassal to offer hospitality to her liege lord. Unless she is declaring herself in rebellion. Is that what she's doing, Ler Ordnoth? *Does her lordship declare herself in rebellion?"*

"No, your grace," Ler Ordnoth said quickly, visibly fighting not to panic as he called out to the gate captain. "Open the gates. We'll be making an exception this time."

The gate captain frowned. "Not sure I have the authority to do that, ler."

Ler Ordnoth gave Aefric a gesture he interpreted as a request to wait, and rode up to the gate.

The gate captain's head disappeared from above the wall. Seconds passed all too slowly. A small window in the gate opened, and Ler Ordnoth said something that looked heated.

Finally, the scraping sound of a metal brace being removed. Then the creaking of ropes as the gates were opened.

Aefric didn't wait for Ordnoth to resume his place. He gestured to Ser Beornric, who gave the call, and the party proceeded through the gates before the gate captain could change his mind.

If Baroness Blaewyn intended to put Aefric on the defensive by taking away his soldiers, she'd made a big mistake. All she'd really done was raise his anger.

Inside the gate, a good deal of the castle space was taken up by a large courtyard. Quintains were set up for jousting practice, though no one was trying them just then.

The keep itself sat toward the back of the courtyard. A hexagonal structure, two stories tall in the main part, but with a central tower standing two stories above that.

Other buildings around the courtyard included a large smithy, barracks, stables, and smaller buildings for craftsmen who worked directly for the baroness.

And all of these workers were busy right then, from the chandlers to the wheelwrights. Interesting.

Ler Ordnoth tried to lead Aefric directly over to the stables to have his horse seen to, but Aefric refused to leave the area of the gates until the last member of his party was safely through.

When it became clear what he was doing, the gate captain sent a runner into the keep.

Countess Faenella and their two knights joined him for this brief vigil. The countess said nothing about his little tirade, but she did give him a nod. Though that might only have been that she approved of his getting their soldiers through the gates.

Ser Beornric spoke to him quietly. "I don't like this, your grace. If she wants to separate you from your guard, I'm thinking you shouldn't go anywhere alone."

Aefric nodded.

Nyorngyth rode up and gave Aefric a quick bow and a big smile. "Thought I might have to find my own lodgings tonight, since I'm not even a retainer. It's an old loophole that sees a noble excepting soldiers from hospitality. Hasn't been done that I've heard of in centuries. Fell into disuse as a clear sign of mistrust."

Nyorngyth bowed and turned his horse then, and rode off to join the others.

When the last of the soldiers were through, Aefric nodded to the gate captain, who closed the gates behind them.

"Your grace?" Ler Ordnoth said, sounding chastened by the whole experience, which Aefric considered a plus.

"One moment," Aefric said, and turned to Ser Beornric. "What of that scout who'd been riding behind us?"

"He took off as we entered Tafarac."

"Good," Aefric said, and turned to Ler Ordnoth.

The ler guided them not to the stables, as Aefric had been expecting, but to the keep itself, where stable boys waited to take the horses of the nobles and the knights.

Ser Beornric seemed to take an inordinate amount of time giving the stable boy instructions about his admittedly impressive steed. But his purpose became clear when four of Aefric's soldiers arrived, on foot, and took up positions around their duke.

"Your grace," Ler Ordnoth began, but Aefric spoke over him.

"Ler," he said, not minding that his words came out a little sharp, "I have been under threat since I entered my duchy. So I take it amiss that her lordship tried to separate me from my guards. And perhaps an indication that I need some close at hand. Which is how things will be."

Ler Ordnoth seemed to take heart from the fact that the countess had only her knight and looked to her for support. But the countess only smiled and said, "I am looking forward to meeting my new neighbor."

Ler Ordnoth surrendered the point then, and led the way into the keep.

THE DOUBLE-DOORS OF THE KEEP LED DIRECTLY INTO THE MAIN HALL. Contrary to the hexagonal shape of the keep, the hall was square, perhaps sixty feet on a side.

It looked surprisingly empty. No tables set up for dinner. No courtiers, neither standing nor sitting along the sides. There weren't even chairs for that kind of sitting.

The stone floors had been recently swept clean. That much was clear. And the walls were decorated with tapestries dedicated to the Ol'Felruun family. A great, spreading family tree on the north wall to Aefric's right. On the wall to his left, scenes of hunting and landscapes of Felspark, always featuring prominently members of the Ol'Felruun family.

And those tapestries on the south wall looked old. As though they might've been brought in by the Ol'Felruun who first built this castle.

At the far end of the room, a dozen soldiers, clad in chainmail and armed with pikes. Short swords at their sides, as well, but the pikes looked more impressive.

The soldiers flanked a simple stone throne. And seated on the throne was the Baroness Blaewyn, with a pair of large, russet hunting dogs at her feet.

The baroness was blonde, like her brother, though she wore her hair straight to the shoulders. She dressed in a fashion similar to her brother as well. She wore a gown of goldenrod that had lace and frills, extraneous buttons, ruffles and more. Her gown was belted at her waist by a cloth-of-gold sash.

Must've taken her ten minutes to put that dress on. And three helpers.

She wore it well, though. That had to be admitted. Diamonds flashed on a gold chain at her throat, as well as in three places on her golden diadem. Perhaps representing the three stars on her banner?

Aefric approached, flanked by Faenella on his left and Ler Ordnoth on his right. Sers Beornric and Arcy followed a step behind and flanking, while Oswen and Sighild followed directly.

Behind him came his four personal guards.

Aefric stopped at what he considered a respectful distance.

"You have insulted me, your grace," the baroness said by way of greeting.

"Then I have only returned the favor," Aefric said.

"We do not allow foreign soldiers in any Ol'Felruun castle," she said. "This has been the rule for generations, and it exists for a reason. The last time foreign soldiers were allowed in one of our castles, they attempted to assassinate my great uncle Leoffrid."

"Then it is good that I have brought no foreign soldiers," Aefric said. "For I have no plans to assassinate anyone."

"They are not *my* soldiers," she said. "Therefore they are foreign."

"This barony is part of my duchy," Aefric said. "And therefore they are not."

"It was not always part of this duchy," she said. "There was a time when this barony was part of the principality of Fyr."

"Those days are long behind us," Aefric said. "Fyr lives only in memory. This barony is part of the duchy of Deepwater and the kingdom of Armyr, and has been for more than a century. Perhaps two."

"The old families of this region have long memories, your grace."

"Nevertheless. Fyr is the past. Armyr and Deepwater are the present. You might argue that Goldenfall's soldiers, or Norra's, are foreign in your lands, and have some cause. But the argument that mine are foreign holds no weight."

"You have forced me to admit soldiers from Fyretti. By your own logic, I could call them foreign soldiers."

Aefric sighed. "You offered the countess hospitality as well as offering it to me. Are your defenses so poor that a dozen soldiers present a threat? Or is your hospitality so poor that you begrudge them a bed and a meal?"

"Your grace insults me again."

"Not at all. I ask questions." Aefric flared a breath through his nostrils and tried to keep his temper under control. "Baroness, I am new to Armyr. I do not deny it. And I can see that you bristle at being asked to answer to a duke you would not choose."

Aefric made the mistake of drawing another breath then.

"Why would I resent being made vassal to the great *Hero* of Deepwater?" she asked, voice full of venom. "Perhaps because my lands were untouched until you drove the borogs south? Perhaps because they took out their shame and rage on us? Killed my people? Burned my fields and towns? Perhaps because I could lay every horror we suffered at your feet? *Your grace*?"

"I knew nothing of this until today," Aefric said, sounding as tired as he felt. "I knew their armies had fled south, but I hadn't really known what that meant. I was no general. I was only a man, trying to save lives the only way he knew how."

The baroness opened her mouth, but Aefric said, "Please, your lordship, let me speak."

Maybe it was his tone. Maybe it was his words. Either way, she nodded, though she still looked at him suspiciously.

"I traveled as an adventurer for many years. I tried to do good, when I could, and I'd like to think I did more good than harm in my travels." He looked up at the baroness. "But always, I was responsible only for myself. I had no one to answer for. No one to answer to."

He made a show of shaking his head.

"That all changed only a few days ago. His majesty King Colm Stronghand named me duke of Deepwater. And now, I am responsible for a countless number of people. Not just their lives, but their fortunes. I have a lot to learn, and I know that. And I cannot promise that I will not make mistakes. But if I can count on the counsel of experienced nobles such as yourself, then perhaps I can speed my learning process, and help us all recover from the horrors of the Godswalk Wars."

Baroness Blaewyn tilted her head as she considered that. She nodded.

"Perhaps, then," she said, "you deserve a chance." Her expression darkened. "But I cannot in good conscience swear the oaths of vassalage until I am confident in you as my liege lord."

"No," Aefric said, shaking his head slowly. "I'm afraid I cannot agree to that. And I believe you know I cannot. Whether you approve of me or not, I am the duke of Deepwater, and your rightful liege lord. I will have your oaths before I leave here tomorrow."

"But you have not refreshed yourself, your grace," the baroness said with a smile. "I would be a poor hostess to consider anything so formal as oaths while you stand there, hungry, and dusty from the road."

She clapped her hands twice, and a series of pages entered.

"Rest and refresh yourself, your grace, then we will dine. And then we will discuss those oaths."

Aefric didn't believe her smile one bit. But the truth was, those oaths were long, and his people were hungry. The oaths could wait for now.

He only hoped he wasn't making a huge mistake.

THEIR ROOMS WERE IN THE CENTRAL TOWER OF THE KEEP, ON THE THIRD floor. The route they followed was up a central staircase, to a small landing. The door there led to an interior hallway, with a series of bedrooms along the outside.

Aefric was interested to note that he, Countess Faenella, Sers Beornric and Arcy, and Oswen and Sighild all had their rooms on the same floor.

Aefric's room was a single chamber. Decent bed, without a canopy. A small armoire. A copper basin of water, with soap and towels. One small window, with a view of ruined farmland. A small hearth, near the bed. The page who led Aefric inside got the fire going before leaving, and brought in an additional four full ewers of water.

The room was an insult. That much was obvious. This was not a room for her liege lord. This was a room for a knight, a ler, or perhaps the children of nobles, such as Oswen and Sighild. But even then, there should have been the offer of a servant. Or at least the offer of a bathtub.

All right. Aefric stopped to check the tally.

The baroness took insult that Aefric had insisted on his soldiers coming in. Aefric had taken insult that they were to be left outside.

The baroness had taken insult at Aefric's questioning her hospitality. So, in response, he was given this room?

All right. Aefric could raise this issue at dinner. Could call her on her insult. But the truth was, he'd slept in much worse conditions over the years.

Besides, if he ignored the insult, he stole its power.

So Aefric whistled loudly enough that anyone listening in would be sure to hear him, as he stripped down and washed the day's travel from his body. He considered changing his clothes, but he'd only brought so many, and he'd forgotten to get them washed in Norra.

So he cheated.

As part of every apprenticeship, young would-be wizards are

expected to do a great deal of cleaning. Every day. Washing tubes and alembics, sweeping and dusting, and generally doing whatever servant work the wizard wants to assign them. Which is often so much that it threatens their studies.

There's a purpose to it, though.

Every apprentice, somewhere along the line, figures out little spells to aid in the cleaning. Often these are the first spells they figure out on their own, which is the whole point of the exercise.

Aefric, properly speaking, was no wizard. But he'd been through the training, and he'd figured out his own version of various cleaning spells.

When he had time, he cleaned himself with water because he liked the feel of the scrubbing. But when it came to dusting, sweeping and such, he vastly preferred magic.

So Aefric went back to his first petty spells right then to clean all the clothes he carried.

Of course, this meant that he could change for dinner, if he felt like it.

But he would not, he decided. Let the baroness notice that his clothes were now clean. This would either make her wonder, or it would remind her that he was a noble who commanded his own magic.

While she, so far as Aefric had seen, had no wizard in her court. Why was that, he wondered? True, wizards were far from common enough to accommodate every noble who wanted one at court.

On the other hand, Norra kept a wizard. What did it say that Norra did and Felspark did not? Assuming Felspark lacked a wizard, and that their wizard was not simply elsewhere...

Merrek, perhaps?

Was that what the baroness had meant by pointing out that Felspark had once been part of Fyr? Was she trying to reform that connection through the family that had once ruled that lost principality? The Fyrenn family? Perhaps through Duchess Ashling of Merrek?

Aefric needed to discuss this. With Countess Faenella. And likely with the knights as well. Ser Beornric knew Armyr in ways he did not.

In fact, Aefric had just finished cleaning himself and dressing — with every intention of summoning those three to his room — when the knock came.

Dinner was ready and waiting.

Aefric wasn't the only one who felt rushed. Oswen and Sighild grumbled that they'd barely had time to wash, let alone change or fix their hair. Even the knights grumbled about not having time to care for their armor.

Ser Beornric had changed into breeches of dark gray, and a fine, tunic-style shirt of canary yellow. Ser Arcy wore breeches of a similar cut and color, though the shirt she'd chosen to go with them was the dark color of rich loam.

Faenella, alone, seemed to have had enough time to prepare herself. She'd even donned the first dress Aefric had seen her wear since his installation — a simple, but flattering gown of a vibrant brown that complimented her eyes, worn with a belt of woven strands of gold. She still wore her boots, but the dress almost hid that fact.

She raised an eyebrow at Aefric's trademark staff.

"Your grace," she said, "are you certain it's wise to bring a weapon to dinner?"

He realized then that — likely apart from concealed daggers — none of the others were armed. Not even the knights. He'd left his own sword in his room, but the Brightstaff...

Aefric frowned, but shook his head.

"Consider it an affectation of the new duke," he said. "I am Aefric Brightstaff, and the Brightstaff goes everywhere with me."

"And the wand?"

"A gift from his majesty, and likely a conversation piece. After all. They seem to love their history here in Felspark, and this wand has history." He held up his left hand, where the emerald glinted on the fancy ring given him by the queen. "As, I suspect, does this ring."

"Your grace knows best, I'm sure," Countess Faenella said, and Aefric heard something in her tone he didn't like.

"Faenella," he said softly. "Don't start hiding behind our roles now. I value your opinion too much."

"The staff, you might get away with, without insulting her. I haven't seen you go anywhere without it, and I'll happily tell her so."

Aefric nodded.

"But that wand," she continued softly. "How did the king's great great grandfather use that wand? Could he have used it against the Fyrenns? I don't know about you, but I'm not certain when the principality of Fyr became part of Armyr, and if that wand was involved…"

Aefric blinked. "Good point. And thank you for your counsel."

He made the pages wait while he put the wand away, and affixed a spell-lock to his door. Just in case.

Oswen and Sighild took the delay as an opportunity to fix something in their dresses, though for the life of him Aefric couldn't tell what had changed.

Not that he would admit that.

"All right," he said instead to the lead page, "take us to dinner."

Dinner in Tafarac that night wasn't held in the great hall of the baroness' castle.

Instead, Aefric and his party were guided away from the main hall and to a side room on the first floor. A room near enough to the kitchen that savory smells made the walk down those stairs worthwhile.

The dining room was small, considering its purpose. No more than ten feet across and perhaps twenty long, with a fire blazing in a hearth at one end. Mats woven from rushes covered the floor, with sweet herbs woven into them and likely strewn underneath them.

The dining table was of a dark wood, and looked to be as old as the keep, though kept polished to a sheen. It was rectangular, with carvings of scenes from great feasts along its edging.

A dozen fat, white beeswax pillar candles lit the room, stationed two by two along the center of the table.

It was set for eight, with antique, chased silver plates, goblets and utensils.

The eight chairs matched the table, and were high-backed, with arms, and cushions.

Aefric was amused to note that the size of the room made the presence of his guards impractical. They'd be constantly in the servants' way. So Aefric stationed two of them just outside each of the two doors that led into the room.

One of those doors undoubtedly led to the kitchen, but that was fine. Threats could come from anywhere, after all, and if he happened to have guards watching the preparation of food and drinks, so much the better.

Pages led the diners to their seats along the long sides of the table, with Aefric seated across from Countess Faenella, the two knights facing each other in the middle, and Oswen and Sighild facing each other. This left the head and foot of the table empty, waiting for their hostess and final guest.

They were not kept waiting long, at least. Aefric and his party had done little more than settle into their seats and begin to study the antique tapestries of hunting scenes on the walls before a herald announced the baroness and her brother.

The baroness took the head of the table, nearest Aefric and Faenella, and her brother took the foot.

Both had changed for dinner. The baroness wore a shimmering gown of ruby red and lemon yellow, those colors being woven together in a complex design that left one shoulder bare. Her blonde hair was woven into braids and studded with diamonds.

The ler dressed to match her, in pants of ruby red and a shirt of lemon yellow. Though his shirt again favored lace and frills, and was open just far enough down his chest to hint at his chest hair.

Ler Ordnoth, Aefric noted, wore his sword to dinner on his cloth-of-gold sash. That made Aefric feel a little better about having the Brightstaff standing beside him while he ate.

Baroness Blaewyn took note of the Brightstaff, but contented herself with a shake of the head, rather than words.

Once she was seated, Aefric took the baroness' hand and kissed it, which she accepted stoically.

"Thank you, your lordship, for your hospitality," he said, still holding her hand. "It is easy to be generous to those you like. Generosity to strangers, and to those ... one has reason to distrust, that is not so easy."

"So," she said, as Aefric released her hand, "your grace admits I have reason to distrust him."

"I understand why you believe you have reason," Aefric said. "I have lived my life as an adventurer. No doubt you expect me to make a capricious duke. Rash, and caring more about personal glory than responsibility."

The first course of their meal was brought in then. A simple salad of mixed green and red lettuces, with sliced vegetables. It was paired with a light white wine, so thin it was almost water.

Once the servers were gone, and the diners had begun to eat, the baroness responded.

"I will not deny that the thought has crossed my mind." She nodded to the Brightstaff. "Your grace certainly does not shy away from flaunting his powerful magic weapon."

"The staff has been by my side since I earned it," he said, and told the tale then.

It was a tale none of the others had heard. Aefric found that the whole of the table was listening as he recounted the battle against that famous lich, Nez'karak, and the events that had led to his gaining the Brightstaff.

"I have not been separated from it since," he said. "It has served me many ways over the years, and it has preserved my life — and the lives of others — when hope otherwise seemed lost. It is no mere weapon. It is a symbol of hope, and power, and light in the darkness."

"You speak well, your grace," the baroness conceded. "But surely you must see that it is still a weapon. And by carrying it with you into my dining hall, how am I to see it as anything other than a threat?"

"It threatens only my enemies," he said. "Are you my enemy, your lordship?"

"How am I to judge that, your grace?" she asked, eyebrows raised. "You *speak* well, but your *actions* have laid waste to my lands. Is that not the deed of an enemy?"

"I did not burn your towns and farms," Aefric said. "I did not scatter salt among your fields. I was one of those *opposing* the borog armies of the Flayer, and doing my best to stop them."

"And yet—"

"I laid my life on the line," Aefric said, cutting off her rejoinder and inadvertently silencing the rest of the table's conversation. "I did so over and over during the Godswalk Wars. I did so for people I did not know, in lands that were not my own. I did so because I had the power to make a difference, and it was the right thing to do."

He leaned a little closer to the baroness.

"I could not save every life. Every farm. Every town. But I tried. And I saved as many as I could. *I am not your enemy.* Not unless you *make me* your enemy. And before you do, you might ask the borogs how well that worked out for them."

The baroness sat back, paling slightly. At the other end of the table, her brother leapt on the opening to tell a long, involved story about a four-day hunt for a boar that turned out to have a magic tusk.

The baroness did not speak again through the salad course. Aefric considered drawing her out, but she seemed to be considering something, so he gave her room to think.

And as he did, he considered his own coming conversational sallies.

THE FIRE ROARING BEHIND THE BARONESS KEPT THE SMALL DINING ROOM pleasantly warm. Down the table, Aefric could hear Ler Ordnoth either boring or enthralling Oswen and Sighild with another of his stories.

The two young noblewomen certainly looked interested in the

ler's story, but that might simply have been the result of good training.

In the center of the table, the two knights, Beornric and Arcy, held a hushed conversation intended for their own ears.

The baroness kept her own counsel for a time. Possibly considering what Aefric had said already. Hopefully coming to agreement.

For his own part, Aefric, through the soup course — a creamy soup, featuring mushrooms and fennel — spoke with Countess Faenella about what she'd done during the Godswalk Wars. She told a story about holding back the borog army at the town of Kidell, in Merrek, and her time spent healing the wounded after the battle.

During the main course — roast loin of boar, served with a spiced potato medley, two kinds of cheese, and a rich red wine — the baroness finally broke her silence.

"Words come easily to you, your grace," she said. "But I cannot know the truth of why you fought in the Godswalk Wars. You spoke of risking your life, but how can I know that you risked your life for others, and not your personal glory? Certainly, you have not refused the king's reward, so how am I to believe that you did what you did for any reason other than reward? How can I trust that you are anything more than a mercenary?"

Aefric was about to answer that, but she said, "Please, your grace."

He nodded.

"We have lost many lives, here in Felspark. And with them we have lost farmland, livestock, and more. We may be facing famine, come wintertime. Now, Felspark is far from alone in its suffering. I know that. Though as *my* responsibility, Felspark takes precedence in my mind. Which is as it should be."

She nodded to the Brightstaff, where it stood beside Aefric.

"You are an adventurer, your grace. By your own admission. And when the Godswalk Wars came, perhaps you did more good than harm, fighting back the forces of the Flayer. And likely fighting other evils besides."

She shook her head slowly.

"But now is not the time for adventurers. Not here in Armyr. Now is the time for nobles. Now is the time for those of us who understand what it means to rule. Who understand how to make the hard decisions. Who understand how to guide our people back from the horrors of war to prosperity."

The baroness gave Aefric a pointed look.

"I am the sixteenth Ol'Felruun to sit the baronial seat of Felspark. You are an adventurer, named for a deed and an object of power. How am I to answer to you at a time like this?"

Aefric considered that through a long bite of boar meat. Meanwhile, conversation around the table had stopped. Even Ler Ordnoth was watching Aefric. Waiting for his response.

He swallowed his bite of boar. Washed it down with a sip of wine.

Then he turned back to the baroness.

"I could give you an answer," Aefric said. "But the truth is, words will not alleviate your concerns. Only deeds will. And there are no deeds I can perform here and now that would prove that I am the right man to steer Felspark — and all of Deepwater — out of this crisis."

"There is one," she said quickly. "Forgo insisting on my oaths of vassalage. Let me withhold them until you prove yourself a man worthy to be called my liege lord."

"Your lordship did not let me finish," he said quietly. Now none of the other diners were even eating. They were too busy watching.

The baroness' lips compressed into a pale line, but she nodded.

"There are no deeds I could perform here and now. But there are two deeds I will point to that have already taken place. I would like Countess Faenella to speak on one of them, and then I will explain the other."

The baroness frowned, and narrowed her eyes in suspicion, but nodded.

"Your excellency, will you tell her lordship about how I addressed the request for aid I received from Norra?"

Aefric knew he was taking a chance here. From the way the baroness had been talking, Felspark might be in league with Merrek.

With that in mind, he sucked in a slow, deep breath then, hoping that Faenella would withhold the portion about the investigator. Just in case.

She didn't.

She explained the problems Norra was having with Motte and with bandits around Kerrik Forest and their quarries — without explicitly blaming Motte for the banditry. She told how Aefric had committed soldiers to aiding with her problems. And she did explain that Aefric had commissioned a special investigator to see about the source of those problems.

Faenella didn't mention or even allude to Merrek, at least. She withheld concerns about a possible need to investigate her own borders. And most important, she didn't mention that she herself was to be the special investigator.

Small victories, but better than the alternative.

"A fair solution, your grace," the baroness admitted, "though hardly an example of the kind of hard decision I was speaking of."

Before she could continue, Aefric raised his hand.

"I mentioned I had a second action to point out?"

The baroness nodded.

"The second action is not one I performed, but it is relevant." He leaned a little closer. The only sound was the fire crackling in the hearth.

"King Colm Stronghand considered his list of candidates, and selected *me* to be the new duke of Deepwater." He held up the emerald ring on his left hand. "And he was not alone in choosing me. Queen Eppida Fyrenn swore the liege-lord portion of the oaths of vassalage right along with him, and gave me this ring herself."

He gave the baroness a moment to study his emerald ring, while he hoped that the queen's last name would help his cause here. The Fyrenns were a family even older than the Ol'Felruuns.

Of course, he was stretching the truth by claiming that the king had his queen's full support in selecting Aefric for the duchy. He didn't really know that. But he had the impression from a few things said by Nyorngyth that her participation in the oaths was unusual.

And considering she personally gave him both the ring and his horse, he felt confident that she had at least some faith in him.

"The king and queen of Armyr say I'm the one to lead Deepwater, its lands and its people, out of these dark times. Who are you, baroness, to gainsay them?"

The baroness opened her mouth to say something, then closed it again.

Aefric leapt on his advantage.

"With this in mind, I trust that your lordship will raise no further objections to swearing the oaths of vassalage after dinner?"

Silence fell on the small dining hall in the castle at Tafarac. A silence so strong that Aefric felt it physically. Later he would swear that even the fire that roared in the hearth behind the baroness had given up roaring and crackling for a time.

Aefric would not break that silence. He stared at Baroness Blaewyn, waiting for the only answer she could legally give.

She had no legitimate reason to refuse him the oaths of vassalage. As a noble sired by a line of nobles, she had to know that. And now he had left no room for doubt that he knew it as well.

Countess Faenella watched Aefric and the baroness in that heavy moment of silence. Nor was she alone. Sers Beornric and Arcy, ladies-in-waiting Oswen and Sighild, and even Ler Ordnoth all watched during that eternal moment.

But it wasn't Baroness Blaewyn who broke the silence. It was her brother.

Ler Ordnoth said, "I find myself reminded of the time a silence dragon came to Felspark. It was not during my own lifetime, of course, but during the rein of King Colm's grandfather King Cainu..."

He launched into full storytelling mode then, and as he did, the world seemed to right itself. The fire resumed its roaring and crackling. The knights returned to their low-voiced private conversation.

And servants cleared the remains of the main course and began serving a small plate of river trout.

Each diner was brought a small antique plate of chased silver, on which sat three small bits of grilled and seasoned river trout, shaped into the Felspark stars. Along with the trout were brought small, two-tined forks.

Aefric, unaccustomed to a course between the main and the dessert, frowned in puzzlement.

"The river trout is served with every formal baronial meal in Felspark," the baroness said. "Trout, because that is the fish that sustained our people during the ancient war between Fyr and Arm, the two principalities that once ruled all these lands. They are shaped into stars to commemorate the three great discoveries of star iron in the river valley. All three were discovered in Ol'Felruun land. Though when they were discovered we still called ourselves Ol'Shasstyr."

She speared one star on her fork and held it up between herself and Aefric.

"Would your grace care to guess the name of the man who discovered those deposits?"

"Felruun Ol'Shasstyr?"

"Precisely," she said, eating that star of trout. Aefric tried his own, and found that the dill spices made the fish quite bitter.

"Served bitter," she said, as Aefric winced at the strength of the dill, "to remind us of the blood spilled in our ascent to the lordship of Felspark."

Aefric nodded, and sipped some of the rich red wine to dilute the dill taste.

"So you see, your grace," she said. "When I say we old families of this region have long memories, I do not only mean of the happy times. We remember the good and the bad. The blood we spilled and the blood we shed. We remember every wrong done us. But we remember every right as well.

"Do you understand me, your grace?"

"I believe so," Aefric said. "You are warning me that the blame you lay at my feet for the evils committed by the borogs during the Godswalk Wars will be held against my grandchildren."

"Yes," she said, with a nod. "That is true. Though if it reassures your grace, we hold even more blame for the borogs. But it also means that the good you do us, should you do us any, will be remembered just as long. And just as vividly. Do you have the stomach for that, your grace?"

Aefric looked her in the eye and ate both his remaining pieces of trout without wincing or turning to his wine. He ate them slowly, savoring the bitter taste. And he gave himself no time between them. No sooner was the first swallowed, then the second was on his fork and entering his mouth.

The baroness nodded, and ate her own trout stars just as slowly. Possibly even slower. And she held Aefric's eye the entire time.

The countess, upon hearing the story behind the trout course, seemed to treat that part of the meal as holy. She closed her eyes, said a small prayer, and ate all three stars every bit as slowly as Aefric had. Not seeking relief from her wine. Not giving herself a break between bites.

While she was busy with that, the knights with their conversation, and the others with the tales of Ler Ordnoth, the baroness spoke softly to Aefric.

"You understand, your grace, that you put me in a difficult position. You are requiring me to swear oaths under duress, and that is no proper way to swear an oath."

"I understand that you are trying to convince me of that," Aefric said, just as quietly. "But we both know the truth of the matter. Your barony is part of the duchy of Deepwater. You owe your fealty to the title, not the man. That you say you distrust me does not give you an excuse to abrogate your leal duties."

The baroness had a rejoinder ready, but Aefric stilled her with a gesture. And since neither of them wanted to raise their voices and draw attention, she nodded for him to continue.

"There are two compelling reasons for you to swear the oaths, and only one reason I can think of not to."

He raised one finger from the table.

"First, as I have established, it is your obligation. And you know I must enforce that obligation, or I will lose control of the duchy. The king and queen have put their trust in me. I will not betray that trust."

He raised a second finger.

"Second, withholding your oaths is shortsighted. The oaths are not one-way. Without the oaths, you would lose access to my protection and my aid, both of which were considerable when I was just an adventurer. Now that I am a duke, they are worth all the more."

Aefric closed his fist.

"And the only reason I can think of for you to refuse me the oaths is if you hope to sever your ties to Deepwater, and seek either independence, or to affiliate yourself with Merrek."

The baroness steepled her fingers and narrowed her eyes at Aefric, while her nostrils flared in a long, slow breath.

"You said you were not a general, your grace."

"I have never served as one. But no adventurer survives long without learning a thing or two about strategy and tactics."

"Very well, then," she said. "Let me ask you this. Have you the stomach for war?"

"I've fought—"

"Not as a warrior, your grace," she said smoothly. "As a general. Have you the stomach to send others to face death in your name?"

Aefric pondered that, and didn't enjoy the heavy way his heart pounded at the thought.

"It is not the first solution I would seek," he said. "But if it becomes necessary, yes." He nodded. "I would."

"Are you certain, your grace? We have just finished the Godswalk Wars. The lands are torn. The people are tired and grieving. None of your people will want war. They will want you to settle. To negotiate. To yield some to preserve peace for all. Can you stand up to your advisers? Your nobles? Your tired troops? Can you stare them down and say, 'We will fight, because our cause is righteous?' and hold to those words?"

She spoke with such intensity. Aefric felt each and every word physically. As though she were jabbing hooks into his flesh and trying to fish the truth out of him.

Aefric stared deeply into her eyes, so dark a blue, yet sparkling reflected gold in the candlelight.

"I would say those words. And I would lead my troops into battle myself."

"Even if the cause is a small strip of land in the least of your baronies?"

"Those who steal from my vassals steal from me. I will not stand for it."

The baroness nodded. She turned and looked up at a servant who had been waiting beside the door. She tapped her forehead.

Servants brought in dessert then. And what a dessert it was. A light, flaky pastry, filled with melted chocolate.

Oh, chocolate. Aefric hadn't tasted it in ages. His most recent memory of it was Keifer's, and that chocolate was mass-produced and sad by comparison.

The chocolate in this dish was rich, dark, and robust, and the pastry around it was light and flaky.

A more comfortable silence fell over the conversation then, broken only by the fire, and by the sounds of pleasure from the diners.

Further, Aefric noted something as the dessert was served. Ler Ordnoth's eyes had rounded and he looked a question at the baroness, who responded only with a slight nod.

The ler looked astonished to see that nod.

When dessert was finished, and all proper compliments on the dinner — especially that dessert — had been given, the baroness stood.

"Your grace," she said, "I believe it is time for me to swear my oaths of vassalage." She turned a smile on the others present. "Will you all consent to stand witness?"

Not one of them objected, not even the ler.

BY THE TIME AEFRIC WAS DONE RECEIVING BARONESS BLAEWYN'S OATHS of vassalage, and swearing his own liege-lord oaths in return, he was more than ready to climb those stairs again and go to bed.

And he was not alone in this. Only the two knights actually yawned, but the countess and both her ladies-in-waiting looked almost ready to fall asleep there at the dinner table.

Even Ler Ordnoth seemed to have tired of speaking, which had to have been nigh unto a miracle.

Nevertheless, before he was allowed to follow a page out of the dining room and up the stairs to his bed, the baroness took Aefric aside for a moment.

"Your grace," she said, and for the first time she made the title sound more sincere than sarcastic. "As you might have guessed from our dinner discussion, Felspark is troubled by more than the aftermath of war."

"I suspected as much," he said. "Do you wish to discuss these troubles now?"

"Breakfast will be soon enough, your grace," she said. "So long as you are willing to delay your departure for our conversation."

"Of course," Aefric said, and managed a tired smile. "Duty must come first."

"Just so, your grace," she said.

He kissed her hand then and they said their goodnights.

Aefric renewed the spell-lock on his door that night, just in case.

He slept hard and heavy, with dreams of blood and warfare, and the baroness' voice saying, "Nobility is forged in blood and war. Have you the stomach for that?"

The knock that jolted him awake in the morning was most welcome.

Aefric hurried through is ablutions, and dressed for the road in his leather pants and the forest green shirt that buttoned all the way up the front. He wore his wand and sword on his belt again, and carried the Brightstaff and his backpack.

Thus attired, he allowed a page to lead him to breakfast. He was starting to feel a little silly about letting four armed guards accompany him, but he could just imagine the complaints from Ser Beornric if he sent them away. So he allowed their presence as he followed the page down the stairs to the first floor up in the central tower, above the main keep.

When they reached the dining room, he indicated with a gesture that his guards were to take their positions without.

This room was an even smaller dining room than he'd seen the night before.

It was little more than a breakfast nook, really, with a small, round wooden table set for two places. Along the two outer walls, four large casements stood open, bringing in fresh spring air along with a view of farms that either hadn't been harmed by the wars, or had been among the first restored.

The baroness was seated and waiting when he entered. She wore a white gown that morning, covered in elaborate embroidery done in golden thread. She wore her hair down, and around her neck a thick gold chain studded with three diamonds.

As Aefric set down his backpack, the baroness arched an eyebrow. "Your grace really must allow the servants to do *some* work for him."

"I've been carrying that backpack so long I only notice it by its absence."

"Nevertheless," she said, with a little less humor in her voice. "You are a noble now, your grace, and should allow others to carry such things for you. As nobles, everyone pays attention to how we conduct ourselves. The more you present yourself as an adventurer, the less they will regard you as a duke."

Aefric frowned and was about to reply, but she smiled and held up a hand in surrender. "Merely a point to consider. You did mention that my counsel might have some value, your grace."

"Fair enough," he said with a chuckle. "And I will take your words under advisement."

"All I would ask."

The servants brought in their breakfast then. A medley of sliced melons, along with honeyed oat bread and slices of sharp cheese. To drink with breakfast, as in Norra, they served water.

And as in Norra, serious subjects had to wait until the fast was broken. Until they finished, the baroness spoke only of the age of the farms, the quality of the grains and green beans they grew, and similar such things.

After the servants cleared away the breakfast dishes, leaving only their goblets of water and a pitcher for more, Aefric spoke first.

"You said something of troubles to discuss, your lordship."

"I did, your grace," she said with a nod. "And thank you for hearing me." She drew a deep breath and let it out quickly. "Your grace, Merrek has been withholding trade from us. I have sent my court wizard, Shaela Ol'Teruun, to negotiate with them in an attempt to make them see reason, but to no avail."

"When did they start withholding trade?"

"Three aetts ago," she said. "When it became clear that we were continuing the trade route up the river into Norra, as we have done for time out of mind."

Aefric sighed.

"Indeed, your grace," she said. "Since the wars' end, Merrek has been pressuring us to cut Norra off from trade. And given us no good reason except the continuance of our own trade."

"And your wizard has had no success in negotiations?"

"No, your grace, and worse." The baroness grimaced. "She overheard a conversation that implied that the duchess is after the Fyrsa River Valley. That would give her the river, along with our most valuable mines, including our star iron. And if she takes that, she'll take the lands south of it as well. More than half my barony, most of my money, trade, and right now most of my food."

"You aren't the only one being pressured by Merrek."

"I didn't think I was, your grace," she said frankly. Apparently she'd heard more in Countess Faenella's words last night than Aefric suspected. "Worse, I have not heard from Shaela since that last report, over an aett ago."

"This was why you were worried about war, then," Aefric said with a grimace.

"Of the three duchies in Armyr, Merrek's land was least harmed by the Godswalk Wars, your grace. And the Fyrenn family memory goes back a very long time."

"All right," Aefric said. "I can't act on this from here. But I assure you now that I will act as soon as I can." He looked her deeply in the eyes. "And I will not yield your lands to Merrek. If Merrek wants a fight, I'll give it to them."

The baroness took Aefric's hand and pressed her forehead to his knuckles.

"Thank you, your grace."

"This does press my timetable a little, so I'll need to send a few rika birds before I leave."

"Of course, your grace," she said, and called for paper and pen.

Aefric wrote three messages. One to the baron of Riverbreak, one to the baron of Havenford, and one to the count of Goldenfall. He invited each to his castle at Behal — at the southern tip of Lake Deepwater — to report on the state of their lands, and to swear vassalage to their new duke.

All three birds should deliver their messages that day. If all three lords left first thing tomorrow, they would all arrive at Behal before sunset. Or at least during the evening, in Havenford's case.

If they delayed — which at least Goldenfall was likely to do — who could say?

Frustrating. Aefric really wanted to get to Water's End. Establish himself in the ducal seat, before he began taking on his heavier duty load.

Now, with Merrek pressing, he had no choice but to get things in motion as soon as possible.

That meant Water's End would have to wait. He'd settle for working out of Behal for the time being.

Assuming, of course, it had survived the war well enough to keep a roof over his head.

8

———————

Aefric was pleased to see that the rains had passed overnight without his noticing. The morning air was sweetly fragrant from the rain, and the spring skies above were clear, warm, and inviting.

If he had to be in a hurry, at least it was a good day to be riding.

To Aefric's surprise, when his party rode out past the gates of the castle at Tafarac that day, they did so to a fanfare blown by a dozen trumpeters.

The citizens of the upper, and older, part of the town took surprise at this, but were quick to cheer and cry praise to Aefric in a way they'd very much *not* done during his ride in the day before.

Little by little, it seemed, he was winning over the people of his duchy. Or at least the nobles. He was three for four so far, and he had ideas about how he might bring Motte into the fold without violence or undue pressure.

Goldenfall was still a question mark, as were the baronies of Riverbreak and Havenford. But Aefric would see about all three of those soon enough.

At least he'd had a look at some of Goldenfall, and he'd get a look at some of Riverbreak that day. Havenford, unfortunately, was well away south and west from the Kingsroad. The only vassal territory he would not see on this journey.

He'd have to make time for a visit. When he could.

He hadn't even claimed his ducal seat yet, but he already felt embroiled heavily in the politics of his new role. The interplay of his vassals. The pressure of Merrek. And what was Duke Wylyn of Silverlake doing during all this?

The part of him that was Keifer felt more than a little overwhelmed.

For so long, he'd coasted along the edges of the world. And yet here he was, in a different world entirely, but thrusting himself into the middle of problems, forming alliances and making enemies.

As Aefric, he was familiar with all these things, but in a very different way. As an adventurer, his allies and enemies, his dealing with problems, that had all been largely on a personal level. A smaller level.

As a duke, everything was already so much more complicated.

With that in mind, he shared with Countess Faenella and the two knights what the Baroness Blaewyn had told him.

"I can't believe Merrek wants another war already," Ser Beornric said.

"I'm not yet sure she does," Countess Faenella said. "I'll still want to find proof in my investigation, your grace."

"Of course," Aefric said.

And then, for the first time when discussing larger matters, Ser Arcy spoke up.

"More like she's counting on everyone else *not* wanting war," she said. "Might be she'll back down if challenged."

"Or she might be after a wedding," Ser Beornric said.

That stilled the conversation for a moment. Aefric could hear strains of the discussion between Oswen and Sighild about whether or not Ler Ordnoth could beat Aefric in a duel with swords.

"Think on it this way," Ser Beornric said. "Ashling's family once held all of Merrek and a good part of Deepwater. She holds Merrek now. If she marries you, your grace, she brings Deepwater back into her family line as well."

"No she doesn't," Sighild said, loudly. She looked pale at drawing so much attention, but Oswen smiled widely and encouraged her to go on.

"You are considered the senior duke, your grace, by right of the size of your holdings." Sighild's words came slowly, as though to keep them steady on her tongue. "If she marries you, your firstborn child together would be named Brightstaff, and inherit your duchy. Your secondborn would be named Fyrenn and inherit hers."

"Which means," Ser Beornric said, darkly, "that the only thing standing between her family and your duchy would be that firstborn."

They all let the implications there sink in as they rode along.

"Whatever her plans," Aefric said at last. "We need all the information we can gather. She's been planning this for a while, and I have a great deal of catching up to do."

"With that in mind, your grace," the countess said, "I think it's best I leave you at the Haven. I'd hoped to accompany you to Deepwater and see Water's End, but time presses. I'll take the river down to my county seat. Establish myself. Make contact with my old traveling companions, and get straight to my duties."

"Yes," Aefric said with a sigh, "I suppose that's best." He'd miss her counsel, but this wasn't the time to say so. She had too much to do, and he would need her information too much.

"I'll have to linger a day or two at Behal, anyway," he continued. "I've summoned Havenford, Riverbreak and Goldenfall to report to me there and swear their oaths."

"The castle at Behal is lovely," Oswen said. "We stayed a night there on our way to Armityr."

"It's intact then," Aefric said, feeling something unknotting in his shoulders. "Good. I knew it was on the map, but so were at least five other towns along the Kingsroad that are no longer standing."

"From what I was told by the castellan, Ser Grey," Oswen said, "the town suffered little and the castle itself wasn't touched."

"Better and better," Aefric said. "Thank you." He turned to Faenella. "Send me a rika when you leave to begin your investigations. After that, I'll contact you nightly for updates."

"Yes, your grace," she said.

"With these things in mind," Aefric said, "we need to make Behal today. So we'll need to push the pace a little. And take fewer, shorter breaks."

"I'll send word back along the line, your grace," Ser Beornric said.

They rode a little faster then, through the bright morning sunshine. With more of them falling into their own reveries and thoughts, until Nyorngyth rode up.

"Why the hurry, your grace?" he asked. "Tis a fine day for a ride. Should we not enjoy it as a blessing from Ulna?"

"Would that I could," Aefric said with a smile at the priest's enthusiasm. "Unfortunately, matters are pressing, and I need to cover more ground today. If this means we must leave you behind, we'll miss your company, but I'll understand."

"No need for that, your grace," Nyorngyth said. "Ulna blesses those who ride with speed when they need it."

He fell back behind into his place in the party then, and Aefric thought about that as they rode.

Ulna would bless speed, as well as blessing those who took their time. So long as they had a reason for the one. Did they need a reason for the other?

Alas, though, such simple thoughts were not his for the dwelling that day. His mind turned to thoughts of Motte, Norra, Felspark, and the role of Merrek in the problems of each.

And perhaps the greatest question of all — where did Goldenfall fit into all this?

They were not riding long before they reached the border between Felspark and Riverbreak. It was marked not by a river or some other obvious land feature, but by a series of marking stones.

The first of these was more than a marking stone. It was a tribute. It stood beside the Kingsroad itself, an obsidian obelisk standing about twice Aefric's height. The face of a thin but determined man was carved on the road-facing side. A story was carved below the face.

In the sixth year of the reign of Queen Ceridwyn, Karmak Ol'Duin was given claim to the lands south of the Kingsroad and east of the Haven, for so far as he could run without stopping.

He ran day and night for two days.

Here, he fell. Exhausted, but newly named Baron of Riverbreak.

That was the last thing Aefric remembered noticing on the first leg of their ride that day. The day was hotter, without the rain chasing them.

Heat and sweat and dirt darkened his train of thought.

Goldenfall. There'd been no word yet about Goldenfall. What did that mean?

If Goldenfall was coordinating with Motte, and Motte was working with Merrek, then it seemed to Aefric that Goldenfall might be applying pressure to Riverbreak. They were neighbors. They shared the Kingsroad, as well as river traffic. With Merrek pushing up from the south, it made sense that Goldenfall might — as Motte did — push down from the north.

The three baronies squeezed between greater powers. Unless their duke protected them.

That was, presuming that Riverbreak wasn't in league with Goldenfall, and working against Felspark and Norra. And perhaps against Fyretti, too. Why not?

And here, Aefric was riding to Behal. A pinch point between Riverbreak and Goldenfall. With every possibility that he was riding into an ambush.

An ambush. With fewer than forty soldiers standing by him. And a small train of non-combatants who'd need protection.

Not encouraging.

But sometimes the only way out was through. And if his new enemies were making their plans, they might not have counted on him speeding his pace today. In fact, he might be outmaneuvering *all* his enemies this—

"Soldiers, your grace," Ser Beornric said. "Coming from the west.

More than a hundred. Possibly two. Supporting more than a dozen mounted knights."

Then again, maybe the trap was coming to him.

***

SCOUTS HAD TRAILED AEFRIC EVER SINCE THE KERRIK FOREST. A SCOUT had been riding somewhere behind them today as well, keeping an eye on his progress.

And now that that he was well clear of Tafarac and support. Now that he and his party of no more than forty capable fighters were alone and isolated out on the Kingsroad, with no sign of support anywhere around.

Now, soldiers approached.

Now, more than a *hundred* soldiers. Possibly twice that number. Plus a dozen mounted knights.

Was Goldenfall making his move at last?

"All right," Aefric said with a sigh. He took in his surroundings with a glance.

It was almost highsun. The morning had melted away while he had ruminated on his problems.

Forest to his left, on the Riverbreak side.

Possibilities?

No. If the enemy was picking this spot for their attack, then they probably had archers in the wood. Or at least more infantry.

To his right, the Goldenfall side ... not much. Not nearby. There was a newly built hamlet in the distance behind him. Maybe a dozen miles back.

Apart from that, some work crews off to the north. Likely surveyors, taking in the state of the land.

He could see the oncoming soldiers now, in the distance. Too far away to see their banners and pennants yet, but they were kicking up a lot of dust. Especially considering the recent rains that had come through.

"All right," he said a little louder. "We'll have to make a stand here. I want the carts and—"

A trumpeter from the distant soldiers blew a series of notes.

"The prince!" Ser Beornric yelled, and the smile lighting up his face shone out through his voice. "The prince approaches!"

"Well," Aefric said, allowing himself a deep breath that lurched his speeding heart down to a more reasonable pace.

Hadn't even realized how his heart had sped. Or how he'd started sweating.

No. He'd been sweating because of the heat.

That was his story, and he was sticking to it.

"Well," he said, louder this time, "then let us ride to meet him."

The whole of his party gave a cheer then, and rode out to meet their prince.

As the distance closed, Aefric could see there were more people riding horses than just the knights.

Then he could see the banners. His own, flown highest. Below it flew the prince's personal banner: crossed swords of gold, points high, on a field of forest green.

Then the prince was close enough to be seen properly, and both Oswen and Sighild sighed at the sight of him. And unless Aefric was mistaken, Countess Faenella might have been stifling a sigh as well.

And Aefric could understand the reaction. Prince Killian had his father's rugged good looks to go with his youthful vigor and a smile that was downright roguish. His hair was jet black, as was his short, well-trimmed beard.

He was dressed in his gleaming, enameled, full plate armor, though without the helm. As though he were expecting an ambush himself.

He picked Aefric out of the group immediately.

"Ah," he cried, leaping down from his horse and striding closer. "The Hero of Deepwater himself! The great Aefric Brightstaff!"

Aefric turned his head away from the compliment as he slid down from the saddle and moved to meet his prince.

Prince Killian wasn't having the show of humility. No sooner did they reach each other in the middle ground of the Kingsroad than he clasped Aefric's shoulder and gave him a gentle shake.

"Don't do that," he said, smiling and chiding at the same time. "You're a hero, man! Enjoy it! I've never gotten to be a hero. Father barely let me see any action during the wars. Now they're done. Most action I'm like to see in the next decade will be on the tourney grounds."

Aefric couldn't help chuckling.

"It's good to meet you, Prince Killian," he said, offering his hand to be kissed.

"Bah," the prince said, knocking aside Aefric's hand. "Today I'm your regent, not your prince, so if anyone's kissing hands right now, you should be kissing mine."

"I think I'll forgo it," Aefric said, shaking the prince's hand instead.

"Probably a good choice. The kiss might be taken as arrogance by the knights."

"Quite a company you ride with," Aefric said, looking out over the crowd.

"Just following your grace's instructions," Prince Killian said with a slight bow, apparently enjoying his role. He pointed to the groups as he named them, starting with the group of mule-drawn carts.

"There are your builders, to finish that fort out past Kerrik. There are your hundred infantry, to make clear whose fort it is." Killian's eyes twinkled as he smiled at Aefric. "Two dozen mounted infantry to help cover your ride home, in case of ... excessive ambitions from your new vassals."

"The others are yours, I take it?" Aefric asked.

"Of course," he said with a nod. "A dozen knights to see to my royal safety, and a small train of retainers to see to my royal comfort. After all, once I officially turn the duchy over to you, I really ought to head back to Armityr."

"Anything pressing I should know?" Aefric asked.

"From your personal lands," — by which Aefric knew that Killian meant the lands held directly in his name as duke and not through a vassal — "not too much damage from the wars. Except for your coastal towns, farms, and villages. I'm afraid they were almost all destroyed during the wars. Only Ajenmoor remains."

Ajenmoor. Ajenmoor had been the biggest of them, but that still meant that four towns along the coast, along with a number of smaller villages as well as all their people, had been destroyed.

"Well, it's survival is a blessing, at least," Aefric said.

Prince Killian nodded, his expression not quite grim, but respectful of the loss.

"I've been sending scouts up to the Dragonscar, keeping an eye on Silverlake, but I don't think Duke Wylyn's tried anything so far. Likely too busy with his own lands. He and his were hit even harder than you and yours."

"And Merrek?"

"Your vassals are having interesting troubles, but nothing I can tie to her hands," he said, actual irritation flashing in his eyes. "She may be my aunt by law, but if I were in your place I wouldn't trust her. She covets your lands and don't think she doesn't."

"I'm taking steps already," Aefric said, "and I'll have to stop at Behal for a couple of days to get more pieces in motion."

"Thought you might," he said. "I told the castellan to prepare for you."

"Thank you."

Aefric didn't want this conversation to end. It felt so good to just talk to someone as an equal. Without having to play games about who wanted what, much less the constant flow of courtesies and titles.

Aefric knew full well that he could only get away with speaking so plainly to the prince because the prince had already established that he was here, today, as ducal regent. Not prince and royal heir.

That meant that Aefric could afford to be casual. It felt so good he didn't want it to stop.

But he felt that itch of duty. It was a sensation that started along his spine, down below his shoulder blades, and worked its way up.

"Your finances are in decent shape," the prince continued. "You'd be richer right now, but I started spending on repairs. Figured you'd approve."

"I do."

"The rest," Prince Killian said, "is in the report I left you. It's at Water's End, I'm afraid, but you can always send a messenger for it. If you need it immediately."

"I probably will, to be safe."

"One last question."

Aefric raised his eyebrows enquiringly.

Prince Killian leaned a little closer. Lowered his voice.

"That letter you sent me," he said. "It just appeared in my hands. And it remains. No illusion." He shook his head. "I've never heard of magic that can do that. And I suspect my father would pay a great deal for its secret."

"Desperation was its secret," Aefric said, just as softly. "I'm not certain I can replicate what I did that morning, let alone codify and teach the technique."

A half-truth. Aefric knew he could cast that spell again, if needed. But he wasn't sure he could teach even the king's wizard to duplicate it.

"Then that's everything for now." The prince drew himself up tall, but before he could say anything further, Aefric interrupted him.

"There is one more thing, if you would."

Prince Killian raised his eyebrows enquiringly.

"If you don't mind the drag on your speed, perhaps you could travel with my infantry and builders out to the edge of Kerrik?"

Prince Killian smiled. "Oh, may I have the pleasure of informing Motte's people of your decision about the fort?"

"You wouldn't mind? I only ask because I suspect Motte's soldiers will be more ... amenable to hearing it from you than from one of my soldiers."

"Less chance of bloodshed, you mean." He nodded. "I agree. Still can't believe Ferrin had the gall to set up a toll gate without even *asking* me." He shook his head. "This will be my last act in your name, then. Otherwise..."

Prince Killian drew himself up to his full height. Aefric felt a small bit of pleasure that the prince wasn't *quite* as tall as he was.

Still, in that moment something changed in the air between them. Some touch of the casualness of before was gone. Now they had to be formal again.

"In the name of the king, I hereby return the duchy of Deepwater to your charge and care, your grace."

"In the name of the king," Aefric said, "I accept the charge and care of the duchy of Deepwater, and shall endeavor to rule with wisdom and mercy."

Aefric kissed Prince Killian's hand. "As duke to regent, I thank you for your service to my duchy."

Prince Killian kissed Aefric's hand. "As prince to duke, I thank you for your service to the crown."

Prince Killian bowed, then straightened with a big smile and gave Aefric a bear hug.

"Wish I had time to spend with you, your grace. I'd love to hear some of your stories."

"Another time, your highness," Aefric. "To be sure."

Then Prince Killian moved off to introduce himself to the countess and her ladies-in-waiting, while Aefric and Ser Beornric got the soldiers joining their party organized and spread out along the lines.

Then Aefric and Ser Beornric went over to speak to the builders and infantrymen who were heading off to the fort. First about their duties at the fort, and then about coordinating with the baroness' forces to deal with bandits in the forest.

Finally, all the orders had been given and it was time, at last, to get back on the road.

The delay had cost more time than Aefric liked, but it was all to the good.

They were perhaps a half hour further down the road when Aefric learned that Nyorngyth had taken advantage of the pause to make sure the horses were tended to, and that food was distributed down the line.

Aefric laughed with pleasure at that, as he munched on cold roast turkey and apples, with a small chunk of a creamy cheese.

Leave it to a priest of the travel goddess to turn even a delay to their advantage.

Aefric might be riding to troubles both known and suspected. But at least he wasn't riding alone.

SOMETIME LATE THAT AFTERNOON, A BOUNDARY STONE ON THE NORTH side of the road marked the end of Goldenfall and the start of the duke's own lands.

Before long, then, off to the north, glistening in the hot, late afternoon sun, Aefric could see the dark waters of the foot of Lake Deepwater.

Lake Deepwater. Largest lake by far in all of Armyr. Possibly the largest in the western half of Qorunn. More than sixty miles long, and more than thirty miles across, as its widest point. There were those who said it was even deeper than it was long.

Some said it had no bottom at all. That it connected directly to the that plane of existence that undines and other water creatures called home.

Others said the Qorunn was round, and that the Deepwater cut straight through the world and came out a lake on the other side, somewhere. On some island or continent not yet discovered.

Aefric wondered if it would be an abrogation of his ducal duties to see if he could personally find the bottom of that lake...

As he considered that, Aefric spotted the first ducal habitations shortly thereafter. Small fishing villages, along the edge of the lake.

Somewhere along the coastline of that vast lake had been the Battle of Deepwater. Somewhere up the eastern shore...

Truth was, he wasn't entirely sure. At the time, in the heat of the battle, he'd thought that vast body of water was the sea.

Now, though, the sight of so much water brought dreams of a bath. And perhaps a properly cooked meal. He was hot and dirty from the ride, and his clothes itched from sweat.

And that creamy cheese had tasted good at first, but now it soured a little on his tongue, as it lingered. And he was growing tired of cold roast turkey.

The setting sun turned the western sky crimson as they reached Behal.

Behal sat just north of the Kingsroad, where the Haven River flowed out of Lake Deepwater. Across the road sat a forest, with the river cutting through a section of it.

The town of Behal had no wall. Aefric found that interesting, until he realized that there were two warships out on the lake. Apparently, the town had been built where it was to take advantage of the quick drop to deep water.

Those two warships had catapults and ballistae, and looked as though they could cover the Kingsroad and beyond.

He wondered if they could sail the rivers, or if they were lake bound...

Possibly. The Haven River looked quite wide here. A massive stone bridge crossed it, Aefric could tell that much in the distance. But he couldn't see it well enough from where they rode to know if it was a moving bridge, which would allow larger ships to sail the river. Or if only those that could sail under its high arch could sail from the river to the lake.

He hoped they could sail the river.

Otherwise, that meant he had two warships that couldn't leave the lake. Was that a good use of resources? Especially when those fallen coastal towns and villages could have used the protection of two more warships?

Too soon to say. He had to understand why things were the way they were, before he started casting blame.

With that in mind, he continued surveying Behal.

This was the biggest town Aefric had seen so far in Deepwater. Not as big as Armityr, but still large enough that it might be a small city rather than a large town. Though that, he supposed, depended on population.

The town spread to both sides of the river, on the north side of the Kingsroad. It didn't cross the road on the east side of the river. That would have taken the town into Riverbreak land. But it looked as though it was preparing to expand across the Kingsroad on the west side of the river.

They'd already cleared the forest out a few hundred yards that direction, and had the logs stacked. Perhaps in anticipation of expansion. Though Aefric wondered how practical that would be, given that...

They were making room for refugees from the coast.

A wave of cold washed down his spine at the thought. He wasn't looking at the expansion of a blossoming city. He was looking at people finding the necessary room to house those who'd lost everything.

Behal Town was mostly built from wood. Buildings up to three stories, in the cases of guild halls, inns and government buildings. There were temples, but those were more often built from stone.

Aefric and his people rode the short, wide road from the Kingsroad to Behal Castle, and the moment people saw his banner they began to cheer.

Locals began gathering. Cheering. Crying out for the gods to bless their duke. Throwing flowers. Youths, laughing, raced along before and behind Aefric and his party, as though trying to turn the procession into a parade.

Aefric managed a shaky smile, and did his best to wave and look confident. He was thinking of Baroness Blaewyn's words. *The more you present yourself as an adventurer, the less they will regard you as a duke.*

These people needed to see their duke. Their confident duke. Their duke who had arrived to see them through the aftermath of the Godswalk Wars.

So many people. Not just those here, now, calling out to him. Blowing him kisses. Crying out his name as though it were a benediction.

So many people throughout all of Deepwater. And all of them, counting on him.

Hot fear twisted in his guts. Filled him with images of these people, dying of hunger and sickness. Of these people around him, shivering in the cold because they had no roofs over their heads.

Aefric's undertaking was no mere dungeon crawl, risking only his life if he failed.

If Aefric failed now, these people — these *innocent* people — would suffer and die.

That thought made Aefric straighten his back, and meet as many eyes as he could on that ride through town under the setting sun.

He wanted to see these people. And he wanted them to know he saw them.

He was here now. They had to know that. They had to understand.

He was here. For better or for worse. And he would do whatever he could for his people.

And he prayed to whatever gods might be listening that he didn't fail them.

BEHAL CASTLE CUT AN IMPOSING IMAGE AGAINST THE SETTING SUN. THE sky behind it, a red darkening down toward purple. And the castle itself, a towering gray edifice perched on a steep, grassy, rocky hill. Up so high that riders — or anyone else following the road — would have to circle the hill three times before reaching the gates.

As for the makeup of that castle, four wide, round towers sat almost outside its walls. Each of them, a good hundred feet tall. The castle walls sprouted out of the backs of the towers, maybe three-fourths the towers' height, and came together to connect.

The main part of the keep stood as tall as the towers. Smaller rounded towers at the corners of a squared body, and a raised section in the middle of the front, likely providing a solid defense of the castle's entryway.

But Aefric noted a detail of Behal Castle that wasn't covered on the map.

The castle was technically out on the lake.

Apparently the hill it sat on was an island in the mouth of the river delta. Two hundred feet of lake water between the mainland and the castle.

Hell of a moat.

Twin stone gatehouses — decent keeps unto themselves — guarded the way to the castle. One on the island and one on the shore. Each controlled half a massive drawbridge.

The bridge was down as Aefric's party approached. Guards at the gatehouse saluted, right fists high in the air, and someone blew a series of notes on a trumpet.

Aefric reined in there, momentarily. There was no need for the additional mounted soldiers to see him to the castle. Through Ser Beornric he had them remain here at the gatehouse, where there would be more than enough room to accommodate them.

Interestingly, the soldiers seemed to expect that. Perhaps the gatehouses served as the local ducal army base? Aefric would have to check on that.

Countess Faenella, perhaps as a demonstration of trust to any observers, offered to have her soldiers barrack here at the gatehouse as well.

So it was a considerably smaller group, proceeding on. Only Aefric, the countess, her ladies and retainers, the two knights, and Aefric's personal guard.

Aefric felt oddly proud and accomplished as the hooves of his party thundered across the drawbridge. He'd made it past the lands that — while technically part of his demesne — were held by others.

Here, everyone's first loyalty was directly to him.

He was riding across his own drawbridge, to his own castle.

Underneath that sense of pride and accomplishment, this moment touched him in two very different ways.

To the part of him that had lived his whole life as Aefric, the experience was surreal. That part of him was still getting used to the idea of entering castles that *weren't* ancient, haunted ruins. And the notion that a castle was not only active and occupied but *his*, well, that would take some time to settle in.

But the part of him that had grown up as Keifer thrilled to this moment. Riding across a drawbridge at sunset. Surrounded by his own soldiers, vassals and people. Entering his very own castle.

This was exactly the kind of moment he'd daydreamed about while clicking the pledge button on Del Baker's Jumpstart.

Riding into his very own castle.

His new home.

Well, sort of. His lake house, perhaps. Since his proper home was Water's End.

But Aefric managed not to let the details get in the way of his feeling good after a long, hard day's ride.

Yes, he was sweaty and dirty. Yes, his legs were sore and his horse needed rest. Yes, his back and shoulders were getting stiff from trying to hold his spine perfectly straight on the ride through town, after a hard day's travel. And yes, his stomach growled in hopes of something more than cold turkey and creamy cheese.

But he'd been riding for seven days to get to this point. And now the sun was setting. His soldiers were smiling as they saluted. And as Aefric rode across the river on that double-drawbridge, he was reaching the end of his...

No.

No, he wasn't.

Aefric was cheered, saluted and trumpeted as he passed through the second gatehouse — just as big and defensible as its twin on the other side of the double-drawbridge — but he realized he wasn't done riding yet.

He had that long, long road yet to go. Three circles of that steep hill yet stood between him and rest, food, and a bath.

He was tempted then to halt. To get out his little magical carriage and just let it zoom him the rest of the way up.

But no. He couldn't do that. The carriage likely couldn't carry more than four — which would mean himself, the countess, and Oswen and Sighild. His personal guard, and the countess' retainers, they'd still have to ride their tired horses the rest of the way. Not to mention the knights.

Not how Aefric wanted to arrive at one of his ducal castles for the first time — setting himself above his people.

So he swallowed his tired frustration, and he rode loop after loop after loop up the hillside, making his way to the castle.

The sunset deepened. The shadows lengthened. Before they would reach the castle's gate, Aefric would have to hold the Bright-staff high and let its light shine out, guiding his party safely through the growing gloom.

The view, at least, was good. The bustling activity of the town down below. No. The small city. He could tell now that Behal was too big to call a town.

Then there was the beauty of the river, the delta and the lake. The dozens of small boats out on the water. Perhaps fishermen hoping for night fish, or pleasure boats, or transport, or something else besides.

The castle's little island had its own docks, on the north side, complete with a dock house. And he couldn't be sure in the growing dusk, but he thought one of the docked boats flew a sigil that wasn't his.

The docks led to a small road that would join the main brick road up to the castle.

Of course, it also passed right by the gatehouse, so it was hardly a stealthy way onto the island. The road was even gated at that spot, to ensure control of who came to the castle from the docks.

Sadly, these views felt like small compensation for yet more delay in a day that had already grown overlong.

Even reaching the top level of the hill wasn't the end of the ride. They came around the penultimate curve — the shoes of their horses clattering on the fire-hardened bricks — to find a large hedge maze. It spread on both sides of the road, connected by arching, vine-covered bridges from one half of the maze to the other.

The hedge maze seemed to go on and on. But finally they came to the last curve, and a flower garden that would probably look gorgeous by daylight, when Aefric wasn't so tired. Benches in that garden probably made for lovely places to look out over the lake.

But this was no time for hedge mazes and flower gardens. He didn't even slow down.

The sky above was deep violet, with the first stars starting to show, when Aefric and his exhausted party reached the castle gates at last.

A ring of torches had been set up outside the wall, just past the portcullis.

Which was down.

Its thick iron bars between Aefric and comfort and food.

Because *of course* there had to be a ceremony first.

Night might not have fallen yet, but it was at least getting a standing eight count. Aefric smirked at that thought. A joke he couldn't share. No one around him would get it.

He was getting punchy. Even his last bite of cold turkey, apple, and creamy cheese had been so long ago now that he would have eaten even those things ravenously right then.

He was tired. He was sore. And the last thing he wanted to do was deal with a ceremony before he could do anything to alleviate his exhaustion, hunger, and soreness.

He knew that the moment he saw and heard the ring of torches outside the closed portcullis. Twice now, he'd seen a ring of torches set up just this way. If this kept up, he'd start expecting formal oaths and promises every time he smelled pitch.

A red carpet had been laid out on the semi-circle of fire-hardened bricks outside the portcullis. And arrayed about looked to be most, if not all, of the castle staff.

There had to have been a hundred men and women of various

ages, all gathered about. Possibly more. Too many to fit on the bricks, let alone the carpet. They overflowed onto the rocks and dirt beyond.

Along with the castle staff were pike-bearing soldiers in chain mail, their tabards proudly displaying the lake and sword of Deepwater.

Aefric could only just hear the rustling of that chain armor under the susurrus of quiet, excited conversation.

And in the center of it all, directly in front of the portcullis, stood a tall, proud woman, wearing the navy blue and gray of Deepwater. She had dark skin, and close-cropped black hair liberally sprinkled with gray. On her back she wore a greatsword, and at her belt a ring of many keys.

She could only be the castellan, Ser Grey.

Aefric, leading the party now, reined in and dismounted.

Ser Beornric blew a whistle that Aefric hadn't known the man was carrying.

"Ser Aefric Brightstaff, Hero of the Battle of Deepwater, and newly made Duke of Deepwater."

With that, the men and women all knelt. Most on both knees, but not all. The soldiers — including Ser Grey, and a half-dozen others who wore no armor but had swords at their belts — knelt on one knee instead, to show that even now they were ready for battle, if needed.

Aefric's personal guard all took a knee, as well, including Ser Beornric. As they did, Aefric glanced behind, to see that Countess Faenella started to take a knee, but Oswen and Sighild stopped her, whispering quickly into her ears. Ser Arcy, also, remained standing.

"Your grace," Ser Grey said, drawing the greatsword from her scabbard and holding it up, spread across both palms. "I am Ser Grey Ol'Ducell. Knight of Deepwater and castellan of Behal Castle. In token of the service I swear to you, I offer my sword."

She bowed her head and lay the blade on the carpet at his feet.

Aefric knew that, as duke, there was something he was supposed to say or do here, but for the life of him he wasn't sure what.

Aefric picked up the sword, which led to a few loudly indrawn breaths around him. Ser Grey, for her part, watched Aefric carefully. And she didn't seem to be breathing at all.

"This is quite a sword, Ser Grey. I can feel the pulse of magic and history in it. Is it a family heirloom?"

"It is, your grace," she said, voice even, but Aefric could hear hesitation in her tone. "My father carried it in service to Duchess Arinda's father, Duke Arallan Soulfist. I carried it in service to Duchess Arinda for many years."

"Then I am both pleased and proud that you now wield it for me," Aefric said, handing it back to her.

She let out a breath and her shoulders eased. Had picking up the sword been the wrong move? He'd have to ask Ser Beornric about it later.

He made a fist, then clutched the wrist behind it in the formal salute from a noble to a knight. "Arise, Ser Grey."

She smiled then, though still looked a little unsure, and led him through the rest of the ceremony.

It turned out that the other half-dozen sword-bearers who'd taken one knee were knights as well, each of whom had to have the formal presentation of their weapon.

And since Aefric didn't want Ser Grey feeling singled out, he picked up each of their weapons before returning it as part of the ceremony. When it was his turn, even Ser Beornric looked puzzled about that part, which meant Aefric had definitely done something ... if not wrong, then certainly unusual.

He'd *definitely* have to remember to ask Ser Beornric about that later.

The soldiers needed only his thanks for their service as a group before they could pick up their own weapons and stand. Though he made sure to call out and address his personal guard separately, to make their role clear.

Ser Grey looked unsurprised that her duke had arrived with his own personal guard, and promised to have his personal sigil added to their tabards first thing.

Then came the castle staff, who just needed a word of thanks and welcome, again as a group.

Finally, Ser Grey said, "You grace, welcome to your castle." Louder she called out, "Your duke has arrived!"

Trumpets blew, ropes creaked and the portcullis was raised. And up above, his personal sigil was raised below his ducal banner, to indicate that the duke was in residence.

At last, Aefric was free to enter his castle. Maybe he'd even get something to eat.

But the part of him that was Keifer slammed down worries about food and rest. This was a big moment, and he wasn't going to miss it.

For so long, the part of him that was Keifer had dreamed of arriving at his very own castle for the first time. As a *duke*. A powerful noble.

As he stepped through the portcullis, he was living out fantasies spurred by hundreds of novels and thousands of games.

For that part of him, this was a moment of indescribable pleasure.

Even the part of him that was Aefric thought it was cool.

He'd imagined wanting a tour of his castle at Behal the moment he entered. Learning its secrets and byways. The names and faces of every servant and retainer. Of truly making it a home, even if it would be a secondary home to Water's End.

But even the bliss of living out a fantasy lasted only so long, while his body was clamoring for attention. He quickly had to admit to himself that those other things could wait.

Right now, all he really wanted to do was eat, sleep, and bathe. In that order.

But that was not how things were done. Ser Grey quietly reminded her new duke of this. And after he'd ... deviated from the normal approach to the welcoming ceremony, Aefric didn't have it in him to mess this up too.

So he agreed that his party should all be escorted to their chambers and given a chance to rest and refresh themselves before dinner.

Inside the curtain wall was a large, brick courtyard, with small buildings around the sides, close to the curtain wall. Different types of smiths and wrights, stables and more.

Aefric and his party had to wait there for a moment, while the servants and soldiers all rushed past them back to their duties. Aefric, however, was expected not to notice this, while Ser Grey pointed out defensive features along the walls, and the catapults at the tops of the towers that could, she said, reach as far as the Kingsroad, if the weather was right.

When it was time to move, at last, Ser Grey herself escorted Aefric through halls and up stairs to his chambers. Along the way, he was immediately struck by a difference between this castle and the baronial castles he'd stayed at over the past few days.

The walls and ceilings of the rooms he passed through here were not bare stone. They'd been covered over with plaster, and painted.

The main hall — which was being set up for a small feast — was painted Deepwater gray with navy blue trim. And though there were very large tapestries on the walls, depicting old battles, there was one space that was visibly empty, up behind the ducal throne.

The ducal throne, at least, was a simple thing. Carved from a plain, dark wood.

Other rooms had been painted different colors, depending on their uses. Some dark browns and oranges, some light yellows, blues and whites. And some of the walls had not tapestries, but paintings.

The stairs were all bare stone, walls and ceiling, but that didn't bother Aefric.

He was only paying half-attention to his surroundings. Tired as he was, he couldn't divide his attention from what Ser Grey was telling him as they walked, surrounded by four members of his personal guard.

"We've had a two rika birds. One from Riverbreak. Baron Karmody will be here by highsun tomorrow. The other from Havenford. Baron Osmaer will be only a few hours behind him. Likely before sunset."

"Nothing from Goldenfall?" Aefric asked. "I sent their bird at the same time."

"Not yet, your grace. I shouldn't read too much into that, though. Count Cyneric is the type to think three times before moving once. If you expect his bird today, you're like to see it tomorrow."

"Not encouraging," Aefric said through a sigh. "I've already been warned to expect trouble from him."

"And you may have it," Ser Grey said with a wolfish smile. "His daughter Byrhta has been at Water's End for three aetts now. Might be Count Cyneric is sending *her* your rika bird, with his response, for her to come down and deliver herself. In fact, I think it was her sloop that docked just before your grace arrived."

"And she means trouble?"

"Well," Ser Grey said, slowly. "Can't say of a certainty, your grace, but I find it interesting that once word got out about who your regent was, the count of Goldenfall sent his second child, his eldest daughter, back to Water's End."

Aefric chuckled. "So you think the count is looking to improve his family's station through marriage?"

"That certainly one possibility," she said, and Aefric could tell there were implications in her words, but he was too tired to worry at them right then.

***

Finally, at the fourth floor, Ser Grey stopped outside a black oak, gilt-trimmed double-door. Two pikemen — both sweaty from having rushed back to their post after the ceremony — stood guarding the doors.

"Your grace," Ser Grey said, taking the key ring off her belt and holding up one key that looked unremarkable, "may I present your ducal chambers."

She unlocked the doors then and threw them open. And what Aefric saw inside lifted his spirits considerably.

The walls and ceiling of his outer chamber had been plastered and painted a soft gray. The floor was covered in white ash floorboards. Two bay windows gave views of the lake, and Aefric could feel that they'd been enchanted to strengthen and harden them.

The room had been arranged into three distinct sitting areas. The first was a casual, comfortable area of padded couches and two large chairs surrounding a coffee table near the windows.

The second was a marble chess set, with two seats. All set up and ready to play. Both the red and white pieces had been intricately carved into what Aefric suspected were likenesses of historically important people.

The third sitting area was a black oak table, rectangular, with eight matching chairs. Fine scrollwork and carvings along the edges of the table and the backs and arms of the chairs.

All three sitting areas had rugs with navy blue and gray chevrons. The Deepwater battle flag.

The walls had landscape paintings of different parts of the duchy, from Kerrik Forest to the Dragonscar to the coast. A large tapestry map on one wall was woefully out of date, listing towns along the seacoast that Aefric knew had been lost.

And one painting above the chessboard drew his eye. It depicted a battle scene, with an immense body of water in the background. Human armies with their backs to the water, looking ragged and troubled. A borog army menacing except...

...except for the sections of their army that were decimated by lightning strikes and fleeing in terror.

In the center of the painting, Aefric, high on a hill. Glowing Brightstaff in his hands, clearly calling down the lighting.

Wasn't a bad likeness...

"Like it?" Ser Grey asked. "The same artist is making a tapestry of the scene to go behind your throne."

"Sounds a bit excessive," Aefric said.

Ser Grey smiled and shook her head. "Not in Armyr, your grace. Excessive here would be covering the main hall in one *giant* depiction of this scene. The tapestry I commissioned in your name is far more tasteful."

Aefric chuckled, despite himself. "I suppose I should trust your sense of the duchy and the nation in this regard."

"Thank you, your grace," Ser Grey said, sounding a little more relaxed. "Right now everyone remembers the Battle of Deepwater. But give it ten or twenty years, you'll be glad the young bucks all have to look at that tapestry when they talk to you. Remind them that you know a thing or two about fighting in the front lines yourself."

Aefric shook his head. "I hadn't even thought of that. Thank you."

"I know it's the habit of new lords to install their trusted friends and allies in all the high offices," Ser Grey said. "But I've lived here in Deepwater my whole life, and can tell you things you won't find in the records. And I keep one ear and one eye on everything that happens in Behal."

Aefric stopped looking around. Nodded thoughtfully at Ser Grey. "I'll keep that in mind, Ser Grey. And I have no plans to replace you. Or any of the staff here at Behal. Not unless it proves necessary."

"I'm glad, your grace." She drew a deep breath. "Many of the merchants and petty nobles are nervous that an adventurer has been given the duchy. Consistency in administration will go a long way toward easing their concerns."

Aefric huffed out a breath and said, shortly, "They can't be that scared of adventurers. Your last duchess was a Soulfist. Hardly the name of some ancient Armyrian family."

"True," Ser Grey said, evenly, "but she was the fifth Soulfist to hold the duchy. It was her ancestor who was the adventurer, and no one living remembers him."

She frowned. "Well. I suppose we may have some eldrani and derekek here and there who remember that far back, but most of your people are humans, and won't remember much past Arinda's father, may he lie quietly."

"Fair enough," Aefric said, looking over the small stage that had been set up in one corner. Likely for musicians. There were also black oak cabinets set up along two of the walls, and a small black oak bookshelf full of books.

Now Aefric knew he was tired. He passed a whole shelf full of books and didn't even pull one down to look it over.

There were three doors that led out of this room, two on one side, one on the other. A glance through the one door on the right-hand wall told him that beyond lay his solarium.

He was too tired to deal with a solarium. It would keep.

Aefric instead crossed his sitting room, tried the door closer to the windows, and wandered into his bedroom.

This room was even larger than the sitting room. With more furniture made from black oak. Armoires full of cloaks and night-shirts, and a small armory with a selection of personal weapons, and space for his sword and staff. More bookshelves in here, he was pleased to note, with more books.

In one corner, a small altar was set up. On shelves above it going up the wall, small icons of the various gods — only the ones Aefric might be expected to offer to, he presumed, since gods like Xazik the Flayer and Kulath the Pestilence were notably missing — while shelves below the altar held a variety of incenses and candles.

Aefric crossed the white ash floorboards and rich, pale gray and navy blue carpets, only half-aware of his surroundings now.

An altar. Candles. He knew what he had to do.

He reached down and took a small, while candle. He set it on the altar, and lit it in silent tribute to Andi. As he did, Ser Grey watched in respectful silence.

Some of the tension in Aefric's back and shoulders relaxed, then, as he turned to take in the rest of the room. More windows of enchanted glass, with views over the curtain wall and one tower to the lake beyond. More paintings of pleasant scenes, as well as two scenes of lovers meeting by a secret pool.

The bed was the second largest he'd seen here in Qorunn. The largest was in that manor off to the northwest, past the Risen Sea, belonging to her lordship, Arawyn of Goldenmoon. That bed had been big enough to sleep eight, and rumors said that it did on occasion.

Though on the night when Aefric had been invited to share it with her, no one else was present.

This bed was big enough to sleep three, with room for them to spread out a bit. He yearned to stretch out in it. Just running his hands across the soft, smooth sheets made his eyelids feel heavy. And testing the soft, thick padding was enough to make him yawn.

Ser Grey cleared her throat.

He shook himself. Right. More to do.

One of the doors out of that room led into his closet. And what a closet. A room unto itself, with couches and full-length mirrors. White ash floorboards, covered with rugs. And racks and racks and racks of clothing. Clothing for all occasions. Footwear too. Sandals and shoes and boots in various cuts and sizes, with differing amounts of elaboration.

And all of it made for a duke, not a duchess.

Aefric looked a little closer.

"These would fit me," he said, surprised.

"I should hope so," Ser Grey said with a smile. "It's a small selection, for a duke, but you'll have a great deal more up at Water's End."

"These would fit *me*," Aefric said again, tapping his chest for emphasis. "I haven't exactly seen a tailor recently."

Ser Grey smiled. "Kainemorton himself brought us your measurements, and every tailor and bootmaker for a hundred miles has worked feverishly preparing a wardrobe for you."

Aefric felt as though there were more he should say, but he closed his mouth.

Two more doors led out of the closet. One led into the sitting room. The other into...

...his own private bath.

A tub built up from stone. Large enough for him to share with guests, if he had a mind to. The bath was built with a view out another bay window, though the view was different. Westerly, across the delta and with views of the lake and the land.

Including the dark sky. But the room was lit. And without any obvious candles or lamps, as he'd seen on the way up.

He shook himself. Lighting spells, attached to disks of glass that hung from the ceiling. They'd had them in each room of his chambers, and they were so like light fixtures that Keifer was used to that he didn't notice them at first.

But the tub was enchanted too. And the water that filled it steamed with heat from spells laid into the stone.

"Right," Aefric said. "Bath first, then clothes, then dinner. Fair?"

"Exactly what I hoped you'd say, your grace."

Ser Grey bowed then, and left Aefric to his bath.

He stripped down and got straight into the tub. The hot water was bliss itself, though the scrub brush was a close second.

The weirdest part about the bath was that servants came in while Aefric was naked and cleaning himself. But they acted as though this was all perfectly normal, so he tried not to let it weird him out.

They brought him scented soaps, so that he could come out of his bath literally smelling like a rose.

More importantly, they brought him a small plate of sliced fruit, which he devoured hungrily. Apples and pears, along with both red and green grapes, and a soft, chewy fruit he didn't recognize, though it tasted sweet and a little tangy.

The hot bath eased relief into his tired muscles. The fruit took the wicked edge off his hunger, but left him ready for more. And the scrubbing and soap left him feeling almost human again by the time he was asking for towels and ready to get out.

Only irritating thing about that was that Aefric had wanted to get to know the servants, especially those who'd be working around his chambers, which seemed to have a mix of both men and women.

But no way was he going out of his way to meet eyes and ask names. Not while he was naked. That could get misunderstood in all the worst ways. Especially since he was the new guy here, in pretty much every sense.

So he accepted his towels and dried off, and walked naked into his closet while trying not to think about the fact that he was naked.

Here, he allowed himself to have a little fun.

He dressed himself — to the chagrin of two of his servants, who had to be mollified with promises that this would not be a habit — in navy blue hose beneath a soft gray shirt, with pearls for buttons, and interesting embroidered patterns at the cuffs and collar. He wore a wide belt of black cloth, that still allowed for his belt pouch and his wand, in its sheath.

Over the shirt, a navy blue vest, edged in gold thread. On his feet, simple black leather shoes.

He did allow the servants to comb out his hair. That seemed to be important to them. Or maybe they were just worried about their jobs.

He left his backpack in a trunk at the foot of his bed, and sealed the trunk with a spell lock. He called the Brightstaff to his hand — getting an appreciative *ooh* from the servants — and finally was ready for dinner.

AEFRIC HAD TO BE LED BACK DOWN TO DINNER FROM HIS CHAMBERS. HE hadn't had attention to spare for tracking the way when he'd come up. The servants seemed to expect it, though, and had a page ready to guide him back to the main hall, where dinner would take place below the dais and the ducal throne.

As Aefric entered the main hall, a trumpet played and a herald called out, "His grace, the duke!"

Clothing rustled and chairs scraped then as everyone stood.

There were three tables in all. The center table, set for twenty-four, and two smaller tables set for a dozen each.

Aefric looked to be the last to arrive. Two tables were full and the central table had one chair empty.

The diners at the first table — none of whom he recognized, but they were all dressed finely enough to be minor nobles, diplomats, or well-to-do merchants — bowed as he passed and took their seats.

Aefric almost frowned, but he caught the expression before it crossed his face. The frown came from concern that he'd have to pass all three tables to get the diners to sit, before he could take his own seat.

He chanced that this would not be necessary.

He stopped in the middle, at the head of the longest table, and looked over at diners of the last table. He didn't know any of them either.

He nodded to them. They bowed and took their seats.

Finally he looked down the long table. Countess Faenella sat at his right hand. A young woman he didn't know sat at his left. They were followed by Oswen and Sighild. After them, more people he didn't know. Sers Beornric and Arcy sat about the middle of the table, and Ser Grey at the foot. But the rest of them, he didn't know.

He chuckled voicelessly through a breath. As Keifer, he'd gone entire weeks without meeting anyone new. Now here he was surrounded by people he'd probably have to meet and remember.

Well, he'd wanted a change.

At his nod, the diners all bowed and sat, and Aefric sat with them.

That dinner was a whirlwind, and tired as he was, Aefric was carried along by the current.

Later he remembered that the food was wonderful. A crispy salad. Magnificent freshwater marlin from out on the lake, served with a potato discs and cheese and...

Oh, there was more. So much more. And later he wondered exactly how much he'd eaten.

The wine was good. A light, white wine, and he'd been smart enough to avoid drinking too much of it. He knew that because he didn't have a headache later. And he knew he always got headaches when he drank too much wine, white or red.

And he remembered *why* he'd watched his drinking.

Byrhta Ol'Caran. Daughter of the count of Goldenfall. Seated at his left hand.

She looked to be about Aefric's own age, but that could have been deceiving, because she plainly had some eldrani blood. And not just in the beauty of her features, which was exceptional enough to make the air seem brighter around her.

Her hair was a dark forest green, which contrasted sharply with her quite pale complexion. Her wide eyes were amber, with flakes of canary yellow.

She dressed in a complex gown of that color, to bring out those flakes in her eyes, and she was adorned tastefully with golden jewelry. A necklace crowned by a ruby. Bracelets sparkled with flakes of emeralds. And small earrings dangled, made from gold and twisted into ornate curves that doubled back on themselves. Likely to keep them from catching on everything that came near.

She was solicitous, asking about his investiture while lamenting that she'd missed it.

She asked about his travels along the Kingsroad, and how he'd found his lands and his vassals.

She was a deft conversationalist. Not nearly so direct as some of those he'd been dealing with so far. Despite Aefric's questions, she gave no hint about whether or not her father would be coming to Behal, or even whether she'd heard that he'd been summoned. And each time, she managed to turn the conversation elsewhere, without looking as though she were trying to avoid a subject.

It might have helped that she had Countess Faenella to use as a foil, when needed, though she also enlisted Oswen and Sighild in her subject changes as well.

Aefric was fairly certain those two had tried to help him keep her on point, but they were no match for the easy way she controlled the conversation.

Always smooth as a glassy lake.

What made gaining information from her even more difficult was that she occasionally *did* answer questions directly. When Aefric asked how she came to be at Behal, she claimed to have sailed down as soon as she'd heard the new duke was due to arrive here.

But when Aefric had asked how she'd heard, she'd only smiled and said, "Leave a girl *some* secrets, your grace."

Now, that could have meant any number of things. Some of them even innocent. And perhaps Aefric wasn't being fair. Perhaps it was exhaustion, or the giddiness of food after that long day's ride and the stressful thinking he'd been doing.

But when she said that, he heard it as, "I have spies, of course."

Not that she would ever admit that.

Still, frustrating as the woman was, at least she wasn't overtly coming on to him.

She'd been paying him a lot of attention, yes, but he was the duke. That was to be expected. But if Ser Grey was right about her having marital intentions, she wasn't coming at him hard and fast.

Which was a contrast with some of the women farther down the table, or seated at one of the other two tables, who tried to catch his eye with smiles.

When dinner was over, he had to beg off of several offers of company — likely just for conversation over wine, but he couldn't be sure of that — because all he really wanted to do was go back to his rooms and relax for a bit before turning in.

This would be his first chance to really stop and breathe, and he wasn't going to miss it.

He did promise Faenella that he would see her off in the morning.

It was Ser Grey, again, who escorted him back to his room. Aefric took advantage of that to deal with a couple of quick matters.

"The countess and her party will be leaving in the morning. Get them a fast boat that can seat—"

"I know the size of her party, your grace, including soldiers. I know just the boat."

"Perfect. Thank you. Has Byrhta Ol'Caran stayed here before?"

"From time to time, your grace. She fostered with Duchess Arinda, and I think the servants are fond of her both here and at Water's End."

"Good to know," Aefric said, with a sigh. "Do I need to worry about my servants telling her what I say in conference?"

"Perhaps, but definitely not the servants who attend you in your rooms," Ser Grey said firmly. "Not here at Behal. I keep a tight rein on them."

"Good. Thank you." They'd reached the door of his rooms, but Ser Grey didn't look inclined to leave. "Was there something else?"

"One other thing, your grace. Not for hallway ears."

Aefric led the way into his chambers. The servants had gotten a fire going, and prepared him a small plate of fruits, cheeses and sweets.

Once the door was closed, Ser Grey said, "There are two secret doors that lead into these chambers."

She led the way over to a cabinet near the window. The cabinet was flush against the plaster. She showed him a hidden catch where the cabinet met the wall. Depressed it.

The cabinet swung into the room, revealing a tight hallway and stairs.

"This is the servants' backway. Runs through most of the castle, though it isn't used much these days. Mostly when the castle is over-flowing with some major event."

She closed it again, then led him into his own bedroom, to a tapestry he'd ignored the first time through. It sat in a corner, and was nothing more interesting than an elaborately done list of the names of every duke and duchess of Deepwater, with his own newly added near the bottom.

Behind the tapestry, since he was looking for it, he could only just see the barest crack in the plaster, running the outline of a doorway.

He couldn't see a latch, though.

"Press your ducal seal to it anywhere," Ser Grey said.

He did, and the door it concealed slid back an inch or so, then swung backwards. Behind it a set of spiral stairs led down.

"This leads all the way down through the keep, past the under-ground levels, and comes out near the docks. It opens at both ends only to the seal, when held in the hand of the rightful duke or duchess. Won't work for me, or even for a regent."

Aefric frowned, puzzled that he couldn't sense the magic of this.

Ser Grey smiled. "No, your grace. You likely can't sense its spells. Pains were taken to hide them. I daresay none but maybe Kainemorton himself could notice them."

Aefric nodded as Ser Grey closed the door.

"Obviously, this one's your bolt hole, if you need one. If bad things are happening and you need to flee, this will take you straight to a ship and safety." She shrugged. "That's the idea, anyway."

Aefric nodded. "Are there other secret passages in the castle?"

"Mostly the servants' backway. But there are a couple of other passages. Short ones, for some purpose long since passed. I can show them to you, if you like."

"Another time," he said.

"Of course. Good night, your grace."

And with that she left him, and Aefric was only too happy to go to bed.

9

Aefric's first full day at Behal started early. He knew the countess would want to leave at first light, so he was up before dawn. He allowed his servants to shave and dress him — which felt weird enough — but despite their pleas that he eat something, he held off breaking his fast for the time being.

Might have helped that he still felt full of marlin. And what had that dessert been? Something like a cherry souffle, and delicious.

The selection of clothes took longer than he wanted it to. He knew that he had to present himself as a duke, so he had to dress finely. But that didn't mean he had to wear elaborate clothing every day of his life.

He was a duke now, but he'd lived most of his life as an adventurer. And there might be some benefit in letting people remember that.

Perhaps simple but high quality clothes would combine both elements. Noble, without being ostentatious.

So he wore knee-high boots, but selected ones that were made from doeskin and tanned so soft that they practically caressed his calves.

He couldn't decide if the duchy's colors should be day-to-day wear, or only for special occasions. So he split the difference. He wore a shirt of a dark, smoky gray, and black pants, both of which were trimmed and subtly embroidered with navy blue.

He wore a cloth belt of navy blue, with his new wand in its place. And as he slid its sheath onto the belt, he reminded himself to find time to experiment with the wand and learn its ways and secrets.

He left his sword behind with a sigh. Carrying a sword might send the wrong message.

In a cabinet in his bedroom, he'd found a selection of ducal jewelry, but decided that it should be for special occasions. The queen's ring and Andi's pendant would be all the ornamentation he'd need.

He did consider wearing the coronet. A simple gold circlet crowned by a dark blue sapphire, it looked light enough to wear for an extended period in comfort.

No. He would wear it later, when meeting with his barons. But he didn't need to wear it just to remind people he was the duke. He needed to develop the bearing that projected his identity without such obvious clues.

While he was looking at it, though, one of his servants — an older woman named Falip — said, "Your grace has a larger version at Water's End, if that's not big enough."

"It's plenty big," Aefric said with a laugh. "I'm just realizing that everything I do today sets the tone for people's expectations. So I'm trying to make sure I know what I'm doing."

"If I may say so, your grace, you'll do just fine." She lowered her voice and stepped closer. "Your grace, if you'd not stopped the borogs at Deepwater, they'd have hit Behal next. And everyone knows it. The castle might've held, but the city would have been overrun. So your people stand behind you, don't doubt that we do."

"Thank you, Falip," Aefric said, returning the smile she gave him.

He retrieved something from his backpack, then spell-locked the trunk once more. Then he called the Brightstaff to his hand, and set out.

Ser Grey was waiting just outside his room.

"How did—" He started, then just laughed. "Let me guess, you knew I'd want to see the countess off."

"Yes, your grace. And I thought you might need me to help set your schedule today."

They fell into step then, proceeding down the hall and stairs, flanked by four of his personal guards. The castle was busy already, with servants and pages moving about on business, and the sounds of work in the background.

Aefric noted that his personal guards already had his Brightstaff sigil affixed below the Deepwater seal.

"You really do carry that everywhere then, your grace?" Ser Grey asked, nodding at the Brightstaff.

"I have for years now," he said. "I feel naked without it. I carried it even into the presence of the king and queen."

Ser Grey's eyes widened a bit, then she nodded acquiescence.

"Then I suppose I can't talk you into leaving it in your room. For appearances' sake."

"No," he said simply. "Yes, it will remind people that I was an adventurer, but I see no reason to shy away from my past. I'm certainly not ashamed of it."

"Fair enough," she said, then bobbed her head back and forth, considering. "It might even help maintain your image as a war hero." She drew a breath then, and changed subjects. "Will you want to meet your barons in the courtyard, with musicians? Or in the throne room?"

"Neither. I'll want to meet with each of my barons privately when they arrive," he said. "In some small meeting room. Myself, you, Ser Beornric, a token guard presence, and the important members of each baron's party."

Ser Grey sounded tentative as she asked, "May I ask why, your grace?"

"In this case, you may," he said with a nod. "I want them to assess me without the pressure of a court crowd around them."

"Are you sure, your grace? There's power in ceremony. Or at least in addressing your vassals from the throne."

"There is," Aefric said. "And there's a time for that. But this is the first meeting. I want them to understand that I don't need to play power games. This is not just a duke meeting a pair of barons, but *me* meeting *them*. If we can't honestly take each other's measure, it'll be harder to work together in the future."

"But you don't work together, your grace," she said. "They work for you. They are not your equals. They hold their lands in your name."

"True," he admitted. "And if I have to remind them of that, I will. But recovering from the Godswalk Wars is going to require a lot of work. I'll get a lot more done with a lot less effort, if I develop a good relationship with my vassals. Where I can."

"That's true, your grace," Ser Grey said, "but keep in mind that there are still the lers and the guilds to consider. They'll need a firm hand to keep them in line, and little displays of power help that."

"I'll be starting that with dinner tonight," he said. "I will be eating in private, with my barons and knights. Over time, I will invite different lers, guildmasters, courtiers and wealthy merchants. Depending on the night. Let dinner with me become something they vie with each other for."

"Setting them against each other, trying to win the favor of the new duke," Ser Grey said with a nod. "Interesting. And it might work." She frowned. "What of the count's daughter?"

"She's a courtier," Aefric said. "She's not invited to my table tonight."

"Well," Ser Grey said with a chuckle. "That'll certainly send a message."

They were joined then, at the first floor, by Ser Beornric.

"I'm glad you're joining us," Aefric said, after they'd exchanged greetings. "I'll want to break my fast with you both after we've seen the countess off."

Out in the courtyard then, Aefric interrupted Ser Grey's call for horses. With a small thrill of pleasure, he set down the tiny carriage the king had given him, and spoke its word of command.

"*Arcoa.*"

The carriage sprang into the air, and with a *pop* became full-sized. It looked to be made entirely of ebony, though trimmed in gold leaf. And the Deepwater seal was emblazoned on the carriage doors, and flew from pennants at each corner.

The whole thing was much bigger than Aefric expected. It could sit eight, four to a bench, and not feel all that tight.

"Allow me, your grace," Ser Beornric said, stepping close to open a door that opened for him before he could reach the handle.

Aefric chuckled and entered the carriage.

Clean, carpeted flooring. Pale gray, padded silken seat covers along both the seats and the backs of the benches. The Deepwater seal had been embroidered into the seat backs.

Aefric eased himself onto his seat with a smile.

"Your grace," Ser Beornric said, from outside.

Aefric looked over, and saw that Ser Beornric was looking at the top.

"There are four guard seats up there," he said. "Belted, to keep them from falling. And more seats on the driver's bench."

"Perfect," he said. "The horses can wait for another trip then. We can all ride my new toy."

That made Ser Grey laugh as she and Ser Beornric joined Aefric inside, at his invitation. The knights sat opposite him.

"The docks," Aefric said, addressing the carriage, and it rolled outward, through the portcullis, and began carrying them swiftly and smoothly down the brick road.

"How does it ride so smoothly?" Ser Grey asked.

Aefric considered how well he could explain shock absorbers. As Keifer he'd known them well, back on Earth, but he wasn't sure when they were developed or how he could phrase an explanation here in Qorunn.

"Magic," he said, and settled back on the seat.

The view from the long, winding road was certainly better when he wasn't exhausted and half-starved. The morning was just taking on the glow of coming sunrise, and when his eyes adjusted, Aefric could see farther than he expected.

From this height, he could see just well enough to imagine the sight across the narrowed part of the lake, off to the east and north, where the Golden River poured in.

The Golden River was the dividing line between ducal lands and Goldenfall, and the river technically belonged to Aefric. Though, of course, traditionally the duke allowed Goldenfall free passage on it.

Up that river was the county seat of Goldenfall. Castle Vabarett. Only hours away by boat.

There'd been a bridge up that river once. Destroyed during the wars.

Aefric pondered that on the ride around the circles and down the hill. Some fairly large ships could sail that river. Perhaps including a pair of warships.

A point for consideration. If Goldenfall wouldn't come to him, Aefric could go to Goldenfall. With warships at his back.

Now *that* would send a message.

The first rays of dawn were just glimmering on the lake when Aefric's carriage arrived at the docks. Bells aboard ships on the water rang out, carrying one message or another. Lake birds up above cried and squawked at each other before taking turns diving for fish.

The sky above was cloudy and trending towards gray. The trade winds were blowing in from the Risen Sea, and looked to be bringing rain with them.

A chilly morning. Aefric should have let the servants give him that fine woolen cloak they'd tried to insist on. But no. The weather had been so nice yesterday.

He'd need to start trusting the locals' knowledge of the weather patterns, until he'd been here long enough to know them himself.

Sers Grey and Beornric had cloaks, but Aefric hoped they had the good sense not to offer them. He'd rather shiver a little than take someone else's cloak.

As he stepped out onto the dock, Ser Arcy was coordinating the loading of the waiting sloop. A fine, sleek-looking boat, that creaked as though eager to be underway.

A boat just big enough for the crowd it would need to carry, once all the horses and soldiers were added.

None of the countess' soldiers were in sight, though. Perhaps they'd pick them up on the way.

Countess Faenella, Oswen, and Sighild stood watching while the boat was loaded. Nyorngyth was with them.

The countess wasn't wearing her armor today, which surprised Aefric. Instead, she was wearing a dress of deep blue. She was even wearing a gold necklace with a garnet.

Apparently she wanted to arrive at her county looking the part of a countess. Probably a smart move.

Oswen and Sighild wore dresses as well — Oswen's a deep, chocolate brown and Sighild's an orange so pale it might have been a whipped topping — but that was less of a surprise. Though Oswen had also foregone the swords she'd worn, while riding.

"Come to see us off, your grace?" the countess asked, smiling.

"Of course, your excellency." He smiled, then said more seriously. "I know the questions at the border feel urgent, but take as much time as you need to establish yourself. If your lers and courtiers see you riding out to adventure first thing, they may think less of you as a countess."

"We'll keep an eye on her, your grace," Oswen said, with a smile.

Countess Faenella laughed. "I think they will at that." She pointed at Sighild and mock whispered, "Especially that one. She can be a right taskmaster about appearances."

Sighild flushed so bright it was hard to tell where her hair stopped and her face began.

Countess Faenella laughed then, and Oswen joined her, but it wasn't a vicious laugh. It was a warm sound, and even got a smile out of Sighild, though she was still a vivid crimson from her neckline up.

Aefric stepped up to Sighild, and mock whispered, "If they're too mean to you, you're free to come hide here as long as you like."

Aefric had thought that Sighild couldn't blush any harder.

He'd been wrong.

She burned so brightly then that he felt the heat of her flush over the foot of distance between them.

Deciding that enough was enough, he turned back to Countess Faenella.

"Have you had any news of your county?"

"No, your grace, though I'll send you a status report by messenger as soon as I have it ready."

"Excellent. Thank you." He turned to Ser Grey. "That reminds me. The prince left his report on the duchy up at Water's End. Send a messenger for it, if you would."

"At once, your grace," she said, and to Aefric's surprise, headed down the dock to another boat.

Apparently there was a frequent flow of boats and ships between Water's End and Behal. Retrieving the report would be a simple matter.

He turned back to Countess Faenella just as the sloop captain called that all was ready.

"Then I guess this is farewell, for now," he said, and kissed her hand. "Though I hope you won't be a stranger."

"I'll be living in a land of nothing but nobles and merchants," Countess Faenella said with a smile and a wink. "I'll need to talk to your grace every so often just to stay sane."

They chuckled, and he turned to Oswen, said a goodbye, and kissed her hand.

"Do you know where the hand-kissing custom in Armyr came from, your grace?" she asked.

"No," he admitted.

"Sighild," Oswen said, "give his grace your hand."

Sighild stood straighter then, and held her chin higher. She looked as though she were fighting the urge to run and hide. She was still blushing, but not so intensely as before.

She gave Aefric her hand. He took it in his.

"She shows you her strong hand," Oswen said. "Her weapon

hand. And it is empty. You are her duke. The superior noble. She is symbolically placing her life in your hands."

Oswen pointed at the knife every noble wore at their belt. Aefric had always worn one as an adventurer as well, so he'd added one to his belt without thinking about it, not even noticing that the servants hadn't tried to correct him.

"If you were angry with her, you could pull the knife from your belt and cut her wrist. You have that right. If you were pleased with her, you could kiss her hand as a blessing."

Aefric kissed Sighild's hand, and pretended not to notice the way she shivered when he did.

"No one expects to be cut anymore," Oswen continued, when Aefric had released Sighild's hand. "The hand-kissing is mostly symbolic these days. But technically you would still be within your rights under Armyrian law to cut the arm of a lesser noble who'd displeased you."

"Cut the arm right," Aefric said, "and they'd die before a healer could save them."

"Yes, your grace," Oswen said. "That's true. And not against the law. Presuming your grace had cause for great displeasure."

Aefric pondered that as he turned to Ser Arcy. He made a fist, and grabbed the wrist behind it in salute. She bowed in return.

Aefric then turned to Nyorngyth, while Sers Beornric and Grey both shook Ser Arcy's hand, before parting.

"Well, Nyorngyth," Aefric said. "Will you be moving on or staying here for a time?"

"I'm torn, to be honest, your grace," he said. "On the one hand, I'd love to see how you settle in here and at Water's End. On the other, a trip down to a troubled border? Clandestine investigations? How can I resist?"

"And you think you'll be invited along, do you?" Countess Faenella asked.

"Depends, your excellency," he said, sounding perfectly confident. "Do you think a priest of Ulna might prove useful on such a venture?"

Countess Faenella laughed. "Come on, then. Ulna won't want us dallying."

"Ah," Nyorngyth said, following her aboard the ship, "but dallying at times is a key part of travel. In fact, we have a song about it."

Nyorngyth began to sing as Aefric turned back to Sers Beornric and Grey.

"All right, sers, we should get moving. We have a lot to do today."

"Might your grace have room for one more in that carriage?"

Aefric knew that deep voice. It sent a shiver of happiness through his system, and had him smiling even before he turned to address the speaker.

"Karbin!" he cried out, feeling like a boy of twelve again as he grabbed his old mentor in a bear hug.

Nothing about Karbin had changed since Aefric had last seen him. His blue-black skin as wrinkle-free as ever, keeping him looking thirtyish in that way wizards have of staying young.

He still dressed in shades of sand and dusk, with four wands at his belt beside that strange obsidian rod he'd found in the ruins beneath Sulkrekeep.

"So you do remember me, your grace," Karbin said with a laugh, while returning Aefric's hug. "I feared that the ducal seal might go to your head."

"No, you didn't," Aefric said, laughing, reluctant to let go for fear he would turn out to be an illusion.

"No, I didn't," Karbin said with a smile as he pulled back from the hug. "In fact, when Kainemorton told me you could use some help, I headed for Water's End straightaway."

"You?" Aefric asked, half-caught between hope and disbelief. "You're the ducal wizard he found me?"

"At your service, your grace," he said with a bow.

"Call me 'your grace' one more time and you'll be nothing but 'lord wizard' for the rest of my life."

Karbin laughed, and said, "You'll have to accept it in formal situations, at the least."

"That, I suppose I can live with, if I get to have you around."

Aefric turned and made the introductions then, not shying away from the fact that Karbin had been his first real teacher, when it came to the ways of magic.

Then the four of them got in the carriage, and Aefric felt a lot better about his chances of coming through this business with Merrek in one piece.

But he knew he still had a long way to go.

Back at the black oak table in Aefric's suite, he broke his fast with Karbin, and Sers Beornric and Grey. They had water to drink while they dined on a medley of fruits, with a hearty rye bread and a selection of sharp cheeses.

All right, there was also at least one creamy cheese on the plate, but Aefric wouldn't have the stomach for any more creamy cheeses anytime soon.

As they ate, Aefric began with small orders, such as having Ser Beornric interview the six knights who'd been present when they arrived the day before. Ser Grey had said they were the ducal honor guard. Aefric wanted Ser Beornric to get to know them and decide if they should be brought in to join his personal guard, or remain strictly an honor guard for formal occasions.

When the small orders were finished, he brought Karbin and Ser Grey up to speed about Kerrik Forest. The reports of the barons of Norra and Felspark. What he knew about Motte, and what he suspected, and where Merrek fit into all of it. He included the mission he'd given Countess Faenella.

"Opinions?" Aefric asked, when he was pretty sure he'd covered everything.

"We need to settle Goldenfall, at speed," Ser Grey said. "Motte and Merrek are bad enough. We can't have Goldenfall making things worse."

"We can't deal with Goldenfall until we know where the two remaining barons stand," Ser Beornric pointed out. "Until we have those meetings today, we have two cards hidden that might be in our hand and might be in Merrek's."

"I'm most worried about the coast right now," Karbin said. "With all the damage Deepwater's coast took during the wars, Merrek is the major source of Armyr's sea power. And you'll be in no shape to compete with her anytime soon. Worse, the number of problems in front of you may embolden her to harry what shipping you have."

"We'll know more about that," Aefric said, "after I meet with Havenford this afternoon."

"I'm not sure Goldenfall can wait," Ser Grey said. "It's your richest county, and Count Cyneric will be only too happy to hang back. Let you and Merrek go after each other while he stands ready to scoop up the leavings."

"The support you've garnered from Norra and Felspark is contingent on your actions," Ser Beornric said. "If they don't see signs soon that you're making good on your promises, they'll lose faith. That could play straight into Merrek's hands."

Aefric shook his head. "With the steps I've already taken for Kerrik, the fort, and Norra's bandits, Norra should be fine."

"True," Ser Beornric said, "but Baroness Herewyn will be expecting your investigator to show sooner rather than later."

"She knows it's the countess," Aefric said. "She'll know that'll take some time."

"I hope so," Ser Beornric said. "But there's a gap between knowing something in your head and trusting it in your gut."

"Herewyn's of an old family," Ser Grey said. "She understands these things, especially when a rival duchy may be involved. She'll give his grace room to maneuver. Given what your grace has already done, Norra is probably a solid ally."

"Can you say the same thing for Felspark?"

"About the age of Baroness Blaewyn's family?" Ser Grey asked. "Yes. As for her patience with her current problems, that's harder to say."

"She's also worried about the possibility of famine, come wintertime," Aefric said. "If nothing else, taking steps to bring in food should assuage some of her fears."

"Might be tricky," Ser Grey said. "Our losses on the coast have cut into our stores and production as well."

"You said Felspark's wizard might be hostage in Merrek," Karbin said.

"Yes," Aefric said. "As of yesterday, Blaewyn hadn't heard from her in over an aett, which is unusual on her current assignment."

"Who's the wizard?"

"Shaela Ol'Teruun," Aefric said with a quick shake of his head. "I don't know her."

"I'm pretty sure I met her once," Karbin said, slowly, "at a convocation down in Sartis. Should be enough of an excuse for me to go looking for her."

"You don't mind?"

"For this, I'll even teleport."

"That would be wonderful," Aefric said.

"Getting Felspark's wizard back," Ser Grey said. "That should pretty much cement their loyalty, while buying you room to find more food, and figure out what's happening on a deeper level. Not to mention how to respond."

"Not to mention how getting their wizard back will add to Felspark's resources," Ser Beornric added.

"Perfect," Aefric said. "I'll want you to get started on that today then, Karbin, if you would."

"Of course," Karbin said, and Aefric would swear that behind that smile lingered a *your grace,* left implicit just to tease him.

"After Merrek, you could check on the coast. See what remains of those fallen towns and villages. Check on Ajenmoor, as well. Find out if there's anyone harassing our shipping."

"Just what I was thinking," Karbin said.

"Then perhaps you were thinking about this, too." Aefric leaned in, leading the others to lean a little closer as well. He lowered his voice. "Once we know how things stand with our shipping, maybe you could find the pirate queen Nelazzi."

"Nelazzi!" Ser Grey said too loud, then lowered her voice. "What do you want with that scoundrel?"

"Merrek is trying to pressure our trade, through my barons. We can't pressure Merrek ourselves right now. But Nelazzi certainly could. And might, if we promise her safe harbor at Ajenmoor, so long as she leaves *our* shipping alone."

"That might work," Karbin mused. "Especially if she can sell her goods there without being questioned about their port of origin."

Aefric frowned, feeling less confident about this option. He'd never loved pirates, but had to admit. "We *could* use the trade…"

"I'm not sure about this," Ser Grey said. "Getting into bed with a pirate is a good way to wake up robbed."

"I'm not looking at a long-term arrangement here," Aefric said. "But right now, Merrek is in a stronger position, and I need to do something to even the odds a bit."

"But pirates…"

"Right now Merrek is making noises about stealing land from one of my barons, and may well be sending soldiers in as bandits to rob another."

"But do we know that for certain?" Ser Grey insisted.

"How about this," Karbin said. "It will take me time to free Shaela, and investigate the coast and the state of our shipping. Once I've gathered my information, I'll stop at Ajenmoor and reach out to you, Aefric. You can update me on Countess Faenella's investigation, and whatever else you've learned. We can decide more from there."

"Good enough," Aefric said, turning to Ser Grey. "If we get proof of shady dealings by Merrek, will you support my offering Nelazzi a letter of mark?"

"Letter of mark?" Ser Grey asked.

"Letter of mark and reprisal," Aefric said. "Basically sanctioning piracy against an enemy, for purposes of war." Aefric drew a deep breath, holding Ser Grey's eyes all the way through it. "Because make no mistake. If Merrek is doing what we think she's doing, then we're at war, whether we say so or not."

Ser Grey frowned, and thought about that for a minute, then slowly nodded.

"I've fought as a knight many times, your grace," she said. "But I've never had to be a general." She shook her head. "I don't like the idea of working with pirates. But I do see the wisdom in it. *If* Merrek is guilty."

"Believe me," Aefric said. "I don't like it either. No one hopes more than I do that dealing with Nelazzi won't be necessary." He shook his head. "But I just got this duchy. I'm not handing it over to Merrek without a fight."

AEFRIC KNEW THAT THERE WAS BUSINESS HE PROBABLY NEEDED TO attend to that morning. Reviewing the Behal accounts, at the very least, or letting Ser Grey review the locally important lers, guildmasters and others whose names he should know.

What Aefric would, himself, have preferred to do was spend the rest of the morning learning the layout of his castle at Behal.

But he couldn't take the time for that yet.

All this talk of Merrek and war made him realize he had a powerful new resource in his hands, and he needed to learn to use it now, before it became necessary.

Thus, he designated the top three floors of the main keep tower near his chamber as his magical laboratory. Those rooms hadn't been used for some time, though they had once served as a nursery for visiting mothers of gentle birth.

In Aefric's opinion, a high tower was hardly a good place for a nursery anyway.

He did allow servants to clear away the two lower levels of his new laboratory, but the top level he cleared out himself through one of his old favorite spells.

The *wizard's valet*. It conjured a bodiless motive force that could tirelessly perform all the basic duties of a servant or laborer.

That spell had saved him *countless* hours, back during his apprenticeship. And come in handy more times than he would have guessed, over his years of adventuring.

While his *wizard's valet* cleared out the room around him that morning, Aefric sat on a simple stool in the middle of the round room, deep in trance, with the whole of his focus on the wand, Garram, in his hands.

This was a trick that no one ever taught the apprentices. They were expected to work it out for themselves. Not that all of them did. Or, at least, Aefric had met several young wizards over the years who didn't seem to know the trick.

And certainly no one ever mentioned it *at all*, to a non-magic-user.

Let the world believe that only costly spells could unlock the secrets of a mysterious enchantment.

Truth was, those expensive spells were fast. But they weren't strictly necessary. A con, to part impatient adventurers from their coin.

Any magic-user past apprenticeship could discern the deeper powers of an item through a type of focused meditation. Projecting a part of their consciousness out through the flows of the magic inherent to Qorunn, and follow those flows into the item and through the depths of its spells.

As Aefric had come to understand the process, he likened it to studying an intricate painting. First truly learning the essence of the image depicted. This was the basic level of what the item could do. Then focusing down into the details.

In terms of a painting, that would mean the sense of depth and perspective, shadings and contrast. In terms of magic items, it meant the character of an item's powers.

Was the item a thing of brute force or subtle manipulation? Was it limited to a single effect, or a series of related effects, or something broader?

Or was the wand simply an amplification of the powers the magic-user himself could bring to bear?

These were the second level of things learned.

From there, in terms of art, it was as going over the canvas inch by inch, finding every brush stroke and blend of paint. Coming to understand the structure underlying the image, and how the artist had brought together her resources to produce the work.

In terms of enchanted items, this was the phase when the individual powers would be understood, as well as how to not just call them forth but to exert fine control over their scope and dimension.

Done this way, it was a long process. But this technique had the advantage of giving the magic-user a thorough understanding of the item and all the things it could do.

Those who settled for the expensive shortcut got only an abbreviated version. The basics, yes, but they would miss the nuances and shadings.

They would never have the fine control and full range of powers that could be drawn forth from the item, by a magic-user who took the time to truly study it.

Aefric could call himself the Brightstaff's master because he'd dedicated an entire season to its deep study.

The wand Garram was not nearly so complicated. He could tell that already. And yet, Aefric was still only in the early phases of the first stage of study when he was interrupted by a knock on the door.

"Your grace," Ser Grey called through the closed door. "The baron of Riverbreak has arrived and awaits your pleasure."

Aefric stretched, ignoring the cracks that came from his limbs and back, which had been held a little too rigid during his study. He'd established so far that Garram held within it a variety of uses for ice and fire magic. Experienced as he was, Aefric could tell that the wand would amplify any fire or ice spells that he knew, though he had not yet reached the controls for that amplification.

Right now, then, it was a tool for emergencies only.

He rolled his neck around and looked critically at the job his invisible valet had done. The two glass windows had been washed. The shutters and casements of the other two windows as well. The white ash floorboards had been swept clean, though the whitewashed plaster of the walls was still dirty from old dust and grime.

He mentally ordered his valet to finish with the walls, then dissolve.

Aefric stood then, sheathed the wand, took hold of the Brightstaff, and followed Ser Grey down many flights of stairs to the room where the baron's party awaited him.

This time Ser Grey seemed to choose a less busy route, with only a handful of servants and pages moving through on their missions.

"How did the baron seem?" Aefric asked, along the way.

"Irritated, to be honest, your grace," Ser Grey said. "Though I don't know the source of the irritation."

"Always be honest with me," Aefric said, drawing a puzzled frown from Ser Grey. He continued, "I know 'to be honest' is a common expression, but it underlies an implication that honesty is at times withheld. I can't have that from someone in your position. If I ask your opinion, I want it. Not whatever you or someone else thinks I might want to hear."

"I'll keep that in mind, your grace," Ser Grey said, sounding pleased, then lowered her voice as she continued. "Then if you don't mind my saying, your grace, I hope we find a way to resolve the Merrek issue without ... the solution currently under consideration."

"That solution is extreme," Aefric said, "as we both know. I'd prefer not to use it as well. But I'm coming into a fight dangerously low on weapons, and I may need to consider some that I'd prefer not to choose."

"Some?" Ser Grey asked. "Not just one, but some?"

"Figure of speech, in this case," Aefric said, hoping that was true.

But the deeper truth was this. So far, he knew at least a little about the wand at his belt and what it was capable of.

He couldn't say the same thing about the duchess of Merrek.

This conflict between them might get very ugly indeed.

Ser Grey led Aefric to a comfortable, informal sitting room. Before he entered, a servant handed him his coronet. Aefric sighed, but accepted that this was a formal meeting, even in an informal space. *Not* wearing the coronet might be taken as an insult.

He slipped it onto his head, and nodded for the door to be opened.

The sitting room had walls paneled in cherrywood, as well as the white ash floorboards he'd grown accustomed to. The floor was further covered in rugs of deep lake blue.

A fire in the hearth chased away the late morning chill, and past the bay windows gray skies had begun a swift, slanted rain.

The baron's party had already been seated on cheerful, padded red couches, giving them a view of the lake and the rain just above the crenellations of the keep walls.

A plate of grapes and a sliced, mellow white cheese sat untouched on the black oak coffee table before them. Their silver goblets of wine sat on the table as well, not in their hands.

Tension sang in the air as Aefric entered the room, while a page announced, "His grace, Ser Aefric Brightstaff, Duke of Deepwater."

Following Aefric into the room, one step behind, was Ser Grey, followed by two members of Aefric's personal guard, who stopped just inside the doorway.

He would have liked to have Ser Beornric along for this meeting, but apparently he was still interviewing the knights.

Just as well, perhaps. The better he knew them, the better he could tell how trustworthy they might prove.

As the page announced him, the baron's party stood.

The baron himself was easily enough spotted. He was almost shockingly pale, his skin a sharp contrast to his hair, which was so dark a black that it had blue highlights.

In his middle years, like the king, the baron was a fit man, with a strong build and an equally strong jaw. And he dressed simply, compared to the other barons Aefric had met so far. An unadorned dark blue doublet worn over a white shirt. Dark brown breeches, tucked into low black leather boots that folded down into cuffs.

His light blue eyes seemed to take in Aefric's measure with a glance, and withheld judgment so far.

He was flanked by two who had to be his children. They had the same pale skin and so-dark black hair.

On his right, likely his son, who looked not much younger than Aefric himself. Same light blue eyes as his father, but a slimmer build and jaw. The doublet he wore over his own white shirt was a deep wine red, though he wore the same style breeches and boots as his father.

The son was trying to give Aefric the same sort of assessment his father gave, but he wasn't as good at it. He looked impressed, despite himself.

To the baron's left, likely his daughter, who looked a few years shy of her majority. She had the lean, coltish look of a young woman still growing, though her delicate chin and high cheekbones promised that she would make an attractive adult someday.

Her gown was as simple as her brother's doublet, and the same deep wine red.

Her hazel eyes assessed Aefric as well, though they danced with mischief as they did.

Standing beside the other couch was a woman who had to have been the baroness. Or at least mother to the baron's children. She looked to be the right age. She also had the same pale skin and the same hazel eyes as the baron's daughter, though this woman's hair was the color of walnuts. She wore a gown of deep lake blue.

She gave Aefric an assessing look with the same neutrality as the baron himself.

They wore little jewelry, but each of them wore a carnelian some-where, set in gold. The baron wore his on a ring, the son on a bracer, the daughter on a brooch, and the likely baroness on a necklace.

The last member of their party stood slightly to one side. He was the only one who hadn't been sitting when Aefric entered, and he didn't have the family look to him.

His skin was tanned, for one thing. And his hair was a more common mousy brown, though cut short in the style of a soldier. He also affected a beard of the style Keifer had known as a Van Dyke, though what they called it here Aefric couldn't recall.

He wore a simple brown tunic and breeches, though the simplicity of their cut belied their quality. Aefric could tell they'd been made from fine material, as had his calf-high leather boots. He wore a thin scabbard at his belt, as for a rapier, though it was empty of its weapon right now.

His only jewelry was a small garnet on his belt buckle.

The garnet. Worn on a belt buckle. That meant something to Aefric, but he couldn't recall what.

His hands looked smooth, but he had a scar on the right side of his chin, of the sort that usually came from dueling, rather than fighting in battles.

Aefric was fairly certain this man had assessed Aefric, Ser Grey, and likely Aefric's two guards the moment they'd stepped into the room.

"Your grace," the page said, "may I present his lordship, Karmody Ol'Karmak, Baron of Riverbreak." The baron presented his hand — a bit grudgingly, from the look of the movement — and Aefric kissed it.

"His wife, the baroness, Montess Ol'Nastath." Her turn to have her hand kissed, though her fingers gently gripped Aefric's as he did so.

"His son and heir, Master Baston Ol'Karmak." The boy's whole body seemed to tense as Aefric kissed his hand.

"His daughter, Mistress Vercy Ol'Karmak." She actually giggled when Aefric kissed her hand, which got her shushed harshly by her mother.

Could this have been the first time her hand had been kissed by a noble?

"And Ser Grud Ol'Garan, of the Order of the Garnet."

That was it. The garnet on his belt represented a knightly order. Odd. The man hardly looked the part. He was lean, but not too well-muscled. And his soft skin hardly seemed hardened by campaigns and battles.

Just what did the Order of the Garnet do?

All the same, Aefric gave him the salute a noble gave a knight. He made a fist and grabbed its wrist. Ser Grud responded with a bow.

"Please," Aefric said, rounding the couches and taking an armchair for himself, "be seated, and refresh yourselves. I hope I have not kept you waiting long. I've hardly begun to settle into my duties, and there's already so very much to do."

"I am curious, your grace," Baron Karmody said, "why it is you saw fit to visit the baronial seats of Norra and Felspark, and yet refused me the same courtesy?"

"Well, to be fair," Aefric said with a sigh, "I didn't visit Felspark's baronial seat at Ruunkeep. I visited her at Tafarac, which was much closer to the Kingsroad."

Aefric held up a hand to forestall the angry objection he saw forming in the baron's eyes.

"In truth, I'd hoped to visit you at Magranus, after stopping here for the night at Behal." Aefric shook his head. "Unfortunately, too much is happening. I needed to be here to begin coordinating ways to help my barons, and to assess and deal with extant threats."

Aefric took a goblet of light white wine brought to him by a page. He took a sip of its sweet, dry flavor while the baron rubbed at his chin, considering Aefric's words.

"Which is why I called you here," Aefric said. "As well as Baron Osmaer of Havenford, and Count Cyneric of Goldenfall. I need the clearest, most up-to-date assessments of yours lands and status that I can get. And I need to get your oaths of vassalage at the same time."

"Has Goldenfall replied?" the baroness asked, while her husband steepled his fingers.

"Goldenfall only seems to employ the slowest of rika birds," Aefric said, which got a quickly stifled burst of laughter from Vercy.

"Control yourself," Baron Karmody growled, "or leave the room."

She bowed her head, chastened.

Baston continued watching Aefric through the whole exchange, as did Baroness Montess.

"Personally," Aefric said with what he hoped was a disarming smile, "I appreciate knowing when my attempts at humor don't go to waste."

"Humor has its place," Baron Karmody said. "What problems are so pressing, your grace?"

Aefric smiled. "A question for later. We have other business before us first."

"But as my liege," the baron said, "your problems are my problems. I only wish to help."

"You have not yet given your formal oaths," Aefric said, "so those problems will wait. And before we get to the oaths, I need to know what's going on in Riverbreak."

"Riverbreak ... abides, your grace," Baron Karmody said. "We were spared a great deal in the Godswalk Wars, when you drove the borogs south well to the east of us. We suffered our share of pains, but I daresay we're in a stronger position than our fellows Norra and Felspark. Alas, I fear I know little of what transpires way out in Havenford."

An odd statement, given that they share the Haven River...

"How much do you know of what transpires in Norra and Felspark?"

"Rumors, only," Baron Karmody said too smoothly for it to be true.

"And trade?" Aefric asked. "How fares trade in Riverbreak?"

"Slow," Baron Karmody said, affecting a sigh that didn't reach his eyes. "The wars have hurt trade everywhere, I suspect. Though our ships stand ready to make up the difference when trade flows steadily once more."

"I'm glad to hear it," Aefric said. "Are there any problems you would bring to my attention?"

"Two," Baron Karmody said, smoothly. "The first is on the matter of trade. My adviser, Ser Grud, tells me that Merrek could be trading with us more than they are, but are holding back, to weaken us." He shook his head. "Though I suspect you have heard the same from Norra and Felspark."

"I'm sorry, your grace," Ser Grud said, and the man had a surprisingly smooth voice, for someone with such a guttural name. He really should have been a skald, rather than a knight. "I'm afraid that

Merrek's duchess is likely hampering trade to try to force you to cut a deal with her that would be to her advantage."

He grimaced, as though his words tasted foul. "I suspect that, given your past" — he nodded to the Brightstaff, standing beside Aefric's chair — "she believes that if she gets you to the negotiating table you will find yourself facing a battle you cannot win."

"And with all due respect, she may have a point, your grace," Baron Karmody continued. "We Ol'Karmaks, on the other hand, have been negotiating trade deals for generations. I would be more than happy to do my duty to the duchy and represent Deepwater myself, in negotiations with Merrek."

"I thank you for that offer, your lordship," Aefric said, "and I will consider it carefully. At the very least, I may wish to bring you in as an adviser, when the time comes to negotiate with Merrek."

"I would, of course, be honored," Baron Karmody said.

"You said there was another matter?" Aefric asked.

"Yes. Before her unfortunate demise, Duchess Arinda had promised herself in marriage to my son, Baston."

"You have evidence of this?" Aefric asked, surprised.

"Alas, nothing so overt was ever written down. The promise was verbal. But witnessed by myself and my wife."

"I was so happy for the both of them," Baroness Montess said, picking up as though they'd rehearsed this. "It was all I could do not to shout it from the battlements."

"Then I am sorry for your loss," Aefric said, "but I don't see how I could help."

"We are both nobles, your grace," Baron Karmody said gently. "A promise from a duchess to a baron is a promise from the duchy to the barony."

Aefric frowned. Could this man be implying...

"You wish me to marry your son?"

"Or my daughter Vercy, if your grace prefers women. The promise could be fulfilled either way."

Aefric frowned deeper, but the baron's entire family looked serious. The hope in Vercy's eyes shone so bright it was almost painful to see.

"I will take this matter under consideration as well. I am still receiving reports about other commitments made by my predecessor. I cannot agree to anything further until I have all my information."

"I doubt the Duchess Arinda would have been so false as to promise herself to another," Baron Karmody said. "But I of course respect your grace's wish to be fully informed before fulfilling her promise to us."

"I thank you for your patience." Aefric stood. "For the moment, though, you could at least take one important matter off my plate."

"The oaths of vassalage," the baron said, kneeling on the carpet while his wife came over to kneel beside him, apparently intent on swearing as well. "Of course, your grace. We are ever your humble servants."

Aefric doubted that a great deal. But he would take their oaths, and hope those oaths were worth more than mere words.

ONCE AEFRIC FINISHED ACCEPTING THE OATHS OF VASSALAGE FROM Baron Karmody and his wife, and offering his own oaths as liege lord, he needed fresh air.

He met with Sers Grey and Beornric on the battlements that looked out over the busy city of Behal. The skies had taken a break from the rain, and hopeful sunshine poked through the gray clouds above and given Aefric at least a taste of warmth, under the strong, cool breeze.

He'd returned to his rooms, though, and added that cloak to his outfit. It was soft and woolen, a pale gray color and marvelous for keeping the wind at bay.

"Your grace should eat," Ser Grey said, first thing. And she had a point. It was mid-afternoon now, and he'd had nothing since breakfast save for a half a goblet of that sweet, dry white wine.

As though echoing his castellan's assessment, Aefric's stomach growled.

"I will," Aefric said, "as soon as we're done here." He squinted down the river to the south. "If those sails mean what I think they mean, Havenford will be here a little early."

"Then let's get to it," Ser Beornric said, then ducked his head and added, "your grace."

Aefric chuckled. "When I'm meeting with the two of you, I don't mind forgoing the courtesies."

"I'll try," Ser Grey said, shaking her head, "but it won't be easy."

"What do you think of those knights?" Aefric asked.

"They're true knights," Ser Beornric said. "All six of them fought at Deepwater, and all six of them would follow you into the Abyss, if you asked them to. I'd have added them to your personal guard already, but it really needs to be you, doing it."

"Right," Aefric said. "We'll arrange that for after I have a bite to eat." He shook his head. "No. We'll call them together, bring them into my personal guard, then I'll share a late lunch with them."

"Good thought," Ser Grey said. "Now, about Baron Karmody."

"Yes, about him," Aefric said. "You were in the room. What did you think? Start with that promise of marriage."

Ser Grey sighed. "I hate to say it, but it's a possibility. Duchess Arinda loved to imply promises and get people's hopes up, before playing one suitor against another."

"She couldn't have been serious about Baston," Aefric said, knowing that disbelief was as visible on his face as it was audible in his voice. "The son of a baron? Marrying a duchess of her standing? Wouldn't she be expected to marry someone closer to her equal?"

"Usually, yes," Ser Grey said. "But in Arinda's case..." Ser Grey sighed. "She ... had her own way of doing things. If she liked the boy's eyes, that might have been enough for her."

"And if she did promise it? Does her promise bind me?"

"If they had it in writing, it would. If it were a written promise, your only semi-gracious way out would be to ask the king to nullify the agreement."

"He'd probably do it," Ser Beornric said. "He's fond of you."

"But he might not, because he might worry I'd do what Arinda did. Consider my options too long and die without an heir."

"There is that," Ser Beornric admitted reluctantly.

"The girl isn't uncomely," Ser Grey said. "Though I imagine you might consider her too young—"

"*Too young*?" Aefric said. "She's a child!"

"Well," Ser Grey said slowly. "*Child* is an exaggeration—"

"*Fine*. If not a *child*, then *certainly* too young to merit serious *marriage* consideration."

Ser Grey cleared her throat. "You're a noble now, your grace. Technically you could be promised to a newborn babe, even if you did not consummate the marriage until she was of age."

"Great," Aefric said, fighting not to roll his eyes. "So they'd expect me to commit to the marriage now, and ... consummate it when—"

"Close," Ser Grey said, though she looked as though what she said pained her. "But not quite. Truce, Vercy's not yet reached the age of majority. But *some* would call her old enough to be wed. And old enough to consummate the union."

"*I* say she's not old enough," Aefric said. "So she's not old enough. I'm the duke here."

"Very good, your grace," Ser Grey said, then realized she'd given him his courtesy again and shrugged. "Habit."

"All right," Aefric said. "I refuse to commit to anything anytime soon. And I don't like the idea of marrying someone just because Arinda *might* have promised to marry her brother."

"Of course," Ser Grey said, visibly biting down the urge to add *your grace*.

"You do risk insulting Riverbreak," Ser Beornric said, "if you refuse the marriage."

"I won't formally refuse it yet, so that's a worry for later," Aefric said, shaking his head. "What about the baron himself, the standing of Riverbreak, and trade?"

"Please tell me you wouldn't let him negotiate with Merrek for you," Ser Grey said.

"Not in the least," Aefric said firmly. "If anything, that offer makes me suspect he's working with Merrek."

"*Possible*," Ser Grey said, "but not a certainty. He may want to handle any trade negotiations to ensure that whatever deal is made at least benefits his barony."

Aefric considered that through a long breath, looking out over the city below. If he tried, he could imagine hearing the sounds of people going about their busy lives, heedless of what went on up here at the castle.

"It is also possible," Ser Grey said, "that the baron was simply being cagey. Unsure how far to trust an adventurer who'd been made his liege lord."

"Does no one care that the king himself selected me?"

"Yes," Ser Beornric said. "But remember that they know the king did so for *his* purposes, which are much larger, and may not always align with what your new vassals consider their own best interests."

"Terrific," Aefric said, shaking his head. "Either way, we'll have to be careful around Karmody and his family. At least until we establish some kind of trust with them. Or get Merrek settled. Or both."

"Did you tell Riverbreak anything of what else is going on?" Ser Beornric asked.

"No. By the time the oaths were done, I'd begged off further conversation over concerns about my duties to the duchy."

"Reminds me," Ser Grey said. "The prince's report is waiting in your chambers, when you want it. And both the mayor of Behal, and a delegation from the Behal Trade Council have requested audiences with you."

"Of course they have," Aefric said with a sigh. "All right. Schedule both meetings for tomorrow afternoon. Mayor first, then trade council."

"I'll make the arrangements," Ser Grey said.

"As for the report, it'll have to wait until after dinner," Aefric said. "All right. So, Arinda may have gotten me into a marriage I need to get out of. Baron Karmody may be in league with Merrek, or may just really not trust me. Have I missed anything?"

"Two things," Ser Grey said. "The first is the presence of Ser Grud."

"Ser Grud?" Ser Beornric asked.

"Knight of the Garnet," Ser Grey said, "and officially an adviser to Baron Karmody."

"Wonderful," Ser Beornric said, rolling his eyes.

"What's the Order of the Garnet do?" Aefric asked.

"The Order of the Garnet," Ser Grey said, "is little more than a jumped up guild of duelists that fill their time between duels with extensive work in trade and trade negotiations."

"Ugh," Aefric said. "And I saluted him like a proper knight."

"It's good that you did," Ser Beornric said, "if he came in with the baron's party. Not giving him his knightly due would have insulted the baron."

"In that sense," Ser Grey added, "they may have brought him along to test you. As well as represent the baron, if a duel became necessary."

"Wait," Aefric said. "Baron Karmody brought a professional duelist along to the meeting where he informed me about this so-called marriage promise? Why don't I think that's a coincidence?"

"Because you have a brain in your head?" Ser Beornric asked.

"In all fairness," Ser Grey said, making placating gestures, "Baron Karmody might honestly employ Ser Grud for his advice on trade matters. Some garnet knights get good at it."

"I'll keep that in mind," Aefric said, fighting the urge to spit. "What's the second thing?"

"The second thing," Ser Grey said, grimacing through a breath. "Baroness Montess."

"What about her?" Aefric asked.

"You are new to Armyr, your grace," Ser Grey said. "Among nobles here ... there is the frank acceptance that marriage is about alliances and offspring."

"So?" Aefric asked, as Ser Beornric turned away, visibly trying not to laugh.

"The act of sex in Armyr — and though this perspective started

among the nobles, it spread to the populace long ago as well — is not
... so tightly tied to marriage, as it is in some nations across Qorunn."

"The *leaba* you were offered in Norra," Ser Beornric added, "is a
reflection of this. Sex for pleasure is part of the culture here, so long
as all involved want it to happen."

Aefric shook his head in disbelief. He'd known that some places
in Qorunn had such views — he'd enjoyed them himself in Goldenmoon — but he didn't remember this about Armyr. And certainly, as
Keifer, he'd never read anything like this in the sourcebooks.

"Jealousy can still occur, of course," Ser Beornric said. "Though
public displays of jealousy are considered quite gauche."

"Among the nobles of Armyr," Ser Grey said, "these things are
especially true." She shook her head. "And from the way Baroness
Montess looked at you, I shouldn't be surprised to hear of her visiting
your chambers tonight."

"What if I offer them *leaba*? The baron and baroness are a good-
looking couple. Surely we could find volunteers here to share their
beds."

"A possibility," Ser Grey said. "But remember that Havenford will
be joining us tonight as well. And *leaba* can be a risky offer. If, for
example, the baroness had volunteers, but the baron did not. Or if
Havenford had volunteers, but Riverbreak did not."

"Not a formal insult," Ser Beornric said, "and nothing they could
properly complain about. But it could lead to hurt feelings."

"If you had stronger relations with Barons Riverbreak and Havenford," Ser Grey said, "then you could offer *leaba* safely and risk little.
But with matters between you unsettled, and yourself a new noble,
they might ... they might believe you were misusing *leaba*. Perhaps
attempting to curry favor through an old tradition. Or worse."

"Lovely," Aefric muttered. "Just what I need. Another
complication."

"I'm afraid that *leaba* is not your way out of a possible visit from
the baroness tonight."

"Can I at least refuse her if she shows up?" Aefric asked, frustrated. "Or am I expected to simply perform on demand?"

"If you refuse her *company* without a compelling reason," Ser Grey said, "she will take it as an insult. You would be under no obligation to have sex with her, though, should you choose not to."

"Well, I'm glad of that, at least."

"Don't be afraid to consider it, though," Ser Grey said. "She's an attractive woman. And ... acclimating yourself to the local cultural mores will help you settle in as duke."

"Plus," Ser Beornric said, "working off some stress through sex it rarely a bad thing."

"Your knights certainly benefit from it," Ser Grey said, sharing a smile with Ser Beornric that left no doubt in Aefric's head that the two of them were sleeping together. "No reason you should not as well."

"And I hate to say it," Ser Beornric said, "but the baroness coming to you tonight may be a good thing. Apart from ... any other hopes she might have ... she'll undoubtedly also try to gain information from you. Might be a good opportunity to spread disinformation."

Aefric was about to object.

"A more palatable weapon, I should think," Ser Grey said, "than a pirate's aid."

Aefric closed his mouth. She had a point.

Aefric might just have to take one for the team.

***

AEFRIC GATHERED HIS KNIGHTS IN HIS SOLARIUM.

The solarium was a large room, five stairs up from Aefric's sitting room. And at least as large as that sitting room. The floor and three of the walls were all paneled in white ash bleached almost to the color of bones.

The remaining wall was a network of windows, all clear as crystal, but enchanted to be strong as stone, or stronger. And those were not the only windows.

The roof of Aefric's solarium was domed, and the dome was made entirely of stained glass in patterns of red, blue and green. A series of low, comfortable couches — upholstered in a soft gray color — had been arranged to maximize their view.

A light tea was kept brewing in here, filling the air with a sweet, gentle smell.

Even with the sky still swirling with rain clouds, the solarium managed to be bright and cheerful. Just entering this room gave Aefric's spirits a lift, and he hoped his knights felt the same way.

There were six of these knights, led in by Ser Beornric, who introduced them down the line.

Ser Leppina, with her tanned skin and her strong build. She wore her brown hair in a long, single braid that fell down to her ribcage. It was said that she only cut her hair short when someone bested her in combat.

Ser Temat, with his dark skin, lean muscles and that wicked scar at his neck. He kept his head shaved "to avoid giving the enemy a handle."

Ser Vria, who looked too small and pale to be a knight. At least until Aefric looked into her golden eyes and saw a will that would not break. It was said that she used her size to her advantage even better than the kindaren. It was also hinted that she had eldrani blood, and given the faint orange tint of her hair, and the fine perfection of her features, it was certainly possible.

Ser Micham, the son of the mayor of Ajenmoor, he had skin toughened by the sea, and he'd lost half an ear to a borog's spear. But he kept his brown hair and beard trimmed as fashionably as the cut of his fine clothes.

Ser Arras, said to be the unclaimed bastard daughter of Duchess Arinda, conceived and born when the duchess was traveling abroad. She certainly had the beauty of the duchess, tempered with a challenge in her hazel eyes that dared anyone to call her pretty. She kept her black hair cut short, and wore simple clothes that were easy to move in. She was also the only knight present who fought with two swords, by preference.

And finally, Ser Wardius, the most scarred of the lot. Both his cheeks were jagged, and he'd lost the tip of his nose and the small finger off his left hand. His hands showed more scars than tanned skin. But he was a wiry kind of tough, and in his eye the certainty of a man at peace with who and what he was.

Every one of these knights only a handful of years past their majority. But they carried themselves as though they'd seen twice as many years. Likely the result of fighting in the Godswalk Wars.

After Aefric improvised a small ceremony for bringing them into his personal guard, it was time to eat. And he was more than ready.

This late lunch took place at the large table in his own chambers, at the suggestion of Ser Grey. She'd said it was a subtle way to honor them, and sure enough, they'd all looked pleased to be invited to dine with the duke in his own rooms.

The lunch itself was surprisingly relaxed and pleasant. Every one of these knights hailed from a different part of the lands Aefric now held himself, rather than those held by his vassals.

Most importantly, they were all so used to only getting asked about wars and battles and tournaments that they seemed thrilled that Aefric was more interested in the knights themselves and the areas where they grew up.

Aefric made it clear that whether they were the children of knights and nobles or of farmers and townsfolk — in which case they'd been knighted for deeds of arms during the Godswalk Wars — their duke wanted to hear all about them and the parts of his duchy he might not see for some time.

Aefric kept them talking all through the meal, and over coffee afterward. In fact, he kept them talking until Ser Grey arrived to announce that Baron Osmaer Greenhand of Havenford had arrived and awaited his grace's pleasure.

Then Aefric, stood, smiled down at his knights, and said, "I hope we will have time to talk like this again soon. I don't know that we will. Events are in motion that may bring trouble."

Each knight thumped his or her shoulder to indicate their readiness, if needed.

Aefric smiled.

"With that in mind, I'll want you all to spend the afternoon drilling, under the direction of Ser Beornric" — Aefric glanced at the knight in question — "who should remember to include himself in the exercises. And I'll want you involved in keeping the soldiers of my personal guard in ready shape, in case they are needed."

They each nodded and thumped their shoulders again.

"Excellent. Ser Beornric, they are yours for the rest of the day. Ser Grey, let's go."

Before Aefric was out the door of his chambers, one of his servants — a young man named Buchmond — cleared his throat and offered Aefric his coronet.

Aefric sighed as he donned it, but thanked Buchmond as he turned to follow Ser Grey to the meeting room.

Along the way, Ser Grey told him she'd arranged for him to meet with the mayor just after lunch the next day, and the trade council later that afternoon.

Administration. Was that really what he, as Keifer, had signed up for?

Part of the job, he supposed. As was going to meet a baron.

AEFRIC WAS MEETING THIS BARON IN THE SAME MEETING ROOM AS HE'D met the last one, as it turned out. Baron Osmaer's much smaller party reclined together on a single red couch, watching the lake as though the two of them were alone in a world of their own.

A page announced Aefric, as he entered followed by Ser Grey and then two soldiers of his personal guard.

"His grace, Ser Aefric Brightstaff, Duke of Deepwater."

The baron and his husband stood and turned, smiling, to bow a greeting to their duke.

Baron Osmaer was a tall man, with dark skin, and his hair a halo of dreadlocks. He wore surprisingly simple clothes. Dark greens and browns, for both his tunic and his breeches, and his low, soft leather boots looked as though he might have walked here in them.

On a leather thong around his neck hung the deer antler pendant of Halstaffur the Green Lord.

And just like that, the man's clothing made sense to Aefric. Priests of the Green Lord rarely cared about ornamentation.

The baron's husband was slightly shorter — if Baron Osmaer was Aefric's height, this man was perhaps a handspan shorter — his hair a deep auburn and his skin a soft brown. He dressed just as simply as the baron — in tunic and breeches — but he favored dark orange and reddish-brown for the colors he brought together.

His boots, though, were newer, and came up to his calves. Interesting.

"Your grace," the page said, "may I present his lordship Osmaer Greenhand, Baron of Havenford."

The baron held his out, and Aefric kissed it.

"His husband, Baronet Gautzelin Sul Lazanae."

After Aefric had kissed the baronet's hand as well, he said, "Please be seated," and stepped around to sit again in the armchair. "I trust I have not kept you waiting overlong. I was meeting with my knights."

"With such a view of the lake," Baron Osmaer said with a smile, "we could have waited all evening without complaint. Could we not, my love?"

"I shouldn't complain if we waited here until morning," Baronet Gautzelin said, taking his husband's hand.

"Then you must take time, while you're here, to visit the garden. The view is even better there, I expect."

"You expect?" Baron Osmaer asked. "You haven't taken it in yourself as yet?"

"Sadly," Aefric said with a sigh, "I've been too busy since my arrival."

"I imagine," Baron Osmaer said. "The death by a million small requests, no doubt."

"Oh, those are still coming."

They laughed, and the baron said, "Your servants were good enough to provide us with this sweet wine, for which we are both grateful."

"It's quite good," Baronet Gautzelin said, taking a sip from his silver goblet, for emphasis.

"However," the baron said, "I would myself prefer something more along the lines of stout beer, if I might ask for one."

Aefric glanced at a servant, who nodded that it could be provided.

"For the both of us, please," Aefric said. "I could do with some beer myself."

"Oh," Baronet Gautzelin said with one hand dramatically raised to his forehead. "Save me from adventurers and their low palates."

The baron stilled, holding his breath.

Aefric burst out laughing.

After days of every noble treading as though afraid of snapping a twig and drawing his wrath, such an easy joke was so unexpected that he needed a moment to stop laughing.

While he laughed, the baron relaxed through a long breath, and smiled himself.

"I'm sorry," Aefric said at last. "Everyone has been so formal with me that I'd almost forgotten what humor sounded like."

"Then you'll have to come visit us," the baronet said, evidently pleased with himself, "whenever you want reminding."

"An invitation I shall remember, I assure you," Aefric said, still smiling, as he and the baron took their beers from a servant, who brought them in silvered mugs.

"A toast, your grace," Baron Osmaer said. "To your health, and to the flowering of Deepwater under your guidance."

All three drank to that.

The beer was quite good. Strong, thick, rich and still crisp. With just enough bite to make one take it seriously.

"Will Ser Grey be joining us?" Baron Osmaer asked.

"As castellan under his grace," Ser Grey said, "my duty here is to witness and record, not to take part. Unless, of course, ordered by his grace."

Baron Osmaer raised an eyebrow. "Seems unkind to have her present and not drinking."

"Please, Ser Grey," Aefric said with a broad smile, "join us, if you would."

She signaled for a mug of beer, and took the other empty armchair.

"Now," Baron Osmaer said, "I imagine you'd like to know how things stand in Havenford?"

"I would," Aefric said. "Very much."

"As you might expect," — he gestured to the token of his god worn round his neck — "our farmland is fine. Bountiful, even. During the wars, our coastal towns suffered, but with so much else intact, I've been able to make good time rebuilding them."

"How is trade?"

"Down, somewhat," Baron Osmaer said, sounding unconcerned. "But mostly because I've needed to keep as many ships as possible close to shore. To ensure safety during our rebuilding."

"If your grace could spare any additional funds to help with fortifications or weaponry," Baronet Gautzelin said, "they would be most welcome."

"I'll have to look into it," Aefric said. "I'll be getting reports soon from up the coast, about how things stand with my own towns and villages, and the state of my own navy."

"The denizens of two of your southernmost coastal towns came into my lands seeking refuge when their homes were destroyed," Baron Osmaer said. "I welcomed them, of course. They've been helpful during the rebuilding. But if your grace wishes, I could send them back to your own lands."

"By all means, let them help you rebuild," Aefric said.

"Thank you, your grace," Baron Osmaer said with an incline of his head. "And once those towns are rebuilt, I'll be only too happy to have my people help those refugees rebuild their own towns in your lands."

"Thank you," Aefric said. "What of any other problems you might be having?"

"Other problems, your grace?" Baron Osmaer genuinely sounded puzzled.

"There have been some reports of Merrek applying pressure through trade. Have you experienced anything along those lines?"

"Not at all, your grace," Baron Osmaer said, sitting back and looking astonished. "In fact, Merrek ships have frequently sailed alongside us. Our greater numbers helping to deter pirates."

"And this has been true even since the war?" Ser Grey asked.

"The practice only really started during the war," the baron said. "Before the war, we all had ships enough that it wasn't necessary."

"Merrek has been nothing but good to us," Baronet Gautzelin added.

"Merrek's navy was hurt by the war?" Aefric asked.

"Oh, indeed," Baron Osmaer said. "Their coast was savaged by the sea devils, even as ours was. I wouldn't be surprised to hear that their trade is in even worse shape than ours."

"Proportionately speaking," Baronet Gautzelin added quickly.

"Yes," Baron Osmaer agreed. "Proportionately speaking, of course. In absolute terms, I'm sure she moves a good deal more cargo than Havenford ships ever could."

"But her trade is likely down," Aefric said, disbelieving. This seemed to go against everything he'd been told so far. "How sure are you of this?"

"I get regular reports from my captains," Baron Osmaer said with a shrug. "And they talk with her captains. Can't see why they'd lie about something like this."

"No," Aefric said, giving Ser Grey a significant look. "I can't see why either."

"Is something wrong, your grace?" Baronet Gautzelin asked.

"Yes and no," Aefric said, "but nothing I can explain right now."

"I'm sure your grace knows best," Baron Osmaer said, and sipped his beer while making a sound of approval. "This really is marvelous, by the way."

Aefric shook himself, and took another sip of beer.

The baron was right. It *was* good.

"I'll have them send a cask home with you when you leave," Aefric said.

"Oh, don't," Baronet Gautzelin said. "It'll be all he drinks until Midwinter."

"Never mind that," Baron Osmaer said, smiling. "Thank you very much, your grace. We're pleased to accept the gift."

Baronet Gautzelin sighed and rolled his eyes.

"On another matter," Aefric said, "by any chance is your lordship fond of travel?"

"Well, I haven't been an adventurer in a hundred and fifty years," Baron Osmaer said. "But I do still love to see the road wide open before me. When I can."

A hundred and fifty years? The man was plainly human, and didn't look a day over thirty. Aefric had thought only wizards held the secret of such extended youth, but apparently priests of the Green Lord knew a thing or two as well.

"Your grace wants to ask about farmland," Baronet Gautzelin said.

"I do," Aefric said. "Felspark worries about famine come wintertime, and Norra isn't much better off. I don't know about Fyretti, Goldenfall and Motte yet, but I know my own farms along the coast would benefit greatly from the blessings of Halstaffur."

"If your grace orders me, of course, I shall obey," Baron Osmaer started slowly. Aefric cut in before he could finish.

"I'm not ordering you. I'm asking for help, on behalf of those who need it. If your barony can spare you."

"Thank you, your grace," Baron Osmaer said with a nod. "In truth, right now, it cannot. Not for long."

Baron Osmaer held up a forestalling hand.

"I have three acolytes who have been training with me," he continued. "All are ready to become priests, and could use this as a final task. I shall send the three of them out to deal with Felspark and Norra first, then return here to Behal for instruction about where they are next most needed. Only send them back to me when they are no longer needed urgently."

"Thank you," Aefric said.

"As for your coastal farms," Baron Osmaer continued, "I shall see to them myself."

"I'm not sure I can thank you enough," Aefric said.

"Rule us wisely, and that will be all the thanks I require."

"I'll do my best."

Baron Osmaer nodded. "Is there anything more, your grace?"

"Only the oaths of vassalage."

"Well then," Baron Osmaer said, sinking to his knees. "Those we can take care of at once."

WHEN THE OATHS WERE FINISHED, TO AEFRIC'S SURPRISE, THERE WAS still some time before dinner, so he returned to the battlements with Ser Grey, this time looking out over the lake.

The sun was beginning to set, burning the distant, westernmost part of the sky a light yellow. What little warmth that sun had brought with it today fled in chill winds, that promised more rain before morning.

Still the lake was busy with boats and ships.

"I'd say Osmaer's on your side," Ser Grey said.

"So far, at least," Aefric said. "What did you think of what he said about Merrek's ships?"

"I agree that the captains weren't likely lying to each other. Not if they were relying on numbers to keep pirates at bay."

Ser Grey held onto her next words as long as she could before letting them out.

"Speaking of pirates—"

"We can't go to Nelazzi," Aefric said. "Not now. Not if Merrek's ships are sailing with Havenford's."

"Good," Ser Grey said through a relaxed sigh.

"You really didn't like that idea, I take it?"

"Your grace must do as he thinks—"

"What did I say earlier about asking for your opinion?"

Ser Grey nodded, chastened.

"I think dealing with pirates is abhorrent. Even if there is some small, short term benefit to working with them, in the long term, they will pay back every good they do us with a thousand evils."

Aefric blinked. "So you *don't* like the idea then."

Ser Grey's mask of distaste cracked in a chuckle. "No, your grace. I do not."

"Noted," Aefric said with a nod. "For what it's worth, I don't like the idea either. But more important is the implication that Merrek's trade is down as well."

"Even reduced," Ser Grey said, "Merrek's fleet is not to be discounted."

"Perhaps," Aefric said, trying to put together the pieces of everything he'd been told so far. From the bandits in Kerrik Forest and greater Norra to the brazen actions of Motte, to trade pressure and possible land-theft in Felspark, and the cagey behavior of Riverbreak.

Merrek couldn't be suffering on one hand, and actively supporting Motte and working against Deepwater at the same time. Something was missing.

But what?

"I wish the countess could get started on her inquiry today," he muttered.

"She probably only got to Fyretti by late morning," Ser Grey said. "And given that she'll need to settle in, as well as send for her companions? She'll likely not leave for four or five days at least."

"Terrific," Aefric said. "Anything special I'll need to know before I meet with the mayor and trade council tomorrow?"

"Only that they'll want money," Ser Grey said with a shrug. "They always do."

"I haven't even had a chance to check on the state of Behal's finances, let alone Deepwater's," Aefric said, shaking his head. "I'll have to..."

"No," he said with a smile. "I'll definitely meet with them before I review the finances. That way I couldn't promise them anything if I wanted to."

"Devious, your grace," Ser Grey said. "Are you certain you weren't born to this?"

Aefric laughed. "More certain than you'll ever know."

"We've had a rika bird from Goldenfall, by the way," Ser Grey said. "Count Cyneric assures you that his daughter can give a true and accurate report on the state of Goldenfall. And while he says he'd love to swear fealty, his county cannot spare him at this time."

Aefric spat over the wall. "Damn."

"What?"

"He just promoted his daughter from courtier to ambassador, didn't he?"

"You're thinking about dinner?"

"I am," Aefric said through a sigh. "I'll need to dine with my barons and their families, tonight, not my knights. And Byrhta has to be invited after all."

"I'll tell the seneschal."

"The seneschal?" Aefric asked.

"The seneschal runs the castle itself," Ser Grey said, "freeing you — and me, in your absence — to handle the larger issues." She smiled. "Your grace doesn't pay me enough to act as both seneschal and castellan."

"Just as well," Aefric said. "You need to sleep *some*time. All right. I'll want to meet the seneschal soon. I should have before now."

"Duchess Arinda never dealt with Behal's seneschal herself," Ser Grey said. "She always left the task to me because, as she put it, 'you don't need me butting in on your working relationship.'"

"A fair point," Aefric said, "but not an excuse not to at least *meet* this seneschal." Aefric grimaced. "Especially since I'm changing the dinner plans again."

"A common occurrence," Ser Grey assured him. "And look at the bright side. Perhaps Byrhta will be charmed enough by you at dinner that she'll show up at your door tonight at the same time the baroness does. You could allay them both with a round table discussion about trade."

Aefric's head drooped as he looked at his castellan.

"You're joking, right? You don't think she'd—"

"You've been ignoring her, which her father won't want. Further, she might have heard by now that Karmody expects you to marry his daughter. Showing up at your door tonight would be one way of grabbing your attention, and possibly convincing you to set aside Arinda's promise, leaving you free to pursue ... other matrimonial possibilities."

Aefric had a horrible thought then.

"You don't suppose Vercy herself would show up at my door?"

"Normally I'd be worried about it. But given the way her mother was looking at you, she'll want to go first."

"By Kalinda's silver eyes," Aefric said, "I'm not some prize stallion to ride."

"Forgive me, your grace," Ser Grey said, "but you are a young, handsome man. A war hero. And now a rich and powerful duke. Every unwed noblewoman and her mother for a thousand miles wants very much to break you to the saddle."

"That's marriage though," Aefric said, his heart pounding as though he were trapped under tons of fallen dirt and ancient ruin once more. Only this time, transporting himself away wouldn't free him from the problem.

"We're talking about sex," Aefric continued. "Am I really to expect a parade of noblewomen coming to my door at night?"

"Did you look about the hall during dinner last night?" Ser Grey asked.

Aefric nodded.

"And how many young women tried to meet your eyes with hopeful smiles?"

The answer was a larger number than Aefric wanted to think about.

"And I'm expected to bed all of them, am I?"

"Not all of them. Not if you don't choose to. Still. I'm sure at least some of them will appeal to you. And with those who do, you should feel free to indulge yourself in what pleasures they offer you."

Aefric shook his head in disbelief.

"Countess Faenella, down in Fyretti. Is she—"

"Getting as many offers as you will?" Ser Grey shrugged. "Likely not *as* many, because you are a duke and she a countess. Your rank certainly doesn't hurt your appeal, and your court holds far more options than hers does. However. Faenella's certainly pleasing enough to look upon. And she has wealth and power enough to tempt even those who prefer their women ... more demure and less strong-willed and muscled."

Aefric didn't know what to say to that, so Ser Grey went on.

"This is Armyr, your grace. As I tried to tell you. Sex is not a big deal here, especially among the nobility. They sleep together freely, regardless of rank or marital status, and refer to it as 'the noble privilege.' Had you stayed a night in the royal palace at Armityr, the queen herself might have come to your chambers."

"And that wouldn't have gotten me into trouble?"

"No," Ser Grey said firmly. "Not if you'd accepted, and not if you'd refused her. You would have been free to decide. Here, the situation is a little more complicated because your vassals are only just getting to know you. Which might be all the more reason for them to visit you in the night."

"As a means of getting to know me?"

"Just so," Ser Grey said with a nod. "And if both Byrhta and Baroness Montess should show up at your door tonight, I say, invite them both inside. Enjoy a night of pleasure with them. It won't obligate you to either Goldenfall or Riverbreak. In fact, it might help your nobles relax, knowing that you're adjusting to the customs here — of which the noble privilege is an important one — rather than trying to impose foreign concepts of morality."

"You're serious," Aefric said. "They wouldn't take that as some sort of promise."

"Your grace," Ser Grey said patiently, "a night of pleasure here is no more an implication of commitment than a discussion over wine would be."

Aefric thought about that for a moment. But the part of him that was Keifer still wasn't sure about the night he'd spent with Octave. To even consider sleeping with someone else? Someone else who wasn't Andi?

Aefric could feel the cycle starting again. That whipping back and forth between the fact that his wife was dead and gone and the part of him that still wanted to be faithful to her.

But before that tsunami could drown and dominate his thoughts, there was a cry from a sweaty, breathless page at the stairs.

"Your grace! Princess Maev arrives!"

The princess? Here?

Then there was only one thing to do.

Aefric stepped up onto a crenellation and prepared to jump.

10

The late afternoon wind whipped Aefric's blonde hair, and he held his cloak in one hand and the Brightstaff in the other as he stepped up onto the crenellations of the battlements, high above the courtyard below.

His eyes tracked across the courtyard, gauging the strength of the wind...

"Your grace!" Ser Grey cried, grabbing him by the cloak and pulling him back down onto the battlements, while four of his personal guards rushed to assist.

"This is hardly a matter meriting suicide," Ser Grey said firmly, her eyes blazing with anger. Likely at what she perceived was a fatal weakness in her new duke.

"Of course not," Aefric said, shortly. "I've faced down a lich, a thunder of giants, an army of borogs and more. I think I can stand up to a princess."

"Then what were you doing?"

Aefric turned to his guards. "Meet us at the bottom." He turned to Ser Grey. "With me, now, and have faith."

He stepped back up onto the crenellation.

Ser Grey looked uncertain, but stepped up next to him, holding her cloak against the wind.

With his free hand, he reached out and grabbed her shoulder.

Before she could stop him, he jumped, pulling her with him.

The two of them plunged over the side.

Aefric muttered a few words, calling forth not the power of flight itself. That would be wasteful for a trip so brief as this one.

No, the power he called forth was that of autumnal leaves, slipping free from their branches and floating gently on the wind until they kissed the ground at last.

And like those leaves, Aefric and Ser Grey drifted on the wind.

Ser Grey didn't scream, as the wind whipped them near the castle wall, then swirled and carried them up and an on course to clear the wall and head over the lake, but the shoulder muscles in Aefric's grip seized harder than a blacksmith's anvil.

Aefric only laughed in what he hoped was a reassuring manner, and pointed down into the courtyard with the yellow diamond atop the Brightstaff.

Instead of soaring up over the wall and away, they began to float gently down to the spot where Aefric was pointing. Not quite cutting through the wind, but more as though they were being tugged through it. The wind's arms ruffling a minor protest en route.

Down in the courtyard below, where workers went about their days and Ser Beornric and the knights of Aefric's personal guard were training, eyes were raised and shouts voiced.

Aefric and Ser Grey landed lightly on the bricks of the courtyard, near the portcullis and the road that led to the gatehouse down below, at the foot of the hill.

"Your grace," Ser Grey said, loudly over the tumult of excited discussion coming from all around the courtyard. "I'd be most grateful if you *warned* me before doing that again."

"Sorry, Ser Grey," Aefric said, smiling, and well aware that he didn't sound sorry in the least. "But with the princess arriving, I wasn't sure we had time. She's not someone to keep waiting."

"Your grace, we had time."

"Are you sure? The page—"

"The page ran with all speed," Ser Grey said, "so that your grace would not have to. He was only telling us that her ship has docked, and that she's likely in her carriage or on her horse, on her way up the hill."

Aefric sighed. "So we *did* have time then."

"Yes, your grace. Your grace might have noticed that ascending the hill to the keep takes rather longer than a handful of breaths. Gives us plenty of warning when someone approaches."

"Of course it does." Aefric gave Ser Grey a pained smile. "I'll try to keep that in mind, next time."

"Thank you, your grace," Ser Grey said, apparently caught somewhere between irritation and amusement. "Now may I see to the arrangements?"

"Please do."

Ser Grey hurried away then, and Aefric smiled and waved at some of the gawkers around the edges of the courtyard. Teamsters, carrying goods up from town. Smiths and wrights whose work had been interrupted by the sight of their slowly falling duke and castellan. Soldiers on guard duty, who yet handled their weapons as though unsure that there was no threat they needed to respond to.

Aefric called out to them, "All is well, men. Sometimes I fear I lack patience for all those stairs."

He gave them a smile. A few of them managed to return it, before offering a salute that their fellows then had to join. Aefric returned the salute, then wandered over to see how his knights were doing.

They were wearing quilted armor and training with blunted, tourney swords, but still looked fairly impressive.

Ser Beornric stood off to one side, and called out specific instructions in the vein of "attackers, come in high," or "defenders, counter mid-line."

When Aefric reached him, Ser Beornric addressed him in low tones.

"Your grace gave us something of a turn."

"You mean you seven are capable of being distracted?" Aefric responded loudly enough for his voice to carry over the clashing of their steel. "I would never have guessed it, and I don't know that I believe it even now."

That got him some chagrined smiles.

"Go clean yourselves up," Aefric said. "The princess arrives, and I'd like my knights beside me to welcome her."

"You heard the duke," Ser Beornric said in his command voice. Then, quieter, to Aefric, he added, "I should clean up as well, your grace, and I won't let them tarry."

"I know you won't," Aefric said, clapping Ser Beornric on the shoulder.

The four guards Aefric had left on the roof joined him then, sweaty and panting from their rush down the stairs, but ready for action, if needed.

"Sorry about that," Aefric said. "I thought we had less time than we do."

"No ... need for apology ... your grace," said the one with the brush-like black mustaches.

What was his name?

Oh, yes.

"Thank you, Tapenn, but it was unkind of me to make you rush for no reason. I'll try not to make a habit of it."

"Keeps us ... on our toes," he said, with a smile.

"All right then," Aefric said with a smile. Then called up to the soldiers on the wall. "How long until the princess arrives?"

"Another two turns up the hill, your grace."

Well. He'd just have to wait, then, and try not to get too nervous. Meeting the prince on the road was one thing. But receiving the princess here? At his own castle? Not even his ducal seat, but a secondary castle?

What if there was a protocol for receiving royalty for the first time? And he didn't know it?

He'd just have to do his best, and hope his people kept him from looking too foolish.

Though he suspected that was asking a great deal.

AEFRIC FELT A CERTAIN SENSE OF DÉJÀ VU.

He was standing outside the closed portcullis of his castle, on a red carpet that had been hurriedly laid out, while a ring of torches had been set up against the graying light of late afternoon.

The portcullis was on the east side of the castle, which meant late afternoon arrivals would always be in shadow. Was that a bad decision, as far as social proprieties went, or a good decision, as far as castle defenses went?

Aefric had trouble deciding between the two. Especially since the answer might have been that both were true.

This time, though, instead of being the one approaching, Aefric stood in the center of it all, just in front of the portcullis. On his right and one step behind stood Ser Grey. Mirroring Ser Grey on his left was Ornella Ol'Narim, the seneschal of Behal Castle.

Ornella was a surprisingly efficient seneschal, given that she was about Aefric's age, soft spoken, and had only been on the job here at Behal for about a year. She was a large woman, who dressed in robes of Deepwater navy blue and gray, and wore her hair in a single brown braid most of the way down her back.

Fanned out behind the three of them were the knights of Aefric's personal guard, their armor freshly polished, and his personal seal already emblazoned at their left shoulders.

The soldiers of his personal guard continued the half-circle from the outer edge of knights.

The gathered crowd featured the barons of Riverbreak and Havenford, their spouses and children. (Or at least Riverbreak's children. Aefric didn't know if Havenford had children). Also included were Byrhta Ol'Caran, as well as the local lers, knights, and other courtiers.

Not the whole of the castle staff, though, so the waiting crowd was smaller tonight.

While they waited, Ornella and Ser Grey quietly went over the proper steps for greeting royalty, and Aefric tried not to get too nervous.

This was the problem with nobility. As an adventurer, whenever something made him nervous, he could deal with it directly. Often with spells or steel.

As a noble, though, he had to refrain from such things. He had to take the less direct and more socially acceptable approach.

That seemed to involve a lot of waiting, which made his stomach churn in discomfort.

Fortunately, the princess didn't keep them waiting too long.

Whistles from the guards along the route called the warning, and the crowd rustled to eager life. People all around Aefric talked to each other, both quietly and anxiously, while he tried to ignore them. He listened instead to the cries of the late afternoon birds, hoping they could bring him something closer to peace.

They couldn't. But they were more soothing than the chatter and speculation of nobles.

Now he could hear the hooves of the approaching horses.

And finally they came into view.

First, the knights of the princess' personal guard, clad in full, shining plate armor, with their helmets on and visors down.

Four such knights, riding two abreast on high-stepping chargers. One carried the banner of Armyr, and beneath it the princess' own banner: a golden bow with arrow nocked, on a field of forest green.

Then, in the center, rode the princess herself, on a brilliant black stallion, that could have been the twin to his own Windsong.

The princess rode not in elegant finery, but dressed as though she were herself an adventurer, like Aefric.

She wore tight buckskin pants, tucked into high doeskin boots. Her shirt looked to be buckskin as well, and left three-quarters of her arms bare all the way to her hands.

Even the laces and ties of her clothing looked to have been made from sinew, rather than cloth.

Her cloak seemed the only thing on her body woven from cloth, rather than tanned from the hides of animals. It was a soft gray, remarkably similar in its way to the cloak around Aefric's shoulders.

For all that, she had the pale skin so beloved of Armyrian nobility, contrasting with the waves of long black hair, flying wild behind her. And with her high cheekbones, large eyes, and delicate chin, Aefric had no doubt that many of the noblemen around him favored dreams of being admitted into *her* chamber door some night.

Four more knights rode behind her. And following them, more horses and carts, bringing up the remainder of her entourage, as well as those things she carried when traveling.

The knights came to a halt, but stayed ahorse while the princess rode between them and slipped from the saddle near the edge of the red carpet.

Aefric could see then that she wore a long, slim sword at her side. A saber or a rapier, most likely.

Her horse stayed right where she left him, even with no one holding his reins. If anything the horse looked about imperiously, as though daring anyone to try to control him.

A reddish-brown, great spotted forest lynx fell into step beside Princess Maev as she approached. The lynx was tall at the shoulder, and she was just short enough — about a head shorter than Aefric, which still meant she was one of the taller women present — that she could rest one hand on the lynx's head.

Princess Maev's soft gray eyes seemed to laugh with pleasure as she stopped on the carpet and took in the sight of the crowd waiting for her.

Her lips curled in a small smile as she looked then at Aefric.

"Well, well," she said, sauntering slowly forward again with the kind of confidence that said she knew every eye was on her, and she liked it. She stopped a dozen paces from Aefric, and spoke.

"Can this man before me be Duke Aefric Brightstaff? Hero of Deepwater?"

But before anyone could think about answering — if, indeed, anyone would have — she stopped, turned to her lynx, and crouched low enough for the lynx to touch noses with her.

"I think he's too handsome to be a war hero," Princess Maev said to the lynx, her words carrying above the breeze, largely because the crowd had grown quiet and hung on her every word. "What do you think, Sylkanis?"

The lynx buffed her chin.

Princess Maev stood and faced Aefric.

"Sylkanis agrees with me that you're quite handsome," she announced as though she weren't saying anything unusual, no matter how bizarre her entrance was to Aefric. "But she believes you are, in fact, who I was told to expect."

She tilted her head. "Are you?"

Well.

This wasn't going at all the way Aefric had been told to expect. One of the princess' knights was supposed to blow a whistle and announce her. Then one of his pages was to announce him. There would be formal introductions then, and hand-kissing, first of Aefric, then of the other nobles and so on.

But Maev had thrown out the script.

And yet, through the pounding of his nervous heart, Aefric found himself meeting those soft gray eyes and smiling back at her.

"I may not be the man you expected me to be," Aefric said. "In fact, I suspect I'm not the man any of these people expected me to be. But I *am* Aefric, known as the Brightstaff, for the staff I bear and the deed involved in claiming it."

Aefric held up the staff, and let its diamond shine out brilliance, banishing any nearby shadows. Princess Maev's smile widened at the sight.

"I did fight at the Battle of Deepwater. And there are those who call me its hero, for the deeds I did during that battle. Though to this day I say that any who fought alongside us at Deepwater should be called heroes."

Aefric extinguished the staff.

"And I was made duke of Deepwater by your father, King Colm Stronghand, so I suppose I must be that as well."

He smiled.

"Now. My turn to ask. Can this lovely forest nymph I see before me truly be Princess Maev Stronghand?"

At that, the air filled with the hushed babbling of nobles. They stilled again as the princess spoke up.

"You were expecting some soft, powdered lass?" the princess asked with a challenge to her smile now. "Perhaps adorning fancy frippery and bedecked with jewels?"

"I cannot claim to have known what to expect," Aefric said. "I was too busy learning what I should be saying right now. *If* we were doing things according to the proper protocols."

The princess laughed, a bright, cheerful sound, and as she did her lynx nuzzled her legs.

"Fah on protocols," the princess said. "I must embrace too many of those back home."

She laughed again. Aefric tried not to laugh with her, but the woman's laugh was infectious. Even some of the shocked nobles around them couldn't stop a chuckle or two.

"And so to the rest of you nobles," Princess Maev said, looking out over the crowd, "I'm sure I shall meet you all properly later. Right now" — she turned her focus back on Aefric — "I passed a lovely looking flower garden a few minutes back down the road. Would your grace be so kind as to show it to me? I bet it will be lovely as the sun sets."

"I'd be only too happy to do so," Aefric said.

And to his surprise, he actually meant it.

MOMENTS LATER — THANKS TO THE QUICK WITS AND LEGS OF A YOUNG groom — Aefric was mounted on Windsong and trotting back down the road alongside Princess Maev, while her lynx capered about the brick road around them.

The early evening wind had picked up, whipping their faces and hair. The skies to the west were burning bright red as the sun began to sink.

Princess Maev laughed into the wind, and Aefric felt certain she was laughing at the burble of scandal he could still hear from the nobles, behind them just outside the portcullis.

Though he might have imagined that he could still hear them, over the sounds of the princess' laughter, and the clatter of not only their own horses' hooves on the bricks of the road, but the hooves of the princess' personal guard, trotting along just behind them.

Well, two of those knights were rushing along the sides of the road to get out in front.

The one thing Aefric was certain he *could* hear from back by the castle was the calling of his own personal guard for their horses.

They'd catch up. Aefric wasn't particularly worried about getting attacked so close to Behal Castle. Especially since he was more concerned about what exactly the princess had in mind.

Was she actually making a play for him? Or was she just shocking the local nobility for her own amusement? Could both be true? Or was there some third option he wasn't considering?

And where did his own feelings lie in this?

There was something about this woman. The freeness of her spirit, perhaps. Certainly she was beautiful, but he'd met several beautiful women since he'd come to Armyr. Her looks alone would not have been enough to bring twinges of guilt when he looked at her.

And he did feel those twinges. And he knew full well that they were vestiges of worry about infidelity to Andi. Even though he knew that word no longer applied.

Andi was dead.

The part of him that was Keifer needed to move on. He knew that. And the part of him that was Aefric, well, to that part of him the matter was even less complicated.

The part of him that was Aefric had never known Andi.

But the Keifer part of him had been there first, underlying everything that Aefric grew to become. Even if it had been suppressed beginning with his youth on the streets of Sartis.

One thing had become clear to him over the last few days —

whether he had been known as Aefric or Keifer, in his heart of hearts, he was still the same man. He had the same underlying sense of right and wrong.

The same basic kernel of self lay behind everything he did and everything he was.

That kernel might be consistent and strong. But the rest of his mind was awhirl.

Confusion and concern.

Infatuation. A matter of the moment? Or something more?

Then there was the dangling Damoclean sword of future visits in the night from women who wanted nothing more than a night of pleasure.

That he lived now in a land where that was normal behavior. Where it would become a part of life.

It was a good thing that Aefric's horse knew the way, because his mind was far too busy picking away at a thousand semi-related concerns to worry about such simple matters as keeping to the road.

BEFORE AEFRIC REALIZED IT, HE AND THE PRINCESS HAD REACHED THE garden, and were dismounting.

She had spoken of wanting to see the garden by sunset. Well, she was rapidly running out of that. And with the wind picking up and the storm clouds moving in up above, it would soon be too cold and dark to go wandering in a garden.

So why had she chosen now, for her visit?

He tied his own horse to the hitching post just outside the low, white picket fence, near the gate. As he did, the knights of her guard were doing the same. His own had not yet caught them up.

But Aefric noted the princess didn't tie up her own horse. Could she trust her steed not to wander off?

He turned to ask her, but she looked out across the lake.

"I see fishing boats," the princess said. "As well as a handful of pleasure barges, merchant vessels, and a few others besides."

She turned to him. "But the only two warships I see fly your flag."

"Warships, your highness?"

She slashed the air between them with an open hand.

"No," she said sharply. "Enough of that. I can get all the courtesies I want from that obsequious lot back there. I was told to expect an adventurer and a war hero, and I'll not have you hiding from me behind the games all nobles play."

Aefric frowned, but nodded slowly. She seemed to be talking about more than titles. She seemed to be telling him to speak plainly in her presence.

Well. He'd try. Knowing she was a princess didn't make that easy, though her tight, buckskin outfit certainly helped. She looked more like someone in his old line of work than she did like a princess.

He took off his ducal coronet — which he'd only worn for the formal greeting — and tied it to his belt, behind his wand.

She nodded. He cleared his throat.

"What warships are you looking for, Maev?"

The princess still looked a bit suspicious, as though wondering if he was humoring her or whether he understood her point. But she nodded again.

"As we rode here, you looked worried enough that I thought you were seeing phantom warships out on the lake. But now I think not. Nor do I believe you worried about the scandalized nobles behind us. What then troubled you so?"

"It's ... a hard thing to talk about."

She nodded, slowly, seeming to come to some conclusion. She smiled. "All right. Let's see these flowers."

She turned and led Aefric into the garden itself, while the knights of her guard spread out around them at a respectable distance. The knights of Aefric's guard caught up and began to do the same.

Sylkanis pranced ahead of them down the gravel pathway, making even less noise than the quiet crunching of his and Maev's own boots.

Maev smiled at her lynx, but if she even noticed her knights, she gave no sign. So Aefric tried to do the same.

The shadows lengthened as they passed the white picket fence and entered the garden.

The roses were first. Only just starting to bloom, but some looked to be early risers, perfuming the air from blossoms of deep red and bright pink. The crowning glory among them was a single blooming rose of emerald green, that spread as wide as Aefric's outstretched hand.

"Magnificent," Maev whispered, leaning in close to admire the emerald rose. "And the fragrance. A touchy spicy, don't you think?"

"I'm not sure," Aefric said, from where he stood, a respectful arm's length away.

"Then come smell it," she said, reaching out to grab him by the shirt and pull him down until his face was close to hers.

"It's lovely," Aefric said. "Truly."

And it was. She was right. The emerald rose had a touch of spice underlying its rosy scent. And Aefric felt his pulse quicken as he realized Maev herself smelled of honeysuckle.

He stood quickly, and made a show of looking at the other roses.

"There's a sapphire blue here that's not quite ready to open," he said. "Another aett or so, perhaps?"

Not that he had any idea when this rose, or any other, would bloom.

Maev was slow to stand, and he thought he felt her watching him as she stepped in close beside him.

She reached out and trailed callused fingertips along the closed bud.

"Two aetts," she said softly. "Perhaps three. Do I frighten you, Aefric?"

His breath caught, to see those soft gray eyes looking at him from hardly three handbreadths away. He could feel his pulse beating in his wrists, at his elbows, in his throat.

He swallowed. She only watched him. Waiting.

Words tangled in Aefric's head. He wanted to deny her question as foolishness. And in a sense, it was. He was Aefric Brightstaff, with his signature weapon in hand. She was an unarmed princess.

Of course he wasn't afraid of her. Not in that sense.

But in another sense...

That quickening excitement. Was it fear? Or was it something else?

Fear would be safer.

But what answer could he give her?

She spoke before he managed one.

"Who was the last woman to share your bed?" Maev asked softly. "One of those prissy noblewomen back there? Perhaps with soft hands and a soft head? I know it wasn't any of the noblewomen you rode with. Sighild had the desire, but not the courage. Oswen would have, I think, if not for Sighild. Faenella likely didn't know it was an option. One of your baronesses perhaps?"

Aefric shook his head. Words finally found their way out of his mouth, though he wasn't sure they were the words he would have chosen.

"A serving girl in Norrtarr. Octave. Offered me *leaba*."

"*Leaba?*" Maev nodded, pensive. "Interesting."

She turned away then. Walked on past the rosebushes, to a bed of chrysanthemums.

"Pretty enough, but not my favorites," she declared and moved on, passing four more colorful beds of assorted flowers, before she reached a bed of experimental violets.

Here were violets in the dozens of shades from pale blue to the darkest of violet. They were arranged in a spiraling pattern that made Maev smile as she traced it in the air.

The breeze was chilly. Aefric knew that. So why did he feel so warm?

"You know they will, don't you?" Maev asked. "Your noble-women, I mean. They'll come to your chambers, hoping to share your bed. Some will hope for favors. Others, just the bliss moment."

She turned quickly to regard Aefric, leaving her features in shadow. Though her eyes glowed green and catlike for a moment.

"What do you think of that?"

Aefric sighed, feeling defeated, and answered with perfect honesty.

"I don't know." He shook his head. "It's a new custom to me. It feels strange to think that women who barely know me — some of them even married — might expect me to have sex with them. And then just go on about our lives as though nothing has happened."

"Adventurers are famous for whoring." She somehow made that sound not like an accusation but a simple statement of fact.

"Perhaps. But I never took to it."

He turned to face the violets as he continued, though their spiral offered him no solace. Though that might have been because the daylight had dimmed too much for him to discern distinctions among their different colors.

"I've been with women, of course," he said. "But almost exclusively when it meant something more than a pastime."

The gravel crunched near him, as she moved to stand closer.

"Are you afraid I'll show up at your chambers tonight? Or afraid I won't?"

"To be honest, I hadn't even thought about it until just this second."

She put a hand on his shoulder. "I don't mind the occasional bedmate. But if this is your worry, let me take it from you. I find you far too handsome and interesting to show up at your chamber, seeking nothing more from you than the bliss moment."

Aefric turned to look at her, but she was shades of gray. The sun had sunk too far now for him to see her features clearly.

"What about a conversation?" he asked softly. "Or a game of chess?"

He felt her smile more than he saw it. "Now if I know that's on offer, I might just show up at your door after all."

She seemed to leave something unspoken there, but Aefric couldn't worry his way through it just then.

"That's good," Aefric said, with his heart pounding so hard he wondered if she could hear it. "I'd like that."

"Tell me, Aefric," she said softly, leaning in even closer. "If you would. What troubled you so, during the out ride here?"

Again, as he turned to her, for just a moment her eyes glowed catlike, though the flare of green was gone just as quickly as it had the last time.

"I was remembering the last woman I talked with happily for hours at a time. She ... died."

"Sometime you must tell me more of her," Maev said softly. Then louder said, "But I think we've seen all we can of this garden tonight. Damn the storm clouds for stealing the moon from us!"

"That's not a problem," Aefric said, then caused the Brightstaff's yellow diamond to light up the garden.

Maev turned away quickly, bending her knees and holding her arms wide.

"A word of warning next time, if you would," she said, wincing. "My night vision."

"You know the Cat's Eyes," Aefric said, amazed. That was a trick of the eldrani foresters. One they refused to share with other magic-users.

"And you now know one of my secrets," Maev said, smiling even as she grimaced in pain. "Help me back to my horse? I'll be some time getting my sight back, and I think I'm ready to eat dinner."

AEFRIC AND THE PRINCESS RODE BACK THROUGH THE GATES AND INTO the courtyard at Behal Castle before full dark had risen. They'd ridden back with their way lit by Aefric's staff, for which both of their knightly escorts seemed grateful.

They'd had torches available, but Aefric suspected that it felt less knightly to ride carrying a torch. And neither he nor Maev had any more of their entourage present, to handle such duties.

The chill was growing in the night air, and they pulled their cloaks around themselves as they dismounted outside the stables.

Ser Grey was waiting for them. She spoke as Aefric handed his coronet to his servant Falip, for her to return to its proper place.

"We've had rikas," Ser Grey said, her voice as grim as her expression. Her eyes shifted to the princess, as though trying to suggest that these messages were for ducal ears, not royal ones.

"If you wish me to leave, I shall," Maev said to Aefric while scratching her lynx between the ears. "But I confess I'm eager to know what news could put such a look on your castellan's face."

Aefric nodded at Ser Grey, who drew a slow breath Aefric had learned to interpret as disapproval, but she held up one message and spoke.

"This one came from Prince Killian, sent first by messenger and then via the rookery at Ironwood Inn."

"Your grace," she read aloud from it. "Motte met us on the road with soldiers and knights. I think only my presence kept them from fighting. They follow us through the forest. I'll be staying with your fort until its finished. Expect more word from me soon."

"*My* brother?" Maev asked, her eyebrows high. "Staying to oversee *construction*?" She shook her head. "That can only mean he expects a battle. But Motte is your own vassal, isn't he? Can matters really be so tense between you?"

"Funny you should ask, your highness," Ser Grey said. "Because the other in my hand is from Count Ferrin, of Motte."

She held that one up and read from it.

"Duke Aefric, how dare you attack my soldiers and seize my fort? I won't stand for this. Withdraw your troops at once or face my wrath!"

Princess Maev laughed. "His wrath! Oh, how I'm sure the Hero of Deepwater trembles in his boots at the very thought of—"

"No," Aefric growled.

"Well, no," Maev said, sounding puzzled. "Of course not. I only meant—"

"No!" Aefric shouted, and all nearby activity halted. The knights, the soldiers, the grooms, even the servants who rushed to fuss over Princess Maev's hair all stopped and stared wide-eyed at Aefric.

The lynx, for her part, only looked at Aefric with a curious expression.

"I will *not* let him spend the blood of my people on his vanity," Aefric said. "I will not let him play these games *his* way."

He shook his head and turned to Ser Grey.

"I'm sorry, Ser Grey. I'm trying. I'm trying very hard to be a duke. But some problems are better solved by an adventurer than a duke."

He turned to the princess, whose eyes were practically aflame as she regarded him.

"I fear I won't be able to join you for dinner. I should be back by dawn. Breakfast, perhaps?"

"Take me with you," she said urgently.

"If I could, I would. But the way I travel now prevents that from being an option."

"Your grace," Ser Arras said, her voice demanding. "Surely you won't leave your personal guard behind."

"I must. But I won't make a habit of it." He turned to Ser Grey. "If it happens that I'm not back by dawn, send troops to Kerrik. And don't take any action against ... the other threat ... without more information. There's a piece missing there."

"Other threat?" Maev asked.

But Aefric had no time for more questions.

He took the Brightstaff in both hands, and summoned the white lightning to surround it. He thrust the staff towards the sky.

White lightning shot upward from the yellow diamond at its tip.

And as this happened, Aefric became the lightning, charging upward and away.

As lightning, Aefric jolted through the sky. Over Deepwater. Over Goldenfall. Over Motte towards its northeastern corner. Until he reached his destination: Castle Kirandai, near the mouth of the Teras River. The county seat of Motte.

As lightning, Aefric blasted through the gates of the keep and into the main hall, where a dinner was just getting underway.

He resumed his human shape, yet aglow with the aftermath of his lightning, and reeking of ozone.

The main hall, Aefric took in at a glance. Stone in shades of brown and red for the floor, walls and ceiling. Three wheel-like chandeliers provided light, while a series of braziers provided heat.

The diners all sat at one long central table. Or at least, they had been before Aefric *boomed* his way into the room.

Now benches were tipped over. Guards were running about. There was a great deal of shouting and screaming, especially from the well-dressed people panicking in the middle of the room.

"Count Ferrin Ol'Nylla!" Aefric shouted, blazing more light out from the yellow diamond atop the Brightstaff.

That stopped everyone in their tracks. All eyes turned to him. Another few brief screams, then silence fell on the diners, while the guards pointed halberds and swords in his direction, but didn't look eager to close the distance.

Ser Pemith — clad in a padded black tunic and breeches, rather than armor — stood near the count, and drew her sword to stand in his defense. Her dark hair bound behind her, and her dark eyes offering challenge.

Interesting that she was here, and not with the count's forces in Kerrik Forest.

The count himself looked every inch a fop. His hair was a dark shade of brown streaked with blonde, and his skin was fashionably pale. His clothes were overwrought, with reds and yellows coming together in ways that Aefric wouldn't have wanted to see. He wore gold at his throat, on his wrists, and on his fingers.

He was staring at Aefric, with his mouth moving like a fish's does, as it suffocates on the floorboards of a boat.

"Tell me, Count Ferrin," Aefric said, slowly walking forward. "Who am I?"

Count Ferrin affected calm through a sigh, but Aefric wasn't buying it.

"You are Duke Aefric Brightstaff," he said. "Or I hope you are, because it is Duke Aefric Brighstaff to whom I intend to send the bill for these damages."

"Quite a tone you take," Aefric said, "with your rightful liege lord, and the overlord of your lands."

"Well," Count Ferrin began, trying for a lazy tone, but Aefric cut across his words.

"You have committed a grievous error," Aefric said, and that he could hear his boots echoing on the stone floor told him that the guests and guards were all watching him. "You trusted to lies. I know who your backer is, and she will not save you."

Count Ferrin's eyes widened then, and his plump lips parted in shock.

Aefric was right, then. The count *did* believe that Merrek was allying with him. A potentially crucial piece of information.

"Arrest that man!" Count Ferrin said, pointing with both hands, lest there be any doubt whom he meant. "For acts of war against Motte."

Aefric caused white fire to coruscate along the Brightstaff. The guards hesitated, looking to each other to see who would go first.

Into that hesitation, Aefric spoke, addressing the knights and guards directly.

"Many of you fought in the Godswalk Wars," he said, his voice ringing out strong in the hall. "Or share blood with those who did. *I* fought and bled alongside you. You all know this. You all know they call me the Hero of Deepwater. And you all know the reason why."

Aefric pointed at Count Ferrin.

"Where was your count during the wars? Fighting alongside you? Risking his own life? Or did he cower here in his castle? Sending others to die in his place?"

Count Ferrin looked torn between the desire to deny Aefric's words, and the need not to get caught in a lie right now.

Aefric continued.

"King Colm Stronghand himself knighted me for my actions during the Godswalk Wars. And more than that, he created me Duke of Deepwater. Thus, though this … 'man' may be your lord, I am your overlord. The loyalty you owe him, you owe first to me."

Aefric met Ser Pemith's eyes now as he finished his point.

"I understand that some of you may be feeling conflicted. But ask yourselves. Which of us has done more to *earn* your loyalty?"

Ser Pemith lowered her sword.

"Stand down," she ordered the guards. "This is a matter between the duke and the count." She looked back at Aefric, but she continued talking to her people. "This is too big for us. Let them decide it."

Aefric nodded, while Count Ferrin howled a protest.

"You have been challenging me since before I arrived," Aefric said, his eyes on Count Ferrin, but his words for everyone. "You built a toll gate without either right or permission. You sanction and support robbery in Kerrik Forest."

"Lies!" Count Ferrin said. "I keep *my* share of the forest free from bandits."

"Not by arresting them," Aefric said, "but by driving them across the Kingsroad into Norra. And I will soon have proof that you profit from this venture."

"Lies!" Count Ferrin said again, but it was weaker. He was cowering on his throne now. And it was the county throne he sat on, with his diadem on his head, even while dining.

"You have done all these things," Aefric said. "And you have done more besides. And I say all of it will stop. Right. Now."

Aefric caused the staff to blaze brighter.

"You have wished to challenge me?" he said. "Well here I stand. No knights beside me. No soldiers. Either challenge me yourself with steel or spell, or drop to your knees right now and swear proper vassalage to your lord and liege."

Count Ferrin's eyes darted about for support. Perhaps thinking to call a champion to stand for him. But whatever he saw in the eyes of those around him stole the last of his resistance.

He sank into himself, and dropped down onto his knees there on the cold stone floor.

"I call on all present to witness," Aefric said. "Recant your false accusations against me."

"I recant them all," Count Ferrin said, sounding broken and on the verge of tears. "All the accusations. Even the ones you didn't mention."

"You will recall the army menacing my people in Kerrik Forest."

"Yes, yes, of course. I'll send a messenger tonight."

"Now," Aefric said. "The oaths. With everyone in your hall standing witness."

The oaths took a long time. Long enough that Aefric could tell the hungry diners could no longer ignore the wind whipping in through the blasted doors of the keep. He heard them shivering where they stood.

Once the oaths were finished, Aefric stood the Brightstaff beside him and held out his right hand.

Bowing his head, but still watchful, Count Ferrin put his hand in Aefric's.

Aefric's left hand went to the knife on his belt. Count Ferrin's eyes widened, and he squeaked.

Aefric leaned down and kissed Count Ferrin's hand, then helped him up. The man was a panting, sweating mess.

"All right," Aefric said. "You will be punished for what you have done. But if you stop working against me, I hope that I can one day call you friend."

Count Ferrin shivered, but looked hopeful.

"For now," Aefric said, dropping his voice so that only Count Ferrin and Ser Pemith, near at hand, could hear. "Your part of dinner is done. Let us go somewhere private. I want a full and complete accounting of your involvement in banditry and other acts against my duchy. And I want the names of those who have been representing your benefactor."

"I know just the room," Ser Pemith said, and led the way.

In some ways, things with Motte weren't as bad as Aefric had feared. In other ways, they were worse. Motte had been siphoning as much money as he could from his benefactor, and using that money for the fort, to hire more soldiers, and to rebuild as much as he could without draining his own coffers.

All told, he'd come pretty far in repairing the damage his county had sustained during the Godswalk Wars.

That benefactor Count Ferrin claimed as Merrek. Aefric had no doubt that the count believed this, but Aefric wondered. He took extensive notes about the go-betweens, including a handful of courtiers who had been present when Aefric burst in during dinner that night.

Whether it was good or bad that those go-betweens had been present, Aefric didn't know. So he had to hope it was good.

The bandits were a wash for Motte, financially. The count supported them, and profited a little from them, but the profit only came out to about what he paid to support them. He'd continued the practice only for two reasons.

One, his benefactor wanted it.

Two, he'd hoped to make Norra dependent on him, both undermining Aefric and increasing his own power and influence.

Aefric commanded him to give up his benefactor, arrest those bandits, and to never work against him again. He even made Count Ferrin swear to that last item, with Ser Pemith as witness.

Of course, Aefric didn't trust the little weasel very far. But right now he was cowed, so he would behave himself for some time at least. Especially when he found out the full price he'd pay for what he'd done so far.

Aefric considered telling him then and there. But that would have been going too far. Even a coward like Count Ferrin would have declared war, rather than pay that price.

But once Aefric was certain he'd wrung all the truth out of the little weasel that he would get — and Ser Pemith had run out of things to add — he left them to their dinner.

Ser Pemith was intriguing. She had, it seemed, objected to a great deal of what her count was doing. But didn't feel she could speak against him, because of her knightly oaths. Once she had been given both reason and opportunity to speak, she'd helped fill in gaps in Count Ferrin's memory about the wrongs he'd been committing.

Even those gaps that might have been intentional.

Ser Pemith might turn out to be an ally here in Motte. She was honorable, and she'd witnessed every oath Aefric had made Count Ferrin swear. And he hadn't pushed those oaths beyond anything reasonable for a liege lord to ask of a vassal, so he hoped she would help keep Count Ferrin honest.

Or at least as close to honest as the little weasel ever got.

Once he was finished there, Aefric lamented that the Brightstaff could call the lightning form only once between risings of the sun. He'd have to get back to Behal another way.

He could try his reverse summoning trick again, but he really wanted to discuss it with Karbin in some detail before attempting it a second time. It just felt too risky.

And true teleportation was still beyond Aefric. Though perhaps he could get his new ducal wizard to teach him the technique...

A hope for later. He still needed to get home. And do so as quickly as he reasonably could. By horse, by *magaunt*, or even by his new carriage, the trip would take days that Aefric didn't have.

Not that he'd thought to bring his carriage along.

So Aefric was forced to resort to his least favorite form of long distance transportation.

He flew.

When Aefric had first learned that there were magical ways to soar through the air like birds or dragons, he'd dreamed of nothing else.

The reality, well, fell short of the dream.

It wasn't that flying was so very difficult, or required immense concentration. No, it was all the other little details about it that he hated.

First, there was the wind.

Aefric didn't mind a little wind in his face. But what he faced while flying, that was like getting constantly slapped by cold, unseen hands. Hands that occasionally smacked him with a bug, or tried to make him swallow one.

Everything attached to his body had to be perfectly secured or it might be lost. The chill of the wind inevitably cut right through every opening in his clothes and ran wild inside.

Often, like tonight, he had to fly through a spout of rain, which left him drenched and made the wind feel icy. Even if it did blow him dry within a few dozen minutes.

Even dry, the cold lingered. Dug down into his bones and set up housekeeping.

And worst of all was trying to gauge exactly where he was, and where he was going.

The reverse summoning, that he'd only accomplished to a location he knew well. And the lightning form, it traveled the same way — as much by thought and will as anything else.

But flying, that was slow enough that he had to trust to his normal senses. Which meant, at night, trusting to his reading of the stars up above. He simply couldn't see landmarks well enough on the ground below to judge whether or not he was going the right way. It was all too easy to veer a few degrees off course.

And even a few degrees off course could mean going miles and miles the wrong way.

In this case, he didn't yet know the duchy well enough to even *hazard* a guess by overland landmarks. He had to follow the tip of the Warrior's Blade constellation which — as he understood the movement of the Warrior's Blade this time of year — should have been due west of him.

The possibility of error — along with his need to hold the Bright-staff tight against the buffeting winds — inevitably knotted every muscle in his body with stress.

And so he felt like a single giant knot of tension by the time he found himself flying over Deepwater and turning south toward Behal.

He finally arrived at Behal Castle somewhere past midnight.

And no sooner did he land on the battlements than he had pages running about to find Ser Grey, and to have food brought to his chambers.

Hot food.

Aefric was clad in a thick, woolen robe and shivering in front of the fire in his sitting room when Ser Grey was announced, and given permission to enter.

"Your grace," she said at once, "that was a foolish thing you did tonight. You shouldn't go rushing off like an adventurer anymore."

"I understand the wisdom of what you're saying," Aefric said, holding up a forestalling hand, "but this was a problem that called for an adventurer's solution. Not a noble's."

Ser Grey grimaced through a slow, deep breath. "Would your grace care to explain?"

"Certainly," he said, and told Ser Grey what he'd done. And when it came to the why, he finished with, "Count Ferrin was counting on my playing the game his way. Playing the game he's been playing all his life, and I'm only just learning to play."

Aefric shook his head. "I'm a duke and he's a count, and my vassal. So I could beat him at that game, but it would take time I don't have. So I cut through the process. The adventurer's way."

"And your grace promises that he won't make a habit of this sort of behavior?"

"It's a tool in my toolbox, good ser, but it won't be the first one I reach for. Or likely the third." He shook his head. "But there are times for it. And when those times come, I won't shy away."

"As your grace told me to speak honestly, I can tell you I don't like it. Not one bit. It's rash, and puts you at risk."

She frowned as she nodded.

"But I *do* understand," she said. "And I hope to provide you with ... gentler means of redress in the future."

"So long as those means accomplish my goals along a timeline that works," Aefric said.

But then his late supper arrived. A roast turkey leg, along with a vegetable and barley soup, honeyed oat bread, and a block of sharp cheese. To drink he was brought both some of the beer he'd shared with Baron Osmaer earlier, and a mug of mulled wine.

Ser Grey left him to dine in peace then, for which Aefric was quite grateful.

Aefric sat at the large, black oak table in his sitting room. Blissfully alone for a rare moment. The only sounds, the happy gurgling of his full stomach, and the contented crackling from the nearby hearth.

He'd dismissed his servants while eating his late-night dinner. Decided that they didn't need to watch him gnaw on a warmed turkey leg, or practically groan in pleasure at the spreading warmth of the mulled wine in his system. Much less the bliss of that vegetable and barley soup.

That soup was so good that even as Aefric remained seated, luxuriating, he was tempted not to drink any more of that good, stout beer. It would drive away the taste of the soup.

Ah. Now *that* was a decision he didn't mind making. No pressure. No lives in the balance. And while the beer might displace the soup taste, it would likely help him ease to sleep.

That would be good. Aefric needed sleep.

Apart from the sheer stress of his day, that trip to Motte, the spells, and that flight home had worn him out pretty well.

Especially since he knew he'd need to rise early again. Ser Grey had already warned him that Baron Osmaer and his husband were returning to Havenford just after first light, to see about sending out those new priests of Halstaffur out to aid the other baronies and counties.

One more yawn, and Aefric would go to bed.

Naturally, this was when a soft knock came at the door of his chambers.

Aefric considered not answering. He didn't want to see anyone.

Didn't want to talk to anyone. And he was wearing nothing but a good, thick, gray woolen robe and slippers.

Hardly the image of the dashing young duke.

But the knock came again.

Aefric sighed, stood, and trudged across the room. He sighed again through a long breath, then opened the door just enough to see who stood on the other side.

Sure enough, it was Baroness Montess. She had her walnut-colored hair down and loose about her shoulders. Her hazel eyes were dark with desire. She wore a dark blue robe, open just enough to let Aefric know that what she wore beneath was gauzy and not at all concealing of the shapely body it covered.

Despite himself, Aefric had to admit. The woman looked good. Especially when he considered that she was nearly twice his age.

Two guards, on either side of his door, stood very much at attention. Visibly trying not to notice the baroness, or the conversation that she began.

"Your grace," she purred, smiling. "As soon as I'd heard you returned from your journey cold and shivering, I knew my duty. As your true and loyal vassal I had to come and warm you myself."

She raised a hand as though to stroke his chest, but held back.

Waiting for permission?

"Baroness," Aefric said, "I am most flattered by your offer. And more than a little tempted, despite my overwhelming exhaustion." He shook his head. "But in truth I can barely keep my eyes open. I would be poor company tonight."

"Your grace will sleep deeper and more soundly, if he allows me to tuck him in properly. I know just the kind of goodnight kiss he needs."

At that image, a part of Aefric very much wanted to invite her in. He girded himself for what he knew he had to say next.

He smiled, and hoped it didn't show that the smile was more of his lips than of his heart. All he really wanted to do right then was go to sleep.

"I am truly grateful for your offer," he said, and reached out a hand to stroke her cheek. "Come to me another night, and I will welcome you properly. And perhaps learn more about this kiss you speak of."

He put his fingers to her lips to stop her from speaking. She kissed those fingers gently.

"But tonight I must sleep all I can," he insisted. "And rise as early as I might. Tomorrow will be a long day."

She shifted her robe to display a little more of what the gauzy cloth beneath didn't quite cover.

"Your grace is certain I cannot tempt him tonight?"

"I do not deny that you *tempt* me, Baroness," Aefric said. "But tonight I have traveled by spell to confront a count in his hall. I have bent wild and untamed powers to my will, and brought a recalcitrant nobleman to heel. And then, I had to fly back many, many miles through rains and winds both."

She made a small sound that was intended either as sympathy for what he'd gone through or an indication that she was impressed by what he'd done. He couldn't tell which.

Her gaze, however, had drifted down to his chest, visible through a gape in his own robe. He tilted her chin up so she met his eye.

"Another night, baroness," he said softly. "Another night. But not this one."

She took his hand and pressed her forehead to it.

"As you wish, your grace," she said. "I shall return another night."

"Good night, baroness."

"Sweet dreams, your grace," she said. And Aefric suspected she would have said or done something more, but he closed the door before she could.

He slid the bolt into place. Wandered into his room.

He fell into his bed, fast asleep.

11

Aefric awoke suddenly. Panting for breath, and covered in sweat.

But there was no threat.

He was safe.

He was in his so-big, so-comfortable bed at Behal. Servants were moving about the room. One was standing over him.

She was a young woman. He'd heard her name yesterday. It was…

"Somer?" He asked.

"That's right, your grace," she said with the kind of bright, pleased enthusiasm that no one should have when it was still dark outside. "I didn't meant to startle you, so. I was told to wake you. Ser Grey awaits without. You have just enough time to bathe and dress before his lordship, the baron of Havenford, departs."

"Thank you," Aefric said, settling down a bit. His heart was still beating too quickly, and he was tense through more muscles than should have been, given that he was just sleeping.

"Unpleasant dreams, your grace?" Somer asked, holding out a dressing gown for him made of soft white linen, so thin it was translucent.

"I'm not sure," he said, fighting a yawn as he stood and donned the gown. He tried not to think about being naked in front of Somer, and the other servants who were busy putting away his dinner dishes from last night. Banking the fire. Cleaning.

What *had* Aefric been dreaming? As he wondered, fleeting images and sensations returned, that gained more solidity in his mind as he gave them focus.

He had been standing just off of a merry-go-round. There was a line behind him. Everyone was waiting for him to get on and take his turn, but all the horses looked like Armyrian noblewomen. And that wasn't right. He'd started looking around for someone to help him.

He'd seen Maev, but she'd just laughed and said, "Ride them all. We'll talk later." And he'd seen Andi, who'd said, "Pick one already, Keifer. It's past time, and everyone's waiting."

He'd even seen Octave. But just before he could hear what she was saying, he'd awakened.

He let out an exasperated breath and shook his head.

The bath helped. Lots of hot water and scrubbing chased away the last vestiges of the previous night's long flight, as well as reminding his muscles that they were allowed to relax and move after all.

In fact, he'd been tempted to linger. But before he could, Somer was there, with towels, saying, "I'm sorry, your grace. But if you're to have enough time to dress properly, you really should get out of the tub."

There was nothing challenging in her words. Yet, at the same time, they held a quality that was not to be denied.

Aefric looked up at her. There was nothing challenging in the young woman's expression either. But her brown eyes were firm and would not yield.

She wasn't giving him an giving him an order. That was clear. Yet at the same time, she made equally clear that he had duties, and that it was time for him to get out of the tub.

Quite a trick, that...

"You have younger siblings, don't you, Somer?" Aefric asked as he climbed out of the tub and began drying off.

"Six, your grace. I helped raise them."

"I thought as much," he said with a chuckle. He hurried through the toweling off process and slipped back into his dressing gown before she shuttled him into his closet, where two more servants had already picked out clothing for him.

Aefric considered picking out his own clothes, just to be obstinate. But when he compared the extent of his available wardrobe to his amount of available time, he sighed and accepted the choices his servants had already made.

A forest green tunic, cut a little low in the neck, with quilted diamond-shapes through the body, and lighter green, almost hose for the sleeves.

The pants they chose for him were form-fitting — which still impressed him, given that he'd never yet stood for a tailor here — of a deep oak brown.

Calf-high boots a shade darker than the pants, which matched the belt they had for him, whose buckle was polished brass, edged in gold.

They'd already attached his wand Garram to his belt by its sheath, which meant they were learning quickly.

The emerald ring the queen had given him had been polished. They offered him a trio of necklaces to choose from, but he stayed with the crystal Andi had given him, on its simple gold chain.

Though in this tunic, the crystal would be visible. He wasn't sure how he felt about that.

Fah. Let the whole duchy see it and wonder.

Today they offered him a half-cloak that matched the soft, gray one they'd given him yesterday. He almost asked why this one, and not the full cloak, but reminded himself that he was going to rely on locals' knowledge of the weather until he came to learn the patterns himself.

Dressed at last, he called the Brightstaff to his hand and came out into the main room, where Ser Grey was waiting. Today she wore navy blue hose and a long, quilted tunic of Deepwater gray. As always, her greatsword hung at her back, and her ring of many keys from her wide, black leather belt.

"We have time, your grace," she said quickly, holding up her hands. Though Aefric thought he saw a spark of mirth in her dark brown eyes. "No need to go jumping off of battlements or disappearing in a flash of lightning."

"Point taken," Aefric said, one eyebrow raised, and together they made their way down to the large front doors of the keep, flanked by four soldiers of Aefric's personal guard.

"You caused quite a stir last night, your grace," Ser Grey said, en route. "First riding off with the princess, then ... your rather abrupt exit. I daresay the castle will be abuzz about it for aetts."

"Well," Aefric said with a sigh, "it was bound to happen sooner or later. Magic is a way of life for me. Eventually I'd cast some spell that drove everyone to distraction. Better to get it out of the way."

"And the princess?" she asked with a raised eyebrow that felt impressively incisive. Aefric felt a small compulsion to answer that had nothing to do with magic and everything to do with Ser Grey's experience as a knight and a castellan.

"You'd have to ask her," he said.

"Does this mean I may join the two of you for breakfast?" Ser Grey smiled. "Or had you forgotten you promised her breakfast?"

"I didn't forget," Aefric said, telling only half a lie, because he hadn't truly *forgotten* per se. He just hadn't thought about the matter since he'd made the offer. He *had* been rather busy. "But I think she expects it to be the two of us."

"And what about Byrhta Ol'Caran? She's actually requested a formal meeting with you. Remember also that you promised to meet with the mayor and the trade council this afternoon."

"Then I'll meet with Byrhta after breakfast," he said. "We need to talk about Goldenfall."

"I agree," Ser Grey said. "Goldenfall must be brought into the fold, and quickly. Not to mention brought to heel, if they try to resist."

She shot Aefric a quick glare.

"Though I hope you don't plan to use the same technique you used with Motte."

"Not unless I have to. Though I must say it did make an impression. How much of an impression, I imagine we'll know soon enough."

Finally they passed through the main hall, which was being set up to provide breakfast for the court, and reached the front steps of the castle.

Baron Osmaer and Baronet Gautzelin were already present, dressed in the same, simple sorts of clothing they'd been wearing when Aefric met them. They had a carriage waiting to take them down to the docks, and their luggage already loaded.

They were talking with Princess Maev, who managed to surprise Aefric yet again. Not just by her presence, but by her mode of dress.

After yesterday, Aefric had expecting her to wear something woodsy again. Possibly made from the skin of other animals killed by her own hand. But no.

Today, she adorned a simple tunic that again left her arms mostly bare, over hose that tucked neatly into her ankle-high boots. Her jet black hair was pulled back and braided down between her shoulders.

Her shoes were black, as was her belt. Otherwise, her clothing matched Aefric perfectly. Her tunic, forest green and her hose that deep oak brown.

It was more the sort of outfit one would expect a knight to wear, than a princess. But it suited her, right down to the sword hanging from her belt.

And from the colors, he wondered if their servants had planned their outfits jointly...

"Aefric," she said brightly, making a small sound with her fingers and calling her lynx back from somewhere near the carriage's horses. "We were just discussing the wild rumors about you. I do hope you'll tell us they're all true."

"I hate to ask," Aefric said through a pained expression that brought smiles to the faces of his listeners, "but what rumors?"

"My favorite," Baronet Gautzelin said, "claims that you called forth lightning demons to tear down Castle Kirandai stone ... by ... stone."

"Come now," Aefric said. "If I did that, what would become of the castle staff? Why should I make them suffer for the foolishness of their count?"

Maev and the baronet laughed, but Baron Osmaer nodded and said, "I approve of your logic. You didn't do that, then, I take it?"

"I demolished the doors as I blasted my way in," Aefric said. "I do confess it. And I imagine I gave a number of people quite a fright. But I didn't harm anyone."

"Not even the count?" Maev asked, almost sounding disappointed.

"I hurt his pride and his ego a great deal," Aefric said. "But I didn't go there to physically punish anyone. I went there to put a stop to Ferrin's idiocy, as well as get his oaths of vassalage, and a few other little things besides."

Baron Osmaer immediately nodded that he understood not to ask any further. His husband drew breath to ask a question, but when the baron squeezed his hand, he frowned and let the breath go.

Maev's eyes blazed with the desire to ask, but didn't indulge herself. Not there and then.

Aefric said his goodbyes then, to the baron and his husband. And he sent them off with two casks of that good stout beer, which brought a wide smile to the baron's face, and an exasperated sigh from his husband.

As they departed, Maev said, "You promised me breakfast."

"And I'm good for it," Aefric said. "Shall we?"

"We shall," she said, taking his arm, while her lynx, Sylkanis fell into step beside her. "And I want to hear *everything.*"

<hr>

Breakfast with the princess was doomed to be a strange experience.

On the one hand, they were to dine in Aefric's solarium, which was really quite lovely just after dawn. The rains had moved through the night before, and the skies above looked to be clear through the whole of the day.

The skies were lovely shades of yellow as the sun rose, and those colors echoed on the glimmering surface of Deepwater Lake. Where the fishing boats were already about their day's business.

The stained glass from the domed ceiling above lent a lovely touch to the morning light.

Aefric was seated on one padded, comfortable chair. Maev was seated on another. A small, dark wood table between them, where servants kept their plates filled with an assortment of fruits and cheeses, along with a breakfast pastry involving eggs and bacon, with a wonderful spiced, melted cheese that made the bites of fruit even sweeter.

To drink they had fresh water, but also available was mint tea. Though the tea was mainly there, Aefric suspected, to perfume the air. He had yet to see anyone in Armyr touch a drink other than water, over breakfast.

Sylkanis lay on the floorboards over near the wall of windows, enjoying a selection of raw lake fish.

This should have been an ideal setting for breakfast with a beautiful young woman. And there was enough truth to that thought to quicken Aefric's pulse and make him sit a little straighter.

Aefric, however, was still getting used to the casual scrutiny of armed and armored knights.

Four of the knights were Maev's. Four of them were Aefric's. All eight stood sentinel off to the sides of the room.

Not in the way, yet looming nonetheless. With that sense of implicit violence Aefric had always felt in the presence of armed and armored men and women.

Aefric finished his second recounting of exactly what he'd done between the time that he left Maev's presence the night before and the time he returned to the castle later that night.

He'd already had to repeat sections of it several times, because she wanted to hear over and over about how he blasted through the doors. About how he confronted Count Ferrin. About how he'd spoken to the knights and guards, and finally challenged the count to single combat.

"The best part about that," Maev said between bites of strawberry, "is that by all rights he could have chosen a champion and made you fight."

She shook her head in amazement. "But you'd already ensured that even his own knights would refuse to fight for him against their overlord."

She popped the rest of that strawberry into her mouth and gave Aefric a soft round of applause.

"Brilliant," she said after swallowing. "Truly inspired."

"I don't know about that," Aefric said. "I shamed and humiliated him. He's going to want to get back at me."

"Of course," she said, shrugging one shoulder and looking over the fruit on the plate. "And when you trounce him a second time, perhaps the lesson will take. Even a foolish young squire learns to keep his shield up, the second time he's unhorsed."

"And yet," Aefric said, "he keeps jousting."

"Fah!" Maev said, waving away what Aefric thought was a legitimate concern. "You push the analogy too far. You won a victory last night. Don't diminish it."

Aefric felt that the matter was more complicated than that, but no matter how he tried, he couldn't get Maev to agree.

"I understand," she said at last, cutting a slice of cantaloupe down to size and not sounding at all as though she understood. "You're his duke, and he's going to be a thorn in your side for some time yet. But make no mistake. He's still smart enough to recognize that you could have done a lot worse than humiliate him last night."

Aefric frowned. He hadn't considered that side of things.

"He may decide," Maev continued, "that falling into line with you will be the smarter move than fighting you. Especially once it becomes clear that the other counties and baronies are flourishing under you."

"Assuming they will," Aefric said, shaking his head while Maev finished off that bite of cantaloupe.

"You've arranged for priests of the Green Lord to restore their farms and pastures. Yes, it will take time, but you've already accelerated your duchy's recovery. And you've only been here, what? This is your second morning at Behal, I think?"

Aefric nodded.

"Have some faith in yourself," she said. "And if you have doubts, remember. I have faith in you. And I'm a smart woman."

Aefric had something clever to say then — he was sure of it — but he was interrupted by a spell.

A message spell, coming in.

It felt like a ringing through his bones, and an urge to turn his head to receive the message.

Maev asked a question then in a concerned tone, but he missed her words. He was too busy listening to Karbin.

"Aefric. Felspark's wizard isn't a prisoner. Out of touch because disease wiped out Fyrcloch's rika birds. We must speak in person. Tell me when."

Fyrcloch Castle. The ducal seat of Merrek.

Tension sang through Aefric's bones. The feel of Karbin's spell, waiting for his reply.

"Come to me when you can," Aefric said. "Sooner is better."

The magic faded then, and Maev looked at him expectantly.

He opened his mouth to tell her, then frowned.

"Before I tell you what that was about — and I promise I will — I need to know something that you can tell me. You sat regent for the county of Fyretti for some time. What's the state of that county?"

Maev frowned for a moment, as though considering pulling rank on him, but huffed out a breath.

"It's in good shape," she said, shrugging one shoulder. "Their two coastal towns were wiped out by sea devils during the war, but they're already rebuilding, because nothing else got hit. Their coffers are reasonably close to full, all things considered. Their farms and such are all producing. All's well there."

"What about trade?" Aefric said.

"Down," Maev said with another shrug. "But only because others are in worse shape than Fyretti. Their boats ply the river as much as they can, and more stand ready for when traffic will bear. They lack ships, right now, for sea trade, but are rebuilding those as well."

"What about Merrek?" Aefric said. "Some of my vassals have reported Merrek applying pressure about trade."

"Not with Fyretti," Maev said firmly. "I shouldn't be surprised if my aunt by law were trying to turn the screws on you, Aefric. But I've seen no evidence of it in Fyretti."

"It's not Merrek then," Aefric said, shaking his head. "It can't be."

"What can't be?" Maev asked, with diminishing patience.

Karbin appeared between where they sat the wall of windows. He wore his usual shades of sand and dusk, and at his belt his obsidian rod alongside his normal assortment of wands.

All about the room, knights drew swords and started calling challenges.

Aefric leapt to his feet and threw his hands out wide.

"This man is my ducal wizard," he said. "And he is here at my invitation. Stand down, all of you."

Aefric's knights sheathed their swords at once. Maev's waited for her nod to do the same.

Aefric made the introductions then, finishing with, "And I apologize for inviting a third to our breakfast. But his news cannot wait, and I presumed you would rather hear what he has to say than—"

"Of *course* I want to know," Maev said, sitting forward, full of excitement. "Don't give it a moment's thought."

"I hate to disappoint your highness," Karbin said, calling over another chair with a gesture so he could be seated. "What I have to say is important, but may not sound like—"

Maev made a sound of frustration. "If the two of you don't stop apologizing and *start* telling me what's going on, I shall become *quite cross* with both of you."

Aefric would have sworn he heard one of Maev's knights hiss in a breath at that.

He nodded at Karbin.

"As I told you in the message," Karbin said. "Shaela wasn't Merrek's prisoner. The negotiations were taking a long time, but she was building the impression it was because Merrek couldn't fulfill the amount of cargo Felspark was asking for. She also thought there might be another reason behind the delay, but couldn't find out what."

"I have some thoughts along those lines," Aefric said. "But was there anything else first?"

"Only one thing," Karbin said. "I didn't get to examine this deeply in the short time I had, but from what I can tell, Merrek is hurting for soldiers. They never had many to begin with, focusing more on sea might than land. But right now, they have only a token number, for defense. And those are spread out fairly thin, and watching their southern border."

"Why is that important?" Maev asked.

"Two reasons," Aefric said, "First it confirms that none of Merrek's soldiers are along her northern borders, harassing my barons. Second, and more important, it means that Merrek could never hope to take and hold the Fyrsa River Valley in Felspark. They had to have been talking about a different river valley entirely."

"There was talk of taking a river valley?" Maev asked, her patience dwindling.

"A discussion was overheard," Aefric said. "And I think misunderstood." He summoned a page. "Send for Sers Grey and Beornric, please. And hurry."

The page was about to leave, but Aefric gestured for a knight to stop him.

"One more thing," Aefric said to the page. "Bring me Byrhta Ol'Caran as well."

Soon the solarium was crowded enough that Aefric moved the conversation to the black oak table in his sitting room. Though considering the political maneuvering involved, he half-wondered if they should have crowded around his chess set.

Sylkanis joined them in the sitting room, but was far more interested in wandering about Aefric's chambers than in any discussion to be had at the table.

The knights of his and Maev's guards came into the room as well, but Aefric turned to Maev and asked a question as quietly as he could.

"We're about to discuss a very private matter. Would I be insulting your knights if I asked them to leave?"

"You would," she said, just as softly, and her eyes danced with what might have been mirth at whispering with him this way. "But they are sworn to keep my secrets, and I will ensure that they keep yours."

"Thank you."

Aefric took his seat at the head of the table then, with Maev and Karbin on his right, and Sers Grey and Beornric on his left. Byrhta sat at the foot of the table, looking puzzled about why she'd been summoned.

She was elegantly dressed, in a bodice of dark forest green that matched her hair, and transitioned smoothly into skirts of sea foam green. Her hair was done up in a complicated style, and kept in place with jade combs. She wore a simple gold chain at her throat, with an emerald dangling down along her cleavage. Two engraved gold bracelets dangled on her left wrist.

"Byrhta," Aefric said. "Thank you for coming. I know the two of us were to meet later this morning, but events have accelerated on me. I will meet with you privately later, if you wish, but there is information I need from you here and now."

Byrhta nodded and folded her hands on the table.

"My father and I are, of course, loyal to our duke," she said. "How may I help your grace?"

"Right now I need to know the state of Goldenfall. Whatever you can tell me."

"There is a great deal to tell," she said, arching one dark, forest green eyebrow above her almost too-perfect features. "Where shall I begin?"

"I know Goldenfall was hit hard by the forces of the Flayer during the wars. But I don't know *how* hard. The extent of the damage."

Byrhta nodded once, slowly, and began to speak.

"Vabarett, both the city and the castle, managed to survive the borog siege. That is the extent of our good news. As for the bad news, the rest of our county was largely decimated before the borogs were driven south. Some four-fifths of our pastures and farmland, ruined. Two-thirds of our towns and settlements, destroyed beyond hope of repair."

Byrhta spoke with a steady voice, but the pain in her eyes was plain.

"Countless numbers of our people were slaughtered," she continued. "Not to mention our livestock. Father has been working tirelessly to keep his people alive, and to begin such repairs as he can. But hunger and exposure are constant threats. To make matters worse, our coffers ebb. And we cannot spare the resources to keep our mines producing."

Her nostrils flared in a quick breath.

"In short, your grace, we have been devastated. My father regrets that he could not come offer his oaths of vassalage, but assures you that he will happily do so at the first opportunity. And he hopes that you will not deny our people aid over a delay their count cannot help."

Holding Aefric's eyes the entire time, she got out of her chair then and dropped down onto her knees on the hardwood floor. She raised her folded hands to Aefric.

She ignored everyone else present. Her eyes stayed locked onto his, and her words, for him alone.

The intensity of her gaze stole Aefric's breath.

"I beg you, your grace," she said. "Aid us. Please."

Aefric found his breath.

"Why didn't you say something earlier?" he asked in disbelief.

"When, your grace? I've spoken to you only at that first dinner.

And there I dared not reveal our weakness. Not in front of so many. And not until I knew what sort of man you were."

She shook her head, without looking away from his eyes.

"I confess. I still do not know for certain that I can trust you. But by all accounts, your sudden departure last night involved sparing the lives of your people. And our people in Goldenfall are your people as well. I beg you. Aid us."

"Of course I will," Aefric said, standing and stepping closer to take Byrhta's hands and draw her to her feet. "Have no fear on that. And please, be seated once more."

Byrhta took her seat again. And if she felt at all ashamed of kneeling and begging, she didn't show it in the least.

Aefric had to admit he was impressed by her dignity.

"There's one more thing I must ask you about," he said. "Because it concerns the whole of the duchy, as well as information I've gotten from several vassals."

"I am yours to command, your grace."

"I need to know how trade is in Goldenfall, and whether anyone has tried to pressure you."

"Trade is but a pittance of what it was. And yes. Motte has tried to pressure us into bad bargains, but my father has rebuffed him." She shook her head. "I don't know how much longer he can hold out, though. There are basics we need that are only being offered by Motte right now."

"I will ensure that Motte offers a fair price," Aefric said. "In fact, I will assign a mediator, who will ensure that the final agreement favors Goldenfall. As part of Motte's punishment for their abuses."

"Thank you, your grace," Byrhta said, a note of hope in her voice.

"Now," Aefric said. "I'm afraid I must ask you to leave for the time being. I have pressing business before me that must be dealt with today."

"Of course, your grace," Byrhta replied, and that note of hope chilled into disappointment.

"But in the interim." Aefric called a page into the room. "This page will take you to my seneschal. I want you to go over the damages and needs of Goldenfall in detail with her. Be as complete as you can. That will go a long way towards speeding my ability to help."

She bowed, but Aefric crossed to her and kissed her hand.

"I swear to you," he said. "Goldenfall does not stand alone. I *will* help you."

"Thank you, your grace," she said, and this time relief flooded her voice. Her eyes shone with unshed tears. She pressed her forehead to his hand, then turned and left with the page.

Aefric turned to a servant then. "Bring in the rest of that breakfast, please, and send for more." He sighed. "Then clear the room except for the lynx and the guards. We have weighty matters before us."

Aefric reclaimed the head of his black oak table, where fruit, honeyed oat bread, and more of those cheese pastries had been spread out before him. Though none of the others, it seemed were hungry. And Aefric himself wasn't sure he could eat, after what he'd just heard from Byrhta.

He turned to Ser Grey, seated at his left hand.

"I want a team of surveyors sent into Goldenfall today. I want a full assessment of the situation there as soon as I can get it."

"If I may," Princess Maev said, from Aefric's right hand. At his nod, she continued, "Father's surveyors have completed their work in the royal lands. Let me send for them, and let the crown pay for the survey."

Aefric frowned, thinking of the length of his own journey from Armityr. But Maev seemed to anticipate his concern.

"There should be two teams near Towerkeep. A rika could reach them late today, and both teams could be in Goldenfall within three days. Two if they push, and I'll make sure they do."

She put her hand on his wrist.

"Please, Aefric. If Goldenfall is so badly off as that, I want them to know that the crown stands behind them as well as their duke."

Aefric nodded. She wrote out the message right there, and Aefric had it sent to the rookery before they continued.

Sylkanis must have sensed that something had changed, because she came over to sit with Maev while she wrote the message, then stayed near her side for the rest of the meeting.

Then, once they, along with Karbin and Sers Beornric and Grey, were seated at the table once more, Aefric began.

"Let us review what we know," he said. "From Baroness Herewyn, we learned the Norra has been troubled by bandits in Kerrik Forest, ranging as far at times as her quarries. Bandits that seemed to have been driven south by Motte. And some of them might have been Motte soldiers themselves."

"What about Merrek?" Ser Beornric asked. "Didn't you say that she suspected Merrek's involvement as well?"

"I did," Aefric said with a frown. "But I must also admit that it was I who asked about Merrek, not her who raised that name."

"Why is that significant?" Ser Grey asked. "Of course a baroness would be hesitant to accuse a duchess."

"Because I'd already fielded warnings to look for trouble from Merrek. I asked, without waiting for her to imply."

"With good reason," Maev said, shrugging one shoulder. "The Fyrenn family has made no secret about coveting your lands in the past. And it stands to reason that Duchess Ashiling would at least test a new duke."

"True," Aefric said. "We'll come back to that."

"So that's Norra," Karbin said. "What about Felspark?"

"In Felspark, Baroness Blaewyn told me that Merrek was pressuring her to cut off trade with Norra." Aefric grimaced and shook his head. "Wish I'd asked who specifically she'd been talking with."

"She also mentioned," Karbin said, "that her wizard had been out of touch, while negotiating trade terms with Merrek."

"Yes," Aefric said. "I'll get to that. First, I should point out that Norra didn't complain about trade. Only about banditry."

"But surely their trade is down as well," Ser Grey said.

"Of course," Maev said casually. "Everyone's is. She probably didn't think it worth mentioning."

"But she didn't mention any pressure about trade from Merrek," Aefric said. "Which means that she didn't know about it. And yet Baroness Blaewyn said the pressure to cut off Norra had been coming since the end of the Godswalk Wars. Why?"

Karbin looked as though he knew the answer, but he nodded for Aefric to continue.

"Trade that continued from Felspark into Norra should be good for Merrek, as well as Felspark and Norra," Aefric said. "To have enough to trade, Felspark would have to buy more from Merrek, yes?"

Maev's eyes lit up as she saw where he was going.

"Merrek couldn't support that much demand," she said, looking aghast. "Admitting to that would be admitting their weakness, so they tried to make it look like political pressure on Felspark."

"Which is why Shaela's negotiations with Merrek on Felspark's behalf have gone nowhere," Karbin said with a nod. "And why she can't get a straight answer about why they're holding such a hard line."

"Exactly," Aefric said. "We know from Baron Osmaer that Havenford's ships have been sailing with Merrek's ships, to protect both from piracy. And if Merrek needs that support, it can only mean that Merrek's sea power was crushed during the wars."

"Merrek's *lands* weren't hit hard," Ser Beornric said. "Everyone knows that. But if she'd invested most of her power in the *sea*. Much more difficult to judge that from here, or from Armityr."

"So Merrek *was* hit as hard as we were," Ser Grey said, wondering.

"Harder, possibly," Aefric said. "Though I can't be sure of that. Especially not with the devastation of Goldenfall."

"What about Motte?" Ser Beornric asked.

"I'll get to Motte in a moment," Aefric said. "First, for the sake of completeness, we should acknowledge that Havenford stands largely intact, and feels no pressure from anyone."

"Which is why you asked so urgently about Fyretti," Maev said, then clarified for the others. "Fyretti was all but untouched by the wars. And with their own riverboats standing ready for more trade than they currently have, no one has been in a position to pressure them."

"That's right. A barony and a county, both handling or ready to handle much of their own trade by sea or by river. And thus no easy avenue for pressure by outside forces."

"Which brings us back to Motte?" Ser Beornric asked.

"It does," Aefric said with a wolfish smile. "Motte has given us half the key, though they don't know it. Motte has been working with a patron. Both for financial support, and to apply pressure to both Norra and Goldenfall."

"Who's the patron?" Maev asked, leaning forward.

"Count Ferrin thinks his patron is Merrek," Aefric said. "And I implied as much before his court last night. So any spies in his dining hall should believe I think the same thing."

Aefric shook his head. "But I don't. I don't believe Merrek has the resources or the interest in helping a weak count who has little to offer in return."

"Who then?" Ser Grey asked.

"I have a theory," Aefric said. "And this theory comes down to what Felspark's wizard, Shaela, overheard about seizing a river valley."

"If Merrek's hurting," Ser Beornric said reasonably, "they're in no shape to *take,* much less *hold,* the Fyrsa River Valley. To say nothing of any other Deepwater lands."

"No," Aefric said. "They're not. But there's another river valley close to Merrek."

"*The Indecisive River?*" Maev said, eyes wide. "*That* river valley?"

"*That* river valley," Aefric confirmed, calling now on the memories of Keifer's old *Torn Kingdoms* sourcebooks. "The Indecisive River. For all its twists and turns, it stays wide enough and deep enough to carry trade access directly from the Risen Sea almost as far as Armityr itself. Between the Indecisive and the Maiden's Blood, which pours into it, smaller ships can carry trade out east past Rethneryl, and up north past the Endless Mountains."

"But, Aefric," Maev said slowly. "That can only mean…"

"Yes," Aefric said, then let out a long, slow breath. "I think Motte's patron isn't the duchy of Merrek. But the *kingdom of Malimfar*. And I think they're tired of sharing that river valley with Merrek. I think Malimfar wants to seize it, and all the trade that goes with it."

"But that would mean war," Ser Grey said, in disbelief.

"Not necessarily," Aefric said. "I think the point behind pressuring my vassals was to build up animosity between me and Merrek. Make me slow to come to her aid, even if ordered by the king. With Merrek's land forces weak, her sea forces devastated, and her nearest neighbor unwilling to help, Malimfar might be able to seize the river valley."

"The king would never stand for it," Ser Beornric said, shaking his head.

"Perhaps not. But once Malimfar's dug in there, they'll be hard to dig out. In the meantime, they can offer a peace settlement to Armyr, aided by the leverage gained by controlling a major trade route."

Maev bit her lip, and nodded. She sighed.

"That might work. Especially if King Eadred first paid some kind of reparations to Father for the land, and second, ceded to Father the rest the river valley from somewhere near the join of the Maiden's Blood. The place where Malimfar's seafaring ships wouldn't be able to sail farther anyway."

"It would be a crushing blow to Merrek," Aefric said. "But it would be an excuse to keep Armyr out of a war it doesn't need."

"I still can't believe King Colm would stand for this," Ser Beornric said, shaking his head even harder. "He may not want a war, but some things are worth fighting over. And we're talking about lands belonging to the queen's own sister."

"The same queen's sister," Maev said, one eyebrow high, "who has been agitating for more land her entire life? The same queen's sister who has been actively arguing that she should be allowed to annex all of Deepwater? Beginning the very day of Duchess Arinda's death? That queen's sister?"

Maev shook her head. "Father might allow this happen to teach her a lesson. Then let a decade or two of reduced income cement that lesson while Armyr licks its wounds. *Then* he might raise an army and either take back Merrek's half of the river valley, or the whole thing. At which point he might raise up a new count to control that river valley, thus permanently denying it to Ashling and her descendants."

"That could be," Ser Grey said, rubbing her chin. She cocked her head at Aefric. "And if that would be the king's solution, perhaps you shouldn't interfere."

"That might be the king's solution if he faces a valley already lost to him," Aefric said. "But whatever grievance he has with Merrek, I doubt he'd *choose* to lose that land if he could avoid it."

"I'll have to contact Father at once," Maev said, starting to stand. "It has to be his choice whether or not to call the banners."

"Wait," Karbin said, looking at Aefric. "We must not act until we bring together all the pertinent information. Some of which we yet lack."

Aefric thought a moment. "Riverbreak. Were they just being cagey? Or are they compromised?"

"Exactly," Karbin said with a nod.

"Shall I summon Baron Karmody?" Ser Beornric asked, rising to his feet.

He stopped mid-movement when Ser Grey scoffed.

"Bring that man into a meeting like this one and a straight answer is the last thing you'll get." She scoffed again. "I've had to deal with Karmody for all my ten years as castellan here, and mark my words. Everything he says in this room will be angled toward his own advantage, even if he must lie to get it."

Aefric sighed and sagged slightly in his chair.

Maev started chuckling, but not as though she found anything amusing.

"I can't believe *I'm* the one saying this," she said, "but you're thinking like an adventurer, Aefric. Direct, and at the problem. But this situation calls for you to think like a noble. Specifically, like an *Armyrian* noble. How *else* can you get information about Riverbreak?"

Maev raised her eyebrows at him.

"She'd be quite flattered, I'd think," Ser Grey said, keeping a neutral expression. "For the dashing young duke to summon her to his chambers for a mid-morning tryst."

Of course. The baroness.

Aefric sighed. It looked as though he had to take one for the team after all.

SER GREY WOULD HANDLE THE DETAILS, AT AEFRIC'S DIRECTION. SHE was to find the baroness, and issue the discreet invitation. She was then to escort the baroness, personally, though less-used hallways to Aefric's chambers.

He'd originally suggested the servants' backway, but Ser Grey had talked him out of it. First, because trysts between nobles were commonplace, and taking pains to hide what they were doing would only draw attention to it.

Second, and even more persuasive — did Aefric really want the baroness knowing how to reach his private chambers through secret passages?

No. No, he did not.

Still. The waiting was a tricky thing.

Aefric wasn't sure what the expected protocol was, when it came to this kind of waiting. And he didn't feel as though he could ask.

Would the baroness expect him to be naked? Wearing something gauzy, as she'd worn the night before? Would she prefer him fully dressed?

This was all so strange and ... calculated. He didn't feel so much as though he were waiting to have sex but to engage in clandestine politics, that just happened to involve nudity and interlocking bodies.

He settled in one of the comfortable chairs by the window in his sitting room. Fully dressed. He had the prince's report in his hands, but he'd gained nothing from his attempts to read it. It was just something to stare at while he waited.

Then, finally, there was a soft knock at his door, and in came Baroness Montess. She wore a gown of deep lake blue, and her hair up in a complicated pile on her head that involved several gold and silver combs.

But there was no mistaking the look in her eyes or the smile on her lips as she closed the door behind her.

Aefric noticed that the servants nearby paid her no attention whatsoever.

"Your grace," the baroness said. "Such urgency. I barely had time to drink my nysta tea. I fear you'll taste it."

He'd drunk a cup of that tea himself, just in case. The last thing he wanted was to get a child on a married woman.

"What can I say?" he said, forcing a smile as he stood and stepped closer. "Once I was rested and refreshed, I found I could not banish the image of you from my head."

He ran his fingers down her cheek, then down her shoulder along the sleeve of her gown. "Such hints you gave me of the wonders beneath this dress. I knew I could wait no longer to explore them."

He kissed her then, and she molded herself to him even while she moaned into his mouth. Her tongue worked as though to distract him from the slightly bitter taste of the tea.

When they parted from the kiss, he scooped her up in his arms and carried her to his bed while she made pleased sounds about the whole thing.

If he'd worried about his ability to perform, he needn't have. She was more than attractive enough to rouse his interest, and a very skilled lover.

And strangely, there was a formality to the whole event that kept emotions at a distance. She never called him anything but "your grace," even while moaning in passion. And she didn't balk at his addressing her only as "Baroness."

After they'd satisfied each other, when they lay naked, perspiring and entwined, she eagerly asked about the night before. Where he'd gone. What he'd done. And she didn't just want facts, she wanted story.

Well, that was fine with Aefric. He'd never intended to keep his deeds in Motte any kind of secret. He wanted people to know what he'd done. Both to show him what he would do to keep his people out of needless conflicts, as well as how he might handle recalcitrant vassals.

And if the story set Baroness Montess more at ease, so much the better.

As it turned out, the story didn't just set her at ease. It made her eager for a second round.

As they lay together afterwards, this time drenched in sweat but still entwined and naked, he started the conversation.

"I must ask, Baroness—"

"Oh, *must* you, your grace?" she teased. "I daresay you should know by now that I won't object."

He kissed her. But before she could try to turn that kiss into more, he continued.

"I will be dealing with Merrek soon," he said. "And I was thinking about your husband's offer to assist in negotiations. I'm not sure it would be a good idea."

"Of course it would," she said, rolling over to look him in the eye, and bracing herself with her hands on his chest. "Karmody has negotiated *scores* of trade agreements over the years. You won't find anyone better."

"But both Felspark and Fyretti lie between your lands and Merrek," Aefric said. "So he's never had to negotiate with the duchess herself." He shook his head. "I'm not sure—"

"Trust me, your grace," she said, bringing her knees underneath herself for support, then smiling as she realized the position she'd put herself in. "We have Merrek right where we want her."

"But how do you know?"

"Oh," she said, smiling lasciviously and reaching behind herself with one hand, "I *always* know when I have someone where I want them."

Their conversation had to wait, then, for the next lull in their tryst. And this time the baroness was panting for breath, as well.

"You see ... your grace ... I know ... what I'm about..."

"In here," Aefric said, encouraging her to pillow her head on his shoulder again, "most certainly. But Merrek is another matter. And I would need some kind of assurances."

"But you've already *met* our assurances," Baroness Montess teased, with a smile Aefric could hear but not see from the angle of her face.

He tilted her chin up so she met his eyes.

"I do enjoy it when you do that, your grace," she said, smiling.

"Good," Aefric said. "Now what do you mean, I've already met your assurances?"

"Well," she said, "maybe I want you to—"

"That Knight of the Garnet," Aefric said, suddenly certain. "Ser Grud. He's your assurance?"

Baroness Montess made a disappointed sound, but sighed and said, "Yes, your grace. He represents the duchess."

"I find that difficult to believe," Aefric said. "Why would she not choose one of her own advisers?"

"I don't know, your grace," Baroness Montess said, kissing a scar on his shoulder. "How did you get this one?"

"I'll tell you that," Aefric said, "if you can tell me how you know for certain that Ser Grud represents Merrek?"

"If I tell you," she said, cocking her head to one side, "I want more than a story."

Aefric grabbed her by the shoulders and rolled over so that she was pinned beneath him. Her eyes rolled wild, her lips parted, panting, and she raised her hands as though surrendering, with her wrists flat to the mattress just outside her shoulders.

Aefric got the hint. Held her wrists down instead. She writhed beneath him in approval.

"Tell me," he said, "and I'll *give* you more than a story."

"Oh, yes, your grace," she said through a pleased sounding breath. "And I do look forward to your marrying Vercy. I think she'd do very well with a man like you."

That comment was just too weird for words. Aefric almost lost his train of thought.

"How," he said, leaning down and punctuating each word with a kiss near her ear. Her skin there tasted of rosewater. "Do. You. Know?"

"He carries a small version of the Merrek seal. I've seen it myself. He's used it to seal messages he sends by rider."

"You're positive?"

"Always has it on his person. I swear."

Her hips tried to urge him to other activities then, but he smiled and made her wait while he told her the story she'd asked for first.

He kept her pinned beneath him as he told her of the siege of Karlton, and the arrow that caught him in the shoulder while he and two dozen battle-weary soldiers held the walls against overwhelming odds. All to buy time so the people could escape to safety through na'shek tunnels.

After the story, she whimpered, and said, "Please. Now, your grace. Unless your grace wishes me to beg?"

He didn't make her beg. Once they were finished, he said, "Alas, now I must wash up. Lunch will be waiting, and I have meetings all afternoon."

"Of course, your grace," she said, as though that were the most obvious thing in the world. "Though I must say I hope we'll do this again sometime. In fact" — she stopped getting out of bed for a moment, holding up one hand as though she'd had a brilliant idea — "if your grace would like, next time Vercy could watch from nearby, and learn a thing or two about the arts of pleasure."

Aefric had always known he had a limit somewhere. This suggestion just went *rocketing* past that limit.

But he couldn't admit that. Not there and then.

"Perhaps," he said through a smile that felt pained. "I shall give it some thought."

He didn't expect he had a choice. He had the feeling he'd be hearing that shudder-worthy suggestion in his nightmares.

At least Baroness Montess did not press the point. And she had no trouble dressing and leaving quickly. Though before she left, she smiled and tossed him her garter.

"A keepsake," she said.

Ser Grey had remained nearby, waiting to escort the baroness discreetly back to her chambers where she could clean up before she was seen publicly.

Of course, a servant could have handled that. Aefric had asked Ser Grey to do the honors so she could call the proper people back to Aefric's sitting room to resume their meeting.

Aefric hurried to wash and make himself ready. As he did, he realized that his old worries about guilt and Andi had never once surfaced during that whole encounter.

Was that because of the odd formality involved? Or were the objections coming from Keifer part of him finally losing some of their steam?

Was he ready to move on?

The sinking sensation in his stomach at that thought told him no.

But the sensation was weaker than it had been before. So perhaps he wasn't ready. Not yet.

But he was getting there.

They were gathered again, at the black oak table in Aefric's sitting room, with him at the head of the table.

On his right, Maev — with Sylkanis flopped on the floor at her feet — and Karbin.

On his left, Sers Grey and Beornric.

Knights of both his guard and the princess' were arrayed around the room, four of each, and alternating.

Aefric had wondered if Maev would look at him any differently. Given that she knew how he'd spent the last couple of hours. But her eyes seemed as bright as ever when they regarded him, and she still gave him a smile when she greeted him.

If she were at all troubled by knowing what he and Baroness

Montess had been doing only one room away, she didn't show it in the least.

In fact, no one at the table seemed to say by their expression that anything unusual had happened. Not even a hint of masculine teasing from Ser Beornric.

He caught them up quickly on the most important bit of information — that Ser Grud claimed to be representing Merrek, and seemed to be carrying a small version of Ashling's ducal seal.

"Ridiculous," Maev said dismissively. "Montess had to have mis-seen something."

"I agree," Ser Grey said. "No way an experienced duchess like Ashling would let some Knight of the Garnet run around with her seal. In fact, if he *does* have it, right now every knight at her command should be combing through Deepwater looking for him."

"Fyretti would be their first stop," Maev said. "And I would have heard before leaving yesterday. Therefore, there is no hunt for him."

"Which means that if he does have the seal," — Karbin held up his hands so that Maev and Ser Grey let him finish his point — "and we need to consider that possibility."

He stared from Maev to Ser Grey to Ser Beornric and back. All three nodded, reluctantly. He checked with Aefric as well, but Aefric had no hesitation in letting Karbin continue.

"If he has the true seal," he said, "it's because the duchess *wants* him to have it. So we need to figure out what it means if he *does*."

"It means," Aefric said through a sigh, "that either some of our information is flatly wrong, or I've taken a wrong turn in my logic somewhere. Because that could only mean that Merrek is behind at least some of our troubles."

"Ashling would never let her seal out of her hands," Maev said with such finality that Aefric had trouble disputing her. "*Least* of all to a foreign knight whose loyalty is first and foremost to his own order."

"Could he have a copy?" Karbin asked.

"Seems unlikely," Maev said. "Where would they get the model?"

"Any edict with the ducal seal," Ser Grey said, "could provide grist for a copy."

"Those aren't very easy for most people to get their hands on," Ser Beornric said. "I've certainly never seen an original copy of an edict, myself."

"Difficult," Karbin said, "is far from synonymous with impossible."

"But the real question here," Ser Grey said, "is *why*?"

Aefric frowned. "You mean, why claim to carry the duchess' seal?"

"Shortsighted thievery," Ser Grey said, "would be the most accomplished. He could falsify a letter of credit, or something similar, but it would only lead to the duchess hunting for him."

"In which case," Ser Beornric said, "why come here? Why not just get whatever cash or goods or whatever and flee before he's caught?"

"He's not running with merchants," Aefric said, beginning to understand. "He came to Riverbreak."

"You think he negotiated a deal with Riverbreak in the duchess' name?" Ser Beornric asked.

"No," Aefric said, leaning forward now. "But he clearly persuaded Riverbreak that he speaks for Merrek. Maybe negotiated some consideration for putting him here with me. Baron Karmody has been pressuring me to have *him* negotiate with Merrek. Presumably, if I agree, *that's* when he'd reveal that we could negotiate the deal with Merrek right here in my castle. With Grud speaking for Merrek. Something along those lines."

"Which would lead to a false deal," Maev said. "But you wouldn't know. Creating more animosity between you and Merrek, when you found out."

"So we're back to Malimfar again," Ser Grey said.

"I think so," Aefric said. "But we need to be sure."

"I don't think Ser Grud will just admit to working with Malimfar," Ser Grey said wryly.

But Aefric was looking at Karbin.

"You want me to go back to Merrek," Karbin said. "Confirm that Ser Grud doesn't have her seal."

Aefric nodded.

"If I fly, I can be there in—"

"Fly back if you must," Aefric said. "But I need that information today."

"I can't get into the habit of teleporting on ducal business," Karbin said. "You know the undue pressure that would put on other wizards."

"I'm trying to avert disaster for my new kingdom, Karbin," Aefric said quietly. "Time is of the essence."

"Very well," Karbin said, huffing out a breath. "But I will hide what I am doing. I'll teleport to somewhere near Fyrcloch, and make sure I'm seen flying in. And please do not let word get out about this."

He looked to the faces of the confused non-magic-users at the table.

"Teleportation," Karbin said, "is dangerous, risky magic. That is truth. The number of wizards across all of Qorunn who can perform the spell in perfect safety numbers less than three score. Perhaps half a hundred. The number who can *attempt* the spell ... is considerably higher."

"If nobles and wealthy merchants see one of their peers benefiting from teleportation," Aefric said, having had this very conversation with both Karbin and Kainemorton in the past, "they will demand it themselves. Wizards will be pressured into working magic beyond their safe limits. The results..."

"Deadly," Karbin said, grimly. "And in some cases, perhaps even catastrophic. *Explosively* catastrophic."

"So we won't mention it then," Maev said simply. "And on behalf of my Father — who will never learn of this — thank you."

"I'll leave as soon as the meeting is done," Karbin said.

"We should call for lunch," Aefric said. "We'll need to discuss strategies for the different possibilities here."

"We can't," Ser Grey said, firmly. "Your grace, you have not taken a meal with your court in more than a day, and you have two meetings this afternoon."

"Those things can wait," Aefric protested.

"No," Maev said. "She's right. You owe it to your court to socialize with them. Lunch is the least you can offer them right now, and it shouldn't be in the main hall. A picnic out by the garden would be good."

"With everything going on," Aefric tried, but Ser Grey picked right up where Maev left off.

"The duke is always busy," she said. "And even when he is not, the people must remember the value of his time. Meals and other social occasions are their primary access to you. And your obligation, as a noble."

"Fine," Aefric conceded through a sigh. "I guess we can meet back here after lunch—"

"Your grace has two meetings this afternoon," Ser Grey said. "And you must keep them."

"Surely they can be postponed," Aefric said.

"Which might tip off Ser Grud," Maev said. "Ser Grey is right. You need to act normally, and that means keeping your meetings."

"Fine," Aefric said, huffing out a frustrated breath. The last thing he wanted to do this afternoon was deal with a mayor and a trade council when he was trying to avert a war. "Anything else we should deal with for now?"

"One thing," Ser Beornric said. "You said Baroness Montess told you she'd seen Ser Grud use the Merrek seal on messages he sent by rider. Where were those messages going?"

"Difficult to find that out now," Karbin said, thoughtfully. "Not unless we can find out from him."

"One possibility occurs to me," Aefric said. "Motte. Could be that Ser Grud has been conveying or relaying orders to Motte, from Malimfar."

"If so," Ser Grey said, "then Ser Grud has been *receiving* orders from somewhere." She rapped her knuckles on the table. "Now *that* I can dig into. If he's gotten any messages since he crossed the Kingsroad, I'll find out."

"Good," Aefric said, standing. "If there's nothing else then, I guess it's time for lunch."

IF AEFRIC HAD BEEN A MORE EXPERIENCED DUKE, HE MIGHT HAVE BEEN able to focus in the moment and make excellent use of his afternoon.

After all, there was nothing more he could really do right then, on the Merrek front. He needed to hear from Karbin at the very least. And he would have preferred to hear from Ser Grey as well.

Once he heard from both of them, he presumed he would be in a good position to deal with the question of Merrek and Malimfar once and for all.

But since he could only wait, it would have made perfect sense for him to put all thoughts of such things out of his head, and focus on the activities at hand.

Alas, though, although a lifetime of adventuring had given him a number of skills that would stand him in good stead in a great many situations, it had not prepared him to make good use of waiting time.

He did his best.

First, there was lunch.

Aefric had taken Maev's suggestion, and arranged a buffet lunch with his court out in the garden, overlooking Lake Deepwater.

The day was beautiful for it. Bright, clear spring skies, and the air perfumed mostly by the roses, but to a lesser degree by the chrysanthemums, violets and others to overlay the meal with a pleasant, floral smell.

The morning chill had burned away, and he no longer needed even the half-cloak his servants had given him earlier.

The luncheon was light. An assortment of small meat pies along with a fresh salad of lettuce and three kinds of root vegetables, washed lightly with an oil that gave them a hint of tanginess.

Diners ate at a series of small, round tables, covered in tablecloths of Deepwater gray. They ate in small doses, entertained by the soft sounds of a string sextet, and intermingling their food with walks and conversation.

Over the course of lunch, Aefric must have eaten with four different groups of courtiers, and talked to some three dozen people.

So many new names, and in his current frame of mind, he had no hope of remembering them all. Fortunately, Maev assured him quietly, they would all expect to have to introduce themselves to him at least two or three times.

There were a few things Aefric did notice over the course of lunch.

First, that Maev made a point of whispering with him now and again. She seemed to be enjoying the effect it had on the observers, who were no doubt curious about the apparent intimacy between their princess and their new duke.

Baron Karmody looked a bit sour about that, whenever he witnessed it, but he seemed more relaxed as he spoke to Aefric about little nothings involving his barony and the past.

Baroness Montess couldn't stop smiling when Aefric was near. She seemed to have wasted no time in making sure word got around that she'd been the first noblewoman in Armyr to have a go with the new duke.

In fact, once Aefric realized the *way* she was smiling, he noticed also that all the nobles seemed more relaxed around him now, compared with dinner the other night. And several of the younger noblewomen, in particular, were being more openly flirtatious with him.

So sleeping with Baroness Montess really had helped ease the fears of his court? Weird. Sex as a statement was just an odd idea to him.

The baroness' behavior, strangely, didn't bother Baron Karmody, or their son, Baston. Their daughter Vercy seemed a little grumpy about it, but made sure to give Aefric a big smile whenever she found an excuse.

A nervous smile, if Aefric was any judge, but he didn't doubt its sincerity.

If Aefric had been worried about not knowing what to say, he needn't have. Everyone wanted to hear about what happened in Motte. And many of them wanted parts of the story repeated.

Of course, some then followed up by asking what Aefric would do *next*, but whenever he got that question, he just gave the asker a smile, and said, "You'll see."

Others took their opportunity to ask about the Brightstaff, ever at hand for their new duke. That was fine, though. Aefric had no reason to hide the story of how he'd gotten his namesake. And he could tell the tale in his sleep.

Strangely, no one raised business. Not even the few merchants who were present. Likely a faux pas to do so, Aefric decided.

He did get the opportunity to speak briefly with Ser Grud, and he spent it asking about Ser Grud's travels. The garnet knight claimed to have spent the last year down around Sartis, negotiating sea trade past the Cape of Teeth.

Of course, he could also have been lying.

Byrhta, Aefric noticed, was absent from lunch. Was she still meeting with the seneschal?

After lunch, Aefric met with the mayor of Behal City.

By design, this meeting took place in a more formal setting than where he'd met with his barons. A windowless room on the second level of the castle's interior.

The floor was tiled in navy blue and Deepwater gray, and the plaster of the walls and and ceiling were painted Deepwater gray, with navy blue trim.

The room was a little too long and a little too wide for the rectangular table in the middle. Made the table look small, and a little lonely.

The meeting table itself was simple ebony with the Deepwater sigil done in bas-relief on the top. It had six matching, unpadded chairs, with the Deepwater sigil done on the chairbacks the same way.

Along the periphery of the room were antique weapons and suits of armor, some of which were still in damaged or ruined states, from battles defending the duchy in years past.

Each piece had a small card alongside it, describing who had wielded or worn it for which battle. And how it had been damaged, if appropriate.

Light came from a wheel chandelier that hung above the table.

Aefric had four knights of his personal guard in the room, two just inside each of the two doors.

Mayor Glauglas Ol'Nastrech was a heavy man of middle years, who moved slowly but smoothly. His skin was deeply tanned, either by natural inclination or long hours in the sun.

He wore a light tunic of pale red silk, and dark brown breeches of similar material. His boots and belt were both cut from the same black cloth, with the boots low and the belt wide.

He moved smoothly as he bowed to his duke before taking his seat. Aefric noted that the man avoided looking at the Brightstaff, instead of staring the way some would in his place.

Most striking, though, was the golden seal of his office, which he wore on a heavy gold chain around his neck.

Aefric should have paid full attention to the meeting. He really should have. He knew that. But his thoughts were mostly with Karbin, and Ser Grey, and Ser Grud. And, to a lesser extent, he had to admit, with Maev, and Baroness Montess, and those other flirty noblewomen, and even with poor Vercy, who really was too young to look at him with such hope in her eyes.

The distraction of those thoughts might have been for the best, though. Because, so far as Aefric later recalled, the meeting came down to a few simple concepts.

Behal City was overflowing with refugees from the coast, and from Goldenfall.

The people needed work, and there weren't enough jobs for them.

The people needed housing, and there wasn't enough for them.

The people needed food, and Behal didn't have enough at this rate to make it through the winter.

In short, each of these things needed money. And Mayor Glauglas plainly wanted that money to come from his duke.

Now, Aefric knew that at least some of that was getting taken care of. After all, he'd seen the trees that had been cleared on the other side of the Kingsroad, and he knew that construction on additional housing was underway.

But the other issues, well, some of that would probably need his help.

He refrained from promising anything, though, on the basis that he still needed a full accounting of both the state of his finances and the state of his duchy's needs.

They must have spent at least an hour just circling these two points. The mayor finding some new way to point out that he needed money, and Aefric finding some new way to say he didn't know yet what he could afford.

Finally, Aefric called a halt to the discussion, thanking the mayor for bringing the matters to his attention, and promising to look into what could be done.

Next, came in the delegation from the trade council. Two men and two women — one of the women a kindaren, which surprised Aefric. So far, humans had dominated his lands. The surprise was a pleasant one, though. With any luck, there would be more kindaren, as well as some eldrani, na'shek, and derekek.

He wanted his duchy to be a place where everyone felt welcome.

Someday, perhaps, when the horrors of the Godswalk Wars had faded into memory, that might even include the taroks, and the borogs.

Someday, perhaps. But not anytime soon.

All four of the delegates dressed in clothes that were nice enough to suggest that they had some money, but not so nice as to draw jealousy from less well-off onlookers.

They were a bit obsequious in their greetings, for Aefric's tastes. But when the meeting properly started, matters got even worse.

These four were prattlers.

They seemed to work together. As though their droning were actually a kind of complicated song. A round, performed for him without the benefit of rhyme or melody.

They sang of the horrors of lost trade. Of the suffering of their guild, and through their guild, all of the families of Behal, and through Behal, all of Deepwater, and through Deepwater, all of Armyr.

They wanted Aefric to build ships. They wanted him to finance caravans. They wanted him to pay for trade expeditions to all the old places from where trade had diminished, and to dozens of other places that might be opened to new trade.

They had complicated schemes for turning the state of trade from its current bare trickle to a torrential waterfall. All of which hinged on two things.

First, that the trade council was in the thick of the process, handling the details and negotiations.

Second, that Aefric pay for all of it. Everything. To hear them talk, they were nearly broke, and Aefric's funding was *crucial* to saving the businesses and crafters of Behal — indeed all of Deepwater — and to turning Deepwater into a trade mecca that would be the envy of Qorunn.

Aefric didn't even pretend to make promises here. He let them present — at length, and in more detail that he thought was seemly when it came to the profits — and then he steepled his fingers.

He looked at them all gravely.

And he said, "I'll think about it."

They tried to push, then. He didn't let them. He called the Bright-staff to his hand from where it stood within arm's reach.

All eight of their eyes widened abruptly.

So they'd heard about Motte. Good.

He gestured to his knights, and a page quickly entered and escorted the delegates away, while Aefric and his knights left by the other door.

Aefric had done his best. He'd hosted a lunch. He'd had his meetings. He'd listened to more ways of asking for his money than he'd realized there were.

But he was done with all that. He wanted answers. He wanted action.

And he wanted them now.

12

———

Aefric grumbled about bureaucrats and money as he made his way through the halls, escorted by four of his knights.

In theory, he was on his way to change before dinner. Which was what his knights told anyone who tried to get their duke's attention as he made his way through halls and up stairs.

Even though dinner wouldn't be for an hour or two, and he wasn't sure where or how or with whom he was eating yet.

In truth, Aefric wanted to get back to his rooms and cast a message spell to see if Karbin had learned anything. To send for a page to get a report from Ser Grey. He wanted to talk to Maev and see if she'd learned anything, because he doubted she'd been idle.

For that matter, Aefric wasn't clear on what Ser Beornric had been doing.

Once safely in his rooms, Aefric let out a groan of frustration about bureaucrats.

"Problem, Aefric?"

Maev's voice, coming from his solarium.

He wandered in, to see her seated comfortably on one of his chairs, gazing out over the lake. She'd changed into an airy, blousy top of daisy yellow, and silken slacks of a dark cream color.

Her lynx was curled up across her lap and part of the chair, contented, while Maev scratched the area between Sylkanis' ears.

A bottle of a rich red wine sat open on the table beside her. Two glasses, both empty, sat waiting.

"Hope you don't mind," she said. "I love this room, and your courtiers are boring today." She looked up at him. "No offense."

"None taken," Aefric said with a snort, then came and sat in the chair next to her, on the other side of the little table. "And you're most welcome here." Aefric frowned. "Is my court talking about Motte? Or, well, the baroness?"

"Both, of course," she said, her gaze still out over the lake. "Though they aren't saying anything interesting. Hope your meetings were better."

"They weren't," Aefric said. "The talk was all about money."

"What did you expect?" Maev asked, giving him a small smile. "A mayor and a trade council? Coming to talk to their duke? They weren't likely to ask after your plans for the Midsummer Festival, or the state of affairs at the ducal capital."

"I haven't even *seen* my ducal capital yet," Aefric said with a sigh.

"The wine is ready by now," Maev said, and Aefric waved back a servant who had stepped forward at her words.

Aefric poured for both Maev and himself.

They each sipped. The wine was robust, with hints of cherry, and it cheered Aefric far more than he expected.

Or perhaps that was the company.

"We could go there," Maev said into the comfortable silence, presumably talking about Water's End. "No more than an hour or two distant by, say, that ship there." She indicated one of the two warships Aefric had on the lake. "That one looks fast."

Aefric wasn't sure he could tell a fast ship from a slow one, but now that he looked at the warship in question — with its several sails, and the way it rode low in the water — he thought she might be right.

It did look like a fast ship.

"I feel like I can't," Aefric said. "Not until this Merrek business is straightened out. Especially since Ser Grey has been such a big help so far."

Maev nodded, as though she expected that answer.

"Perhaps," she began, but Karbin teleported in, standing between them and the window.

The guards all tensed, but none of them drew weapons this time.

Sylkanis, however, leapt down, disgruntled, and moved off to find a sunbeam.

Maev regarded Karbin with one eyebrow imperiously high. She sighed. "I do wish you had better timing."

"My apologies, your highness," Karbin said, looking grim. He turned to Aefric. "I got to meet with the duchess."

"And?" Aefric asked.

"It's as we expected. She didn't give him her seal. In fact, she claims never to have met any Ser Grud. But that's not the problem."

Aefric got a sinking feeling in his stomach. "No."

"Yes," Karbin said, nodding. "She's coming here. And not quietly. She's bringing advisers, knights, and more. A full formal visit, complete with entourage."

"Why is that bad?" Maev asked, frowning. "If Ser Grud isn't her man, she can lay to rest all suspicions. And help us plan what to do about Malimfar."

"She's coming in force," Aefric said. "Word will get out. How long do we have?"

"Before she gets here?" Karbin nodded his head back and forth. "It's a good distance, upriver all the way. Normally I'd say two to three days. But if her court wizard calls wind spells—"

"Then she'll be here sometime tomorrow, and everyone between here and there will see her coming."

"Exactly," Karbin said.

"We'll need to keep Ser Grud under surveillance," Aefric said, turning to have a page summon Sers Grey and Beornric.

But before he could, there was a knock at the door of his chambers, and both those two knights gained entrance to his sitting room before quickly joining the others in the solarium.

"Frustrating, your grace," Ser Grey said. "No signs of the man receiving any kind of messages since he reached the ducal lands. No riders that anyone's seen, no rika birds. Nothing."

Aefric's sinking feeling was replaced by a dropping sensation, as though he'd been thrown off the battlements without benefit of a spell to slow his fall.

Cold sweat broke out on his forehead.

"None?" Aefric said sharply. "You're sure?"

"We checked everywhere," Ser Beornric confirmed.

"If he'd gotten a message," Ser Grey said. "We'd know. So he must be up here on his own."

Aefric exchanged a look with Karbin, and from the grim look in his old mentor's eye, he'd reached the same conclusion.

"Not if he gets his orders by magic," Aefric said. "We need to seize him. At once."

***

Securing Ser Grud was now Aefric's top priority. That Knight of the Garnet might hear word of the duchess' coming at any time, which could be enough to make him bolt.

If they lost him, they lost their best link to Malimfar and its plans.

Aefric, of course, wanted to lead the search. But between him and the door out of his solarium, he was intercepted by Sers Grey and Beornric, Princess Maev and her lynx Sylkanis, and even Karbin, his old mentor and now, trusted ducal wizard.

"It's all right, your grace," Ser Grey assured Aefric, both hands raised to physically grab her duke, if necessary. "This is why you have soldiers and knights. Let them handle Ser Grud."

"She's right, your grace," Ser Beornric said with an arched eyebrow. "This is mine to handle."

Ser Beornric turned then and quickly left the room. No doubt to dispatch knights and soldiers, and lead the search throughout Behal Castle. Likely also to send word down to the castle gate, and beyond it to the gatehouses on both sides of the double-drawbridge.

At least, those were the things Aefric wanted to be doing. Should have been doing. In fact—

"*We have time,*" Karbin said, empty hands raised to show no threat — or prepare a quick spell, if necessary. "You might have noticed that I teleported back here? Even if some Malimfari spy cast a message spell to warn Ser Grud *while* I was still meeting with Duchess Ashling, he'd still need time to extract himself from whatever he was doing. Gather his things. Retrieve his horse. And I don't know if you noticed this, but the ride down to the gatehouses is not a matter of seconds."

"No it is not," Maev agreed.

"Unless he skipped the horse and clambered down the side," Aefric growled. "I might, in his place. Not faster, maybe, but stealthier. And stealth is as good a weapon against guards as speed."

"Aefric, this is the role of nobility," Maev said. "To make the decisions, and take the chances. It is the role of your people to enact those decisions. You must let them have their role, or everything breaks down."

Maev said those words with perfect sincerity in her voice. And Aefric didn't believe for a moment that she meant them.

He turned a look of pure disbelief on her, and noted a hint of mischief in her eyes.

"Oh, all right," Maev said, laughing. "I'm no better. I want to be out there on the hunt, too, and so does Sylkanis."

The way the lynx's ears twitched then. Was that agreement? Did Sylkanis understand her?

"But it's true that's how it's supposed to work," Maev said. "Or at least, that's what Father keeps telling me."

"Leading from the front inspires the troops," Aefric said to ... well ... to all of them. "So leading this search myself—"

"Is not the same thing," Ser Grey said. "The commander doesn't scout his enemy. The commander doesn't select the campsites. Your people do their jobs. And you have to let them."

"But—"

"We don't even know that he's running, Aefric," Karbin said. "You and I both assume he's been getting instructions by magic, because that's how we think. Magic is our primary tool. Doesn't mean it's the only covert way to send instructions."

"And other ways are bound to be slower," Ser Grey said. "We may be worrying over wine not yet spilt."

"If this man is an agent of a foreign power," Aefric said, "they have a vested interest in his not getting caught."

He gave a serious look to each of them in turn. Including Sylkanis, just in case.

"Are you telling me," Aefric said, "that a country like Malimfar would take the chance on a lesser means of communication? To handle a matter that could lead to *war*?"

"If it is Malimfar," Maev said, "and if they're using magic for communications, then why has Ser Grud been sending messages by rider?"

"Depends on where those messages were going," Aefric said. "He wouldn't need the seal to send messages to Malimfar…"

Certainty caught Aefric's breath.

"Motte," he said. "Has to be. He must have been sending messages to Motte by rider, using the Merrek seal."

"That could be," Ser Grey said, slowly. "Count Ferrin is a coward. He wouldn't risk challenging his own duke unless he was certain of his position."

"Written messages, bearing the ducal seal of Merrek might do the trick," Aefric said. "And Ser Grud might have been sending them."

"Risky, th—" Maev started to say, then shook her head. "No. No it isn't. If Malimfar is behind those messages, even if the rider were intercepted, Malimfar's goals would be accomplished."

"Exactly," Aefric said. "Word would reach me that Merrek was trying to undermine me. And I'd be given the evidence of a written message, complete with Merrek's seal."

For a moment, the only sounds Aefric could hear were the movements of knights and soldiers out in the hallway.

"It's a lot of supposition," Ser Grey said.

"We need Ser Grud," Aefric said, itching for action.

"Perhaps it would be acceptable to have your court wizard aiding the search?" Karbin suggested.

"Go," Aefric said, before Ser Grey could complain, though she nodded agreement a moment later.

Moments after the hallway door closed behind Karbin, someone pounded on it. The knights of both his and the princess' guard both whirled to face the sound, hands on their hilts.

A servant, Falip, looked through the solarium door to Aefric, who calmly nodded. "Bring whoever it is in here. And they'd better have a good reason for this disturbance."

The moment the hallway door was open, Baron Karmody came charging in, his face contorted in rage, and his eyes all but screaming for blood.

Behind him came his son, whose expression was similar. Then Baroness Montess, who looked worried. Then finally poor Vercy, who looked aghast.

"*What are you playing at, your grace?*" Baron Karmody thundered.

Ser Grey was instantly between Aefric and the storming baron, with one hand on the hilt of her greatsword.

"Your lordship would do well to address his liege in a civil manner," she said, her stance ready and her tone on the frosty edge of menace.

Four knights of Aefric's guard moved to surround their duke, while the princess' knights moved to surround her.

"By the oaths we both swore," Baron Karmody said, his tone acid, "I *will* be heard."

"You will," Ser Grey said, unmoving. "*If* the duke grants you leave. And if he does, I *strongly* suggest you maintain your temper."

Baron Karmody opened his mouth wide to say something, but Baroness Montess put one hand on his shoulder and whispered urgently into his ear.

Baron Karmody closed his mouth. Flared his nostrils in two deep breaths. Then he nodded at Ser Grey. Ser Grey nodded back.

"Your grace," she said, without turning away from the baron, "will you hear your vassal, the baron of Riverbreak?"

"I will," Aefric said.

Ser Grey stood aside, but stayed near.

"Your grace," Baron Karmody said, sounding a little more controlled, at least. "I demand to know—"

Ser Grey cleared her throat.

Baron Karmody turned to Ser Grey with fire in his eyes.

"Finish your thought, your lordship," Aefric said calmly.

The baron frowned, but turned back to Aefric.

"I demand to know why you have *soldiers* hunting a member of my entourage."

"Have you seen Ser Grud recently?" Aefric asked, trying to sound casual instead of eager.

"We were speaking not half an hour ago. Then, suddenly, he remembered an appointment he'd made with..." He frowned. "Well, who the appointment was with doesn't matter."

"It might," Aefric said, pressing to keep his voice casual despite the pounding of his heart. "Who was it with?"

"Some jeweler in town," Baron Karmody said, sounding irritated at the distraction from his point. "Something about a piece Ser Grud was commissioning to give her grace for her nameday."

"So you and he were deep in conversation when suddenly he remembered this appointment," Aefric said. "I take it he rushed to meet his ... jeweler?"

"Yes," Baron Karmody said, eyes narrowed with suspicion. Then he seemed to remember he was furious. "And he was not five minutes gone when *your soldiers* came through *demanding* his whereabouts. As though you would *arrest* a member of *my* entourage."

"Did you tell the soldiers where he'd gone?" Aefric asked, sounding far calmer than he expected to, all things considered.

"Of course not," Baron Karmody said, stiffly. "It's none of their business."

"They are my soldiers," Aefric said. "Are you saying it's none of *my* business?"

"Your grace's words," Baron Karmody said with a humorless smile. "But his point is well made."

Maev came closer to Aefric now and whispered into his ear, "What if they're working with him?"

Aefric shook his head. He didn't believe it. Or at least, he didn't want to.

Nevertheless, he had to ask.

"You say Ser Grud is a member of your entourage. Do you consider him a member of your household?"

"He is of my entourage. That is sufficient. If your grace has a problem with Ser Grud, he should bring that problem to me first."

"Very well," Aefric said. "My soldiers are pursuing Ser Grud because I believe him in the employ of a foreign power working against Armyr, and thus guilty of treason."

***

SILENCE OPPRESSED AEFRIC'S SOLARIUM.

Baron Karmody attempted to stare down Aefric, but Aefric, his face impassive, matched his glare.

Baron Karmody's son Baston emulated his father's furious glare. His efforts fell short.

Maev stood beside Aefric, considering. She ruffled her fingers together, to call Sylkanis to her, and the great forest lynx padded over, threading between the legs of Maev's knights to reach her side.

Aefric's own knights surrounded him, hands on the hilts of their swords. Ser Grey, standing slightly to one side, had removed her hand from the hilt of her greatsword, protruding over her right shoulder, but she looked ready to go for her weapon if she needed it.

Aefric found that he was holding the Brightstaff, though he didn't remember calling it to his hand from where it had stood beside his chair, several feet away.

Baroness Montess, one hand on her husband's shoulder, whispered urgently into his ear.

Standing behind the rest of her family, their daughter Vercy frowned in thought.

Baron Karmody finally broke the silence, laughing.

"Ridiculous," he said, shaking his head and patting his wife's hand absently. "I know that your grace is accustomed to a life of adventure, but that does not mean that spies and conspiracies lie around every corner of his duchy."

"I don't recommend condescending to me," Aefric said, his tone frosty. "Rarely goes well."

"But this is *absurd*," Baron Karmody said. "Ser Grud is no more a traitor than I am."

"I'd be careful saying such things, your lordship," Ser Grey said quietly.

"Grey," Baron Karmody said in disbelief. "Surely *you* don't believe this nonsense. You know the Knights of the Garnet. They're often hired for trade work. And often so they can handle such matters with discretion."

Baron Karmody turned back to Aefric.

"I understand that your grace is new to these sorts of dealings, but really. That's all the more reason he should allow me to handle trade negotiations with Merrek."

"Why?" Aefric asked. "Because you've already begun those negotiations? With Ser Grud representing Merrek?"

Baron Karmody turned his thunderous expression on his wife. "You told him?"

Baroness Montess' eyes widened, and her already pale complexion turned ghostly white. "Karmody, I swear—"

"She told me only that Ser Grud carries the ducal seal of Merrek," Aefric said.

"More than she should have said," Baron Karmody said, then grumbled something to his wife.

From the way her right hand tensed, she had to resist the urge to slap her husband. She did step away from him, and drew a long, slow breath.

"Ser Grud," Aefric said, "does *not* carry the ducal seal of Merrek."

"Yes, he does," Baron Karmody said, impatiently. "I've seen it myself. And yes, your grace, I know what the ducal seal of Merrek looks like. My family has held Riverbreak for generations. I've had many opportunities to study edicts and formal proclamations displaying the seals of every major duchy and county in Armyr. Including Merrek."

"That's as may be," Aefric said, still trying to keep his voice calm, though it wasn't easy. "But the seal is a forgery."

"No, your grace, it is not," Baron Karmody said, biting irritation through every syllable of his words.

"*Baron,*" Aefric said sharply enough to put some anger back in Karmody's eyes. "I am telling you that I know for certain that it is a forgery."

"Aefric," Maev said, holding up a hand before he could add anything further, but keeping her eyes on the baron and his family. To them, she said, "Why is your lordship so certain that it *is* legitimate?"

"That I recognize the seal should be enough," Baron Karmody said, and Aefric heard then what he suspected Maev had already spotted.

The baron was pushing too hard on this single point.

He met Maev's eye. She gave him a bare nod.

Aefric sighed. Perhaps Ser Grud was no more a traitor than Baron Karmody after all.

"This has gone far enough," Baron Karmody said. "Your grace has insulted me through this baseless attempt to seize a member of my entourage. I and mine will be taking our leave of Behal and Deepwater at once. And I shall be complaining to the king about his new duke at my first opportunity."

Baston looked just as angry as his father about everything. Both their shockingly pale complexions had darkened red with fury. Baroness Montess hung her head, positively morose. Vercy's eyes were wide, and she had one hand to her mouth, as though to keep herself from talking, while her eyes darted back and forth between her father and Aefric.

Aefric knew what he had to do. And he didn't like it.

"No, your lordship," Aefric said, through a sad sigh. "You won't."

He nodded to Ser Grey, who called in more of Aefric's personal guard from the hallway outside his door.

"Baron Karmody Ol'Karmak," Aefric began, with a heavy heart, "you have given me no choice but to—"

"Wait, your grace," Vercy cried out. "Please!"

Aefric held up one hand to stall his guards and knights from taking the baron's family into custody.

But it wasn't Aefric Vercy addressed then. And it wasn't her father. It was her brother Baston.

"Is his grace right, Baston?" she asked. "Is the seal a forgery?"

Baston's normal pallor darkened somewhere past mauve in his fury. He looked positively apoplectic.

But it was Baron Karmody who snapped his fingers to silence his daughter. "Vercy, I'll not have—"

It was Vercy herself who cut him off, speaking over her father.

"His grace seems *awfully* certain that the seal is a forgery," she said, her eyes still watching her brother, who had his arms tensed as though it was all he could do not to reach out and strike his sister.

Baron Karmody opened his mouth to say something, but Aefric said, "I will hear the words of your daughter."

Vercy nodded her thanks to Aefric, looking more confident, as she did, than she had in any interaction with him so far.

"Mother," Vercy continued, "you've ... spent more time in the duke's company than the rest of us. Does he strike you as a man to claim certainty if room for doubt remains?"

Baroness Montess slowly shook her head.

"Well, Baston?" Vercy asked. "Anything you want to say? Perhaps *before* our new duke arrests our entire family for treason against Armyr?"

It was a good thing that Baston had never studied magic. His glare alone was almost enough to sear his sister's skin.

"I imagine," she continued, "that after we're convicted, our family will face execution in Armityr. Pity. I've always wanted to see Armityr. But not like that." She looked up at Ser Grey. "If you're the next baron of Riverbreak, I do hope you'll—"

"Enough dramatics," Baron Karmody said. "You've played your game to impress your betrothed. Not that I retain any desire for you to marry him."

He turned back to Aefric. "Fine, *your grace*, arrest us. When we are exonerated, and you are banished in shame, perhaps—"

"Oh, by Elbar's Blood," Vercy swore, shocking Maev's eyes wide and making Baroness Montess whirl around to censure her daughter.

But Vercy's attention was all on her brother.

"If you don't start talking, Baston, I'll tell the duke everything I know. *And* everything I *suspect*."

At those words, Baston paled so fast he staggered a step and Aefric worried the boy might pass out.

"You will do *no such thing*," Baron Karmody started, but Aefric silenced him with a small clap of thunder from the Brightstaff.

"Baston Ol'Karmak," Aefric said. "Have you anything to say?"

Baston shook his head.

"I believe you were arresting us on patently false charges," Baron Karmody said to Aefric.

"Ser Grey," Aefric said, "keep the baron, his wife, and his son right here. "Vercy Ol'Karmak, if you would come with me, please."

"Y-yes, your grace," she answered, drawing herself up straight and tall. And shaking only a little.

"May I?" Maev asked, and Aefric nodded that she could come along.

Aefric led them into his sitting room, and over to the comfortable, padded couches and chairs by the windows, looking out over the walls of the keep to Lake Deepwater beyond.

He seated Vercy on one couch, where she perched on the very edge of her seat, her posture pristine and her head held high.

Aefric sat on the couch facing her, and Maev sat beside him.

With a gesture, Aefric closed the door to his solarium.

"What do you have to tell me, Vercy?"

"A few aetts ago," she said, "while the prince sat regent at Water's End, father grew tired of waiting for trade with Merrek to reopen. He sent Baston to Castle Fyrcloch to see what he could do."

"Did your father first reach out to the regent?" Aefric asked.

Vercy shook her head.

"Baston was gone for almost two aetts, and returned with Ser Grud. He claimed that he'd met Ser Grud at the duchess' court. That he was an important adviser to Duchess Ashling, and that she trusted him so much she'd given him the seal of Merrek. Ser Grud has been with us ever since."

"That's what you meant by what you *know*," Aefric said.

"Well," Vercy said slowly, "there is one more thing. Once Ser Grud had been with us for a few days, I mentioned him in a letter to a friend of mine at court in Fyrcloch."

Vercy drew a quick breath, and glanced at the door to the solarium.

"My friend told me that no Knights of the Garnet had been at Fyrcloch in at least six seasons. And certainly none with the dueling scar I'd described."

Aefric and Maev shared a glance.

"And that's not all," Vercy added, sadly. "My friend ... my friend sounded surprised to hear that Baston had been to court."

She looked up at Aefric, eyes shining with unshed tears. "She never saw him. Or even heard that he'd been there."

"Did you mention these things to your father?" Aefric asked.

"I mentioned them to Baston," Vercy said, looking out the window. "He told me to mind my own business, or" — her eyes flicked to Aefric's, then away — "well, he threatened me to ensure I kept my silence. So I did. But I held onto those letters."

"What more do you suspect?" Maev asked.

"Forgive me, your highness, your grace," she said. "But if this is a matter of law, then my suspicions should not be considered. Only evidence I can swear to."

"I was hoping you wouldn't think of that," Maev admitted. "I'm dying of curiosity."

Vercy shook her head. "I'm sorry, your highness. I only said that to try to make Baston do the right thing."

"Well," Aefric said, "*you* have done the right thing. And I appreciate that a great deal."

Vercy gave him a shy smile.

"Do you have any evidence one way or the other about what your father knows?"

She shook her head. "I can't believe Father would commit treason against Armyr." She frowned. "In fact, your grace, forgive me, but I don't see how carrying and using a false ducal seal constitutes..."

Her eyes rounded so wide Aefric worried her eyeballs would fall right out of her head.

"Oh, Baston, you fool," she said. "You vainglorious *fool*." She looked up at Aefric and spoke rapidly. "I swear to you, your grace. Neither of my parents could possibly know the extent of Baston's treachery. They are good nobles. Loyal to their duke, their king and their country."

"They may leave me no choice," Aefric started, but Vercy's urgency was so great that she actually cut him off.

"I beg you, your grace. Let me tell them what I told you. Let me—"

"I can't," Aefric said, sadly. "For all we know, they know already. I'll give them one more chance. And if necessary, ensure they get the fairest trial I can arrange. That's the best I can do."

AEFRIC LED MAEV AND A DEJECTED VERCY BACK INTO HIS SOLARIUM, where Baron Karmody was arguing heatedly with Ser Grey, and Aefric's knights kept guard on Baroness Montess and Baston.

"You do this," Baron Karmody was saying, "and you'll go down for it just like that fool will. Do you hear me?"

"That fool hears you," Aefric said, cutting off whatever rejoinder Ser Grey had ready. "Not that he favors being called such."

"Oh, forgive me, *your grace*," Baron Karmody said, his voice dripping with sarcasm as he sketched a mock bow. "I shall endeavor to remember to give *your grace* his *courtesies* even when he is absent from the room."

"*Enough*," Aefric said sharply, letting the yellow diamond atop the Brightstaff flare momentarily. "Baston Ol'Karmak. I have heard what your sister has to say. Combined with what I already know, it will be more than enough to convict you, when the time comes."

"Rubbish," Baron Karmody said.

"Your last warning, Baron," Aefric said, not looking away from Baston. "Not another word until I give you leave."

Aefric turned back to Baston.

"The only question now," he said, "is how much your parents know."

Baston looked away, out over the lake.

"Your fate is already sealed," Aefric said. "If your parents are complicit, they will be executed alongside you. You must know that. But if they are innocent, this is your only chance to save their lives. Once I have you sent to your cells, it will be a matter for the king's law."

"And the king's justiciar is on his way," Maev said quietly. "I've already sent for him."

"Baston?" Baroness Montess asked softly. "What have you done?"

"What *he* was too weak to do!" Baston said, whirling and pointing an accusing finger at his father. "Oh, Riverbreak. Great Riverbreak. Our *tiny* little *nothing* of a barony. We don't have Felspark's mines or Norra's ironwoods or even Havenford's sea access."

Baron Karmody's mouth worked as though he wanted to say something but no words came out.

Just as well. Baston kept going.

"Karmak Ol'Duin pushed himself half to death! Every step of his *two-day* run another yard of land he handed down to his descendants. To us! And what have we accomplished since? Nothing! Not an inch more land! Hardly a silver's more income! We're no better off than we were *generations* ago!"

"What did you do?" Baroness Montess asked again.

"Well I didn't waste time going to Fyrcloch!" He shook his head.

"As though an arrogant bitch like Ashling would make time for the heir of a barony so small she's probably never even heard of it."

"Where *did* you go?" Aefric asked, voice quiet.

"You already know where I went," Baston sneered. "I went down into Malimfar. To—"

"Stop talking," Baron Karmody said, looking and sounding absolutely stricken. "This isn't true. It *can't* be true."

"*Of course it's true!*" Baston shouted at his father. "*One* of us had to be strong enough to take a chance. *One* of us had to do something."

"What did they offer you?" Maev asked. "In Malimfar?"

"I am accepted as a citizen of Malimfar and soon to be made *count* of the whole Indecisive River Valley," he said proudly. "And you, *your grace*, have no authority to arrest a foreign noble—"

"You *idiot*," Vercy said, rolling her eyes. "How can you get even that part wrong? *Father* might not have the authority to arrest a foreign noble, but the duke has the right of *high justice*. He judges with the king's voice. Even if you *were* a foreign noble—"

"Which you're not," Baron Karmody said venomously. "*You are my son!*" He turned to Aefric. "Your grace, I cannot apologize enough. Obviously I had no idea—"

"Yes," Baroness Montess said in a small voice. "You did. You had some idea. We both did. We just didn't want to admit it. Not even to ourselves."

"What?" Baron Karmody said, whirling on his wife, who looked as though she'd rather be anywhere else, doing anything other than what she was doing right then.

One of Aefric's knights, Ser Leppina, interposed herself between the baron and his wife.

"What do you mean, Baroness?" Aefric asked, keeping his voice calm.

"Perhaps Karmody didn't know the truth," she said. "I'd like to think he didn't. But I know we both suspected that there was more to Baston's story about Ser Grud than he was letting on."

Baron Karmody tried to say something. Aefric silenced him with a warning gesture.

"Go on," Aefric said.

"I am quite proud to be baroness of Riverbreak, your grace," she said. "And I don't think I'll surprise you when I say that my husband is proud of both his title and his lineage. But we both know what Riverbreak is."

She looked at her husband. "We both knew what Duchess Ashling would see if she bothered to look at us. A small barony, with no special resources beyond a few artists and artisans of note."

She looked back at Aefric. "She had no reason to take interest in us. Certainly no reason to send with Baston a retainer so important that he was allowed to carry her seal."

She looked back at her husband. "We both knew it was too good to be true. We just didn't want to *admit* the truth, because it would be admitting that Riverbreak was just what Baston called us. A nothing little barony."

Baron Karmody's nostrils flared in a slow, deep breath, and he nodded.

"It's true, your grace. When I say I *suspected* nothing, it's only because I wanted Baston's words to be true." He shook his head. "But I must also admit. As time passed, and I had the opportunity to study the seal that Ser Grud carries, I convinced myself that it was real. That it was all true."

He turned to his wife. "And you came to believe it too. Didn't you."

"The seal looks so authentic," Baroness Montess said. "And Ser Grud didn't abuse it. Didn't charge things to her grace. Insisted that any new trade deal had to involve the new duke of Deepwater."

"He acted his part well," Baron Karmody said, sadly. "If he was acting."

He gave Aefric a look of raw pain.

"Couldn't it be real, your grace? What if Baston met Ser Grud in Malimfar because Ashling was negotiating with them?"

Baston laughed viciously at his father. "Look at you. Clinging to broken dreams." He spat. "Pathetic."

"*He's* pathetic?" Vercy asked in disbelief. "You're the one who doesn't seem to realize he's lost, and living out numbered days."

"I've lost nothing," Baston said with an evil smile. "Arrest me if you want, *your grace*, but Armyr is in no shape to stop the might of Malimfar. And as soon as Malimfar takes the river valley, I become count. And King Eadred himself will demand my release."

He cocked an eyebrow at Aefric. "Really. You ought to just release me now and spare yourself time and trouble."

"And what makes you think your precious King Eadred won't just let you *rot*?" Vercy said harshly. "And why should he give a county to a traitor from a so-called nothing barony, when he could give it to one of his loyal courtiers?"

"That's enough," Aefric said, cutting off Baston's reply. He gestured, and soldiers took the fool away.

"What about them?" Ser Grey asked softly, nodding at the baron and baroness of Riverbreak, who held each other as they watched their son and heir get arrested.

"Confine them to their rooms for now," Aefric said through a sigh. "The king's justiciar" — he glanced at Vercy and back — "will want to at least question them."

"And her?" Ser Grey asked, nodding at Vercy.

Aefric turned to address Vercy, but before he could open his mouth she spoke, in a sad voice.

"I'm more than willing to be confined to my rooms as well, your grace," she said. "I know the justiciar will want to hear my words and read those letters I mentioned."

She shook her head. "And even if your grace would give me freedom of his castle, I shouldn't use it. I have no stomach to face the things his court will be saying."

"Very well," Aefric said, then specified to Ser Grey, "but she is to be allowed any visitors she is willing to see."

"And I will be one of them," Maev said, getting a sad smile from Vercy before she and her parents were escorted away and back to their rooms.

Aefric watched them go, wondering if he should have done anything differently.

***

Aefric felt like a caged dragon. He paced his solarium, watched with vague interest by Sylkanis and Maev with almost identical expressions.

Ser Grey stood nearby, clearly trying to think of some way to reassure or calm her duke.

The four knights each of his and Maev's personal guards had retreated to the sides of the solarium to maintain their vigil.

The sun continued its slow descent in the western sky, while news was in short supply.

"Damn it," Aefric said finally, whirling on Ser Grey. "Someone must know something! It's been well over an hour. How long—"

"Does it take to search a castle?" Maev asked, her voice lazy. "Quite a while. Quite a while indeed. Especially one this size. In fact, to search the royal palace at Armityr would take—"

"Maev," Aefric said, "please."

She shrugged, and smiled. "Just making conversation. Waiting will take what it will take, Aefric. Perhaps you could tell me the story of how you got that wand you wear."

"That wouldn't take long," Aefric said impatiently. "It was a gift from your father."

"Is that the wand, Garram?" She nodded slowly. "Father *does* favor you. He doesn't give away family weapons lightly."

That thought made her look contemplative enough that Aefric almost asked a follow-up question. But Ser Beornric came in, and Aefric swiftly crossed the floor to him.

"What news? Is he arrested?"

"We ... cannot find him, your grace," Ser Beornric said. "I apologize. But we are expanding the search. We *will* find him."

"What *do* we know?" Ser Grey asked.

"Not much," Ser Beornric said with a sigh. "From the sound of things, he must have received a message by magic, as your grace suggested. He was mid-conversation, when he claimed to suddenly remember and appointment and fled."

"That much we knew from Baron Karmody," Aefric said. "What else?"

"I think..." Ser Beornric grimaced. "I think your grace was right that he eschewed speed for stealth. His horse remains in the stables. And so far as we can determine, he didn't even retrieve anything from his room."

"So," Aefric said, thinking quickly. "That means he likely climbed down, instead of taking the road. Likely dove into the river, rather than let anyone see him at the docks, or the gatehouses. That would take quite some time, but he's still at least somewhere in the city by now."

"Where he could hire or steal a horse," Ser Beornric said. "But we can watch the roads and the river."

"Any word from Karbin?"

"He surveys from the sky. He'll signal with green fire if he finds Ser Grud. My people are watching for it."

"Wait," Aefric said. "You said his possessions are still here? Take me to his rooms at once. And have Vercy fetched and brought as well."

In short order, Aefric, Maev, Sylkanis and Ser Grey were among the lesser guest rooms of the castle's second floor. Here the plaster on the walls was painted Deepwater gray, and decorated only with occasional vases of flowers on small, mahogany tables. The white ash floorboards of the hallway enjoyed no carpeting.

Two guards arrived moments later with a confused Vercy.

"Vercy, good," Aefric said, while Ser Grey got out the keys to Ser Grud's room. "Has Ser Grud ridden the same horse the entire time you've known him?"

"No, your grace," she answered, puzzled. "He favors no special horses, and he's changed saddles at least twice that I've noticed."

Ser Grey opened the door. A warm lake breeze immediately came in through the room's small, open window.

"What about his clothes?" Aefric asked, as he led the others inside. "Anything special there?"

"Only what he wears every day," Vercy said. "His belt and boots. His sword. The rest" — she shrugged — "Baston bought him a whole new wardrobe just before we came here."

"A few days at the most," Aefric muttered. "Not strong enough."

"If I may ask, your grace," Vercy said, while Maev merely watched, with interest. "What is this about?"

"I need you to look through those things Ser Grud has abandoned," Aefric said. "If you can, find me something he wore often, or better, something you know is important to him. Doesn't matter what."

Vercy shrugged helplessly.

"I confess, I paid him no special mind," she said, as she went through the armoire, and then the small chest of drawers beside the bed. "He tried to flirt with me. To imply that I should welcome him as a visitor in the night, even though he was nothing more than a—"

She stopped. Frowning. Leaned down into the space between the small chest of drawers and the bed, which wasn't all that much larger.

"Nothing more than a what?" Maev asked, one eyebrow raised and mirth in her voice.

"This," Vercy said, holding up something perhaps the length of her thumb, that glinted in the sunlight.

It was a golden pin, with a tiny garnet for the head.

"He always wore this somewhere on his tunic," she said, shaking her head. "I guess he couldn't find it this morning."

"You're certain," Aefric said, trying to keep his voice calm, even though his heart was pounding harder now. He could almost taste the hunt. "He wore this every day. For several aetts."

"Positive, your grace," she said, handing over the pin. "I don't believe I ever saw him without it."

"Perfect," Aefric said, and now the fire of the hunt was spreading through his veins. He turned to Ser Beornric. "Green fire, you said?"

"Yes," Ser Beornric said, suspiciously, "but—"

"Then take a squad of my personal guards to a boat, and be ready to move after green fire when you see it. Go now."

"But—"

Aefric raised an eyebrow.

"Yes, your grace," Ser Beornric said with a slight bow, then turned and left.

Aefric turned to Ser Grey. "Send a rika to Countess Faenella. Tell her not to bother with the investigation we spoke of. Tell her instead to gather her troops and head south. But she is not to cross over into Merrek until she hears from me."

Aefric turned to Vercy. "I need you to write to your castellan at Magranus. Tell him to gather Riverbreak's troops and sail south to the southern border of Fyretti, where they are to join with the countess' forces, under her command."

"Your grace, that should really come from my father."

"It will come from you, by order of your duke," Aefric said. "And if they try to argue—"

"If they try to argue," Vercy said, eyes blazing, "I'll remind them whom they serve."

"Well said," Maev said.

"Go," Aefric said to her, and she left, with two guards remaining her escort.

Aefric turned back to Ser Grey, before she left as well.

"One more thing. Send rikas to Felspark and Norra. They are also to gather their troops and join with the countess at best speed." He clapped Ser Grey on the shoulder. "Then, once I return with Ser Grud, tell Ser Beornric to gather my own troops, and head for Fyretti's southern border."

"All your troops?" Ser Grey asked, confused.

"All but a skeleton guard presence here and at Water's End. The rest will be needed. Trust me."

"But the duchess—" Ser Grey started, but Aefric finished.

"—will see my troops on the move as she comes upriver. But I will explain when she arrives. Now I must go."

"Wait," Ser Grey said.

"You're not leaving me behind," Maev said.

"This time I am," he said. "I'm sorry."

Aefric turned and ran for the stairs to the battlements.

AEFRIC FELT AS THOUGH HE TOOK FOREVER TO REACH THE battlements, even though he'd only had to climb four or five flights of stairs to get there.

He came out through that last door into the heat of late afternoon, mitigated only slightly by the breeze blowing south across the lake.

No more than a token guard presence remained on the walls. The rest must have been off hunting Ser Grud.

Well, Aefric would find that missing knight soon e—

He turned to the south-facing battlements, and found himself face-to-face with Princess Maev, who had retrieved and was wearing her sword belt, as well as her bow and quiver of arrows.

She leaned against an upjut of crenellation, giving him a haughty expression. Seated beside her, looking equally haughty, was her forest lynx, Sylkanis.

"How did you beat me here? How did you even know I was coming here?"

"I am a huntress, Aefric," Maev said simply, as though she'd answered both questions. "I thought you'd figured that out. And if the nobles are to go a-hunting, you'll not leave me behind."

"I'm to go *flying*," Aefric said. "Do you want me to carry you?"

Maev cocked her head to the side and smiled. "Do you even have to ask?"

Aefric fought against the blush that was heating his neck.

"Well, I can't carry both you and Sylkanis."

"And I'm sure you'll make it up to her later. Perhaps by taking us both hunting in those lovely woods just south of the city." She stepped up to him. "Now. How are we to do this?"

"First things first," Aefric said, then took that pin that Vercy swore was Ser Grud's constant adornment.

He held the pin up, and mumbled the right words while channeling just a flicker of his own power through the pin. Tightening the connection between the pin and Ser Grud.

Aefric felt it tugging him to the west.

West? Why would Ser Grud go west?

Made little sense, but it was either correct, or the pin belonged to someone else. Someone west of here.

With another word, he affixed the pin temporarily to the Brightstaff's yellow diamond, and held the Brightstaff up to lead the way.

He slid his arm around Maev's waist, taking a good handful of her belt.

"Hold on tight," he said, his voice a little rough and his heart beating so hard he could feel it in his throat.

"Happily," she murmured, and wrapped her arms around him, taking firm grips on his shoulder and belt.

A simple spell then, and Aefric and Maev took off into the air, while below them Sylkanis yowled an objection at being left behind.

Maev called an apology back to her lynx, but Aefric had to keep his attention on the tugging of that golden pin. It was leading him to the northwest, perhaps by the Kingsroad?

He and Maev whisked through the air, buffeted by winds far gentler than those Aefric had faced during his long flight the night before.

Not to mention that visibility was vastly improved by afternoon sunlight, over what he'd been dealing with last night in the clouds and rain.

On the other hand, he had an additional distraction this time. Maev.

He was torn. On the one hand, he wanted to hold her as tightly as possible, to ensure that he didn't drop her. But the tighter he held her, the more aware he was of how good she felt pressed against him.

If Maev felt the same way, Aefric couldn't tell. She was staring at the world in wide-eyed joy. Taking in everything she could see from their vantage point, hundreds of feet up. And commenting the whole time of the wonders of the experience.

He couldn't really hear her over the wind. But that was just as well. She might have been on a pleasure flight, but Aefric's sole concern was catching Ser Grud.

And he tried to keep his attention on that.

It helped that as they flew, the tugging of the golden pin grew stronger.

Stronger still as they soared over the grain and bean farms west of Behal City. Farms that had come through the wars fully intact.

Soon enough, Aefric saw a lone rider, pressing his frothing horse along the Kingsroad down below. The tugging of the pin left no doubt that this was their quarry.

"Is that him?" Maev yelled.

Aefric nodded. Began their descent.

"Help me get my bow," Maev shouted.

Now they were low enough that Ser Grud heard her voice, if not her words. Looked back over his shoulder. His only reaction, a nod.

Aefric flew lower. Only maybe fifty feet above the Kingsroad now. He knew a spell that would paralyze the man, but it wouldn't affect the horse. He didn't want to hurt the horse, but he might not have a—

Maev released Aefric's shoulder, reaching for something.

The shift in weight threw them off. Made them roll sideways at an angle.

Aefric had to grab Maev in both arms, to keep her from falling. Almost cost him his grip on the Brightstaff.

He had no choice but to slow their flight and regain control.

Ser Grud sped away from them.

Now Aefric was holding her not to his side, but right face-to-face with him. He could see shock and fear in her eyes. The knowledge of how close she'd just come to falling to her death.

Aefric opened his mouth to say something reassuring.

Maev kissed him. Hard. Frantic. Her arms and legs trembled as they clung to him with all her strength.

The kiss was amazing.

Lightning had been Aefric's major weapon from the time he first picked up the Brightstaff. But this was the first time he himself felt thunderstruck.

Somewhere inside him, the part that had been Keifer reeled in confusion, but offered no objection.

When the kiss broke, Aefric and Maev were hovering in place, perhaps a dozen feet above the ground.

"I almost died," she said softly. "You saved my life."

Aefric nodded. Swallowed. Finally managed to say, "Don't do that again."

"No?" she said, giving him a saucy look. "I rather thought you enjoyed the kiss."

"You know what I..." He trailed off as she smiled, then gave him another quick kiss.

"It seems we're no longer moving," she said.

"Well, it's hard with—"

"I noticed."

The blush roared over Aefric from the neck up.

"I meant that it would be easier to fly with you at my side, instead of ... your current position."

"Is *that* what you meant?" she asked, then adjusted herself to his side again, as they resumed their previous grips. "Better?"

"For flying, yes," Aefric said, which got a laugh from her as they took off flying once more.

Aefric and Maev flew lower now, though the warm afternoon sunlight. They no longer saw any sign of Ser Grud or his horse, but Aefric's spell of tracking was still working, so he had hopes of finding the missing knight yet.

Before long, the trail led them off of the Kingsroad and along a smaller road that led out to the coast.

The coast. Where the towns and villages had all been destroyed. All but Ajenmoor. But Ajenmoor was further north.

Well over a day away, even pushing his horse as hard as Ser Grud was.

In fact, that horse probably couldn't take much—

Practically as Aefric thought that, he spotted the dead horse on the side of the road. The poor thing had been ridden to its last breath.

The tugging of the pin led Aefric south off of the road, now, toward pastureland.

He flew a little higher then, over a copse of maple trees, and felt Maev grip him even tighter. He hoped she hadn't lost all her joy of flying, but he couldn't worry about that right now.

Any more than he could worry about how much he enjoyed her scent. Like honeysuckle.

Soon, the pin led Aefric to a ranch house. A rambling, one-story wooden structure that looked to have been built decades ago or more. It was weathered, and hadn't had its red paint freshened since before Aefric had left Sartis.

It was a cattle ranch, and the cattle had already been brought in for the day. He could hear their gentle lowing in the background.

More disturbing was the lack of busy ranch hands. Aefric had always heard that the work never stopped on a farm or ranch. And yet, he couldn't see anyone loitering, much less working.

The conclusion was easy, and Aefric didn't like it at all.

Ser Grud was holed up in the ranch house. With hostages.

Aefric landed just shy of the dirt area before the front door of the ranch house. He landed at the edge of the grass, where it still grew rich and green and thick, likely from generations of encouragement.

He could smell horses and hay, and he thought he heard them whickering in a barn to his left. To his right, a chicken coop. And he could hear the occasional bells of some of the cattle somewhere on the other side of the ranch house.

What he could not hear were any particular noises coming from the ranch house. But the tugging of the pin left no doubt.

Ser Grud was inside.

"Ser Grud Ol'Garan," Aefric called. "The hunt is up. Your master is unmasked. Your plot is foiled. Surrender peacefully, tell all that you know, and you may yet get to keep your life."

"I have a dozen of your people in here, your grace," Ser Grud called back. "I have no wish to harm them, but I will if I am not guaranteed safe passage to my ship and away."

"Truly?" Aefric taunted him. "Some knight you are, Ser Grud. Threatening the lives of peasants to save your own skin."

"And what are you?" Ser Grud called back, sounding angry. "A jumped-up adventurer. Handed a duchy he had no right to by a foolish king who dreams of living in stories."

Aefric racked his brains, trying to think of some spell that would take down Ser Grud without harming any of the peasants. Unfortunately, while he was quite good at dealing a great deal of damage — with a fair amount of precision — the list of effective, accurate things he could do without a clean line of sight were sadly few.

"So *your grace* wishes me to be *knightly*?" Ser Grud taunted, from somewhere behind that front door.

If only Aefric could be certain that the man wasn't holding up peasant as a human shield...

"When your cause is lost, there is no shame in surrender," Aefric said, nodding at Maev for her to stalk around, looking for a vantage point where they might learn something more.

The woman moved as quietly as her cat.

"I've heard it said," Ser Grud called, "that King Colm knighted your before ennobling you. Is that true?"

"It is," Aefric said. "He said I should have been knighted at the end of the Battle of Deepwater, and he wanted to correct that oversight."

"Well then," Ser Grud said, sounding triumphant. "Knight to knight, I challenge you."

"I am a duke," Aefric said. "You have no standing to challenge me."

"I have no standing to challenge a duke, yes. But your grace has acknowledged that we are both also knights. And one knight may always challenge another."

Aefric had never heard that. But then, he hadn't been a knight *or* a noble very long.

He would have asked Maev, but he was no longer sure where she even was. He certainly couldn't see her.

"Come, Ser Aefric," Ser Grud said. "You wanted to save the lives of these worthless peasants. This is the only way you can, short of giving me what I want outright."

"What are your terms?"

"If you can beat me or disarm me," Ser Grud said, "I will surrender and answer any question you put to me completely, without amendment or hesitation."

"And if you win, you want your safe passage to your ship?"

"I do."

It occurred to Aefric then that, as the challenged, he had the right to choose weapons.

This might not be such a bad idea after all.

"Very well," Aefric said. "I accept your challenge. Come out and duel me."

Ser Grud opened the door and stepped out, drawing his rapier in one hand and a dueling dagger in the other.

The door closed quickly behind him, and Aefric heard a bar drop into place.

He smiled and allowed the Brightstaff's yellow diamond to begin glowing.

"Oh, no, your grace," Ser Grud said with an evil grin. "A challenge between knights is a challenge of honor. Using magic is cheating." He nodded to Aefric's belt. "You must use that sword you carry. If you know how."

He chuckled as he moved into position about seven steps away from Aefric.

He saluted with his blade.

Aefric sighed and set the Brightstaff aside. He drew his sword.

He worried now about his chances. He knew how to use his longsword, yes, but he was far better with spell than with steel. And the man he faced was a professional duelist.

This did not bode well.

At least, not if Aefric fought fairly…

"Are you ready, Ser Aefric?" Ser Grud taunted, his arms wide and weapons pointed away.

Before Aefric could answer, two arrows thumped into Ser Grud's back, in rapid succession. One took him in the right shoulder — his sword arm — and the other in his left thigh.

Ser Grud fell bleeding to the ground, but held onto his sword.

From her perch on the roof of the ranch house, Maev called down, "As a knight, his grace may have been required by honor to wager your escape on his sword arm. The crown, however, considers your crimes to have stolen your honor, Ser Grud Ol'Garan."

She jumped down, one arrow still nocked as she approached, ready to ensure Ser Grud's surrender.

"The crown says you have no standing to make such a challenge." Her tone grew positively frigid as she said, "Drop. Your. Weapons."

Ser Grud, bleeding profusely and writhing on the ground in pain, did as he was told.

Aefric, uncertain whether he should feel relieved or insulted, moved in and searched the fallen garnet knight for the Merrek seal.

It wasn't there.

13

It turned out that Ser Grud had ditched the Merrek seal somewhere along the road. It might have been lost forever, except that Ser Grud had made a habit of carrying it about his person on a steady basis for several aetts.

Aefric was able to use an inverted version of his finding spell — fueled by some of the fresh blood Ser Grud was liberally supplying, before he was bandaged — to soar through the air back along the road, until the spell led him to a pile of manure.

This, however, was why every caster worth their spellbook held onto the little tricks they learned during apprenticeship. Scooping away handfuls of manure, from a distance, was no more difficult for Aefric than closing a door from across the room.

The search did take time, but at least he didn't have to dig his hands through a pile of manure.

Once he retrieved the seal, he smiled and rendered it spotlessly clean with the same spell he used regularly on his clothes when he traveled.

That spell worked as well on manure as it did on dirt, dust, sweat and blood.

The darkness of night was rising by the time Aefric and Maev got Ser Grud back to Behal Castle.

Aefric then wanted to call a priest to heal the poor man's wounds properly with divine aid. They'd been languishing under bandages and simple poultices for hours.

Maev, apologizing, overruled this. Ser Grud was the crown's prisoner, and she didn't want him at full strength and capable of escape before the justiciar arrived.

"As he is," she said, "he's not going anywhere."

She did have a point about that. So they sent Ser Grud a field surgeon instead.

They each retired to their rooms then, to clean up.

Aefric changed into red silk robes over a brown tunic and breeches of the same material. Maev, when he next saw her, had changed into a simple, but elegant gown of deep blue.

And he next saw her at dinner, at his black oak table, where Ser Grey and Karbin both joined them, dressed as they'd been all day.

Ser Grey didn't even waste breath arguing that Aefric should dine with his court that night.

Matters had grown beyond such niceties, for the moment.

The dinner was a rich, savory roast, with a selection of sautéed root vegetables, a salad of mixed greens, and a bottle of fine, rich green sharabi.

There was little news, over a tense dinner.

"The duchess approaches even faster than we expected," Karbin said. "She may be here tonight."

"We've heard back from your vassals," Ser Grey said. "Your armies are on the move."

"Good, on both counts. We may be pressed for time." Aefric shook his head. "Malimfar's army is likely already in the field, if not already in position."

"They couldn't be in position yet," Maev said reasonably, though she still sounded distant, as she had since she took down Ser Grud. "Ashling would know, and she wouldn't be coming this way."

"Are you sure you don't want to order troops from Goldenfall and Motte as well?" Ser Grey asked.

"No," Aefric said, shaking his head. "Goldenfall can't spare them. And Motte might switch sides. I need Ferrin more settled before I can trust him."

"Reminds me, Byrhta wishes to speak with you at your first convenience," Ser Grey said. "And Ornella has written a report of their meeting. It sits over with the prince's report, on the table near the window."

"Thank you," Aefric said, feeling tired down to his bones, and knowing his work was not yet finished. "I'll talk to her ... sometime after dinner."

"Your grace," Ser Grey said slowly. "If Baston and both his parents are convicted of treason, most of your people will expect—"

"I won't take the barony from Vercy," Aefric said. "She stood up to her family for the sake of us all. I'll not punish her for that."

"And if the justiciar decides that she's guilty as well?" Ser Grey asked.

"Well," Aefric said slowly, "obviously I cannot overrule the crown. But I will still speak on her behalf."

Had Maev flinched when Aefric said "the crown?"

"Aefric," Karbin said. "I apologize. I should have thought of using a tracking spell."

"When you left," Aefric said, "speed and the vantage point of flight seemed more than enough to do the job." Aefric snorted. "I wasn't even sure Ser Grud would have left us something that could be *used* for a tracking spell."

"It did sound as though he tried to avoid it," Maev said. "At least, I assume that's what he was doing, if he kept changing horses, saddles, wardrobes..."

"Exactly," Aefric said. "Anything he's been in touch with for enough time could be used to find him, at a distance. The more contact, the better."

For a moment, mirth danced in Maev's eyes, as though she

wanted to make a joke. But then she frowned, and turned her attention to her meal.

The whole meal went that way. Observations or apologies. Half-hearted attempts to make plans, though there wasn't much they could do. And they all knew it. Not until the duchess — and possibly the justiciar — arrived.

Dessert was a cherry pie, which was probably delicious. But none of them had the stomach for it that night, and left their slices untasted.

Then dinner was over, and Karbin and Ser Grey took their leave. Maev stood to do the same, but stopped short of the door and turned around.

"Aefric," she said, her voice as serious as he'd ever heard it. "I'm sorry. You accepted a duel of honor, and I stole it from you. I shouldn't have done so. I know that. I should have trusted you to beat him, instead of waving my rank like a weapon. I..."

Pain filled her large, soft gray eyes. "Please don't hate me."

"Hate you?" Aefric crossed the room until they were standing so close he could almost taste her breath.

"Yes," she said, softly. Not meeting his eye. "I know what honor means to men like you. And I'm sure you could have beaten him. I—"

"I'm not sure of that," Aefric said, and Maev frowned at him.

Aefric shrugged.

"I thought that, as the challenged, I would have had the right to choose our weapons. He said that no, we had to use swords." Aefric chuckled breathlessly. "I have no illusions about my sword work. Especially if I'm not supposed to use magic. I'm not even sure I can *do* that. Most of what I know of swordplay, I learned as a dweomerblade. And if I managed to restrain my instincts and fight without *any* magic at all..."

Aefric chuckled.

"Am I good enough with a sword to fight for my life in a tight spot?" he asked with a smirk. "Sure. Am I good enough to take down a professional duelist who's been killing with the sword since before I had hair on my chest? While fighting down my own instinctual use of magic? He'd have killed me. Wouldn't have taken long, either."

Maev frowned again, searching Aefric's eyes for the answer to some unspoken question.

"I don't think honor is about fighting duels I can't win," Aefric said. "I think honor lies in doing what's right. To the best of my ability. To the last breath in my body."

"So..." Maev said slowly, but before she could get her next word out, Aefric spoke.

"I had to get him out of that house. Away from those hostages." He quirked a self-effacing half-smile. "If you hadn't hit that bastard with arrows, I'd've paralyzed him with a spell."

Maev huffed out a breathless laugh. "Really?"

"Of course. I'm many things, but I'm not an idiot."

"So you don't hate me?"

"I don't think I *could*."

"And you're not angry with me?"

"Not at all."

"Not even for pulling rank on you?"

Aefric held her eyes as he shook his head.

"Then why..." She bit her lip, then continued. "Then why did you just take off like that? After Ser Grud was down. You rifled his pockets then flew off before I could stop you."

Aefric smacked himself in the forehead.

"I'm sorry," he said. "I needed to find the Merrek seal. It wasn't on him."

And Aefric told her the story of how he'd dug through the manure pile for that abandoned seal.

He told it right. She laughed twice, and by the end she was smiling so wide she practically sparkled.

"So," she said hopefully, "we're all right?"

"Better than all right, I hope," Aefric said softly, taking her hands. "Unless that kiss was just a fleeting fancy."

"I meant every moment of it."

"Me too," Aefric said, girding himself against an onrush of guilt from somewhere deep within him.

But that onrush didn't come.

Aefric reached out with his right hand and swept Maev's long, jet black tresses back behind her shoulder. Nestled his fingers into the warmth behind her neck. He moved in to kiss her.

She tilted her head to meet him.

Someone knocked at his door.

Both Aefric and Maev stopped the forward progress of their lips. He held his breath while a servant opened the door just enough to speak quietly with whoever was on the other side. The door closed just as quietly.

"Your grace," Somer said apologetically. "Mistress Byrhta Ol'Caran is here to see you."

Maev chuckled through her nose. Aefric joined her.

"I wonder what she could want?" Maev teased softly. "Coming to your rooms after dinner this way."

"I'm sure she just wants to talk," Aefric answered, just as softly.

"I'm not sure of that," Maev said, one eyebrow cocked, then put her fingers to Aefric's lips. "And that's all right. I don't mind if you have fun with her." Maev's voice lost its tease as she continued. "But if she decides she wants more from you than the occasional bliss moment, well, then she and I might have to talk."

"I'll keep that in mind."

"See that you do," Maev said with a smile, and started to turn away. Over her shoulder she said, "Until later, Aefric."

The way she said his name then felt like a caress.

He tried to give her the same effect when he said, "Until later, Maev."

But he knew he fell short.

AEFRIC WAS STILL COLLECTING HIMSELF WHEN SOMER ADMITTED Byrhta to his sitting room, announcing her as she did.

Byrhta wore a soft-looking dress of a pale yellow-green chiffon that brought out the canary yellow flecks in her amber eyes. The dress was sleeveless, with the bodice cut low, and skirts that played down around her calves. On her feet, dark, forest green slippers that matched her hair, which she wore down, tickling the pale skin of her bare shoulders.

She was carrying a bottle in one hand.

"Good evening, your grace," she said. "If I may say, you look dashing in red."

"Thank you, Byrhta," Aefric said. "And you look stunning in, well, everything, I expect. But most certainly that dress."

As she smiled at that, he indicated the armchairs and couches over by the window and said, "Shall we sit?"

"Thank you, your grace," she said, and as she crossed the room with him, she offered him the bottle in her hand. "I brought a small token of Goldenfall's appreciation for your coming aid."

The bottle was a dark green color, and twisted along the neck with a series of small corks among the twists, before reaching the mouth, where it was sealed with golden wax.

The design looked familiar, but the bottle bore no label.

"What is it?" Aefric asked, as he gestured for her to have her choice of seats.

She sat on one couch, with her right side to the window and the night sky beyond. Aefric sat facing her on the other couch, which she noted with an eyebrow raised the barest fraction.

"Only the finest alcohol brewed anywhere in your grace's duchy. Has your grace ever tasted *flisnaath*?"

"I have," Aefric said, appreciation clear in his voice. "Though not since the beginning of the Godswalk Wars. When I traveled with a group of eldrani spellsingers for a time."

"And does your grace speak the True Tongue?" she asked, in High Eldrani.

"Passably," he said. *"Though not as well as I speak a few other languages."*

"You have a touch of a Thunderwoods accent," she said with a pleased smile. "My grandmother was from the Thunderwoods. One of the few eldrani settlements within a forest."

"The city they call *Thundersong*," Aefric said, which word sounded like Ahlisklasach to the ears of most other races, which was why that city was widely known as Alisklask. "I've been there. It's beautiful, especially by morning sunlight. The amber of the towers seems to glow."

He called Somer over to bring them two small glasses for the *flisnaath*, then opened the bottle himself. Each cork, from lowest to highest, had to be removed slowly, then its left open for the space of five heartbeats, before moving on to the next.

Only once all the corks were removed, and placed in sequence around the bottle, could the wax seal be broken and the final cork removed.

He hoped he remembered the proper words to say as he broke the wax seal.

"Nil sachassa ne vili."

It was an old blessing, from an archaic form of High Eldrani, and the verbs — as far as Aefric could tell — were irregular. The closest he could come to a meaning was "No glory greater than true friendship." But "friendship" in High Eldrani could mean many things, depending on context.

Whatever they truly meant, he must have said the words properly, because Byrhta said them along with him, and smiled as the cork came out.

He poured them each two fingers of the dark red brew, and was amused to note that it matched his robes.

"Je sinilich toh," she said, as a toast, which meant, "To both our long lives and fortunes."

They sipped then. The *flisnaath* was warm on Aefric's tongue at first, and tasted of spiced cinnamon. Then it cooled, shifting its taste to more of a peppermint. A moment later, as the alcohol in the brew began to make itself felt along his tongue, the liquid warmed again as its taste shifted back to spiced cinnamon.

Flisnaath was meant to be held on the tongue through five shifts of temperature and flavor, though the exact details of the flavors and temperatures varied from brewer to brewer.

This *flisnaath* was excellent. The flavors were pure and crisp, and the temperatures shifted by a wide margin. With the spiced cinnamon warm as good bathwater on a chilly night, and the peppermint cool as a refreshing dip in the hot summer sun.

Between sips, Byrhta said, "Your grace has had something of a busy day, I understand."

Aefric chuckled. "From what *I* understand, you probably know almost every detail of it already."

Byrhta smiled, and even without considering the sheer beauty of her smooth, eldrani features, she had a good smile.

"I have lived in Water's End and Behal for almost half my life," she said. "And almost exclusively since the end of the War of Red Gold."

"Is that why Duchess Arinda took you to foster?" Aefric said, surprised. "As a hostage against your father's good behavior?"

"I think that's how it started," Byrhta said, apparently unconcerned about such a notion. "But in time, I believe Arinda came to love me. To perhaps look on me as the daughter she hadn't had. I know I came to look on her as a second mother."

"You're still in mourning," Aefric said, even as the realization occurred to him. "Her death was ... what ... a year ago?"

"One year, ten aetts and three days," Byrhta said with a sigh. "But who counts them?"

Aefric considered that through their next sip of *flisnaath*. But before he could find any words to express his sympathies, Byrhta changed the subject.

"To answer your grace's implied question," she said, "I know that Ser Grud was arrested. As was the family of Baron Karmody Ol'Karmak. Though I know not why."

She tilted her head to the side. "I have also heard whisperings of war drums, and armies wending their way south. Though I note that none of those armies hail from Goldenfall."

"You are indeed well informed."

Byrhta raised her glass in silent toast.

"I have even heard," she said, "that the duchess of Merrek sails this way. Though, as with the arrests and the armies, I've not heard the whys and wherefores beyond rumors too wild to be believed."

"And those are?"

"I should have thought that obvious," Byrhta said with a smile. "That your grace means to install some old adventuring partner as the new baron of Riverbreak, and seize Merrek by force."

Aefric laughed so hard he almost spilled his drink. He had to set down the glass before he could stop his humor.

By the time he got his breathing under control, Byrhta was looking at him with amused eyes.

"I take it," she said, "that those are not the real reasons?"

"No," Aefric said, checking himself from dissolving into laughter. But then he frowned a little more seriously. "I'm not sure how much I can tell you."

"I understand if I have not yet earned your trust, your grace," Byrhta said with perfect calm. "I am not offended. Though I would appreciate being enlightened about the exclusion of Goldenfall from your plans, if I might."

"Goldenfall is not excluded," Aefric said firmly. He sighed. "I didn't summon armies from Goldenfall because, from everything you said earlier, you couldn't spare the people."

"Is that truly the reason, your grace?" Byrhta asked. "No other?"

"No other," Aefric said with a shake of his head. "If this comes to battle, and I hope it doesn't, people will die. Goldenfall has seen so much death already. How could I ask you to suffer more?"

Byrhta nodded slowly, eyes pensive.

"Then why have I also heard that Motte has not been called to war? They seem to have troops to spare right now."

"They do," Aefric admitted. "But could I trust their commanders? I shamed Count Ferrin just last night. Right now I wouldn't put it past him to switch sides in the middle of a battle."

"So the stories of what you did in Motte last night are true?" Byrhta asked with a smile.

Aefric nodded. Told her the story himself, then they shared another sip of *flisnaath*.

After, Aefric decided that one detail of the arrest would become public soon enough, if it wasn't already. So he said, "Ser Grud was arrested for carrying a forged duplicate of Merrek's seal."

Byrhta's forest green eyebrows shot up.

"So you *don't* know everything," Aefric said with a smile. "Good to know."

"And the Ol'Karmaks," she said. "You had to arrest them for aiding and abetting him?"

"They are under suspicion only, pending a full investigation."

"By the duchess?" Byrhta asked. "Is that why she's coming?"

"She might think so, but no. The king's justiciar has been sent for."

She lowered her voice. "But your grace has the right of High Justice."

"I do."

Byrhta's nostrils flared as the implications sank in.

"I believe I'm ready for another sip," she said.

"As am I," Aefric said.

They sipped again, and then they spoke of lesser things. Aefric told a tale or two from his travels. Byrhta spoke of happier times in Goldenfall and Water's End and Behal.

They talked, and they sipped, for quite some time. Telling stories. Singing snatches of song. They laughed together, and shifted from the common tongue to High Eldrani and back easily as they spoke.

And though the *flisnaath* was strong, that they drank it the proper way, slowly and interspersed with a good deal of conversation, ensured that they never became drunk.

All in all, it was a far more pleasant, relaxed evening than Aefric expected. And he found himself quite enjoying Byrhta's company.

Alas, though, the hour grew late as the bottle slowly emptied.

"Thank you, Byrhta," Aefric said, when they'd finished the last drop. "This has been a most enjoyable evening."

Byrhta's eyes widened a touch, as though in disbelief. A smile played about the corners of her lips.

"And is the evening over, your grace?" she asked softly.

"Well, we're out of *flisnaath*. I could have something else brought—"

Byrhta chuckled. "Does your grace find me less appealing than the baroness Montess?"

"Your beauty," Aefric said with more honesty than he intended, "is the stuff of legends and songs."

"And there is more of it that you haven't seen," she said, softly, as she stood. "More of it that I would share with you this night."

Aefric swallowed as she sauntered closer, her hips shifting. Truly, she was like some artist's masterpiece come to life. The part of him that was Keifer could only compare her to fantasy artwork created by the likes of Larry Elmore.

But Byrhta was no mere painting. She was a living, breathing woman. Perfection made flesh. Irresistible.

And she was looking at Aefric with heat beyond anything he'd tasted in the *flisnaath*. The amber in her eyes, almost hypnotic.

Aefric was standing before he knew it. Closing the distance between them.

Taking her in his arms.

"Your grace," Somer called from the hallway door. Her voice so strained and urgent that it cut right through the need growing inside him.

It took an effort of will for Aefric to turn his head and learn what Somer wanted.

"Duchess Ashling of Merrek," Somer said. "She's here."

Frustrated desire rushed out of Aefric in a breath, as he forced his arms to release Byrhta. Though he noted that her arms lingered about him. And the look in her eyes was, if anything, even more frustrated than he felt.

"I'm sorry," he said. "I must—"

"You must go receive the duchess," Byrhta said, sounding as

though she were re-donning her armor of nobility even as she spoke. "I understand."

Aefric started to turn away.

She turned him back with a soft hand on his cheek.

"But your grace," she said, meeting his eyes with heat once more. "Promise me we will continue this another time?"

Answering words came out of Aefric's mouth before he could even consider whether or not he should say them.

"I promise."

"Then I shall look forward to that time," she said with a smile, "your grace."

"As shall I," Aefric said. And he knew he would.

Once more, Aefric found himself standing before the portcullis of Behal Castle. His ducal coronet on his head. A red carpet under his feet. A ring of torches providing light, as well as a little heat in the cool, midnight air.

Though both tastes of the *flisnaath* lingered on his tongue.

The cool night air helped with the heat lingering from those final moments with Byrhta. He caught himself surreptitiously checking for enchantment, but he found no trace of any spells or influences lingering about his person.

He'd just been reacting to the woman herself then. He needed to figure out what that meant.

In the background of his mind, he felt a swirl of conflict about Byrhta, but it stayed in the background. And to help keep it there, he focused on where he was and what he was doing.

The crowd outside the portcullis was much smaller this time. Most of his soldiers were gone, so there was only a token guard presence. Mostly his personal guard, anchored by two of his knights and four of Maev's.

Ser Grey was back a pace, on his right side, and Ornella mirrored her, on his left.

Maev stood beside him, still in her gown of deep blue. Though she'd added a touch of jewelry. A gold pendant featuring a dark blue opal.

A handful of courtiers were out of bed and freshly dressed as well, chief among them Byrhta, who had changed into a complex gown of dark russet, with matching shoes.

The duchess arrived by carriage, followed by a train of knights and retainers.

She wore a gown of black silk, trimmed in gold, that somehow made her look like a pirate queen as she stepped out of her carriage and went through the formal greetings.

With her agreement, an abridged version of the formal greetings, which no doubt left many of the courtiers wondering why they'd bothered getting out of bed. They never had even a moment to meet the duchess' eye or exchange a word of well-wishes.

Soon enough, Aefric and the duchess adjourned to the same meeting room where Aefric had met his mayor and the delegates of the trade council.

The tiled floor in navy blue and Deepwater gray. The old arms and armor around the Deepwater gray walls. The ebon table with the bas-relief of the Deepwater sigil, surrounded by six matching chairs. The wheel chandelier above them.

This time, however, four braziers surrounded the rectangular table, to chase away the chill of midnight air. Aefric found something reassuring about the scent of their burning coals.

He sat at the head of the table, Duchess Ashling at the foot. Maev sat on his right and Ser Grey on his left. A balding old man with a long white beard, in robes six shades of gray, sat to Duchess Ashling's right.

Aefric knew the man almost at once. They'd met briefly several years ago, while Aefric traveled with Kainemorton.

This was the wizard Sirondfar. A *ventavis*, more commonly thought of as a specialist in the magic of birds and weather.

So that was how they got here so quickly.

On her other side, a knight whose few remaining hairs were gray, and whose plate armor yet had dents under its polish. She had a grim expression, and Aefric would have sworn that her eyes alone were accusing him of some great wrongdoing.

This woman was introduced as Ser Limic.

Once they were all seated, and a light white wine provided to them all in crystal goblets, Aefric began the conversation.

"I confess, your grace, I didn't expect you to come."

"It's *my* seal the man is said to be carrying," Duchess Ashling said with a finely sculpted, raven black eyebrow raised. "*My* justice he should answer to. I appreciate your arresting him and informing me, of course. And I trust you won't object to my taking him back to Fyrcloch for trial."

"I certainly would not object," Aefric said. "If Merrek were alone in injury in this matter."

"Malimfar." Duchess Ashling breathed the word, more than said it. Her voice only just audible over the low flames of the braziers. Louder, she said, "What do you know already, your grace?"

"Know? Little. I suspect more, though." He shook his head. "But I would prefer to hear you speak on the subject first."

Duchess Ashling considered that through a sip of her wine, while Ser Limic whispered in her ear.

Duchess Ashling shook her head. Whispered something back. The exchange continued a moment, before Duchess Ashling turned back to Aefric with an apologetic smile.

"My war counselor doubts your good intentions, your grace," the duchess said. "And as she has advised me for many years—"

"If I may," Maev said, raising a hand.

Duchess Ashling nodded. "Of course, your highness."

"I have not known his grace long, but I have watched him cope with crisis after crisis and maintain a cool head and clear vision. If your war counselor suspects him of plotting against you, she is in error."

Aefric would have sworn he heard Sirondfar mutter, "I told you as much."

"Then if I may ask, your grace," Ser Limic said in a rough voice.

"Why is it my scouts tell me of troops mustering as though they intend to move south toward Merrek?"

"Not to fight against Merrek," Aefric said. Then nodded his head from side to side. "Not unless I am gravely mistaken about what's really going on here."

Duchess Ashling nodded. "Your grace is not mistaken. Right now my brother Ser Mekel rides south at the head of my own armies, to stop Malimfar from snatching my half of the Indecisive River Valley."

"I thought as much." He briefly told her how and why he believed that Malimfar had been trying to divide him from Merrek, and how he was sending troops south to her aid.

Duchess Ashling looked at Aefric in silence for a long time then. Twice one or both of her advisers tried to say something, and both times she waved him to silence. Her eyes locked on Aefric's, as though trying to strip secrets directly from his mind.

He found himself surreptitiously checking for magic. She used none. Save perhaps the magic of her own intellect.

"You are truly doing this?" Duchess Ashling said at last. "You are riding to my aid? Unbidden? With no promises in the offing? No demands for gold, or land, or special considerations?"

"I have not been a duke for long, your grace," he said. "I do not know how such things are usually done. But I was raised to believe that when your neighbors are in trouble, you help them. And I'd like to think that if I find myself in trouble one day, maybe you'll ride to my rescue."

Duchess Ashling quirked a small smile at that.

"Perhaps I will at that." She nodded. "I have misjudged you, your grace. I apologize for that."

"Adventurers have something of a ... grasping reputation in some circles," Aefric said with a smile. "I know. But not all of us condone such behavior."

"So I see," she said, her smile a touch wider now. "What shall we do about Ser Grud?"

"I've already arrested him in the king's name," Maev said. "And sent for the justiciar."

"Does the king also know what's going on with the Indecisive River Valley?" Duchess Ashling asked.

And Aefric could have smacked himself that he hadn't asked that same question, hours ago.

"He does," Maev said. "Or he will soon. I sent rika birds not long after lunchtime."

"Colm will come a-marching then," Duchess Ashling said with a small chuckle. "He loves to play the hero." She looked up at Aefric. "Then there is no pressing need for me to be here, much less remain for the long visit I expected."

She nodded. "I shall sail south for the Indecisive River Valley in the morning. Would you care to accompany me, your grace?"

"I would," Aefric said. "And I'll bring my court wizard, if you don't mind."

"Not in the least." She turned to Maev. "Your highness?"

"Absolutely," she said. "And if one of you can give me a squad of scouts when we get there, I'll get you better intelligence than you could possibly expect."

"I've little doubt," Duchess Ashling said before Aefric could.

"Then I suggest we make an early night of it," Aefric said, standing.

They said their good nights, and left to be escorted to their rooms.

Once Aefric and Ser Grey were more or less alone and moving through the halls of the fourth floor, Aefric said, "This may be our last night in a castle before we fight for our lives. What do you think of offering her grace *leaba*?"

"I think it's a good move," Ser Grey said. "She's of an old family, and she's just starting to think well of you. This should cement you in her mind as trying to move from adventurer to noble. Especially if you share your logic with her about the dawn of battle nearing."

Ser Grey smiled. "And I guarantee she'll have plenty of volunteers."

"Do you know her tastes?" Aefric asked.

"I have an idea or two."

"Then would you handle the selection? I'd hate to get this wrong."

"Of course, your grace," Ser Grey said. "I'll consult Ornella as well, in case she has any thoughts."

"Good idea."

Ser Grey hesitated before asking her next question, and the words seemed to resist leaving her mouth.

"What about her highness? Do you wish to offer her *leaba* as well?"

Aefric sighed. "I confess that I'd rather visit her chambers myself..." He winced. "But she said she would never see me for just that. And I don't think I could bear it if she sent me away."

Ser Grey said nothing for a moment, though Aefric would have sworn that words were trying to wedge her mouth open and escape.

Finally, she straightened as though a thought had occurred to her.

"You told me to always speak honestly, your grace, did you not?"

"I did," Aefric said, though his thoughts were elsewhere.

"Well, I think that if her highness would welcome anyone to her chambers tonight, she would welcome you."

"I'd like to think that," Aefric said. "I truly would. But even if she didn't send me away, what if she thinks I only came to her because we might die soon? What if she thinks..."

He shook his head. Sighed once more.

"No," he said. "The only thing worse than her sending me away would be her thinking I only came to her because we would soon face death."

Ser Grey sighed, her mouth wide in a grimace.

"So *leaba* then?"

"Offer it," he said. "And ensure she's told my logic as well." He sighed. "Even if it's not with me, she should have one more night of pleasure before she stands to battle."

AEFRIC ARRIVED ALONE BACK AT HIS CHAMBERS. SOMER OPENED THE door for him, and he would have sworn her smile was knowing as she stood aside to give him entrance.

"Sleep well, your grace," she said, and perhaps he was hearing things, but he thought he heard a teasing quality to her voice.

But she'd never spoken to him that way before. He must simply have been tired. The day had been long, and tomorrow looked to be even longer.

Those reports sat waiting for him, but he shook his head. Weary to the bone. Better that he sleep. Yes. Better that he sleep.

Aefric wandered into his closet and stripped out of his clothes. An older servant, a man named Mak, offered him a dressing gown, but Aefric waved it away.

It was late. He was tired. And he didn't need a dressing gown. No one would care if he was naked.

Aefric wandered into his bedroom. The rugs soft under his bare feet. The fire in the hearth warmed the chamber, and scented the air with cherry.

The blankets and sheets of his bed had already been turned down for him.

And Byrhta Ol'Caran lay naked on those sheets, smiling at him.

Her beauty was staggering. Aefric found himself staring. Frozen in place. His heart raced. The hot rush of his blood, louder in his ears than the whistle of the wind outside or the crackling of logs in the hearth.

This woman was the pinnacle of feminine magnificence, from head to toe. Her proportions generous, but not excessive. Her smooth, flawless porcelain skin, almost glowing by the firelight.

The mere sight of her chased away Aefric's weariness and replaced it with a blaze of passion, surging through him, head to toe. Every inch of his skin yearned to touch such a wonder. To prove that this was no figment, no dream, but a woman of flesh and blood.

And her smile made clear that his touch would be welcomed. Reciprocated eagerly.

There was no magic to her. No illusion or glamour. He would know. He would sense it. And part of him tried again, out of sheer disbelief.

Byrhta simply possessed physical beauty beyond anything he'd ever seen before. Ever imagined before. And that seemed incomprehensible. How could this be?

Aefric had known eldrani women, in his time. Full-blooded eldrani women, of a race noted for such glorious beauty — both men and women — that it was often said their race was formed from the very dreams of human beings.

And yet, somehow this incredible woman outshone them all?

"How..." Aefric started, raw desire driving his voice low and rough.

"How did I come to be here? All the servants in Behal know me, your grace," she said, every word sounding like temptation. "And I believe those who serve in your chambers favor my being here tonight as much as I do. Or *almost* as much."

Her eyes trailed slowly, hungrily down Aefric's naked body, from his broad shoulders to his muscled calves, before coming to rest somewhere below his abdomen.

"And unless my eyes deceive me," she said, her amber eyes dancing, "my presence does not displease you."

She was right. Much as part of him wanted to be with Maev, another part of him had very much enjoyed his evening with Byrhta, and wanted to see it through to its natural conclusion.

A natural conclusion that Maev had already approved...

Aefric smiled then, and joined Byrhta in his bed.

He dreamed that night. Not of Maev, or Byrhta. Not of Octave or Baroness Montess. Not even of battles to come or strange merry-go-rounds.

He dreamed of Andi.

Just the way she'd looked, mere months before her death.

She was wearing that soft, strapless summer dress she loved so much. The one that had started life all the shades of sunset, but she'd worn it and washed it so many times since college that the colors had lost some of their coherency. The reds had bled into the oranges. The oranges into the yellows. And down near the end of the skirts, it looked an almost muddy brown.

But Andi was wearing it. And walking barefoot with him along the warm, dry sands on the beaches of Lincoln City, Oregon. Her hair loose and free in the ocean breeze. Her skin bronzed by the sun.

She was laughing. Maybe at the way Keifer always kept one eye on the ocean, worried about sneaker waves.

Andi always swore no wave would take her life.

A joke, of course. She knew how dangerous sneaker waves could be. The joke was her way of saying that she trusted Keifer to keep her safe.

At least she'd been right about the waves.

But the car that would take her life was months away.

It was August.

Andi was still with him. She was laughing in the afternoon sun. Under the heat of the day and the scent of the ocean, Keifer could smell her sunscreen with its vague hints of chemical coconuts.

And she was more beautiful in Keifer's eyes than Byrhta could ever hope to be.

They weren't alone on the beach, but they might as well have been. The crowds around them were playing and chasing and doing all the things people did when they visited the ocean shore.

But he didn't hear them. Didn't see them, except as blurred shapes. Background. Out of focus.

The whole world was out of focus except for her.

Except for Andi.

He remembered that day well. They'd been hunting for those colorful blown glass globes that local artists hid on the beaches, for tourists to find.

They didn't expect to find any. It was just an excuse to stroll along the beach. To crouch over patches of wild grass, and poke around huge logs that had been thrown onto the beach by waves.

To sneak hot kisses and touch sunscreen-slicked skin, playing as though they had to hide what they were doing from the other beach-combers.

Just another of their little games.

In waking life, on that actual August day, they passed a pleasant afternoon, then wandered into Moe's for a dinner of clam chowder in sourdough bowls.

But the dream deviated.

Andi poked into a knothole in one of the logs. Pulled out a translucent, sea-green glass globe as wide as her splayed hand.

"Hah!" she said triumphantly. "I found it. Now I get a wish."

"And what does milady wish for?" he asked, smiling.

"A kiss, of course," she said, as though he should have known that already.

No one else's kisses were like Andi's. They'd been kissing for enough years that the dance should have been familiar. And in truth, the dance of their kisses always used the same steps. And yet, she always found some new way to vary her movements in some unexpected pleasure.

Every time he kissed Andi was as exciting as the first time.

He found that he stopped caring about the other beachcombers. There was a patch of wild grass nearby where their big red beach towel was already spread out and waiting.

He turned them so that her back was to the towel. Began moving them that direction as they kissed.

She pulled back from the kiss.

"There isn't time for that," she said, teasing. "Or I wouldn't have spent my wish on a kiss."

He tried to reason with her. The sun was still high. No one was near them. And even if they were, let them watch. Maybe they'd learn something.

But before he could get any of those words out of his mouth, she stilled him with one finger to his lips. The way she always did when she had something important to say.

"It's time," she said.

He didn't understand. Or at least, he didn't want to. His heart started thumping harder in his chest.

The ocean. He wasn't watching the ocean. First rule of walking the beaches in Lincoln City — always keep one eye on the ocean. It can turn on you when you least expect it.

Fear seized him. He wanted to turn. Needed to turn. The ocean. Sneaker waves might be coming. And they were right next to a log. A big one. And more logs. The ocean might pick them up. Slam them around. Kill Andi and Keifer both before anyone could shout a warning.

Yes. That must be why cold sweat broke out all over his skin. Why he tasted something metallic on his tongue. Why his stomach quivered, and his pulse raced faster still.

"It's time," she said again, and softly as she said those words it was a wonder he could hear them over the roar of blood past his ears. Over his shaky breaths.

No. Something bad was about to happen.

The ocean.

That car.

Something.

"I have to go," she said. "And you're finally ready to move on."

He wasn't. He couldn't be. He could never be ready to "move on." How could anyone ever move on from the perfect woman? From the love of his life?

No. She was wrong. He would keep the flame of their love alive forever. He would. He *would*.

"No," she said, smiling sadly. "You mustn't. And you know you mustn't."

No. She was wrong. He loved Andi and only Andi. There would never be anyone to replace her. Never be anyone to—

"Shhhh," she said, stroking his face with one hand. "It's all right, love. It's the way of things. Of life. And you are still very much alive."

No. He had power now. He had magic now. So much magic. And he had her crystal. Maybe there was a way to bring her back. Maybe he could—

"Don't," she said, her eyes shining with tears, but still she smiled that sad smile. "You know you shouldn't. I'm dead, love. I'm no longer an option. It's time for you to say goodbye, and move on."

No. He wouldn't. If he didn't, she wouldn't leave. He would still have part of her here with him. She would always be part of him.

"You can remember me, of course," she said. "I'd like that. But you *must* say goodbye."

Ridiculous. Impossible. He wouldn't. He couldn't.

"I know it's scary," she said. "But you know I'm right. It's time, my love. Give me one last kiss, and say goodbye."

Kiss her. He could do that much. That would be easy.

He wrapped his beloved Andi in his arms once more. Held her tight as he could. And with his kiss he tried to tell her how much he loved her. How much she meant to him. How he had missed her and mourned her. How...

...how she was right.

Something broke inside him. Still kissing her, he was crying now. Trembling.

The kiss ended. Andi smiled at him once more, and touched his cheek as she began to fade away.

He fell to his knees there in the hot sand. Wracked with sobs.

But he made himself say it.

"Good—

———

"—BYE," HE SAID, WAKING UP.

He was in his bed in Behal Castle. Sheened in sweat. His cheeks lined with tears. His blonde hair matted to his skin. He trembled. Shivered, as though cold, though the room was warmed and the air cherry-scented from the low fire in the hearth.

But there was an unfamiliar lightness to him. As though his heart had been holding up the skies themselves for nearly two years, and finally been allowed to lay its burden down.

He felt wonderful. A little giddy, even.

His next breath came easy. His shoulders felt relaxed. He felt almost as though he could float about the room without even a hint of magic.

He laughed softly, without being able to express why.

Byrhta, sleep-tousled and heavy lidded among the sheets beside him, stirred.

"Your grace?" she asked, blinking against the dim firelight. "Are you all right? Did you have a bad dream?"

"No," he said, then chuckled. "No. I think it was a very good dream. A dream I needed."

"I don't understand, your grace," she said, her amber eyes looking more awake now.

"Nor should you," he said, then smiled. "And I'd like you to call me Aefric."

Byrhta smiled. "Well, then, Aefric. Seeing as we're both awake..."

She didn't need to finish the thought.

When he leaned down to kiss her, there wasn't even a hint of conflict within him. And he didn't expect one.

He was moving on at last.

14

———————

Not long after dawn the next morning, Aefric stood on the deck of a swift, two-masted sloop belonging to Duchess Ashling.

He was accoutered for battle. Good, strong leather boots that came almost to his knee. Tanned, dark brown leather pants, and a dark red shirt of strong cotton that Byrhta had suggested (though all three of Aefric's dressing servants had agreed it was the best choice). He wore a soft, gray wool cloak, and his old backpack waited for him belowdecks, with his luggage.

His shoulders itched for that backpack, but he knew he shouldn't carry it himself. Not until they were actually in the field, when it would at least be *more* appropriate for a duke to carry his pack.

He had the Brightstaff in hand, of course, and both his sword and the wand Garram on his belt.

All about him on the deck, sailors busied themselves with the rigging and the sails, preparing to leave the dock at Behal, cross the mouth of Lake Deepwater and sail down the Haven River.

Among the high decks, aft, Karbin stood beside Sirondfar, deep in conversation.

Maev and Duchess Ashling were talking near the prow. Maev, in her freshly laundered buckskin tunic and breeches (and boots, apparently, though the boots still looked like doeskin to Aefric), with her rapier and dueling dagger on her belt. Standing by her side, and gazing Aefric's direction, was her great spotted forest lynx Sylkanis, with the early sun bringing out the reds in her reddish-brown coat.

Duchess Ashling wore a sturdy, but fashionable dark yellow dress. Though her nod to the coming possibility of battle was a breastplate fastened over the bodice, and a rapier on her belt.

He noted that she also wore boots beneath her skirts, not shoes or slippers.

Deciding he was in the way of the deckhands, where he stood, Aefric joined them at the prow.

"Ah," Duchess Ashling said giving Aefric a big smile, "and here's our most excellent host now. Good morning, your grace."

"Good morning, your grace, Maev," Aefric said, chuckling slightly at the overpowering goodwill in the duchess' aspect, and the humor in Maev's eyes. "I trust you slept well?"

"*Marvelously*," the duchess said. "I find myself far better rested and refreshed than I could have expected. And I find you a more gracious and knowledgeable host than I could have *guessed*. I haven't been offered *leaba* in *ages*. In fact, please, call me Ashling."

"And you must call me Aefric," he said, smiling.

"I don't know where you *found* that girl," Ashling continued, "but she was a *delight*. I do hope she'll be available the next time I visit you."

Girl? Well. Then it was a good thing that Aefric had let Ser Grey choose the volunteer for Ashling's *leaba*.

For that matter, he couldn't remember anything from Keifer's sourcebooks specifying Ashling's sexual preferences one way other the other.

"That would be telling," Aefric answered her, which got a laugh from Ashling.

"Your highness?" Ashling asked, turning to Maev. "Did you enjoy your *leaba* as much as I did mine?"

"I declined it," Maev said with a one-shoulder shrug. "The offer was a generous one, and the man certainly comely enough. But I prefer to go without when I am heading into trouble. Keeps my edge a little sharper."

"So you really intend to go into the field?" Ashling asked. "You know your father will have my hide if anything happens to you."

"My father knows full well that I will not sit in the grandstands while others risk their lives in defense of our lands and people," Maev said, one eyebrow cocked. "I fought in the Godswalk Wars, and if this comes to war, I will fight again."

"Then I need to send a rika before we leave," Ashling said, turning to Aefric. "With your permission, of course."

"Of course," Aefric said, and gestured to Ser Grey, who was seeing to the final stages of preparing the ship to leave.

As Ashling left with Ser Grey, Aefric turned to Maev.

"I almost came to your rooms last night," he said softly.

"And why didn't you?" she asked, just as softly.

"I..." He couldn't bring himself to mention the possibility of her sending him away. "I didn't want you to think I was only there because we might die in the coming fighting."

"And you would rather, instead," she said, "go face your death without having sampled my charms? Oh, that makes *perfect* sense."

Her tone was droll, but there was a smile in her eyes.

"Well, I—"

"Since I was bereft of your company last night," Maev teased, "at least tell me that the lightness I see in your step means that you shared a bed with Byrhta."

Aefric blinked in surprise.

Maev laughed. "Oh, come now. Even a blind woman could have seen the sheer frustrated desire in Byrhta's eyes, while we waited for Ashling's carriage last night. Her gaze practically incinerated your pants. Or at least your robe."

She shook her head, still amused. "I never doubted for a moment that after we left that meeting, Byrhta would come a-knocking on your door."

"She was waiting for me in my room."

Maev chuckled. "The servants here do like her, don't they?"

Aefric shrugged. "She says she's lived here and at Water's End for about half her life."

"And she *is* a charming one." Maev nodded. Then quirked a smile and poked Aefric in the chest with one finger. "Remember. Share the bliss moment with her all you want. Gods know she's the most beautiful woman you're ever likely to find."

Aefric tried to object. Maev didn't let him.

"Don't waste your breath," Maev said, shaking her head. "Her beauty is unquestionable. Famous, even. Though perhaps not as famous as her grandmother's."

"Oh?" Aefric said.

"Didn't she tell you? Her grandmother is Lylasalaas."

Lylasalaas. Well, perhaps that explained Byrhta. Lylasalaas was known throughout Qorunn as the most beautiful eldrani woman ever born.

It was said that she was so beautiful that no wild creature would harm her. That even monsters like the manticore and the great mindless wyrms of the southern wastes would lay themselves at her feet, rather than strike at her.

"So by all means, enjoy her charms all you like," Maev said, then poked him in the chest with a finger again. "But if she ever starts wanting more from you than the bliss moment, you need to tell me. And she and I need to talk."

Aefric quickly agreed. Maev narrowed her eyes at him, then nodded, as though satisfied with his response.

"I do have to ask, though," Aefric said, his voice hushed again.

"Do you?" Maev teased.

"If I *had* come to your rooms last night. Would you have welcomed me or turned me away?"

"Aefric," she said, stroking his face. "You won't know that unless you try."

And she turned away then, and left him standing there at the prow. Wondering.

With Sirondfar providing the sloop a strong wind, they sailed swiftly south that morning, first along the Haven River, then at the river junction, southeast along the Tainfyr River.

Aefric remained near the prow, staring along the wide, swift river into the distance.

He stood there alone, at the moment. Ashling was in conference with Ser Limic. Maev was playing with Sylkanis, keeping the great cat occupied on the ship.

He could have joined her, but he liked the prow. Here, he was out of the way of the sailors, busy about their jobs.

Though it did nothing to soothe his nerves.

Armies were on the move. Some of them his.

He'd stood to battle so many times before. But always before, just as an adventurer. Even in the Godswalk Wars, he'd been nothing more than an itinerant magic-user, doing his part where he could.

He'd rarely had to worry about more lives than perhaps a handful at a time.

He'd never had to give orders to throngs of people who would live or die by his command.

And he'd never had to worry about the repercussions of what he did. Every decision he'd make in the coming battle, every order he'd give, would ripple through the lives of countless others.

So much responsibility. All on his shoulders...

Only hours ago he'd shared a breakfast pastry with Byrhta. A fluffy thing, that pastry. Filled with eggs and sausage. Byrhta had hand-fed him bits of fruit in between bites, along with smiles and kisses, and a good deal of talk about nothing important.

At the time, it had seemed a lovely breakfast.

Now, the food sat like lead in his belly.

They were passing lands that were part of his duchy. Fyretti was on his right, with the county seat, Siarhal, coming visible. Riverbreak on his left, farmland and river towns.

But Aefric had no mind for sightseeing. He didn't want to look at Riverbreak's lands and people, much less Countess Faenella's castle.

The latter sight would just make him wonder where she was.

How her troops progressed. Whether there was anything he could do to speed their progress.

Many of his Deepwater troops were somewhere ahead of him. He knew that. Those who had mounted and taken ships south at his order yesterday, with Ser Beornric leading them.

That was good.

But it was no more than a fraction of his own troops. The others were still mustering. Massing and moving close to five thousand soldiers was not the work of a few hours.

Faenella was already on the march. He was sure of that. She was the sort who would have called a general muster to review her troops as soon as she claimed her county seat.

Hers would already be mustered and ready to march.

Of course, she only had perhaps a fifth as many total troops as Aefric did. Still. Maybe he should have done the same, when he first sat at Behal. Called a general muster. Reviewed the whole of his armies.

Oh, how much good would that have done? Behal wasn't Water's End. He could have mustered all the troops near Behal and it would have been no more than a third of his total complement of soldiers.

And what of the barons? How quickly would they muster and march? How many could they move by river?

The southern border of Merrek was a long, long march from Aefric's lands. Nearly a hundred miles from the Kingsroad. Four, five days maybe?

If Malimfar was already in the field, all of Aefric's work would be too little, too late.

If Malimfar was already in the field.

This waiting would kill him. He needed action.

He found Karbin up on the high deck to the aft, near where Sirondfar was keeping up the wind spells that whipped Aefric's clothes and had necessitated putting Aefric's blonde locks in a braid.

Oh, yes, and filled the sails with speed.

Karbin was watching the weather mage about his work. Studying his technique, perhaps.

Here it was too noisy to talk. The moaning winds too brisk. The chanting of Sirondfar too loud. And the shouts of the sailors, about their work, lending an undercurrent of cacophony to it all.

Aefric drew Karbin back to the prow with him, where he could hear himself think. And possibly make himself heard.

"Can you think of any way to speed our troops in the field?" Aefric asked. Loudly.

"None," Karbin answered in kind. "Far as I know, no wizard has ever ... felt motivated to research magic along those lines. Wouldn't be used for anything but to promote war."

Aefric sighed. "Or *prevent* one."

Karbin raised that damned eyebrow again, the way he always had when Aefric was his apprentice. The way he did whenever he felt that Aefric wasn't picking up a point fast enough.

"And which way, do you suppose, it would see more use?"

"Fine," Aefric grumbled. "Do you know if we have any wizards among our soldiers?"

"Of course," Karbin said. "I *am* your court wizard after all. Keeping track of the magic-users in your duchy is part of the job."

"And?"

"Approximately one hundred among your own troops. Considerably fewer among your vassals."

"How good are they? What should we expect?"

"No better than you were when you started traveling with me again after your time with the Iron Wands." Which meant that they knew a few battle spells, but would mostly fill a supporting role. "And they'll do their jobs. Though I don't know how well your captains and sergeants have been trained in the application of magic to the art of war."

Aefric thought back to what he'd seen during the Godswalk Wars. He shook his head.

"That's what I'm afraid of," Karbin said. "Likely only a very basic approach to their skills. We'll need to see to that, once this business is finished."

Aefric nodded, then had a horrible thought.

"It doesn't matter," he said, and he could have slapped his own face at his idiocy. "I ordered all those troops to stop at the Merrek border and wait for my order to proceed."

"That will leave them some two days from the river valley."

"They need to not stop. They need new orders." He clapped a hand on Karbin's shoulder. "And I doubt there's any way to reach them by rika bird."

Karbin grimaced. "You don't mean…"

"I do." Aefric shook his head. "I'm sorry, old friend, but I need you to do this. The delay in getting them the order to move might be critical. You know how important timing is, when it comes to battle."

"And I know how long it takes armies to move," Karbin said. "It will take Malimfar just as long to—"

"Malimfar knew they were doing this aetts ago. Maybe a season ago. Baston is the only one I know who's been down there recently, and he seemed pretty damned confident in Malimfar's chances of taking that river valley."

"Baston is a fool," Karbin said.

"Yes," Aefric said. "But I'm not willing to wage everything on his being *that* big a fool. I need you to go to my armies in the field, and bring them my orders."

Karbin drew a deep breath, looking as though he'd swallowed something foul.

"You know," he said, "when I took this post, I imagined it would involve a good deal more feasting and consulting than it would gallivanting around your duchy delivering messages."

"And I hope the position soon lives up to your expectations." Aefric held up a hand before Karbin could raise the next, logical objection. "Once this is over, I will arrange a better means of sending urgent messages myself. But for the moment, I need you to do this. I'm sorry to ask it of you. I truly am. But I need it."

Karbin drew a long, slow breath, and blew it out just as slowly. He nodded.

"Write the scrolls. I'll fly down, find your armies wherever they are, and deliver your orders. I'll meet you back at the ship, oh, probably sometime around *twilight*."

"I know," Aefric said. "It's a lot of flying, and a lot of hassle, and I greatly appreciate it."

"Who thought it would be a good idea to ennoble you anyway?" Karbin asked, but when Aefric turned at his friend's sharp tone, he was met with a smile.

"What?" Karbin asked in mock innocence. He shrugged. "I just think they made a good choice."

Aefric shook his head. And went to write up those scrolls.

This much, at least, he could do.

AEFRIC LUNCHED THAT DAY WITH MAEV AND ASHLING BELOWDECKS, IN Ashling's own cabin. Cramped, but for a cabin on a ship this size, it was almost expansive. It was long enough and wide enough for a good seven of Aefric's strides.

It mostly felt cramped because the ceiling beams were a scant handspan above his head.

Carpets covered the floorboards, though, and colorful sheets draped the walls in light cream. Oil lamps hung from the wooden ceiling.

Ashling had a bed, rather than a hammock, and though the mattress was not overlarge, it did look comfortable.

The three of them dined at a small, round table near her desk. Their plates and goblets were wood, though smooth, and finely shaped and engraved. The flatware looked to have been made from tin, or something like it.

Lunch was a savory roast chicken pie, filled with gravy and soft vegetables, served with a good fruity red wine that brought out the flavor in the chicken.

Other than the food, that lunch was a meal Aefric could have happily skipped.

It seemed that at some point that morning, Maev had mentioned to Ashling ... how Aefric had passed the night before.

And with whom.

"Byrhta Ol'Caran," Ashling said longingly, for at least the fifth time. "Oh, those eyes. That hair. That face. That *neck*." She sighed. "I could go on."

She had already. Twice, at least. Possibly three times. Aefric was losing count.

"No," Ashling decided yet again. "*You* go on, Aefric. Tell us everything, and don't spare the details."

Perhaps if he had, there could have been a change of subject. But he'd demurred. Again. This simply wasn't the sort of thing he talked about.

So once more, Ashling went on in his place. At length. Varying at times in her tone, from jealousy to admiration to joy on Aefric's behalf. But always on the same subject. The beautiful Byrhta Ol'Caran, and the extreme good fortune Aefric had enjoyed in sharing a bed with her.

That was all Ashling would talk about.

All. Through. The meal.

Not Malimfar. Not troop movements, or coordinating their forces. Not planning or looking ahead of any sort.

All she wanted to talk about through that lunch was Byrhta Ol'Caran.

And Maev, for her part, seemed to find the whole situation amusing. Including Aefric's discomfort at Ashling's ... enthusiasm for Byrhta's charms.

Aefric, for his part, did keep trying to change the topic to the coming confrontation with Malimfar.

Their armies could already be on the move. They likely were. There existed the distinct possibility that Malimfar would beat them to the field. Might even sack Merrek's towns and ports along the Indecisive River and seize the whole of the river valley before any troops could oppose them.

But every time Aefric tried to press those points, Ashling would say something like, "Mekel will have my troops in place by now. We should be able to hold off Malimfar for a few days, then crush them once your troops arrive. They can't be much better off than we are. They were hit by the wars too, after all, and our scouts don't believe they can field enough troops for a sustained conflict."

Inevitably, before Aefric could reply to that with a sensible counterargument, Ashling would get that longing look again and say something like, "Tell me at least this much. When her eyes burn with lust, do they grow more amber? Or more yellow?"

It was hopeless. He had no chance of turning this conversation anywhere useful.

He had to *do* something. Perhaps Ashling was confident in her brother's troops and the arrangement of her forces, but it sounded too easy to Aefric.

Malimfar shared a border with Merrek. Surely they had scouted the whole of the river valley and beyond for aetts in advance. Perhaps even surveyed Merrek's lands. Assessed the troops she could muster.

It's what Aefric would have done.

Malimfar had been working towards this for some time. They wouldn't invest so much unless they were confident in the outcome they could achieve.

And Aefric found he could not simply sit and wait while they sailed down the river. He needed information. Solid information about the state and arrangement of Malimfar's forces. How things stood in the Indecisive River Valley.

But there was no quick and easy way to get that information. No one in place whom he knew at all, much less well enough to reach with a message spell.

And seeing at such a distance without an object enchanted specifically for the task was a rare and difficult magic. Even Kainemorton might not have been able to do it.

No. If Aefric wanted solid information, he knew only one way to get it.

Shortly after they finished lunch, Aefric soared off into the air and flew directly south.

Sirondfar's winds buoyed him at first, but soon he'd left the river and was flying over rolling hills and farmland in Fyretti, making towards the border separating his duchy from Merrek.

Castle Fyrcloch was somewhere to the south, along the Tainfyr River, not far from the Indecisive River Valley.

That was about all Aefric knew of the local geography offhand. And he certainly couldn't go back for the map in his backpack. But he couldn't believe he would need a map.

He just had to fly south until he was flying over the Tainfyr River once more, after it bent back southwest. Then further still until he crossed the Kingsroad South.

Then, well, finding a river valley as big as the one he sought wouldn't be hard.

He passed the ships carrying Ser Beornric and about a thousand of Aefric's own troops. Good. That was good.

Still. His nerves were on edge, as he flew. Anticipating trouble. What if Malimfar had struck some bargain with the borogs, or the taroks?

Or worse, what about the dybbungstad? They'd resurfaced during the Godswalk Wars from their hidden places deep underground. What if Malimfar had cut some sort of deal with them and their demon twins?

They might have necromancers, calling back to a mockery of life those who'd died during the Godswalk Wars.

They might have invited sea giants to wander in from the beneath the waves, promising homes along the river if they helped seize the river valley.

He could imagine so very many ways this could all go horribly wrong.

He was just flying over the Tainfyr River once more when he felt the ringing warning through his bones of an incoming message spell. But the skies about him were clear, and he flew well above the tree lines of the nearby groves of oaks and madrones, so he didn't slow as the message came in.

The voice was Sirondfar's. "Your grace. Are you safe? Where are you? All are worried."

He felt the singing tension in his bones of the spell waiting for his reply. He shouted over the winds of his passage so he could hear himself, though the spell would have heard him even if he whispered.

"I am safe. I fly south as an advance scout. I shall return when I know the status and position of Malimfar's troops."

He flew on then.

Crossing the river.

Crossing the Kingsroad South.

He reached the Indecisive River Valley, and immediately saw the Ashling had been at least partially right. He could see ... approximately two thousand troops flying the Merrek battle flag, descending chevrons of red and gold.

They were arriving at the northern lip of the river valley, and had bivouacked there. Likely sending scouts ahead and waiting for a report before moving down into the valley itself.

The valley was such a lush, green place. The picture of bucolic happiness.

Aefric shuddered to think of such beauty being destroyed by greed.

He flew higher, hundreds of feet up to keep himself safe from arrows, and proceeded across the river valley to see just how ready Malimfar was for this conflict.

Aefric barely had to cross the twisting, turning Indecisive River itself to see his answer.

There, just over the southern lip of the river valley he could see the arrayed forces of Malimfar.

No sea giants. No borogs or tarok or dybbungstad. No hordes of undead abominations.

Only soldiers.

Miles and miles and miles of soldiers.

So very many soldiers. There had to be ... twenty thousand, at the least.

And yes, all flew the wide red X on the pale blue background of the Malimfar battle flag. But underneath it, in many places, Aefric could see the flags of mercenary companies. Upwards of a dozen of them.

But if Malimfar was truly as badly hurt in the Godswalk Wars as Merrek — and surely Ashling's scouts would have known that — then how could King Eadred plan on paying so many…

Spoils. He was going to pay them in the spoils of the Merrek's towns and farms and people.

There was no time for the bulk of Aefric's forces to get here. Much less King Colm's. There might not even be time for the thousand-odd troops sailing with Ser Beornric to arrive.

Ashling's brother Mekel would have to try to stand against Malimfar on his own.

Two thousand troops, against more than twenty thousand?

No tactical genius could save this battle. It would be a slaughter. Then the pillaging would begin. Thousands would suffer.

And Malimfar might not stop with the river valley.

No.

Aefric could not allow this to happen.

AEFRIC SOARED HIGHER INTO THE MID-AFTERNOON SKY. HE NEEDED elevation. He needed to see the whole of Malimfar's forces at once, and he needed to be out of range of even their siege engines. Of which they had more than they could possibly need to take this river valley.

No. That they were bringing more than a dozen ballistae and a score of catapults with them suggested they might intend to push on to Castle Fyrcloch. Perhaps even Armityr itself.

With King Colm on the march, new gates under construction, whole sections of wall still down and a good portion of the royal palace still recovering from the Godswalk Wars, Armityr could be all too vulnerable.

Aefric had to shake himself to stop that train of thought. It wasn't productive. He needed to deal with what was in front of him, not what might be.

What lay before him was a mass of soldiers larger than anything he'd seen since the height of the wars.

And all he had to stop it was his own command of magic, and the Brightstaff.

Aefric's command of magic was far from inconsiderable. But this. This would have been beyond even Karbin. Perhaps beyond even Kainemorton himself.

Well. Perhaps if Kainemorton had all of the Silver Arrows fighting alongside him…

But Kainemorton wasn't here. The Silver Arrows weren't here. Karbin wasn't here.

Aefric had only himself.

No time to seek help. He needed to act. Now. Before they crested the lip of the river valley. Descended the trails. Spread out and began their unchecked reign of terror.

Even the Brightstaff could not help him here. He could call lightning nonstop from now until dusk, and not do much more than bloody that army's nose.

But there had to be something he could do.

And he would have to come up with it quickly. The sky around him was empty of all but a few fluffy white clouds. If he just hovered here, eventually someone would notice him. Then, perhaps, they had a wizard or two who might come and challenge him.

Damn that empty sky. Rains had come through recently, up north. Why where there no rains here? Why couldn't the skies be roiling with thunder and lightning all on their own. Not lightning to strike and slay, but a torrential downpour to turn their march into a slog, or…

Snow.

Snow would be even better than rain. A snowstorm. To freeze soldiers and ice the ground. To stall siege engines, or even warp their wood.

Yes. What he needed was a blizzard.

But how?

Aefric knew that forcing a springtime blizzard was possible through weather magic. But he knew little weather magic himself. Karbin had never taught him any. Likely didn't know any. The whole branch of magic had fallen out of fashion decades ago, when someone decided that it was better for all if weather was allowed to set its own course.

But surely a situation like this. Surely this was an acceptable situation for—

The wand Garram. The wand wielded so well by King Iounn Stronghand. That specialist in the magics of ice and fire, who had lived and worked his will long before the fashions had changed.

Garram had to be the answer. Aefric had not been able to take much time to study that wand's magic, but he understood at least its basics.

It was within the wand to call forth a blizzard. Perhaps even a blizzard such as Aefric would need. He had no doubt that King Iounn could have done it.

But could Aefric? Was his meager command of Garram's magics enough to halt the advance of Malimfar's forces?

It would have to be.

He had no other choice.

He transferred the Brighstaff to his left hand, and drew the wand Garram in his right.

He held the wand before him, pointed at the skies above.

Aefric then chanted an ancient word of power he knew. It was a word not of ice or fire or wind, but of pure magic. The sort of power that many wizards drew upon only for those spells of pure force. Those spells that moved great objects at a distance, or erected physical barriers of pure magical energy.

Aefric chanted the word for a very different reason.

He chanted that word because of a secret he had discovered during his apprenticeship period with the Iron Wands.

That chant called forth not only the ancient power of the word itself, but also resonated with the magic in Aefric's blood. A resonance that built swiftly.

Aefric pushed the power built by that resonance now, even unto pain. He pushed it until he felt the power of that chant burning through his veins. Singeing his lungs. Seizing his muscles.

The power raged to be discharged. To be given form and purpose.

But his spell was not ready.

So Aefric gritted his teeth and, drenched in sweat, he honed that seething power through an ancient kindaren song in praise of the stars and skies, and the powers they too contained.

Aefric sang that song over and over. His lips and tongue forcing out the syllables through clenched teeth. His every muscle locked and trembling to hold back the power that seemed now to be brazing his muscles, bones, and sinews. His heart tried to burst with every frantic beat.

Still he focused on that song. Beating the power within him into shape and form through his guttural butchering of the lyrical kindaren verse.

And as he did this, he wedged free part of his mind, and sent it into the wand Garram. Calling forth all it knew of ice and snow and blizzard.

And of these things, Garram knew a great deal.

With Garram to aid him, Aefric's spells shaped and honed this power to a fine edge, preparing to send it forth into the skies, where it would storm down upon the forces of Malimfar with frozen fury.

But it would not be enough.

Aefric could sense that. Taste it, with his instincts as first of the dweomerblood. He had called together all the power he could handle. Enough power to call a good-sized blizzard through his current command of this wand.

But not enough.

If he had known more of weather magic, what he had might have been enough.

If he had had time to properly study and practice with Garram, what he had might have been enough.

But he had neither of those things. And now he could only fall short. Now he could only fail, and leave these poor innocents to suffer.

No.

If he didn't have enough power, he would have to find more.

But how?

The answer was in his left hand. The Brightstaff. Its spells, on their own, would not serve him here. But perhaps he could twist the powers it called to his purposes?

Only one such power could possibly provide enough. Arguably the Brightstaff's most dangerous power.

This was madness. Aefric knew that. Logically, what he wanted to do shouldn't work.

But when it came to magic, improvisation bridged many more gaps for Aefric, than logic would otherwise allow.

And he had no other options.

So as he kept up his chant, and held his place in the wand, he forced his mind to handle a third demanding task.

He reached into the Brightstaff for the power to become lightning itself.

Wild energies jolted through him. Power that tried to shape him into a bolt of lightning and send him screaming through the skies in a flash of light and thunder.

Aefric grabbed that power as it came through.

Pain tore through him. Through his body from his hairs through his toenails. Through his mind, from his earliest memories through the very will that he relied on to shape and force that wild power to serve him.

Pain tore even through his soul itself, as though his very essential nature had been submerged in a vat of acid.

But Aefric's desperate will held.

He shaped that power to serve his spell.

He channeled that spell through the wand Garram, and up, up, up into the skies above, where he felt it take and begin its work.

But Aefric was spent beyond spent.

He had nothing left for his flight spell. Nothing left to cast another. Nothing left to even hold him to consciousness.

As his limp body began to fall, his mind raved. Afterimages of the sun became as two silver eyes. The whipping wind of his descent, for a moment, seemed as a kiss on his forehead.

Then, there was only blackness.

15

Aefric was aware of pain before he was aware of anything else.

On some level, part of him thought that was a good thing. If there was pain, it meant he wasn't dead, didn't it?

Unless he'd managed to condemn himself to one hell or another. To an existence of nothing *but* pain...

Certainly, the pain he felt was more than enough for him to be in some kind of hell.

Saying that everything hurt didn't begin to cover the extent of the input Aefric was getting from his senses.

It wasn't just that his arms and legs hurt beyond anything he'd known before. Or that his back and his head hurt just as much. And his neck.

No. It couldn't be that simple.

Every single part of Aefric screamed with intense pain. Even places he wasn't normally aware that he could feel at all.

Aefric could feel quite distinct pain from his earlobes and toenails. From his arm hairs. From the insides of his eyelids, and the underside of his tongue.

He was pretty sure he was also feeling pain from his blood vessels, and quite possibly from every nook and cranny of his lungs.

He tried moaning.

Didn't help. Just made him aware of pain in his dry lips and his diaphragm and...

Mercifully, he passed out without ever trying to open his eyes.

He went through two more awakenings into worlds full of pain. The first of these added enough brightness to blind the sun. The second added a cacophonous racket loud enough to deafen an avalanche, or perhaps a hurricane.

The next time he realized he had any awareness, though, wasn't so bad.

Well, everything still hurt as though he'd been beaten by an army of shillelagh-wielding pixies, who each were assigned a separate inch-wide section of his body and given instructions to beat him until their arms could beat no more.

But compared to what he'd been going through previously, it felt almost tolerable.

Why, his mind could even process a sensation that *wasn't* pain. He was smelling something herbal. Couldn't tell what yet. Just that it was herbal and wasn't pain.

Aefric tried moaning.

Nothing got worse.

In fact, he would have sworn, as consciousness faded again, that he heard someone say his name.

Sometime after that, he realized that he'd been awake for a few moments without any pain at all.

He could feel that he was lying down on something padded. That there was a blanket over him. He could even tell that he felt warm.

No pain though?

He didn't trust it.

Clearly this was a dream.

But then, why he should dream of red-tinged darkness and the sounds of an army camp, he couldn't imagine.

What if he was awake?

He could open his eyes and find out.

Then again, if he *was* dreaming, opening his eyes might break the dream. Then the pain would be back.

Should he chance it?

"His breathing has changed." A male voice. Eldrani? Likely. Had the slightly higher pitch, and that lyrical quality to the voice that they all seemed to have.

He didn't recognize the voice though. Nobody he knew.

"I think he wakens," the voice continued.

"Aefric?" Soft tone. A woman's worried voice this time.

Maev?

Aefric opened his eyes. Winced against the brightness, but compared to what he'd been experiencing, the stab of pain was almost a soft caress.

He was in a canvas camp tent, lit by a small oil lamp that hung from a hook above his surprisingly soft bedroll.

Maev's pretty face looked so worried. Her soft gray eyes, filled with concern. He wanted to reassure her. Tried to smile. Tried to speak. Didn't manage either beyond a rough cough.

His hand was raised by someone else's soft touch. Not Maev's. A tin cup was pressed into his hand. Its contents warm.

"Drink." The eldrani man's voice.

Aefric hesitated. Taking drinks from strangers wasn't high on his—

"Please, Aefric," Maev said, putting her hands around his on the cup. "Drink."

Aefric drank. It was an herbal concoction that tasted vaguely of rosemary and orange peel.

Oh, but it was like washing soothing pleasure right down his poor, abused throat.

As he drank, he heard the eldrani man chanting softly, and felt that soothing warmth spread from the drink through the rest of his body. And maybe even past his body to some of Aefric's deeper hurts.

By the time he finished the cup, he could sit up on his own. Managed a weak smile.

Aefric could see the eldrani man now. He had the almost overwhelming beauty of all the eldrani, from his cheekbones to his corn-flower blue hair and periwinkle eyes. He was dressed in yellow robes bearing the hand symbol of the goddess Nilasah, patroness of healers and physickers.

And he could see that Maev was still dressed in her buckskin clothes, with Sylkanis pacing the dirt behind her.

"Ashling's brother Mekel had scouts in the valley when you flew past them," Maev said. And she paused with a frown then, but shook her head against whatever editorial comment she had in mind, and continued. "They saw you fall from the sky. They ... they thought they'd find you dead. Your body broken."

Maev steadied herself through a quick, deep breath.

"They found you unconscious, but apparently unwounded. They brought you back here. Jilskaana here has been treating you ever since."

"Four days," Jilskaana said. "Four days and more you have been in my constant care, and only now do I believe you strong enough to move about. Limitedly."

Jilskaana shook his head. A slow, measured shake of disapproval.

"I know not what you managed to do to yourself," he continued, "but your body was wounded from within. And your mind. And I believe your soul as well. I have done much to set you on the healing path, but you will be some time in recovering completely."

He held up a warning finger.

"Whatever it was you did to put yourself in that state, never do it again. Even Nilasah can do only so much about rampant stupi—"

"*Enough,*" Maev said, in a sharper, more commanding tone than Aefric had heard from her before. Sharper even than when she'd spoken to Ser Grud, while taking him prisoner.

"You know of the snowstorm hammering Malimfar," she said to the healer. "Well this man is clearly its author. We all owe him a great debt of thanks, and I'll not have you insulting him."

Jilskaana's mouth drew wide in a line as he took a slow breath through his nostrils. He nodded.

"Of course, your highness," he said finally. "I will leave you with the patient for now, and see to him later." He glanced at Aefric in disapproval. "He can move about, if he must. So long as he attempts nothing ... *heroic* anytime soon."

With that, Jilskaana left the tent, closing the flap behind him. As he left, he was swearing in High Eldrani about the arrogance and stupidity of wizards.

"A skilled healer, and so pleasant to look upon," Maev muttered, glaring after the eldrani, "but the bedside manner of a borog."

"How—" Aefric started, but Maev turned back to him with eyes blazing.

"*You left me behind,*" she said.

Aefric felt slapped.

"I didn't think there'd be trouble. I—"

"You. Left me. Behind."

"And if I hadn't," Aefric said, "you'd be dead."

"Maybe," she said, crossing her arms. "Or maybe I would have helped you come up with a better plan. One that didn't leave *you* for dead on the battlefield."

Sylkanis stepped up beside her and gave Aefric a look that left no doubt that she was on Maev's side in this matter.

Exhausted and outnumbered, Aefric surrendered.

"Maybe," he said, nodding. "I'm sorry. I shouldn't have left you behind."

"Why did you then?" She sounded a little mollified, but not much.

"I don't know," Aefric said, shaking his head. "I think I was just frustrated with Ashling over lunch. I mean, we could have been planning or at least discussing what we'd find down here, but all she wanted to talk about was—"

"Byrhta?" Maev asked in mock innocence. "Yes, I imagine that must've been annoying for you. Imagine how much worse it would be if you *married* Byrhta. People forever wanting to talk about her, and not about whatever—"

"Are you jealous?" Aefric asked, wonder in his voice.

"Not at all," Maev said primly. "Of course, had you come to *my* chambers the night before, perhaps you would have been spared Ashling's thorough jealousy."

"Perhaps," Aefric said. "If you didn't send me away."

"There is that," she said, chin high. "Perhaps I would have sent you back to your bed alone and lonely."

"No," Aefric said. "You would have sent me running back to Byrhta." He attempted a teasing smile with tired lips. "Byrhta, with her—"

"Don't you *dare* finish that sentence," Maev said.

"Give me a reason not to."

Maev grabbed Aefric's head in both hands and kissed him urgently. A kiss that told him just how worried she'd been.

But then the kiss slowed into something more pleasurable and languorous. And when she pulled back, she smiled and ran her fingers through Aefric's hair.

"I thought you weren't jealous," Aefric teased.

"Of you sharing the bliss moment with Byrhta, I'm not." Maev tilted her head from side to side. "I just know how charming she can be. And I don't like the idea of you considering what kind of duchess she'd make, or what kind of children she'd give you."

Aefric drew breath to answer that, but the tent flap flew open. Ser Beornric came in, with Karbin right on his heels.

One day. One day Aefric would get to *finish* a conversation with Maev. At least, he dearly hoped he would.

THE SMALL CANVAS TENT WHERE AEFRIC LAY CONVALESCING FELT positively crowded now, with Ser Beornric and Karbin bursting in, both so full of energy and news.

So long as neither of them tried to make him get up, or make Maev move away from him. If either of them did that, he'd be looking for a new captain of his personal guard, and a new court wizard.

And possibly a new way to dispose of two bodies...

"Your grace!" Ser Beornric said. The knight was in his full plate armor, and accoutered for battle. "You're alive! You're awake! Thank Nilasah. What happened?"

"I already told you what happened," Karbin said, turning to Aefric as though to give a refresher lesson to his former apprentice. "Every wizard has limits about how much magic they can work. How much power they can control."

Karbin shook his head and grimaced. "Now in the case of our duke here, those limits are harder to gauge, for reasons he well knows."

Aefric gave his old mentor a sheepish grin, while Maev sat up and pillowed his head on her lap. Her fingers gently stroked his forehead.

"But it is clear," Karbin continued, "that his grace pushed himself well beyond those limits." He frowned at Aefric. "You should be dead. You should have burned yourself out from the inside. And even if you didn't, that fall should have killed you. I know you couldn't have managed to slow your fall magically."

"You sound displeased that your duke still lives," Maev said, archly.

"Not displeased," Karbin said quickly. "Believe me. That last thing I want to do is bury my old friend, Aefric." He shook his head again. "But I don't understand how I'm talking to a living man and not a corpse."

"I don't know," Aefric said, frowning. "Last thing I remember is falling. And my mind playing tricks on me. Images of the sun, like two silver eyes. The wind like a kiss on my forehead."

"Silver eyes?" Karbin asked pointedly.

"You think?" Aefric said. "But why would she?"

"Why would who?" Maev asked impatiently. "Don't tell me you have another suitor."

"If she's his suitor, your highness, no mortal woman stands a chance," Karbin said with a smile. "I'm talking about Kalinda. She who became the goddess of magic at the end of the Godswalk Wars."

"But why would she?" Aefric asked again.

"Perhaps she approved of the risk you took, and the reason for the risk."

Aefric frowned, disbelieving. The gods had never come to his aid before, except through the work of their priests.

Still, that raised an important question that had yet to be answered for Aefric.

"Did my spell work?"

The other three all smiled at each other.

"Why not come see for yourself?" Maev asked, and helped him up.

It took longer for him to stand than he liked. And he was glad to have both Maev and the Brightstaff to help him walk on unwilling legs.

Aefric was stopped just outside his tent by several other well-wishers. All soldiers and knights of his own personal guard, who wished to offer their thanks and praise that their duke was alive and returned to them.

Beyond his personal guard, though, and the princess', there were not many in this encampment. So where was everyone?

He was led to a ridge overlooking the river valley, and down below he could see the fires of the camps of ... at least six thousand soldiers, on this side of the Indecisive River.

"How long was I out?" Aefric asked.

"Four days," Maev said. "Down below, you see Ashling's forces under the command of her brother Mekel, and your own, under the command of Countess Faenella."

"More are still coming," Karbin said. "The troops from River-break, Felspark and Norra arrived only today and are still setting camp there, to the west. Havenford's troops are due to arrive by river at first light. And the king's forces have been sighted to the east, pressing their march through the river valley. At least eight thousand strong. Should be here by evening."

"Then I did it?" Aefric asked, with a breathless laugh of disbelief. "I bought enough time for our forces to get here?"

"You did more than that, *your grace*," Karbin said, handing Aefric a spyglass.

Aefric raised it to his eye and looked across the river valley.

He started in amazement.

The valley itself was still lush and green. But up the ridge he could see glinting crystals of frost. The passes that led down into the valley were all choked with snow. He had no clear object for comparison, but his guess was that the snow must've been ten feet deep.

And from what he could see up above the rim, Malimfar beyond the valley had turned to a world of ice and snow.

"From what I heard from Mekel's scouts," Maev said, "the blizzard came down fierce and strong. And it didn't stop. It continued dumping snow down on them for days. I don't think it's stopped yet."

"It's stopped," Karbin said. "It stopped," — he looked significantly at Aefric — "as our duke here regained full consciousness."

"They must be freezing to death up there," Ser Beornric said.

"Assuming they haven't retreated," Maev said. "They'd be fools to stay."

"Retreat isn't easy for them," Ashling said, approaching on foot, flanked by Ser Limic and Sirondfar. "My wizard here tells me that even their exit is choked by snow."

"His grace," Sirondfar said, with one eyebrow high, "was quite thorough."

"They can retreat," Ser Limic said, sounding unconcerned. "In fact, I'd be willing to bet that the mercenary companies have fled already. Possibly looting the countryside as they go, to make up for their lost wages."

"Safe bet," Ser Beornric said, frowning. "Most mercenaries would run from any enemy that could call a storm like that as its opening strike. They'd be terrified of what could follow. And clearly Malimfar's own forces are in no shape to make them behave themselves as they leave."

"My brother," Ashling said, sounding amused, "is torn between being furious with you for stealing his chance for glory and honor, and grateful that he was spared leading his men into a slaughter."

She shook her head. "I'm not sure which way he's leaning right now."

"Gratitude," Ser Limic said in that rough voice of hers. "I had a chat with him about the price of glory."

"It seems I owe you an even greater debt than I expected," Ashling said, looking at Aefric thoughtfully. "I'll have to come up with some way to thank you."

"I'm sure that's not—" Aefric tried, but Ashling spoke over him.

"And rest assured, I won't forget this. Twenty-four thousand soldiers, at last count. Plus the siege engines, and more." She shook her head, gazing at the land around her. "Eadred would have rolled over the river valley and kept going. Might not have stopped until he reached the Threepeaks."

"If then," Ser Limic said. "I still think he would have turned east toward Armityr."

"I *will* find a way to thank you, Aefric," Ashling said. "But for the moment..."

She shook Aefric's hand, kissed him on both cheeks, and gave him a small gold brooch, studded with sapphires.

Aefric's empty stomach growled so loudly that Ser Beornric laughed before he could stop himself.

"And perhaps something to eat," Ashling said, smiling.

AFTER A SUPPER OF ROAST BOAR, SERVED WITH SLICED APPLES IN trenchers of honeyed oat bread, Aefric felt ready to go back to sleep for another aett or so.

The sun hung low in the western sky, looking as sleepy as he felt. As though it didn't have enough energy to make the rest of the trip down below the Risen Sea to the west, and might just lie where it was for the night, if no one minded.

Aefric understood the feeling. He sat leaning on a camp chair, fairly certain that he was being held up by the plate-armored leg of one of his knights.

He wasn't even sure, in the moment, which knight. He could look, but he knew they didn't like him to draw attention to them, when they were on duty.

Which was also why he couldn't ask Ser Beornric, who sat to his left, laughing at some joke made my Ser Limic, who sat facing the knight across the small camp fire.

Maev, to Aefric's right, and Ashling, directly opposite her, were both laughing as well. Must've been a funny joke.

Well, perhaps not so funny as all that. Sirondfar and Karbin weren't laughing. So maybe it wasn't a joke that was funny to magic-users. Maybe that was why Aefric wasn't laughing.

Or maybe he was just too tired.

Certainly Sirondfar was staring pensively at Aefric, and Aefric wasn't even sure he wanted to ask what that was about. Even though he was quite sure that he would normally have asked.

Right then, it seemed like too much trouble. He had a belly full of boar, which had been served with a good, dry wine. He was warm from the fire and warm from the sun. But not too warm because of a slightly chilly breeze coming from the south.

He felt good. As though he should either go to sleep, or maybe say something sweet to Maev. Maev. Who'd worried about him so. She deserved to have him say sweet things to her.

But what?

Maybe something about her eyes. Those big, soft gray eyes of hers. Like soothing mist maybe.

Aefric opened his mouth to say something to Maev about her eyes.

A trumpet blew a fanfare, and a herald called out from somewhere not *too* awful near, "Make way for his majesty, the king!"

Then everyone was standing up, so Aefric had to stand too, which just felt like way too much work. Sitting back down sounded like a much better idea. Lying back down sounded like a better idea still.

So why was he standing?

Wait. He wasn't just standing. He was walking. Well, shuffling along, helped by the Brightstaff in his hand. Yes. The Brightstaff was in his hand, and the wand Garram was in its sheath at his side.

How the heck had he held onto those things while falling unconscious for several hundred feet?

That question spiked wakefulness all through Aefric's system. He would have sworn, just for a moment, he heard silvery, ethereal laughter.

So. His life had been saved by the goddess Kalinda, huh?

Right then it didn't seem so hard to believe.

Aefric was standing now on a hard, rocky trail at the edge of their small encampment. The trail would lead all the way down into the valley. And coming up the trail was King Colm on his white destrier, surrounded by knights in gleaming armor, two of whom carried the royal banner.

One banner the golden oak tree on a field of forest green. The other, the Armyr battle flag: a wide golden X on a forest green background.

Beyond the king, in the valley below, Aefric could see that the king's troops were setting up their camp for the night, right up against the river.

"Well," King Colm called as he leaped down from his steed. He was wearing plate armor of blued steel, enameled with the royal crest. Though he wasn't wearing the helmet right now, he had been recently. His black hair with its smattering of gray still bore the creases.

At his side, he wore a heavy broadsword.

"What's this I hear?" King Colm said, with a big smile that stretched wide his bushy mustache. "I ride all this way to aid my duchess in her hour of need, and here my new duke has already won the day?"

"Well, your majesty," Ser Limic started, but he waved her to silence.

"I already know everything," he said. "Between the reports of my wizard and my scouts, I'm very much up to date about what Malimfar is doing at present."

He laughed. "And what they're mostly doing is turning tail and running. Their morale is broken. Their mercenaries have deserted them. Yes, I think Eadred is in a right fix."

"Then what shall we do about this?" Ashling asked. "How shall we make them pay for what they've done? Trying to turn Aefric's vassals against him? Trying to turn Aefric against me? Trying to seize lands and more from us both, including some of your royal lands?"

"I think they're paying a fairly steep price right now," King Colm said easily. "This little venture has cost Eadred plenty, and will cost him even more before those mercenaries are gone from his lands."

"Not enough," Ashling said, steel in her eyes. "Not enough by half."

"I suppose you'd have me seize their half of the valley," King Colm asked, amused. "Is that it?"

"Seems only fair," she said.

"No," King Colm said. "It's too much. If I do that, Eadred will have no choice but to try to take it back. Then the wars would go on for years. The valley would be ruined."

He looked into the distance for a moment, then shook his head firmly. "No. That's not the way."

"What then?" Ashling said.

"Is this yours to decide," King Colm asked, matching the steel in Ashling's eyes, "or mine?"

She didn't give an inch.

"It is yours, of course, your majesty," Ashling said. "As your most *humble* and *loyal* vassal, I seek only to know how my liege lord will ensure that his vassals are not abused again next spring."

Gods, the sword that could have been forged from that woman's words.

"That's more like it," King Colm said, apparently ignoring Ashling's tone and focusing on her content. "Eadred, of course, shall pay us the cost of mustering, marching and feeding our armies as we came here to stop his unwarranted invasion. I'll see to that."

"He'll argue the point," Aefric said. "Since he never left his own territory. He may even argue that you, through me, struck first."

"Let him try," King Colm said with a laugh. "He mustered some twenty-five thousand soldiers, many of them mercenaries, at my southern border. There's not a court in the land which will believe he had anything in mind other than invasion."

He clapped Aefric on the shoulder. "No, my friend. Your actions will not turn the other kings and lords against me. If anything, they're likely to improve their estimation of us."

"What about Malimfar?" Ashling asked. "Surely you have something more in mind than a little gold."

"I do, as a matter of fact," King Colm said with a smile. "Until today, we've shared the mouth of the Indecisive River with Malimfar. As of today, that ends. I intend to march right down the river and take possession of *both* sides."

He cocked an eyebrow at Ashling. "I trust you will not object to this small gain in land?"

Ashling's eyes glinted at the promise of such a gain.

Not much land, true, but a large increase in her power. She would control all trade between the Indecisive River and the Risen Sea.

"Your majesty's wisdom knows no bounds," she said, sounding much more sincere and offering her hand.

King Colm gave it a perfunctory kiss.

"As for you, my friend," King Colm said, turning to Aefric, "I'll have to find a way to thank you." He nodded his head at Ashling. "And so will she."

"As I've already told him," Ashling said pointedly.

King Colm laughed. "Just making sure. And now, unless I'm very much mistaken, that can only be my daughter, dressed as though she intends to lead a scouting party once more?"

Maev stepped forward.

"Father," she said, "Surely you did not expect me to sit idly by while a foreign power—"

"Of course not," King Colm said, waving away the idea. "You're a Stronghand, after all. Like your brother, you're probably irritated that Aefric here has stolen the day's thunder and left none for you."

"Not at all," Maev said, smiling at Aefric.

But Aefric had a different question. "Prince Killian is here?"

"Here and arguing with your Countess Faenella for the right to command all your troops," King Colm said with a laugh. "The boy was *supposed* to come home as soon as you reached Water's End." He cocked an eyebrow at Maev. "Much as *his sister* was supposed to return home, as soon as the countess reached her castle. And yet I find both of them here in the field with you."

He turned and clapped Aefric on the shoulder.

"They're too much like their father," King Colm said. "Always going where the action is."

He turned back to Maev, who looked relieved about something.

"You can ride with me out to the coast, but this will be your last scouting assignment for a while. I have a mission for you." King Colm smiled. "The new king of Varondam, Dalius Swiftblade the Third, is very much interested in an alliance with Armyr."

His smile widened while his daughter paled.

"I think you'll like him. I got to meet him during the Godswalk Wars, while his father was still king in Varondam. He's a rather dashing young man. Quick with both wit and blade. Fond of hunting, as well."

Maev closed her eyes and said, "You mean…"

"Yes," King Colm said. "We've begun negotiations for you to marry him. I think you'll make an excellent match. And with Malimfar trying to cause us trouble, an alliance with Varondam would serve us well."

He turned to Aefric. "In case you don't know, Varondam is Malimfar's southern neighbor along the coast, and a sea power in its own right." He smiled at Ashling. "We'll have Malimfar in a pincer. Eadred wouldn't dare object to our taking the mouth of the Indecisive."

He clapped his hands together. "It's perfect."

"Yes," Maev said, hollowly. "Perfect."

When Aefric met her eyes, she looked trapped.

"Your majesty," Aefric began, but Ashling spoke quickly over him.

"Yes, Aefric, I know. We're all eager to see this wrapped up. But with the king's forces here, I'm sure he'll give you and yours leave to go home. He certainly can't say you haven't done your part."

"Your part and then some," King Colm said with a smile. "By all means. Send word to your armies to break camp and return home at first light. Ashling and I can handle it from here."

"I…" Aefric started, but Ashling frantically shook her head where King Colm couldn't see. He puffed out a breath. "Thank you, your majesty. We'll do that."

"Excellent," King Colm said with a smile. "And don't worry, my friend. I'll find some way to repay you."

He turned and made a point of cocking an eyebrow at Ashling. "And so will my wife's sister."

"As she has already said she will," Ashling said, matching his raised eyebrow.

The king smiled again, and turned back to his daughter.

"Now, Maev, come along. We have a great deal to discuss."

King Colm put an arm around his daughter and led her back to the horses, where Aefric noted that an extra horse sat ready for her. Sylkanis trotted along beside them.

Maev gave Aefric a wistful look over her shoulder as King Colm led her away, still talking.

Aefric was pretty sure he mirrored Maev's expression as he watched her walk away.

***

THE SUNSET WAS JUST TURNING RED.

The warmth of the day was beginning to cool, warning of the onset of evening.

Aefric stood on the rocky outcropping where he and the others had been dining. Most of them laughing, even. All of them celebrating his recovery with boar and good wine.

Then the king had arrived, and everything changed.

He'd opened negotiations toward a marriage for Maev.

And Aefric couldn't even talk to her about it. Because King Colm was taking her with him out to the coast, while Aefric had been told to take his troops and go home.

Aefric watched as Maev mounted the horse that had been brought for her. She gave him one last longing look before giving him a small wave goodbye.

Aefric waved back. His hand lingered in the air even after she'd turned away.

Their horses trotted away down the pass toward the river valley below.

Aefric stared after them. After Maev.

And then they rounded the first turn and were gone.

Maev, with her teasing smile and her love of action.

Gone. Off to be married, with no idea when he would see her again.

And Aefric had just let it happen.

He didn't just feel tired now. He felt numb.

Ser Beornric cleared his throat from off to Aefric's left. "I'll, uh, go see to giving the orders, your grace."

"Yes," Karbin said, "I'll join you."

Ser Limic and Sirondfar departed as well, leaving Aefric more or less alone with Ashling.

Aefric turned from the trail at last to look at the duchess, whose blue eyes regarded him with sympathy.

"Why?" Aefric asked. "He said he owed me."

"He does," Ashling said, putting a reassuring hand on Aefric's arm. "As do I. And neither of us will forget it. And the truth is, if you asked him for Maev's hand right now, he might grant it. Colm can be impulsive that way, especially when he's feeling generous."

Aefric frowned. "Then why—"

"Two reasons," Ashling said, "and the first should be obvious to you."

Maybe it should have been, but Aefric was too thoroughly exhausted to think of it. He shook his head.

"Tell me, Aefric," Ashling said gently. "Have you ever discussed marriage with Maev?"

"No," he said, then grimaced as realization spread through him.

"Ah," Ashling said with a sympathetic smile. "I see you under-stand now."

He nodded. "If I'd asked her father for her hand without asking her first, she'd never forgive me."

"Just so."

"I could have asked for something lesser, though, couldn't I?" Aefric asked. "The chance to get to know her better and—"

"No," Ashling said. "That isn't how life works for nobles. Marriage is about alliances and children, not love or other emotions. Nothing less than an offer of marriage would have placated Colm. And asking for it without talking to Maev first would have enraged her."

Aefric frowned as he thought about that. What was that phrase Kainemorton used to use for that kind of trap?

Oh, yes. He was caught between the kraken and the ocean floor.

He sighed. "What's the second reason?"

"The second reason," she said, then sighed herself. "This is one I didn't expect you to get. You're too new to your title and position."

She frowned, considering her words.

"Suppose you had talked to Maev in advance and asked Colm for Maev's hand. Suppose also that Colm granted it."

"All right," Aefric said, not seeing where this was going.

"This marriage, it might be good for you, personally. And it would likely good for Maev, personally, as well. I've seen the way she looks at you, after all."

Ashling shook her head. "But the marriage would be a disaster for Armyr."

At Aefric's puzzled expression, Ashling drew a long, slow breath and put one arm around his shoulders.

"An alliance with Varondam could be very good for Armyr. And if Colm gave Maev's hand to you, a mere duke, by preference over another king, he'd *insult* Varondam's king. Thus, increasing the chances that Malimfar could manage an alliance with Varondam in our place."

Aefric sighed, and might have drooped if not for Ashling's arm around his shoulders.

"I suppose you're right," he said.

"I am right, I'm sorry to say. It's the price of our titles." Ashling gave Aefric a gentle shake. "Look at the bright side. Maev is a clever girl. She might find a way to create the alliance without marrying King ... what's his name? Dalius?"

Aefric nodded. Ashling shuddered.

"Horrible name," she said. "If Maev prefers you to him, she might find a way to create the alliance and still get out of the marriage."

"Do you think?"

"If anyone can do it, Maev can," Ashling said. "The trap hasn't been built that that woman can't get out of."

"So there's hope," Aefric said, with a tentative smile.

"There's always hope," Ashling said, giving him another shake.

"Then I owe you a debt of thanks, for helping me keep my mouth shut."

"Think nothing of it," Ashling said, her voice getting lighter as she spoke. "And if Maev *does* marry him, perhaps you could consider taking Byrhta Ol'Caran as your bride."

She shrugged. "Or if not, perhaps we could marry each other. You're really fairly attractive, for a man. Though far too masculine for my usual tastes, of course." She smiled. "Still. We'd produce gorgeous, powerful children, you and I. And just think of all the will-ing, beautiful women we could share. They'd be lining up from our castles to the sea."

Aefric laughed, which, from the look in Ashling's eyes, had been her goal.

"And I can promise you," she said, leading him back towards the main part of the encampment. "For the chance to investigate the mysteries of Byrhta Ol'Caran's beauty, I'd be more than willing to bring you the bliss moment myself, from time to time."

Now they were both laughing.

"Oh, Byrhta Ol'Caran," Ashling said with a sigh. "Is her skin truly as soft as it looks? I keep thinking that it can't be. That no skin could possibly be so soft. But then I look at her again, and I can't help thinking that hers might be. Is it? Tell me, Aefric, please."

He didn't tell her, of course, but that may not have mattered, really. Ashling may well have been going on about Byrhta just to give Aefric room to think about all the things she'd told him about Maev, Varondam and marriage.

She would make a strange friend, Duchess Ashling Fyrenn. But far better to have her as a strange friend than a crafty foe.

16

The Nilasah priest Jilskaana might have been done praying over Aefric, but he'd been good enough to leave behind a supply of that marvelous, blessed herbal mixture, along with instructions. Aefric was to drink a cup on sleeping, on wakening, and with every meal for the next three days.

So when Aefric awoke in his canvas camp tent, stiff and sore in every part of his body, he was only too happy when a servant handed him a steaming tin cup of the rosemary and orange peel brew.

There was more to it than those two ingredients. Aefric knew that. But those were the major tastes and smells he noted as he drank it down. And those were the tastes that lingered as ease and warmth spread all through him, diminishing his stiffness and soreness, if not banishing them completely.

Aefric frowned, though, at the sight of the servant. He hadn't seen any around camp the night before, and had the impression that his personal guard had been handling all the camp details without even the aid of squires.

Further, this particular servant was dressed in royal livery.

Well, that at least explained why Aefric didn't recognize the young man.

"Thank you," Aefric said.

"Of course, your grace. I was instructed to see to your breakfast this morning, while your people break camp, as well as to give you this."

He bowed as he handed Aefric a letter, then left the tent.

The letter was addressed to him and sealed red wax, impressed with the bow and nocked arrow of Maev's personal sigil.

Aefric broke the seal, and spoke a word to fill the dim tent with more than enough light to read Maev's words.

My dearest Aefric,

Would that we were not parted tonight.

More than that. Would that I could have lingered long enough in your duchy to play out our game of hunter and prey the way it was meant to be played. With us sharing both roles over another aett or two, until the heat that burns in us both grew white hot, all but searing everyone around us.

To finally lie with you after such a chase would have been truly glorious.

But as we now lack that time, tonight I would have come to your tent. So that I might not have to travel to Varondam without first knowing the bliss of your sweetest touch.

Presuming, of course, that you did not turn me away. That might have served me right, for the way I have teased you.

Alas, though, Father will not allow me to leave his camp. Perhaps he fears I would vanish into the countryside, where his trackers would never find me.

Perhaps I would. Perhaps Sylkanis and I would make our way north all the way to Water's End.

I can just imagine the look on your face, when we turned up at your castle gate with no warning. With the whole of the countryside out seeking us.

Perhaps, instead, I would linger in the woods near Water's End. Waiting for you to go riding or hunting, only to make you my quarry.

Yes. That thought pleases me. I hope it pleases you too.

But it is not to be. This time it is I who must leave you behind.

I ride at first light with Father's forces to claim the river's mouth for

Armyr, and for Merrek. And after that, I must sail for Varondam, and meet my would-be betrothed. This King Dalius.

Father believes you almost asked for my hand tonight. I told him you would never have done such a thing. Not without discussing the matter with me first.

Nevertheless, as I write this, he bids me thank you for not doing so. The request would have put him in a difficult position.

And now I must go.

It seems so unfair that this letter is all I get for a goodbye. I cannot even kiss you before I leave. So I will have to hope our last kiss burns as brightly in your memory as it does in mine.

And remember — if Byrhta Ol'Caran makes clear that she seeks more from you than the bliss moment, you must tell me. She and I will have to talk.

For do not mistake our hunt for finished.

I am far from done with you, Aefric Brightstaff.

Yours most truly,

Maev.

The letter smelled of Maev's honeysuckle scent.

Aefric read it three times before the servant called him to breakfast. Then he had to dress hurriedly, in a simple cotton shirt of Deepwater gray with his ducal sigil over the heart, and navy blue pants of the same material.

Camp clothes, fit for fighting. Fair enough.

His usual boots were waiting for him, though, and a cloak of soft gray wool, to which the brooch that Ashling had given him had been affixed.

Aefric enjoyed a quick breakfast of fried eggs and crisp bacon, served in a trencher of honeyed oat bread. He ate sitting at a small, collapsible camp table under torchlight, for the sun was just now beginning to rise.

As he broke his fast, all around him his personal guard broke camp and prepared to leave. The sounds of their work, and their calls to one another as they did, gave Aefric the strangest sense that he was still fighting the Godswalk Wars.

That the wars had never ended, and everything since — his title, Maev, Byrhta, all of it — had been nothing more than a dream.

An uncomfortable thing to ponder, as he wolfed down his breakfast, washing it down with good, clean water from the river.

As he was finishing, Ser Beornric approached.

"Good morning, your grace," he said with a big smile, then paused as Aefric started laughing in relief. "Are you well, your grace?"

"Fine," Aefric said, shaking his head. "First camp I've been in since the wars."

"Ah," Ser Beornric said in commiseration. "I had the same feeling my first morning here. I assure you, though. The Godswalk Wars are over, and you haven't dreamed being made duke, or ... well, any of the rest of it."

Was Ser Beornric actually reddening a bit?

Oh. Aefric still had Maev's letter in one hand, where he would normally have been holding the Brightstaff, which stood tall beside him instead.

Aefric folded the letter, and replaced it in its envelope. He tucked it safely into a wide pouch on his leather belt. It was a pouch he usually used for scrolls, but it would hold a letter just as well.

"How close are we to leaving?" Aefric asked, thinking of that letter's author. Perhaps, while camp was struck, he could take a quick flight down—

"The camp and your troops will be ready to leave before the sun finishes rising. I presume that, before we leave, you'll want to thank your vassals for hurrying to your aid?"

Aefric sighed. Duty first.

Karbin joined Aefric and Ser Beornric and two of the soldiers of Aefric's personal guard as they rode from camp to camp. He first thanked Countess Faenella, then Baroness Herewyn of Norra, Baroness Blaewyn of Felspark, and Baron Osmaer of Havenford.

Faenella seemed pleased to have been provided a way to test the discipline of her new troops without having to blood them.

Herewyn was glad to know that her recent troubles with banditry were ended.

Blaewyn was pleased to hear that her river valley was safe, and that trade pressure would stop.

Osmaer was glad they'd avoided any killing, though he lectured Aefric about the potential damage he'd done with that blizzard.

"However," he said, after Aefric had patiently listened to the lecture, "in this one instance, your actions saved a great many lives, and likely a great deal more damage to this beautiful river valley. Therefore" — he swirled his hand through a gesture of benediction — "in the name of Halstaffur the Green Lord, I absolve you of any harm committed by your blizzard."

He then winked. "Just don't go making a habit of it."

Strangely, even though there was no magic to Osmaer's gesture and words of absolution, Aefric found himself feeling lighter. Easier.

It might have helped that each of his vassals lauded him for calling the blizzard and sparing their troops the battle. Each of them also promised him a proper feast of celebration, the next time they hosted him.

Then, it was time for Aefric to ride to the last baronial camp among his troops. Riverbreak.

He paused then, frowning as he looked over the camp, with its at least several hundred soldiers.

"Who commands here?" Aefric asked Ser Beornric.

Ser Beornric didn't get to answer. Before he could, a short fanfare was played, just as had happened with the other camps...

...where a noble commanded.

And out of her tent stepped Vercy, dressed for battle. She wore a chain shirt and hauberk over a simple cotton tunic and leggings. At her belt she wore a pair of whip-thin rapiers, one slightly shorter than the other.

For a young woman still shy of the age of majority and obviously still growing, she moved quite comfortably in her weapons and armor.

"Your grace," she said, bowing and doffing a chain greave to offer her hand for a kiss. "The forces of Riverbreak are yours to command."

Aefric kissed her hand, then said, "Why are you here, and not at my keep under guard?"

A short, slender, orange-haired knight stepped up beside Vercy. The knight smiled with the beauty of the eldrani in her features.

Ser Vria, of Aefric's own personal guard.

"She is and has been under guard, your grace." Ser Vria said with a small bow. "It occurred to me that there was no point wasting a guard on her at Behal, when she could be fighting for her duke and for her family's honor."

Ser Vria smiled at Vercy, who held her head high and looked pleased.

"An offer I was most happy to take, your grace," Vercy said. "Just as I shall now be happy to return to Behal now that the day is won, and await the king's justiciar."

Aefric chuckled. "Well, done, Vercy. I'll expect you on our ship when it leaves. And I trust you'll have no need to come armed."

"As I shall not be riding to battle, I shall dress as a proper noble-woman, your grace."

"I have no doubt," Aefric said. And he gave her and her troops his formal thanks for swiftly answering his call to arms in defense of king and country.

Then, as he rode back toward his own camp, he asked Ser Beornric, "Did you approve Ser Vria's decision?"

"I was already sailing south at your command," Ser Beornric said with a grin. "But Vria told me Ser Grey approved it."

"I hope so. We can't have my knights making decisions that big. I approve in this case, but still." He shook his head. "How did River-break's troops respond to taking orders from Vercy?"

"Ser Vria tells me they followed without question. Though she also tells me that Vercy needs to listen more to her advisers on military matters, until she has some seasoning of her own."

"Eager to prove herself?" Aefric asked. "Or something more worrying."

"Ser Vria believes the former."

"Good. Not that I'm in a hurry to season any of them." He looked out over all the troops that had ridden, marched, and sailed in his name. "I'd much rather see us enjoy a nice, long peace."

"As would I, your grace," Ser Beornric said. "As would I."

AS THE TROOPS BOUND FOR THE RIVER'S MOUTH WERE MARCHING OR riding — not sailing — Ashling lent Aefric the skills of Sirondfar, to see him swiftly and safely back up the river to Behal.

Ashling even gave Aefric kisses on both cheeks after they shook hands, before parting. He'd have to remember to ask someone what that gesture meant.

Ser Grey. Ser Grey would know.

Aefric was impressed at the speeds Sirondfar's winds could drive them up the Tainfyr River. Not so great as the speeds they'd managed on the way down, of course. They sailed against the current this time.

And yet their speed was such that Aefric could tell the trip would not take two full days.

And his ship was not alone in enjoying these magicked winds.

The ships that had carried his troops south from Behal now sailed the same winds back north, and rode the river not far behind their duke.

Aefric spent the trip resting in his cabin. That blessed herbal concoction did good things for helping him heal, but he still felt exhausted most of the time.

In truth, he knew it was good that he hadn't tried to fly to Maev for at least a kiss goodbye. He wasn't sure he could have survived the flight there. Let alone the flight back.

The rest, and the warmed herbal drink, did him a world of good though. By the time they docked at Behal, he felt almost himself again.

Not that he skipped even a single dose of his drink. The last thing he wanted to do was go against the orders of a priest of Nalasah. They had forgotten more about the healing arts than most ever learned.

It was late afternoon of the second day, by the time Aefric was riding Windsong up the long, winding road from the docks to his castle at Behal.

He rode through the portcullis to a twelve-trumpet fanfare, and all his courtiers cheering and throwing roses as he passed.

Aefric wanted nothing more than a bath and a change of clothes. But as Ser Grey greeted him, she made it clear that he had to stop and let his people praise him for winning another war.

Hardly how Aefric would have put it himself. It seemed that his deed had grown with the telling. His courtiers here at Behal buzzed about how he'd frozen Malimfar's army solid, and that the whole of that country was now mired in deepest winter.

So many names and faces. So many people in the warm, late afternoon sun. All wanting to offer words of thanks and praise. All wanting their hands kissed. Most of them hinting that they wanted other things as well, whether patronage or financing or simply his attention and company.

Several of the young noblewomen had lingered nearby through Aefric's arduous process of arriving. All of them perfumed and wearing flattering spring dresses, with their hair artfully arranged. Each with a glint of hope in their eye.

Which might have been why Byrhta Ol'Caran waited to be the last to greet Aefric.

She wore a light chiffon gown of canary yellow. A simple thing, with little more adornment than a small emerald hanging on a gold chain around her neck.

When she walked up, smiling at Aefric, two-thirds of the lingering noblewomen abandoned their vigil in a huff. Half of the remainder left when they saw Aefric's return smile.

Much as he missed Maev — and that was a great deal — he had to admit he was happy to see Byrhta again.

"Aefric," she said, and when the last lingering noblewomen heard her call their duke by name, they turned and left.

"I'm so glad you're alive and safe," Byrhta continued. "I prayed nightly to Vera the Watchful for you, and now I must make an offering of thanks that she has heard my prayers."

"And my thanks to you for your prayers," Aefric said, kissing her offered hand. "Will you dine with me tonight?"

"Happily. And I was hoping we might share a bottle of *flisnaath* in celebration of your victorious return. I do hope to hear all about your triumph."

"Your grace," Ser Grey said, speaking low and stepping in close. "It would be most meet for you to host a feast of celebration tonight, for your victory."

"I would certainly understand," Byrhta said quickly.

"No," Aefric said, shaking his head. "No feast until my work is done. I sail tomorrow for Castle Vabarett in Goldenfall, to meet with the Count Cyneric."

"May I accompany you?" Byrhta asked.

"I was hoping you would," Aefric said with a nod, while raising one hand to forestall an objection from Ser Grey. To her, he said, "After I am done there, I will sail, at last, for Water's End."

Aefric drew a deep breath and sighed.

"*There* I shall host a feast, celebrating both my victory" — though in Aefric's head, he said *survival* rather than *victory* — "and my finally claiming my rightful ducal seat."

"Of course, your grace," Ser Grey said with a nod.

"And now," Aefric said, "if you will excuse me, Byrhta, I need a *bath*."

Byrhta laughed, and for a moment he thought she might ask to join him. She didn't though, and he was grateful.

Then Ser Grey was escorting Aefric to his rooms, along with a small complement of his personal guard, while Ser Beornric saw to the getting his troops properly dispersed to their normal assignments.

"Did you approve Ser Vria taking Vercy down to the river valley?" He asked her along the way.

"I did, your grace," she said. "Should I have kept her here under guard?"

"Under most circumstances," Aefric said, "probably. But in this case I'd say you did the right thing. This was a rather unusual set of circumstances."

"Indeed," Ser Grey said. "Though I must admit that the king's justiciar wasn't best pleased with my decision."

Aefric stopped walking. "The king's justiciar is here?"

"Yes, your grace," Ser Grey said, then grimaced. "Forgive me. I got distracted when you spoke of changing Ornella's plans for your dinner tonight."

"Take me to the justiciar," Aefric said, with a sigh.

They were already on the second floor of the castle when Aefric said that. Which meant that Ser Grey had to lead him back down to the first floor, then down a narrow hall to a guarded door.

The door led to a narrow, winding staircase, descending past the normal basement level with its storage to a lower, subbasement, where only prisoners were held.

It was cold down here. Grimy stone floor, and unrelieved stone walls and ceiling. Dark, too, lit only by periodic torches. The smell of mildew and less pleasant things.

They passed a half-dozen stout wooden doors, each barred from the outside, to reach one where Aefric could hear more behind the door than the scuffling of rats.

This door was guarded by two well-groomed soldiers in the king's livery and bearing patches at both shoulders displaying the three-edged sword of Taesark, the god of justice.

Behind that door, Aefric could hear voices.

"Ser Aefric Brightstaff, Duke of Deepwater, to speak with the justiciar," Ser Grey said to the guard on the right.

She nodded. Knocked a four-beat square on the door, and called through it in a high, clear voice.

"Duke Aefric to see you, justiciar."

She went back to guarding.

A moment later, the door opened a crack.

"Come in."

This was the first time Aefric had heard the voice of a justiciar. It was of a middle pitch, but just as he'd always been told, it had no character beyond that. Not masculine or feminine, not pleased or irritated or anything else.

Well, anything else except spooky. To hear a voice so empty of emotion.

Two pitch torches burned in sconces to the left and right, providing both light and heat for the small cell.

Ser Grud, looking pale and wan and wearing only undyed rough-spun, lay back on a stone couch.

Standing over him, the justiciar.

Middling height. Middling build. Brown tunic, breeches, gloves, belt and boots, all of simple roughspun and leaving not an inch of skin showing.

The justiciar's brown cowl was of roughspun as well, and worn drawn down so low that nothing could be seen of the person inside it.

The justiciar gripped an actual triple-edged greatsword in both hands. A simple iron hilt, but a gleaming blade. Held point up, as though in salute.

Aefric could feel Taesark's cold power radiating from that sword.

Addressing Ser Grud, the justiciar said, "You will remain as you are, and you will hear nothing of my converse with his grace."

The justiciar turned then, and still Aefric could see nothing of the person inside the deep cowl.

"Your grace," the justiciar said. "Have you brought Mistress Vercy Ol'Karmak back with you?"

"I have," Aefric said. "She is under guard in her rooms, near her parents. I apologize for—"

"No apology is merited," the justiciar said. "You have returned with her before the investigation concluded."

"May I ask how the investigation proceeds?"

"This one has a strong will," the justiciar said without respect, irritation, or any inflection at all that Aefric could hear. "But I will have the last of my answers before the coming dawn."

"What of the baron, his wife, and their son?"

"You already know the answer about the son."

"Of his guilt, yes, but not his punishment."

"He shall be beheaded for treason, which punishment shall take place in the public square at Armityr."

"And the parents?"

"The crime is severe, but their contribution to it, and thus their guilt, is lesser. And as they are your vassals, I allow you to choose their punishment. Your choices are execution or exile."

"Exile," Aefric said without hesitation.

"So be it. When I leave for Armityr at the conclusion of the investigation, his lordship, Karmody Ol'Karmak, Baron of River-break, and her lordship, Montess Ol'Nastath, Baroness of River-break, shall be stripped of all lands, titles and possessions, both baronial and personal, and exiled from Armyr. Not to return on pain of death."

Aefric's stomach soured. That sounded more severe than he had in mind.

"But—" He said, though he wasn't really surprised when the justiciar spoke over him.

"This is the ruling of the king's justice, as guaranteed by the power of Taesark. Knowing that, would your grace prefer they be executed?"

Aefric sighed and shook his head. "No."

"Then all shall proceed as I have said. Your grace may rest assured that they shall be given simple clothing, a knife for protection, and enough food and water to last an aett. After that they are no longer the crown's concern, or your grace's."

Hearing those words from such a flat, toneless voice gave Aefric no reassurance at all.

"What of the daughter, Vercy?" he asked.

"Unknown," the justiciar said. "I must first investigate. You shall have your answer by dawn."

Aefric nodded. "May I speak on her behalf?"

"Not until I have investigated. Only then will your opinion be entered into consideration before the ruling is finalized."

Aefric frowned, but couldn't think of a way around that.

"Now," the justiciar said, "I return to my inquisition."

"Ser Grud's guilt is unquestionable, is it not?" Aefric asked, surprised.

"Unquestionable," the justiciar said. "But I will have all his crimes from him. I shall balance all wrongs he has committed against the lands and peoples of Armyr. This is the way of justice. The way of Taesark."

"I'll ... leave you to it, then," Aefric said, fighting a shiver, but the justiciar had already turned back to Ser Grud.

As though Aefric were no longer there.

He lost his fight to that shiver, then, and decided that he never wanted to see a justiciar again, if he could avoid it.

Something about even the echo of the justiciar's regard made him feel guilty. Even if he couldn't think of any wrongdoings.

Yes. A bath was definitely in order. And the bathwater better be hot.

<hr>

THE BATH HELPED, THOUGH AEFRIC HAD TO SOAK AND SCRUB A GOOD deal to rid himself of the cold, penetrating regard of that justiciar. And he had a feeling he'd be hearing that toneless voice again in nightmares through the years.

Fortunately, his dinner that night was a quiet affair, with only Byrhta for company. He was still drained by his healing, and after that encounter in the dungeons, he could not have tolerated a loud, raucous feast. He even refused Ser Grey's offer of a minstrel playing the mandolin in a corner.

Byrhta, though, was good company. Aefric felt relaxed with her, and found her very easy to talk with.

The dined in his solarium, seated on large, comfortable chairs, looking out at the ships staying late on the Deepwater, and watching the stars slowly come out in the darkening night sky above.

Their plates shared the small table between their chairs. They dined on marlin steak, served in a tangy sauce, along with a salad of mixed fruits and vegetables, and thinly sliced honeyed oat bread.

They drank only water with dinner, forgoing wine to keep their palates clean for the *flisnaath* later.

Over dinner, he told her all about the river valley. About how he'd flown south, impatient for answers. What he'd seen massing over the ridge in Malimfar. How desperately he'd reached for more power than he'd ever drawn before, and how he'd called forth a torrential blizzard that had hammered Malimfar's forces for four days straight.

She was such an attentive, appreciative audience for the story that he found himself telling her of those silver eyes he'd seen, and that twist of wind that felt strangely like a kiss on his forehead.

"Does it surprise you that the gods take an interest?" she asked, between bites. "They're said to be fond of heroes and madmen."

"And which am I?" he asked, laughing.

"I'm not sure it's possible to be one, without being at least a little bit of the other," she said with laugh.

Aefric was still chuckling about that when Byrhta said something he didn't expect.

"Is it true? What I've heard about Princess Maev being promised to King Dalius of Varondam?"

Aefric could only shake his head in appreciative wonder.

"I'm surprised you aren't the royal spymaster," he said. "As well-informed as you are."

"Who says I'm not?" she said with a saucy glint in her eye. "It's true then?"

"It's true that negotiations have begun," Aefric said, "but matters are far from finalized."

Byrhta considered that as she swiped up a bit of the marlin's sauce and nibbled it from her bread.

"You have sufficient rank to marry her," Byrhta said, then, one eyebrow slightly raised. "If you wondered. Though an alliance with another country would be better for Armyr, the people would support their princess marrying the Hero of Deepwater."

She gave him a wicked grin. "Or what is the new one they're calling you? The Hero of Frozen Ridge?"

"They're *not*," Aefric said.

"They are," she said, with a slight shrug. "Or perhaps it's Hero of the Battle of Frozen Valley. Not sure the skalds have settled on which."

"Skalds?"

"Oh, the songs are being written as we speak." She reached over and patted his arm with a hand that was softer than Ashling would ever want to know. "If you're going to do heroic things, you'll have to accept having songs written about you."

Aefric shook his head. "I believe I'm ready for the *flisnaath*."

"Good," she said. "So am I."

Their dishes were cleared away quickly by Falip, who then brought forth the bottle of *flisnaath* that Byrhta had provided.

She took her turn opening this one, and Aefric noted little ways she differed in how she removed the many corks. Fine details in how she positioned those corks around the bottle before breaking the wax seal.

He was pleased, at least, that he said the words properly when he spoke them with her, as the final cork was removed.

"Nil sachassa ne vili."

This bottle came from the same batch as the previous. It had the exact same dark red color, and varied much the same way from warm cinnamon to cool peppermint and back several times with each sip.

"Have you ever met a justiciar?" Aefric asked.

"Once," Byrhta said with a shudder. "When Arinda was in a dispute with Duchess Ashling. Disturbing creatures. Did you know that they're said not to be of any of the known races?"

"I've heard that," Aefric said, with a nod, "but I don't know that I believe it. Any more than I believe that anyone who willingly picks up their three-edged sword becomes immediately transformed into a justiciar."

"Would save them the time and costs of training up acolytes," Byrhta said, smirking, and Aefric found himself caught up in laughter that hung on longer than he expected, before it finally abated.

"While I'm always glad to have my jokes appreciated," Byrhta said, her eyes narrowed. "I'm not sure this one was *that* funny. Are you mocking me?"

"No," he said quickly. "I think it's just…"

Aefric sighed out a relaxing breath and settled in his chair. "It's been a hard aett. And to come back from that valley and meet a justiciar first thing…" He shook his head. "I'm exhausted. Strained. Still healing. And I feel like parts of me are clenched that may never unclench again."

She nodded, then gave Aefric a small smile. "Perhaps you're ready for another sip?"

"Definitely."

They sipped then, enjoying the shifting sensations and tastes. And between the next several sips, Byrhta led the conversation for a time. Telling of goings on at Behal while Aefric had been off to the south. Of this minor noble and that one, petty disputes and worries about how they might impress their duke and more.

And yet, Byrhta told it all in such a way that they seemed comical. She exaggerated and imitated and kept him laughing.

Finally, they were down to almost the last sip of *flisnaath*, and Aefric was feeling much better. In fact, he asked a question without even thinking about it.

"What does it mean in Armyr when someone kisses you on both cheeks?"

Byrhta pondered that for a moment. "It can mean a couple of things. Most often, these days, it's a blessing given to parents when a child is born."

"Not in this case," Aefric said. "At least, it better not be."

Byrhta made an amused sound. "The kiss on both cheeks can also be a public declaration of friendship, when done between peers among the nobility."

She gave Aefric a sideways look. "Duchess Ashling kissed you on both cheeks, I take it?"

Aefric nodded. "More than one occasion."

"It's an old custom," she said. "Long out of fashion. But then, so is *leaba*."

"So does anything that happens here escape your notice?"

"Not if it's interesting," she said with a half-smile. But then she gave Aefric a more serious look. "You saved her. She knows this. And she's making sure that everyone around knows she knows it."

Aefric started to ask a question, but Byrhta shook her head slowly.

"I need to tell you something that Arinda used to tell me," she said. "Duchess Ashling always has one eye on the future. And she is always alone at the center of what she sees. Please be careful how you trust her."

Aefric pondered that through their last sip of *flisnaath*.

When that sip was finished, Aefric drank his dinner's portion of that odd healing potion. As he finished it, Byrhta spoke.

"You invited me for dinner, Aefric," she said softly. "Dinner is finished, as is our *flisnaath*. Shall I leave, or may I stay with you tonight?"

"Answer me something first?" he asked, just as softly.

"Anything."

"Why did you point out that I have enough status to marry Maev?"

She sighed. "In a way, you just answered your own question." She gave him a small smile, that didn't look humorous or lighthearted. "Over the years, Princess Maev has granted a number of nobles the right to address her by name alone. Every single one of them has quickly disappointed her and lost that privilege. Every single one. But you."

Aefric blinked as he thought about that.

"It is clear how she favors you," Byrhta continued. "And if you marry her, your children will have blood ties to the crown of Armyr *and* the crown of Rethneryl. Add to that the dowry she'd bring, and you would be a prince in all but name. You'd be a fool not to marry her, if you could."

Aefric made a sound of breathless puzzlement. "I guess I just thought—"

"That I aspire to marry you myself?" Byrhta asked, and her smile looked more natural now. "My father certainly has hopes that direction. You're a powerful duke, and they say your very blood is magic."

"And do your hopes align with your father's?"

"Perhaps," she said with more mystery in her smile than Aefric expected. But then she shrugged. "But whether they do or not, I am not a fool. I know well that I am the daughter of your vassal, and not even set to inherit my father's county. I am below your station. And in the aftermath of the wars, have nothing worth mentioning to offer you for a dowry."

She shook her head and frowned. "As wise as you would be to marry Princess Maev, you would be as much a fool to marry me."

Aefric thought of several questions then, but none of them sounded right to ask. So he settled for saying this:

"Maev told me that if you ever seek more from me than the bliss moment, I am to tell her. And then you and she must talk."

"Well then," Byrhta said. "As I enjoy your company even when we're clothed, I suppose sometime in the morning you must send her a rika. And then, when we can, she and I will have to talk."

She stood and gave Aefric a smile that set his heart to racing. A smile that suggested many wicked ideas.

"But as for tonight," she said, sauntering closer, "I have a few ideas about the bliss moment..."

* * *

AEFRIC HAD DEVOUTLY HOPED TO SLEEP IN THAT NEXT MORNING. HE was still recovering, after all. But he was shaken gently awake by candlelight, and as he blinked his eyes open he could tell that the sky past his bedroom windows was still black with night.

"Your grace." Somer's voice, whispering. Which meant that the gentle hand shaking him was hers. "The justiciar is asking for you."

Aefric nodded. Sighed. Moved sore muscles, then regretted it when his little movements caused Byrhta to stir beside him, and make soft, inquisitive sounds.

"Shh," he said, leaning down to kiss her gently. "Go back to sleep."

She tried to pull him back into her warm, sleepy embrace. And Aefric had to admit that her option sounded a great deal more appealing than getting up and dealing with the justiciar.

But he had duties. He gently extricated himself from her grasp, and climbed out of bed.

Somer helped him into a white, muslin dressing gown, then pressed a warm cup into his hands. The twin smells of rosemary and orange peel hit his nose, and Aefric eagerly drank down the healing brew.

Sore muscles eased once more, though he still felt sleepy. But then, the stuff could do only so much.

Aefric followed Somer and her candle through his bedroom, out through his sitting room, to the black oak table near the hallway door, where the justiciar stood waiting.

As Aefric entered the room, the three-edged greatsword appeared in the justiciar's hands, held point up.

"Your grace," the justiciar said in those creepily neutral tones. "You asked to speak on behalf of Mistress Vercy Ol'Karmak. Now is the appropriate time to do so."

Aefric shook away the last of his sleepiness.

Vercy. Right. He could do this. Even though, the way the justiciar currently regarded him, he felt as though a company of dragons sat slavering, waiting for him to say one wrong word so they could devour him in the messiest way possible.

In fact, it was likely an effect of that regard that chased away the last of Aefric's sleepiness. He felt a kind of pressure, closing in on all sides. Demanding truth from him.

He drew a deep breath, and spoke.

"Vercy Ol'Karmak did, of her own volition, bare witness to me of her brother's crimes, and offered such written evidence as she had to support her case. She made no apologies for his behavior, and in no way attempted to bargain on his behalf or lessen his sentence.

"She first attempted to persuade her brother to admit to his crimes himself, and that he did not was not her failure, but Baston's. She made clear that she did all she did because it was right, and she openly fretted about the harm her brother was doing to my duchy, to Merrek, and to Armyr.

"Furthermore. When I was required to call Riverbreak's forces to war, she willingly stepped up to lead when the chance was given. She donned armor and weapons and would have led her troops into battle herself on behalf of Deepwater and Armyr, had such become necessary. And when the matter was settled, she volunteered to return to captivity and await the crown's investigation and judgment.

"In my opinion she has, at every junction, demonstrated her innocence, and conducted herself as befits a noble of Armyr."

The moment he finished, the three-edged sword disappeared.

The instant it did, Aefric sagged forward, panting, as he finished speaking. The pressure was gone, a slight ache in its place.

The words he'd spoken were all his, but he'd felt as though they'd been pulled out of him.

He shivered, at the unnaturalness of the whole experience.

The justiciar's hood twitched in what might have been a nod.

"The investigation is now complete. Mistress Vercy Ol'Karmak is hereby judged innocent and cleared of any and all crimes against Deepwater, Merrek, and Armyr. It shall be left for your grace to determine if she should keep her barony, or if the deeds of her family require her barony to pass to another family line."

"I would have her keep it," Aefric said.

"So be it," the justiciar said. "Your grace is hereby reminded to assign a regent to rule in her stead until she comes of age."

"I'll find one."

"In the matter of Ser Grud Ol'Garan, he is guilty not only of the crimes for which you summoned me, but of others besides. I shall leave a full report with your seneschal. Compensation for his crimes shall be forthcoming."

"All right," Aefric said, uncertainly. He almost asked what those crimes were, but decided reading about them would be more comfortable than hearing the justiciar recite them.

"Does your grace wish me to adjudicate any other matters in the name of the crown?"

"No," Aefric said quickly.

"Then I leave at once for Armityr, taking with me Ser Grud Ol'Garan and Baston Ol'Karmak."

"May Vercy say goodbye to her parents?"

"She may have until Ser Grud is brought up from the dungeons and her parents are called for."

Aefric nodded to Somer, who whisked out of the room to see to it.

The justiciar continued, "At which time they shall be escorted under guard to Ajenmoor and placed on the first available departing ship."

"No matter the destination?"

"So long as the next port of call is not in Armyr, no matter the destination. Until next time, your grace, farewell."

"And you," Aefric said.

The justiciar left then, and Aefric was only too happy to return to bed. Not for more pleasure. Just for the comfort of being held while the sensation of being locked in thrall by the justiciar's sword faded.

Though more sleep, at that point, wasn't going to happen.

17

———

Always so much to do, first thing in the morning. It seemed that the moment he finished enjoying his breakfast of fruit and cheese with Byrhta, Ser Grey was there making sure Aefric took care of a dozen things before he sailed off to Goldenfall.

Aefric and Byrhta were still in their dressing gowns, and he was already getting to work.

It would have been nice to at least watch her dress one more time. After she found out part of what he had to tell her father, she might not be so eager to come to his chambers again.

In the meantime, the chief of the matters for his immediate attention, of course, was designating a regent for Riverbreak, to guide the barony for the two or three years that remained before Vercy reached the age of majority.

Ser Grey had a list prepared, of course, of some fifteen candidates. All of whose names started with "Ler" because they had lands of their own. But none of them were from other baronies, much less his county or ducal lands.

When Aefric asked about that, Ser Grey said, "Each person on this list holds lands in Riverbreak. Lands that will do better if Riverbreak prospers. It's always risky, assigning a regent. The power can ... influence their thinking."

"I want to make sure the regent will train Vercy properly," Aefric said, "as well as taking into account Vercy's views. She's young, but she's not stupid."

Ser Grey grimaced. "Would you prefer to interview them personally? I'm not sure you—"

"Byrhta," Aefric said, seeing her come out of his closet, clad in that canary yellow dress from the night before.

"Afraid I'd leave without giving you a kiss?" Byrhta asked with a smile. "Never fear on that front, Aefric. Though I'll have to sail home on my family ship. I'd like to give the crew a chance to see their families."

Oh, but her kiss was sweet and lingering. And as always she smelled of something spicy and exotic. Something he couldn't quite place.

When she pulled back from the kiss, Aefric said, "Actually, I was wondering how you'd feel about serving as regent in Riverbreak?"

"Me?" She asked.

"Her?" Ser Grey asked.

"And why not?" Aefric asked. "She was fostered by Duchess Arinda herself. And Byrhta, I would trust you to not only do your best for Riverbreak but to also train Vercy as Arinda trained you, and take her views into account regarding what the barony needs."

Byrhta frowned, considering.

"I'd have to spend a lot of time at Magranus."

"You'd still visit, I hope."

"Of course, Aefric," she said, then smiled. "If you are asking me formally..."

"I am."

"Then I am both pleased and honored to serve you as regent of Riverbreak, your grace."

She offered her hand for Aefric to kiss. He did so happily.

There was a knock on the door, and a guard called in, "Mistress Vercy Ol'Karmak to see you, your grace."

"Send her in," Aefric said, exasperated. He wasn't even dressed yet.

Vercy entered, looking pale and somber in a dress of dark blue velvet. She approached with rapid steps. Her soft leather shoes and velvet gown hushed an accompaniment to her movements. Her wide eyes gazed at the floorboards the whole way.

She took Aefric's hand from Byrhta. Pressed her forehead to his knuckles urgently.

"Your grace." Vercy looked up at him briefly, then pressed her forehead to his knuckles once more. "I was told you spoke on my behalf to the justiciar. And decided yourself to grant me the barony. I cannot thank you enough."

Before Aefric could get a word in edgewise, she dropped to her knees there on the white ash floorboards.

"I am ready to swear my oaths of vassalage."

"Not until you're of age," Byrhta said swiftly, taking a puzzled Vercy by the hands and bringing her back to her feet. "And not until you're formally made baroness of Riverbreak."

Vercy looked flustered, but Byrhta whispered quickly into her ear. Vercy nodded.

She composed herself through a quick breath. Offered her hand for Aefric to kiss, and after he did, she took his hand in both hers and pressed her forehead to it once more.

"I cannot thank you enough, your grace, for all that you have done for me," Vercy said in formal tones. "But know that I and mine are at your service. Now and always."

"Better," Byrhta said softly.

Ser Grey cleared her throat.

"Vercy," she said, "I suppose this is as good a time as any to tell you that his grace has named Mistress Byrhta Ol'Caran as your regent, to guide Riverbreak in your name until you come of age, and to teach you the ways of nobility."

"Oh," Vercy said, eyes wide. Then she gave a small, shy smile. "Thank you, your grace. Thank you, Byrhta. I know you will serve Riverbreak well, and I look forward to working with you."

"And now," Aefric said, "if you don't mind, I need to get dressed."

"Of course," Byrhta said. "Come, Vercy, we have much to discuss."

"Before I go," Vercy said, taking her hand from Byrhta and turning back to Aefric. "Your grace. Obviously, in light of the actions of my brother and my parents" — her eyes shone with unshed tears, but she held her voice steady as she continued — "your grace can no longer be held to the arrangement that would have seen us wed."

Byrhta's eyes rounded wide with surprise. Aefric had to suppress his amusement at finding out the woman *didn't* know everything.

"I'm glad you understand that," Aefric said.

"With that understood," — Vercy continued staring Aefric straight in the eye — "I still aspire to be your duchess. I shall strive to prove myself worthy of consideration as your bride and as the future mother of your children."

"I ... have no doubt that you will bring great honor to your family," Aefric said, while Byrhta frowned in thought.

"Thank you, your grace," Vercy said, and pressed her forehead to his hand again.

She was waiting for dismissal, so Aefric gave it. Byrhta looked as though she wanted to say something, but changed her mind with a shake of her head.

Instead of whatever she was thinking, she said, "Give my apologies to my father, please, Aefric, but I think it best if I take up my new post right away. Mustn't let the baronial courtiers get to thinking they can make decisions without us."

She did give him another kiss, though, before leaving. And there was something more to that kiss than a simple farewell.

As she left, Ser Grey said, "I hope you know what you've just done."

"What?" Aefric asked, starting toward his closet, with Ser Grey following. "I think she'll make an excellent regent."

"Oh, I don't doubt it," Ser Grey said. "You just also proved to her that you consider her important. Not just for her beauty, but for her intelligence and her judgment."

"And?" Aefric asked. "She's already proven both, I think."

"She has," Ser Grey agreed with a nod. "Arinda said so many times. But how many *men* do you think have shown such confidence in her?"

"Few?"

"If any." Ser Grey clapped Aefric on the shoulder. "And then, in her presence, you allowed a vassal, without contradiction, to suggest that she could prove herself worthy to be your bride."

"What should I have done?" Aefric asked. "Dithered about dowries and alliances?"

"Most would have, in your place, if only to assert the realities of the situation." She smiled at Aefric. "Not contradicting Vercy there was a very kind and romantic gesture. One that was not lost on Byrhta. Whose family would make no great alliance for you. And who has hardly any dowry at all, after the wars. Which you would know, if you read Ornella's report."

"I intend to read both hers and Prince Killian's during the trip to Goldenfall." He shook his head. "Wait. I thought you said Byrhta already hoped to marry me."

"I think she toyed with the idea to please her father," Ser Grey said. "But *now* I think she'll take it very, very seriously."

Something to think about, while Aefric got dressed.

AEFRIC WOULD HAVE LOVED TO GET DRESSED ON HIS OWN. TO THINK about Maev, and Byrhta, and marriage and more, with no one to intrude on his thoughts.

But that was not to be.

And so he allowed his servants to outfit him in a long shirt of Deepwater gray over hose of navy blue, bound in the middle by a good strong belt, with his sword and the wand Garram already in place. Low, soft leather boots for his feet, with cuffs that turned down.

And while this happened, he listened to Ser Grey bring him up to speed on the latest news and rika birds.

Count Ferrin, apparently, was humiliated that Motte hadn't been summoned down to defend the border from Malimfar. There'd been a flurry of rikas about it.

First, objecting to being left out. Then, promising to come anyway. Then, wondering who would *pay* for his troops to march all that way.

Finally, apparently before Ferrin ever got around to leaving his castle, he must have received word about what happened down at the river valley.

Because his next three rikas were all effusive with their praise of Aefric's power and wisdom, and their promises of Motte's undying service and fidelity.

"He's terrified of you," Ser Grey observed then. "I do hope you'll take advantage of this before it passes."

"I will," Aefric promised, then listened to more reports that were less interesting and amusing, but likely important in their own ways.

Finally, dressed once more and with the Brightstaff in his hand, he rode down to the docks with Karbin, who would be coming with him to Castle Vabarett in Goldenfall.

The morning was warm already. Could it be that spring was already passing its midpoint? No. Certainly that would be marked with a midspring festival of some kind. Just a warm spring, so far. Though if he was not mistaken, he saw hints of rain in the distance.

"I have updates," Karbin said as they rode, "from the front."

"How?" Aefric asked.

"Sirondfar," he said. "I assumed you'd rather have those updates come to me, rather than have his message spells interrupting your day at odd hours."

"Thank you," Aefric said, with a good deal of feeling.

"Of course," Karbin said. "What is a court wizard for?" He immediately raised a forestalling hand. "And don't you dare say flying and teleporting all around to act as a messenger boy, because if you do, I'll quit."

"What does Sirondfar say?"

"They've taken the river's mouth. They managed to push a march through the night and catch Kivash by surprise. They surrendered, rather than risk being sacked."

"Kivash?"

"That's Malimfar's port city on the south side of the river."

"So it's done? They're finished?"

"It's done."

Which meant Maev was now sailing for Varondam.

Which meant Aefric needed something else to think about.

"Did you ever make it out to the coast?" he asked.

"No," Karbin said. "You recalled me. Still need me to check it out?"

"After we get to Water's End and have a few days to settle in," Aefric said. They were in the middle of the second turn down the hill, and he smiled at the sights and sounds of a busy city down below.

Down there were people who needed homes and work. He'd have both for them soon.

"Thank you," Karbin said, with feeling.

"It's less pressing at the moment," Aefric said. "Plus, I expect Osmaer will be a good deal of help there."

"I have to ask," Karbin said.

"If you must," Aefric answered, with a teasing smile.

"Did you send me off to deliver messages to your armies just so I wouldn't be there to stop you from doing something foolish?"

Aefric laughed. "When have I ever planned that far ahead?"

"Too true," Karbin said with a laugh. But then looked at Aefric more seriously.

"You'll have to start, you know," he said. "Lots of people are counting on you."

"I'm trying," Aefric said with a sigh. "Got any wizardly wisdom to help with that?"

"Yes," Karbin said as though he'd been expecting the question. "If you find yourself considering an action that you know will get you killed, *don't do it*. There's probably a less lethal way to accomplish your goal."

"Wizardly wisdom at its finest," Aefric said drolly.

But then they were laughing, and talking of less consequential matters as they rode the rest of the way down to the docks.

Waiting for them was one of the two warships Aefric had seen on the waters of the lake. The *Lake Monster*. A three-masted beast with a pair of stout catapults aft and another pair of ballistae forward. Just sailing it required a crew of at least fifty, and it could carry at least another hundred troops.

Fittingly, it had a stylized lake monster as its figurehead.

Aefric hadn't been sure about sailing a warship to the home of a vassal, but Ser Grey had sworn it was expected. That Arinda only ever sailed to Vabarett aboard a warship.

Well, then a warship it would be.

He could only hope that wouldn't lead to ... misunderstandings.

ONCE ABOARD THE *LAKE MONSTER*, AEFRIC SPENT THE TWO-DAY VOYAGE in his large, comfortable cabin. Reading and rereading the reports he'd kept waiting.

Prince Killian's report about the state of his duchy. Killian had been right. Apart from the coast, the ducal lands were in good shape. His vassals were behind in their taxes, but only because everyone was hurting from the wars.

Killian recommended forgiving the lapses. Aefric would consider that, for all of them except Motte. Motte would pay every copper.

The treasury was a little low, but not as bad as Aefric had expected, from the way everyone had been lamenting the state of trade. He felt he could afford to begin repairs in several places. Especially after he settled certain matters.

Of course, It would help that he intended to plan twice and pay once.

As for Ornella's report on Goldenfall, that county was a mess. And not just according to Byrhta, though Aefric would have been inclined to take her word. The early reports from the royal surveyors confirmed everything she'd said.

Goldenfall was in terrible disarray. Its coffers close to empty. Its people close to starving, and many wanting even a solid roof over their heads.

Perhaps harder still, so many of their people had died during the wars that they could no longer work all their farms and mines and more.

The county stood on the precipice of complete ruin.

That report alone had been stark enough to bolt Aefric from sleep several times that night. And each time he woke suddenly, in a cold sweat, he would have sworn he heard the justiciar's voice.

Guilty of incompetence. The sentence is death ... for his subjects.

But he could do little about any of it from the cabin of a ship sailing up the Golden River.

So it was with relief, then, that he emerged onto the deck during the afternoon of the second day of travel to find that they were approaching Castle Vabarett.

Ser Grey had written that Aefric was coming, but he could hardly tell by looking at the state of things.

The docks were in desperate need of repairs. Not from damage, but from disuse. And the boats and ships that filled only half of the piers looked almost as disused as the docks themselves. Masts hung bare as winter trees, their sails missing or badly patched. No one swabbed decks, or cleaned and tarred hulls. Several of the hulks listed even at dock.

Somewhere behind that port was a city, and a castle. Both of which had survived a siege and come through the wars more or less intact. At least, from what Aefric had been told.

And yet, *this* was the state of their port?

How much worse must the city and castle be?

No. He would not look. He would not see Vabarett like this when he saw it for the first time. He would see it for the first time when it was a sight worth seeing again.

He kept his eyes to the port and the docks.

"Feels like sailing into a ghost port," Karbin said, shivering. "Did I ever tell you about the ghost port I found out east?"

"Another time," Aefric said, looking down to the docks where a small party awaited him.

An older man in the center wore red and gold clothes that looked as though he hadn't changed them in days. Something similar could be said for the man himself. He looked as a man who had once been stout with muscles and laughter, but now he looked wasted. His flesh hung off him, as his clothes did. His hairs were gray, and half of them missing.

He could have been fifty or seventy. Aefric couldn't tell. And he had the horrible sensation that this was what had become of Count Cyneric Ol'Caran.

Of course, if that was the count, part of the problem with his appearance might have been his choice of places to stand. He stood beside a young, fit man who was, in his way, as staggeringly beautiful as Byrhta.

In fact, Aefric could hear some of his knights sigh with longing.

The man had Byrhta's forest green hair. Her perfection of form and skin and feature. He looked like a storybook hero clad in the red and gold colors of Goldenfall.

Apart from the two obvious nobles, and one page carrying a trumpet, the entire receiving party consisted of four county guards, dressed in chainmail that showed signs of rust.

Ser Beornric grumbled at the sight of those guards, but Aefric thought more about how this little party was Goldenfall in a nutshell.

In desperate need of help.

The *Lake Monster* docked. Aefric descended the ramp flanked by Karbin and Ser Beornric, and preceded and followed by his shining knights. A stark contrast to the party waiting for them.

The page played a short fanfare on his trumpet.

"His grace, Ser Aefric Brightstaff," announced Ser Beornric. "Duke of Deepwater, Hero of the Battles of Deepwater and Frozen Ridge."

So that Frozen Ridge thing was sticking. Ah, well.

"It is a pleasure to receive you, your grace," the older man said, then confirmed what Aefric had worried about. "I am Count Cyneric Ol'Caran, and I hereby welcome you. Goldenfall is yours."

Aefric kissed his hand then, and when the man next him was introduced — Count Cyneric's son and heir, Taeric — Aefric kissed his hand as well.

"Your grace," Count Cyneric said, "I apologize deeply for not coming to you at Behal, but—"

"Think nothing of it," Aefric said. "Your daughter Byrhta answered my questions most ably, and she has given me an excellent picture of the state of Goldenfall. As has the initial report of the crown's surveyors."

"Is my daughter with you, your grace?" Count Cyneric asked, hopefully.

"Alas, she is not," Aefric said. "She sends her regrets, but was eager to take up her post. She is newly named regent for the barony of Riverbreak until its heir, Vercy Ol'Karmak, comes of age."

Taeric started to ask a question — likely about the news that Vercy, not Baston, would next hold Riverbreak — but the count stilled him with a raised hand.

"You honor her, your grace," Count Cyneric said with a small bow. "And through her, my family. I thank you."

"It is no more honor than she deserves," Aefric said. "I have every confidence that she will make an excellent regent."

"Thank you, your grace." Count Cyneric frowned. "You give me yet another reason to hold a feast in your honor. But alas I cannot feast you properly, I fear—"

"No need," Aefric said. "Although I confess I would love to guest with you for a proper visit, under the circumstances I cannot bring myself to lay that burden on you."

"Your grace finds us unfit hosts?" Taeric asked archly.

"Not at all," Aefric said. "But only a poor guest abuses his host's hospitality. You both have a great deal to do. And if I'm going to help you, so do I. That means we all have better ways to spend our time and money right now than pomp and circumstance."

"What does your grace have in mind?" Count Cyneric asked.

"Come aboard my ship," Aefric said. "There we can exchange our proper oaths and discuss your county. When we are finished, I shall sail for Deepwater, and not take more of your valuable time."

"Your grace will not allow me to host him at Vabarett for even a night?"

"Your excellency," Aefric said, trying to make clear that he meant no insult by any of this, "please understand. You have nothing to spare right now. We both know this. If I eat a crust of bread in Vabarett, it is only because I take that bread from the mouth of someone who needs it more than I do. And that I will not do."

"Your grace—"

"Let me promise you this," Aefric said. "Once you and I have restored Goldenfall. Housed and fed its people. Gotten them work. Begun to properly rebuild. *Then* I shall come for a full visit, and you may show me Vabarett as the gem of Goldenfall that it truly is. And, if you wish, all the wonders of your county. For I know it has many."

Count Cyneric smiled. And unless Aefric was mistaken, it looked as though the man was blinking back tears.

"*Thank* you, your grace," Count Cyneric said. "I shall look forward to that day."

"Now," Aefric said. "Let us adjourn to my cabin and see to those oaths."

IT WAS A GOOD THING THAT AEFRIC'S CABIN ABOARD THE *LAKE MONSTER* was large. For during the oaths it felt fair to bursting with people.

Aefric, Count Cyneric, and his heir, of course. But also Ser Beornric and Karbin. And all six knights of Aefric's personal guard, along with the four sad-looking soldiers of the count's guard.

They had to crowd around Aefric's large bed — yes, like Ashling, Aefric had a bed, and he'd discovered that it could tilt to compensate for movement of the river — and his desk, as well as his square dinner table.

The smell of sweat and dirt was strong, and seemed somehow appropriate.

Rather than trust to lamps in a room this crowded, Aefric lit the scene from the yellow diamond atop his Brightstaff.

The Deepwater gray rugs were thick and padded, which was good. Otherwise Aefric would have worried about Count Cyneric's knees through those long oaths.

Once they were finally finished, Aefric helped the count up and over to the table, whose legs were bolted down and knotted to the chairs to keep them in place as well.

Aefric sat facing the count. Karbin sat to Aefric's right, facing Taeric across the table.

"Now," Aefric said. "First, you need food. Havenford and Fyretti have more than they need. I'll see to it that they begin sending you shipments."

"But the cost—"

"I will pay it for now," Aefric said, cutting off the count. "The amount will be tracked, of course, but I won't charge you interest."

Count Cyneric nodded. "Thank you, your grace."

"What about a loan?" Taeric asked bluntly. "So we can negotiate for our own food and more. And Motte—"

"Taeric," Count Cyneric said. "You're not count here yet. Hold your tongue or wait outside."

"Motte," Aefric said, "I will be dealing with. In fact, Karbin, I'd like you to oversee the trade negotiations between Goldenfall and Motte, and ensure that the deal is not just fair, but favors Goldenfall. And make sure Motte knows why."

"Why?" Taeric asked.

"Out," Count Cyneric said.

"But Father—"

"Out," Count Cyneric said again, steel in his voice.

Taeric left in a huff.

"I apologize for that," Count Cyneric said. "I've had to give the boy more responsibility, and now he seems to think he's ready to take over."

Aefric let that pass without comment.

"As for Motte, Count Ferrin made the mistake of working actively against me, and must be punished. This trade deal is only one part of his punishment."

"Of course, your grace."

"Now," Aefric continued. "On to work, and the rebuilding of your economy." Aefric drew a deep breath. "You're not going to like part of this."

"I take it your grace intends to assert that the Threepeaks are and always have been ducal territory, thus reclaiming their mines as well?"

Aefric had to check himself from overreacting to that. How had the man known? Was he so clever that he puzzled it out? Was he so well-connected that he had spies even in Behal?

Or was the move simply that much more obvious than Aefric had thought?

Hoping he hadn't given his thoughts away through his expression, Aefric nodded. "What do you think of that?"

"I expected nothing less," Count Cyneric said with a sigh. "I believe we both know, your grace, that Ferrin and I only claimed those lands in the first place because Arinda was busy with that pirate queen and could not stop us."

He shook his head self-deprecatingly. "We both knew we had no proper claim to them. And I would be a thankless vassal if I quibbled over them now while begging for your help. Especially since I don't have enough people to work those mines properly anymore."

"Do keep in mind in the future," Aefric said, "that I am not Arinda. Don't try pulling something like that on me. You won't like the results."

"I heard about your ... visit to Castle Kirandai, your grace," Count Cyneric said. He *sounded* impressed, but Aefric couldn't tell whether or not the man truly understood Aefric's warning.

He decided he had to take the chance, for now. To do otherwise would lead to Goldenfall's people suffering even more than they had.

And the man had *said* all the right things.

"All right," Aefric said. "As you suspected, I am reasserting ducal claim to the Threepeaks, including all mines. I'll need miners to get those mines working again, and that will mean work for some of your people. As well as some of mine."

"Thank you, your grace."

"There's more," Aefric said. "I intend to lease ten silver mines back to you for a period of eight years. At a reasonable rate."

"Your grace," Count Cyneric said slowly, "I've never laid claim to any of the silver mines in the Threepeaks."

"No," Aefric said, smiling, "you haven't. Those are mines Motte used to claim. His people will continue to work them, and you'll pay them. They need the jobs. But the silver will go to you and the leasing fees will go to me."

Count Cyneric laughed delightedly. "Part of Ferrin's punishment?"

"Yes. As well as helping you get your people through this dark time."

"That silver will go a long way, your grace."

"See that it does. And so you know, the terms of that lease would have been much worse had you argued against my reclaiming the Threepeaks."

Count Cyneric's eyebrows raised the barest fraction, but then he nodded sagely.

Perhaps Aefric's lesson would sink in after all.

There were more details to cover then. More about trade, and especially lumber and seed. But Count Cyneric now seemed to be working with Aefric more eagerly.

Aefric could only hope that the goodwill — and the lesson — would last.

⁂

When Aefric was finally finished going over everything with Count Cyneric, it was well into the dinner hour. He considered offering to feed the count aboard the *Lake Monster*, but didn't want to risk insulting him.

And so, they parted ways instead.

Count Cyneric left the *Lake Monster* with a spring in his step, looking years younger than he had when Aefric had arrived that afternoon.

It might have helped that he didn't leave alone. Karbin accompanied him. He would stay with the count at Vabarett until trade negotiations with Motte were complete.

In fact, as they left in the cold, evening breeze, Aefric could hear Count Cyneric already recounting Motte's more egregious demands in a loud, angry voice.

That would go well. It would go even better when Ser Beornric arrived in Motte with a company of troops and delivered Aefric's edict about the Threepeaks Mountains.

That should happen in about ... another four or five days, by Aefric's estimate.

Pity that the troops would be necessary. He should just be able to send an edict like that with a messenger. But Ferrin had already proven himself too impulsive.

Aefric would have to find a way to make Motte reliable. But that was a problem for another day.

Still. Aefric was too worked up to eat, so he returned to his cabin for a time, and continued his investigation into the wand Garram. He knew he would still not properly progress beyond the lesser understandings of an item of such power. Not here on the ship. But there was no rush. And everything he learned now would make the wand easier to use next time.

When he was done with that, he slept, and continued his meditations on the wand for much of the next morning and afternoon.

When he stepped forth finally onto the decks again, stretching his arms and legs and back, it was nighttime. The *Lake Monster* had emerged from the mouth of the Golden River and into Lake Deepwater.

The winds were cold, and he held his soft, gray, woolen cloak tight as he crossed the deck to the prow and looked out over the waters ahead of him.

Behind him, Aefric heard the soft steps and rustling leather and metal of his personal guards, taking up posts nearby.

The waters ahead of him were dark, as were the skies above. Storm clouds had moved in, blotting out the moon and stars, though they had yet to take further action.

Aefric considered all that had happened since taking up his duchy. The fort and toll gate at Kerrik Forest's edge. Confronting Ser Pemith on the road. Norra, its baroness, and that sweet young woman named Octave. Felspark, and the challenge in the eyes of its towns-folk at Tafarac. Its baroness, and winning her over.

Behal. Maev. Byrhta.

Riverbreak. Havenford. Merrek and more. So much more.

Now, at last, he was sailing for Water's End. For his ducal seat. And he would arrive knowing he had the oaths and support of all his vassals.

Well, the oaths, at least. And the support of all but Motte. And Motte would fall in line soon enough.

Aefric would be arriving at Water's End as a duke in more than just name.

The storm clouds above began sending down scouting parties of slight rain.

It smelled wonderful. And its kiss felt familiar on his face. It reminded him...

It reminded him of a distant basketball court. Where he lay upon the tarmac, drenched in sweat and rain, trying to recover his strength for one more game before the rains made it impossible.

That had been ... what ... a few aetts ago? Or weeks, as time was reckoned in that world?

Had it really been such a short time ago that Aefric had no greater worries on his shoulders than his next game of basketball?

Yes, and no, of course. A few aetts ago, Aefric had been busy traveling, working to stop those marauders who'd been raiding towns trying to recover from the wars.

Back before Kainemorton found him. Brought him to Marrisford, and then to Armityr.

As Keifer, though, he was right. He'd been a man lost in memories and death, with nothing more to look forward to than his next basketball game and his next roleplaying game.

"You're contemplating the changes you've gone through. I can tell. You got the same look when you were an apprentice, trying to remember potion ingredients."

Kainemorton's voice, coming from just behind Aefric, to his right.

He heard the telltale hiss of swords yanked from scabbards, and lit up the Brightstaff's yellow diamond for attention.

"Stop," he told his guards. "This is Kainemorton. He's a friend."

Kainemorton in his orange robes, sat on a stack of crates that was held in place with hempen rope. His eyes twinkled, as they always did. He puffed that pipe of his, and the faint scent of herb-laced tobacco mingled with the gently falling rain.

The guards relaxed, sheathing their swords and moving back to give their duke room to speak with his friend.

Back behind them, the ship's night watch went about their work.

Aefric slowly dimmed the Brightstaff to help them all ease back to their night vision.

"You're right, as always," Aefric finally said with a sigh. "Exactly what I was thinking about."

"You've been busy," Kainemorton said. "I heard about what you did at ... what are they calling it now? Frozen Ridge?"

Aefric scoffed and turned back to the lake waters ahead of them.

"I did what I had to do."

"I understand the princess is quite taken with you," Kainemorton continued. "And that she might have competition from a few others."

Aefric let that pass without comment.

"I understand also that you are already earning respect as a duke, not just as a dweomerblood."

"If you understand all these things," Aefric said, "why do you need to mention them? Surely you must know that I know them already."

"So I do," Kainemorton acknowledged, then puffed on his pipe. "But a short time ago I brought to my tower a man unsure of his decision. I would know how that man feels today."

"That man was unsure of a great many decisions," Aefric said. "And he clung to old pain and lost love. This man has finally released both."

He turned to Kainemorton. "I am quite happy with the decision you refer to."

"Good," Kainemorton said with a smile. "Then I shall leave you to it."

"I trust you won't be a stranger, old friend."

"Of course not," Kainemorton said.

Aefric could hear the sounds of Kainemorton coming to his feet.

"Oh," the old mage said, affecting that he just remembered something. "I should also tell you. I have personally seen to delivering your trunk of memories to your chambers at Water's End. It awaits you, and will open only to your touch."

Aefric straightened, surprised, but smiling. He'd all but forgotten that trunk.

"Thank you," he said.

"Of course," Kainemorton said, and Aefric suspected from his tone that the trunk would not have been delivered until the old mage felt Aefric could view its contents in the right frame of mind.

"And one more thing," Kainemorton added. "The next time someone makes you fight a duel with a sword in your hand, for Kalinda's sake, use *all* your training. Your foe won't suppress any of his skills, and you shouldn't be expected to either."

"How did you know about..."

Aefric let his words trail off as he regarded the smile in those twinkling eyes. He knew because he was Kainemorton.

"Farewell for now," Kainemorton said gently.

And before Aefric could respond, the old mage was gone. No

incantation. No flash of light. The old mage's skill at teleportation surpassed any other Aefric had ever heard of.

And Aefric himself didn't even know the spell.

Ah, well. He had time to learn it later.

For now, if he shaded his eyes against the drizzle, he thought he could just make out the lights of Water's Edge in the distance.

At long last, he was truly coming home.

SIGN UP FOR STEFON'S NEWSLETTER

Stefon loves to keep in touch with his readers, and loves to keep you reading. The best way for him to do both is for you to sign up for his newsletter.

Sign up at http://www.stefonmears.com/join

If you sign up for Stefon's newsletter, you get...

- Monthly updates about his publishing and travel schedules
- His latest news, in brief, and answers to reader questions
- A free short story for signing up
- List-only offers and occasional specials
- Plus a free short story every month!

ABOUT THE AUTHOR

Stefon Mears has gamed in the Torn Kingdoms. Stefon has more than thirty books to his credit, and he never stops writing. He earned his M.F.A. in Creative Writing from N.I.L.A., and his B.A. in Religious Studies (double emphasis in Ritual and Mythology) from U.C. Berkeley. He's a lifelong gamer and fantasy fan. Stefon lives in Portland, Oregon, with his wife and three cats.

Look for Stefon online:
www.stefonmears.com
himself@stefonmears.com